⤙ Callis & Toll ⤚
The Silver Shard

—✛ Callis & Toll ✛—
The Silver Shard

NICK HORTH

BLACK LIBRARY

A BLACK LIBRARY PUBLICATION

First published in 2018.
This edition published in Great Britain in 2019 by
Black Library,
Games Workshop Ltd.,
Willow Road,
Nottingham,
NG7 2WS, UK.

10 9 8 7 6 5 4 3 2 1

Produced by Games Workshop in Nottingham.
Cover illustration by Even Mehl Amundsen.

A CIP record for this book is available from the British Library.

ISBN 13: 978 1 78496 856 4

See Black Library on the internet at

blacklibrary.com

Find out more about Games Workshop
and the worlds of Warhammer at

games-workshop.com

Printed and bound by CPI Group (UK) Ltd, Croydon, CR0 4YY

From the maelstrom of a sundered world, the
Eight Realms were born. The formless and the divine
exploded into life.

Strange, new worlds appeared in the firmament, each one
gilded with spirits, gods and men. Noblest of the gods was
Sigmar. For years beyond reckoning he illuminated the realms,
wreathed in light and majesty as he carved out his reign. His
strength was the power of thunder. His wisdom was infinite.
Mortal and immortal alike kneeled before his lofty throne.
Great empires rose and, for a while, treachery was banished.
Sigmar claimed the land and sky as his own and ruled over a
glorious age of myth.

But cruelty is tenacious. As had been foreseen, the great
alliance of gods and men tore itself apart. Myth and legend
crumbled into Chaos. Darkness flooded the realms. Torture,
slavery and fear replaced the glory that came before. Sigmar
turned his back on the mortal kingdoms, disgusted by their
fate. He fixed his gaze instead on the remains of the world he
had lost long ago, brooding over its charred core, searching
endlessly for a sign of hope. And then, in the dark heat of
his rage, he caught a glimpse of something magnificent. He
pictured a weapon born of the heavens. A beacon powerful
enough to pierce the endless night. An army hewn from
everything he had lost.

Sigmar set his artisans to work and for long ages they toiled,
striving to harness the power of the stars. As Sigmar's great
work neared completion, he turned back to the realms and saw
that the dominion of Chaos was almost complete. The hour
for vengeance had come. Finally, with lightning blazing across
his brow, he stepped forth to unleash his creations.

The Age of Sigmar had begun.

Chapter One

Sunlight trickled down through the canopy of violet leaves and crystalline tree trunks to cast a shimmering amethyst glow across the jungle floor. Shev Arclis knelt, stretched out a hand and let the light play across her fingers. Around her, a cacophony of life screeched, clicked and howled. Disc-shaped beetles buzzed by, mandibles twitching. She waved a hand to shoo them away, and their iridescent bodies flashed from blue to a bright red as they zoomed off into the treeline.

Truly, the jungles of the Taloncoast would be a beautiful place, if they weren't quite so intent on killing her. She reached back and unclipped a flask from her belt. It was worryingly light in her hands. The journey had taken far longer than she had hoped, and the sweltering heat had hardly helped. She let several drops of precious water drip onto her tongue.

Scuffed footsteps sounded behind her, and a familiar stench of stale sweat and gunji-smoke wafted through the trees. She sighed, and turned. There he was, of course. Her shadow. His beady, rheumy eyes narrowed in a suspicious frown, while he panted like a hound worn out from the heat, exposing a row of blackened teeth.

'What're you sneakin' off for, aelf?' he hissed. 'Tryin' to leave us behind, I reckon.'

'Where exactly would I run off to, cretin?' she snarled back. 'In case you hadn't noticed, Howle, there's several hundred leagues of lethal wilderness between us and any scrap of civilisation.'

Howle's eyes narrowed even further and, as if by magic, a crude, saw-bladed dagger appeared in one hand and a barbed hook in the other. He trembled with barely contained rage.

'You speak to me like that again, I'll carve up the other side of your face,' he said. 'You won't be even half pretty by the time I'm done with you.'

Shev rose slowly, moving one hand to her belt and the dagger stowed there. She smiled through the cold rage that filled her, and felt the familiar tautness on the left side of her jaw, where a web of scarred flesh met her upper lip. She'd had just about enough of Howle's taunts, muttered threats and stares. Shev didn't know quite why the old brute had it in for her so badly, but her patience was at an end.

'You don't frighten me, Howle,' she said. 'So why don't you–'

'Enough,' interrupted a voice, soft and measured. Not a threatening sound, but both she and Howle took a step back nonetheless.

The Golden Lord stepped into the clearing. Despite the stifling heat, he still wore thick black robes and an undercoat of leather, revealing not a hint of bare skin. An impassive death-mask of gold gazed at them both as the figure leaned upon his black-iron staff. Not for the first time, Shev felt a shiver of unease trickle down her back.

'We are near,' said the Golden Lord. 'I require you to be alert and attentive, not with daggers at each other's throats. The city of Quatzhymos awaits. Madame Arclis, please lead the way. Howle, sheathe your blade.'

The man had never once raised his voice in her presence, never threatened or struck anyone. And yet a murderous piece of filth like Howle, a thug who'd spent his entire life killing others for profit or enjoyment, obeyed the order at once. That disturbed Shev more than any grandiose posturing or outburst of sudden violence could have.

More figures appeared, filtering through the crystal trees. Her companions. Thieves, fugitives and killers to a soul. They were dressed in a variety of hides, leathers and scraps of metal, and doused in sweat and grime. The journey from Magger-horne had been long and hard, and only around fifty or so specimens remained – the toughest of the Golden Lord's band. They were among the most repulsive men and women Shev had ever had the misfortune of encountering, and in her line of work, that was a truly impressive feat. Not for the first time, she questioned her wisdom in agreeing to this commission before striding off through the wilds.

Think of the prize, she reminded herself. Quatzhymos – the ancient library-city, final resting place of Occlesius the Realms-Walker. It was here, somewhere in this valley, and she never would have found it without the Golden Lord's knowledge. How the reams of dusty tomes and yellow maps had entered his possession, she could not say, for they were relics of a bygone age. Combining these priceless treasures with her own research, a lifetime's worth of exploring ruins and long-abandoned tombs across the wilds of the Shattered Coast, of studying, recovering and analysing, they had pieced together the truth – the true location of the Realms-Walker's tomb.

It had not been easy. These lands had changed so much, even in the last few hundred years. It was the way of things along the Taloncoast, far to the north of Excelsis, outside the great city's sphere of influence. Mountain ranges erupted from the land like enormous fangs, breaking the verdant earth then swallowing it beneath their rocky mass. The raging seas gnawed at the coast, opening new tributaries and headwaters. Maps became hopelessly outdated in only a few decades as this endlessly predatory realm devoured then reshaped itself.

Yet some things survived. Like this hidden valley, encircled by jagged cliffs, locked away from the world. Quatzhymos, where great scholars from across the Mortal Realms had once gathered to store and disperse their knowledge amongst peers. Where the body of Occlesius, the most prestigious thinker, scientist and inventor of his age was interred.

Shev's steps grew lighter as she thought about the secrets that awaited her. The fresh mysteries that would inevitably arise from her discoveries.

'I apologise for the quality of servants I must rely upon,' came a voice at her side. It was the gold-masked lord. 'Reliable souls are a rare breed these days, and so we must... compromise.'

Shev shook her head. 'You're clearly a learned man. How did you ever find yourself working with this scum?'

There was a muffled choking sound, and Shev glanced at the man. She realised it was laughter – coarse and painful.

'I ask myself that very same question every day,' he said. 'The truth is that we do not live in an age of enlightenment, Madame Arclis. Reasoned, thinking people such as we are so few. Killers, however? They abound. We live in an age of war and bloodshed. In such times, we must be realistic.'

He rested a hand on her arm. The metal was icy against her bare skin. This close to the man, she could smell scented oils and a faint whiff of smoke, as if someone had stirred the ashes of a dead fire. She glanced into the black recesses of his mask's eye sockets, and despite herself, she couldn't suppress a shiver as she glimpsed a pair of cold, flint eyes staring back. She had never dared to ask why the Golden Lord did not reveal his face. She presumed he bore the scars of a hard life, much as she did. Yet Shev had never felt a desire to hide her disfigurement from the world.

'These brutes will earn their gold, and go back to their wasteful, cruel lives a little richer,' he whispered. 'You and I will discover the truths that are buried here. And then we will move on, seeking the answers to the next mystery. *This* is how we change the world.'

Chapter Two

For hours, they walked on through the stifling humidity, too hot and miserable to speak. Shev struggled up steep slopes of stinking clay, trying to ignore the barbs and thorns that tore at her clothes and flesh. That same clay came in particularly useful when they passed a dozen bloodwasp hives, smearing the stuff all over their bodies to avoid the insects' agonising stings. Of course, once out of danger they were forced to endure the itching as the stinking mess dried on their skin. Shev counted herself in good health, but soon even she was panting as she hacked her way through the tangled undergrowth. Howle kept close, as he always did, and she was uncomfortably aware of his dead-eyed gaze despite the fact she never turned to meet it.

After some time, they heard the trickle of running water. Some of the others sighed in relief, and she heard the clinking of metal as they retrieved their flasks and waterskins, hoping to refresh their dwindling supplies. Shev paused, hunched down and surveyed their surroundings. The thickest of the jungle had recently given way to a sparse woodland, dotted with tall, thin blackwood trees. Purple and red leaves pooled around their ankles. They were traversing a shallow incline, at the foot of which ran a brook of crystal-clear water. The air was entirely still – quiet save for the occasional avian trill. Too quiet.

'Wait,' she said, softly. 'We should take care here. Check the area before we–'

Guirre, the big Sayronite, shouldered her aside. His great, bald dome of a head glistened in the sunlight, and he hefted his great poleaxe as he strode towards the stream, waterskin in hand.

'You wait,' he growled. 'We've been walking for days. We stop here and drink.'

Several others followed him, stowing blades and blackpowder pieces. The Golden Lord appeared by her side, grasping his staff tightly.

'You see something?' he asked.

'No,' Shev replied, frowning as she watched two sellswords laughing raucously and splashing water at each other. 'But we should move away from here. This is the only source of water we've seen in two days. Every predator within fifty leagues will know of it.'

'Nevertheless, we need water,' said the masked man, addressing those who had stayed back. Many of the Golden Lord's band had learned to heed Shev's advice. 'Let us refill our skins, but Madame Arclis is correct. Do not lower your guard.'

More men and women bounded down to the stream. The Golden Lord stayed at her side, however, observing from a distance. Shev's parched throat ached as she watched the sellswords gulp down handfuls of water, but she had long ago learned to trust her instincts, and right now every fibre of her being was screaming at her to leave this clearing.

Two of the Golden Lord's men began to trudge back up the hill to re-join the main group. They were chuckling at some joke and brushing the remnants of smeared clay from their bare arms.

Out of the trees, a creature with a horned, quadruped form barrelled into them. Its horns locked under the first man's legs, and the huge, grey-skinned beast bucked its head, sending him soaring a dozen feet into the air. It reared up and raked two great claws across the second man's chest. There was a spurt of crimson, and the unfortunate sellsword toppled to the ground, ribs exposed through his torn overshirt. The beast roared triumphantly. Beneath its horned brow was a broad, flat snout and a maw filled with jagged teeth. It was large, but not bulky, instead possessing the sleek muscles of a hunting feline. Several strange, perforated chimneys made of bleached bone rose along its flank. They seemed to pulse with a dim orange light.

A brachitor, Shev realised with a shiver. She'd heard trackers speak of the beasts often, and always with a tone of dread.

'Don't get close to it!' she shouted.

Guirre and his band already had their weapons in hand. If they heard her, they showed no sign of following her advice. They started to loose crossbow bolts at the creature, which pressed itself close to the ground and then bounded into the stream, battering one unfortunate woman with its great, curved horns. She flipped over in the air, then splashed into the water and did not move. Guirre ducked the swipe of a clawed forelimb, and hacked his poleaxe along the beast's flank. It screeched in pained fury as more sellswords darted in to score slashes across its hind legs. More warriors began to sprint down the slope towards the melee, sensing an easy kill and perhaps a chance to claim a trophy.

They were almost upon it when the strange growths lining

the beast's hide erupted, sending a great cloud of fiery dust into the air. The sellswords staggered to a halt. Gasping, they clawed at their eyes and throats. A number toppled to the ground where they rolled and twitched as if struck by invisible blades. Then the screaming started. Guirre, who had been immediately beside the beast when it had released its spores, was the loudest. He dropped to the soil and curled into a foetal ball, his weapon forgotten, bellowing like a frightened auroch. The brachitor lowered its head over the prone Sayronite, and there was an audible crunch of bone. His screams cut off abruptly.

'Please stay here, Madame Arclis,' said the Golden Lord, hefting his staff. It was an unnecessary order. Shev had no intention of getting in that thing's way.

As they watched, astonished, the masked man strode through the swirling spores, showing no sign of discomfort or pain. He stood there, amidst the orange haze, and slammed his staff upon the ground. Once, twice. Three times.

The brachitor raised its great head and growled. Its jaws were smeared with blood, and its eyes, small and beady in the centre of that great maw, were pinpoints of blazing yellow.

It sprang towards the Golden Lord, a flashing blur of grey. A dozen paces away, it leapt, soaring through the air with its razor-edged claws outstretched.

The Golden Lord moved with almost unnatural speed, raising his staff in two hands and shouting a single word in a language that Shev did not understand. The hairs on the back of her neck rose. There was a crack like a gunshot, and a blinding flash of light. When Shev had finished blinking away the afterimage, she saw the small man standing there, totally unperturbed. The brachitor was several feet away, slumped on its side, its grey hide blackened and scarred as if left to char on a fire. Wisps of smoke rose from its broken body.

Shev carefully made her way towards the Golden Lord. He was leaning heavily on his staff, but otherwise seemed unharmed. He gazed at her as she approached.

'Is it...' she began.

'Quite dead, I assure you.'

She crept closer to the smoking body of the creature. Bones showed through its blasted flesh. She took in the great, flat head, tipped with those curved horns, the teeth as big as daggers.

'An extraordinary creature,' said the Golden Lord, sounding entirely unimpressed. 'It discharged some form of... poison, yes? A method of debilitating its prey, I would assume.'

'It's a powerful hallucinogenic,' said Shev, running her hand across one of the brachitor's strange growths, and examining the powder-like substance that surrounded the polyps. Unable to resist, she pulled a small vial from her pocket and brushed some of the dust into it. Even from this distance, it had a powerful smell, like sulphur mixed with rotten meat.

'I think it's more for defence,' she continued. 'It disorients and confuses attackers, letting the brachitor escape.'

'Which rather begs the question, what has such a remarkably dangerous specimen to fear?'

The groans and shrieks of the remaining stricken sellswords went suddenly silent. Shev turned from the corpse of the beast, and glanced back at the rest of their band. Howle stood next to one of the downed warriors, wiping blood from his blade. He glanced over and met her stare, utterly untroubled, as if he had just swatted a fly.

She started forwards, but the Golden Lord laid a firm hand on her shoulder.

'Madame Arclis, we do not have the time or resources to care for the wounded.'

'But we can't just–'

'Their screams risk bringing more hostile creatures to our location,' the masked figure continued. His voice was firm, and for the first time she heard a hard, uncompromising edge to his words. 'This is for the best. Carrying the wounded would simply endanger us all.'

The Golden Lord nodded at Howle, and the sellsword bent down and drove his blade through the last of the twitching victims. The woman rasped a final breath and went limp. Shev wanted to vomit. She looked imploringly at the nearest sellswords, but saw nothing but grim resolve and indifference. No one else seemed to care at all that they had just killed five of their own.

'Take their waterskins,' said the Golden Lord, before striding off and leaving the corpse-strewn stream behind. 'And leave the bodies, we've no time for looting. There will be more than enough compensation for you all once we reach Quatzhymos.'

Howle gave Shev a black-toothed smirk before he and the others strode after their leader. Shev looked at the littered corpses, their glazed eyes staring sightlessly at the azure skies above, and then spun to follow.

Chapter Three

They trudged onwards through the fading light, cursing and grunting as the land became rougher and steeper with every step. Shev could not dispel the image of Howle culling their injured companions from her head. In this job, it paid to be practical, she told herself. Truly, what could they have done? Dragged half a dozen mortally wounded souls through this death-trap of a jungle? Or left them behind, to suffer a slow and painful death, rotting in the heat like overripe fruit? The reality was, out here in the wilds, you had to accept a number of uneasy truths. It was better this way, for everyone.

So why did she feel so godsdamned low?

'My lord,' came a voice from way up ahead. It was Kurdh, one of their trackers – a thin, wiry Excelsian covered with tattoos. He carried a battered but well-crafted sabre and a red and green checked sash that marked him as a former Freeguild man. How he'd come to be out here, she had no idea, but decided it was probably best not to ask.

'I believe we've found it,' he said softly with wide eyes.

Shev bounded up the steep incline towards the man, zipping past several sellswords grappling with the tangled undergrowth.

Clambering over the ridge, she saw what had taken Kurdh's breath away. Ahead of them, the ground fell away into a vast, circular pit, a rent in the earth several thousand paces across. Shards of broken rock circled the rim of this crater, and limbs of ancient trees jutted out from the earth, dangling over the precipice like a giant's crooked fingers. At several points, streams of water poured over the edge, gleaming and glittering as they tumbled away into vast channels far below. The city of Quatzhymos spread out ahead of them. A sprawling ruin littered with shattered buildings, tumbledown spires and great marble columns half-devoured by vines and creepers. At the rear of the canyon the ground sloped away, disappearing into darkness. It was as if the earth had opened its maw to devour the city whole.

Kurdh whistled softly. 'That's a view you don't see every day.'

'Madame Arclis, I knew I was right to put my faith in you,' said the Golden Lord, kneeling down beside them. If he was at all tired from their long march, he showed no sign. He showed no outward sign of emotion either, but she could hear an excited tremor in his voice. 'Quatzhymos, the fabled library-city. I have searched for this place for a very long time. Let us see what secrets it conceals.'

Several sellswords brought up silkhemp ropes and grapples, and found a firmly lodged cluster of thick oaks that hung out into empty space over the drop. They looped and secured them with thick iron bands, and several men and women strapped on gloves and boots tipped with thick metal spikes. Even Shev, no stranger to heights, felt her stomach swirl queasily as several of the climbers let themselves fall into empty space, dangling on harnesses and digging crampons into the face of the rock.

The work was slow, but after a few hours the climbers made the pit's floor, and signalled up that the line was secure. Shev didn't wait; she pushed forward to claim her spot on one of the lines, securing her belt to the rope with a clamp, and strapping on a pair of fingerless auroch-hide gloves. The sooner the descent was over, the better. She gritted her teeth, banished a sudden rush of vertigo, and slid over the precipice. Foot by foot, she descended. The crater's wall was rough and full of torn roots and gaping holes. Several times she reached for a grip only to tear loose a cluster of soil and rocks, which tumbled away into the gloom below. A squat, oval-eyed lizard gazed at her disinterestedly as she lowered herself past its lair.

'Sorry for the intrusion,' she muttered.

The lizard ran a long, blue-tipped tongue lazily over its eyeball.

Suddenly, it disappeared in a snap of fangs and spurt of blood as something with too many eyes and stretching claws burst out from the darkness.

Shev's heart somersaulted. She let out a squawk of horror and hurled herself to the side as the wall exploded in a shower of soil and gore. She dangled there, spinning and cursing, her heart hammering in her chest. Then the screams started. She glanced up and saw a sellsword scrabbling for his blade. He'd barely drawn metal when long, barbed pincers reached out from the wall to snatch him away into darkness. His frenzied, awful screeches cut an icy hole into her heart, until they abruptly cut off. Soil and rocks rained down into her hair and her eyes. Something fell past her, shrieking, close enough to make her ears ache. Desperately, she began to climb down. Abandoning caution for haste, she missed a grip and fell, scrabbling for a handhold. Her head struck something hard, and stars exploded behind her eyes, but by some miracle she managed to hold onto something firm and gnarled, jutting out of the wall. The impact sent a shock of pain up her arm, but she clung on, opening her eyes. A tree root. She wrapped herself around it, holding on to it like a shipwrecked sailor on a piece of driftwood. There was more screaming, and the snap-click of crossbow bolts thudding into solid surfaces. Blearily, she looked upwards and saw at least a dozen sellswords descending at speed as the cliff face erupted to life around them, insectile appendages darting out in search of prey.

She had to get down. Below was only a long drop to certain death. Those fortunate few who'd managed to get down safely had crossbows and repeaters drawn, but what could they do, really? If they fired a hail of bolts, they'd be as likely to skewer their own as strike one of the creatures.

Another cloud of sun-baked mud exploded outwards to Shev's left, and she caught sight of one of the beasts for the first time. It had a long, segmented body like a centipede, bedecked with barbed armour plates that shone razor-sharp in the sunlight. Its head was small, bulbous – like that of a spider, with hundreds of pitch-black eyes and a pair of snapping mandibles. Its fore-legs were long, thin spears of jet-black chitin. It swept those enormous limbs around while a pair of curling antennae whipped at the air. She clutched her lifeline even harder, frozen in both terror and indecision. Yet, even though she was only a few feet away, the beast did not seem to notice her. It was blind in the sunlight, she realised with a surge of relief. As long as she stayed corpse-still, maybe she could survive this yet.

The branch groaned beneath her, and there was a crack of splintering wood.

Of course.

With a shriek, the tunnel-horror stabbed its claws out at

the sudden sound. Shev rolled, hanging by her aching fingers underneath the drooping tree branch. She tugged at the rope secured to her belt. It was hopelessly tangled, pulled so taut that it was cutting into her stomach. All she could hear was the frenzied hissing of the tunnel-horror and the thunk as its spear-limbs thudded into the branch that held her. It swiped a leg across horizontally, and snipped clean through the silkweave rope. The pressure on her abdomen was blissfully released. She fumbled, unhooking the slack, which fell away. Now at least she could move. Unfortunately, she was also now hanging free a few feet above cold, hard rock, with a frenzied monster doing its best to eviscerate her.

First things first. She snapped her head around, looking for some escape. There, below her and to the left, was another jutting root, maybe large enough to hold her weight. Maybe not, of course, but Shev knew sometimes you had to take your chances. She waited until the thing had stopped thrashing, slipped her flask free from her pack and hurled it over the monster's head and into the canyon wall. The tunnel-horror whirled its many-eyed head about with a rattling hiss. Shev hauled herself up onto the branch, swaying as it dropped lower. It splintered, and she saw a jagged line zig-zag down the length of the wood. The tunnel-horror spun back around, its limbs raised high.

She took a step and flung herself into space. Something whipped past her head, close enough to brush her scalp. There was a moment of stomach-churning vertigo, and then she struck rock hard enough to blast all the air from her lungs, hard enough that she very nearly lost her grip entirely. Wheezing and spitting blood, she wrapped her legs around her new home. She lay there for a few blessed moments, whimpering softly, clutching her bruised ribcage. Then her new home started creaking too. Of course, she thought with a sigh.

She dragged her aching bones upright, looking around desperately for another escape route. Below, possibly too far away for her to reach, was a pool of glittering green water covered with algae and drooping vines. It looked deep enough, but there was a good to fair chance that it was merely disguising a cluster of sharp rocks. There was a chorus of hissing behind her, and two more insectoid monstrosities hauled their chitinous bodies free, antennae lashing, razor-tipped legs gleaming wetly in the fading light.

That made her decision to jump much easier.

She ran and leapt high into space, tucking her arms across her chest, pointing her toes and screaming so loudly it hurt as she plummeted down.

She struck the pool of water like an arrow. The chill made her reflexively gasp, and she swallowed a brackish mouthful. Her foot struck soft, muddy earth and stuck fast, and she kicked and struggled in panic, swallowing more water. Finally, her lungs burning, she tugged her foot free of the sucking morass and darted for the surface. One hand scrabbled for a hold, and she raised her head into daylight, spitting out the rancid liquid.

Strong hands grasped her under the arms, and she felt herself being lifted free of the pool. She blinked foul-smelling water out of her eyes, and a figure swam into focus. Kurdh. He was shaking his head.

'Sigmar's teeth,' he said, with a chuckle. 'You're a mad one, aelf. You're godsdamned lucky you didn't splatter all over the flagstones.'

'Every inch of me hurts,' she groaned.

'Yeah, well. It could have been worse,' he replied.

She hauled her aching body to its knees and looked around. Barely twenty souls remained of their brave fellowship, and at least a couple of them were sporting deep lacerations across their arms and chests. She was irritated to see that Howle was one of the survivors, though she noted he was nursing a nasty gash across his upper arm and grimacing in pain. The tunnel-horrors had disappeared back into their lairs, presumably having gorged themselves to their satisfaction. Shev decided not to think about how in the eight realms they were going to make it back up that cliff face later.

The Golden Lord was there, somehow unharmed and barely out of breath. He muttered an arcane phrase, and the tip of his staff began to glow with a soft yellow light, bathing the weathered stones beneath their feet in a warm amber haze. The ground on which they stood sloped away into a wide avenue, which led further into the ruins.

'We are near,' he said. 'Follow me.'

They began to walk down what was once a central thoroughfare, and now a stretch of broken flagstones lined with toppled statues, invaded on all fronts by thick, barbed gorse and patches of yellow-green grass. The statues were of men, aelves and duardin, but not warriors or rulers as you might expect from a city this size. All of them bore the trappings of inventors and scholars. A man reaching out towards the heavens, a bizarre, mechanical contraption in one hand, wearing what seemed to be a pair of many-lensed goggles. There was an aelf, wielding nothing more than a long feathered quill, a look of intense concentration upon his angular face, slightly ruined now by the smears of verdigris that covered his body like a rash.

'I don't think it was a battle that caused all this,' Shev said, wondering aloud. 'There's no sign of weapons, no skeletons lying in piles on the streets.'

'I would estimate this city to have had a population in the low thousands,' said the Golden Lord. 'It is indeed strange to see so few remains. Most likely, Quatzhymos was abandoned.'

'If so, what caused them to leave?'

'Let us continue on. Perhaps we may find answers within.'

The Golden Lord kept up a fearsome pace, hardly caring to take in the wonders that surrounded them. That seemed strange to her, considering how effusive he had been about discovering this place. Perhaps the dangers they had already faced had robbed him of his excitement. They continued on, tramping over scattered masonry, shards of age-old glass and broken pottery. All around them was the spectre of destruction. Entire avenues of columned halls lay crumpled and crushed, as if they were the abandoned playthings of some vast titan.

After what seemed like several hours of travel, Howle held up a hand.

'Listen,' he growled, kneeling to press one hand to the ground.

They fell silent, weapons drawn, gazing around at the ghost of Quatzhymos uneasily. The light was fading now, and shadows crept from doors and hallways like questing fingers.

After a moment, Shev could hear the sounds. Drums, beating to a frenzied, staccato rhythm. Low, guttural sounds, like bellowed chants. They were only a few hundred paces from the far side of the canyon now. The sheer cliff face rose above them at an angle, and the city descended beneath it, into darkness. It was as if the earth itself was opening its jaws to devour Quatzhymos, and the ruins of the city were sliding slowly down its gullet.

'We're going down there?' said Howle. Even the old mercenary's voice was hesitant.

'We are,' said the Golden Lord, who showed no sign of fear or trepidation. He might as well have been announcing a camping trip.

'You heard the drums,' said Howle. 'There's something down there.'

'Then we shall take great pains to avoid it, if it poses a threat to us. We have suffered greatly to get here, my friends, but we have made it. Within lies our fortune, if we only have the fortitude to seize it. Are you with me?'

There was a mumbled sound of assent, decisive if not particularly enthusiastic.

Chapter Four

'Well, that complicates things,' said Shev, staring down at the clusters of roaring fires in the clearing below. Hulking figures whirled and bellowed around the flames, casting flickering shadows across the ground. Their skin was dark green, covered with thick smears of warpaint in all colours, while they carried crude clubs or axes made of chipped stone. Around these capering figures loomed the broken spires of the shattered city, great arcing gateways rent and torn, the skeletons of burned-out towers and piles of scattered rubble.

The orruks had found Quatzhymos, and they had indulged their passion for thoughtless destruction on this ancient place of learning. The light of their roaring fires danced across the cavernous ceiling of the chamber, high above their heads.

'They have been here for many years,' said the Golden Lord, kneeling beside her. 'This devastation is decades old. Perhaps centuries old.'

Leering, bestial faces were carved into the walls in this

corner of the city, and great totems of bone littered the chamber, painted garishly with lurid colour. The place stank of sweat and filth.

'More and more of 'em every season,' said Howle, spitting in disgust. 'Come pourin' out of the jungles, chantin' like mad folk. Port Crassin fell not two months past, burned to ashes.'

'The men of lightning defeated them at the battle of Blistersand,' said one of the Golden Lord's hirelings, a pockmarked youth named Feghel, with an air of sage wisdom. 'They killed an orruk the size of a mountain, so they did. My uncle told me. He fought there.'

Howle snorted. 'Your uncle's a drunk or a liar. Besides, there ain't no defeating greenskins, not for long. You just kill as many as you can. Enough that they don't rise up again for a good, long time.'

'There must be a hundred of those creatures down there,' muttered Shev.

'Then we are fortunate we have not stumbled upon a full war party, armed and ready for slaughter,' said the Golden Lord. 'We can avoid them.'

'You think Occlesius' tomb still stands?' asked Shev.

'It must,' the masked man snapped. Shev raised an eyebrow. It was the first time she had heard him lose his composure. He shook his head, and glanced at her.

'I apologise, Madame Arclis,' he said. 'It is simply that we are so close to our goal, and to be foiled in our quest now would be the harshest of punishments. Please, enlighten me. Where do you believe the tomb is located?'

She turned, and scanned the encampment below. The orruks' fires occupied a central square, what she assumed would once have been a plaza or some kind of forum. The buildings had once been impressive structures, towering spires and great archways of gleaming marble. Most had been levelled long ago, torn down and claimed by the ravenous wilderness. Yet not all had suffered such a fate. Far across the way, beyond the hollering bands of orruks, stood a building larger than any other. It was tall and angular, in the style of many Sigmarite cathedrals she had seen, but there was a wide range of clashing architectural styles visible even through the damage it had suffered. Sweeping buttresses supported a central spire, which tapered to an iridescent spiral of dully gleaming crystal. The windows were circular portals in the fashion of the ancient Azmahari churches. They were almost all smashed. The roof, meanwhile, seemed oddly organic – an almost chitinous shell of disc-shaped tiles, arrayed in yet more spiral patterns. There were many gaping holes in the building, and the main archway lay shattered and broken on the steps leading to the main entrance, but the place retained a sort of tragic grandeur despite the savage desolation around it.

'If I know anything about Occlesius, it's that for all his genius, the man was monumentally self-obsessed,' she began. 'There's no way he would opt for a quaint, quiet burial place.'

She gestured to the grand building across the way.

'I'd bet a hundred gilden that we'll find his mausoleum in there.'

'I concur,' said the Golden Lord. 'Let us be cautious lest we bring the orruks down upon us.'

He turned, and gestured their band forwards. Howle led them down the nearest incline, a steep ravine that dropped between the spines of two broken buildings, crafted from green-black stone. Everyone had their weapons drawn, a wicked assortment of blades of all shapes and sizes. Some carried crossbows and alley-pieces, but all those who bore firearms kept them tucked in their belts and holsters. A single shot here would bring hordes of greenskins down upon their heads. The drums of the orruks were like a hammer in their skulls, and their stamping feet seemed to echo around every corner. Silhouettes leapt and spun across the dusty road ahead as they crept ever closer to the orruk warcamp. They could hear the creatures' idiot howls and the clash of weapons, and see glimpses of their bodies through the skeletons of the ruined buildings.

Ahead, the cover of the ruins broke for a dozen or so paces, and to their left they could see the orruks' camp. In groups of two or three they dashed across the open ground, fortunately bathed in shadows now in the receding light. Dozens of orruks were slumbering next to crude huts fashioned from cured skins and bound bone. These lairs were festooned with skulls and ribcages, some human but mostly the large, broad bones of fellow orruks – victims from an opposing tribe, no doubt. Other greenskins still capered, swirling around the campfires in their insane dance. It should, perhaps, have been a ridiculous sight, but their muscular, war-painted bodies and totems of bleached bone gave their display a kind of primal ferocity. As Shev watched, a fight broke out, and two enormous warriors began to clash their heads together violently, blood spurting from their brows and noses as they battered each other senseless to jeers of their kin.

Ahead, a Kismenite with a short hunting spear and a forked beard bound with brass rings was gesturing furiously at her to move. She slipped out from the ruins' shelter and skittered across the open ground, rolling into the shadows on the far side of the clearing. Her heart was hammering in her chest, but the orruks seemed oblivious to their presence still. Ahead loomed the great central tower.

They drifted through the campfire light cautiously, approaching the structure. Howle was leading, and even Shev had to begrudgingly admit that the killer knew his trade. Despite his age, he moved with agile grace, hardly making a sound. As they neared the broken steps leading up to the ruined gatehouse, he dropped low and raised a hand sharply to signal them to halt. They crouched low, blades and bows ready.

Ahead, two orruks rounded the corner, stumbling and teetering, clutching spears that ended in heavy, jagged shards of black stone. They were clearly inebriated, grunting at each other in their harsh tongue. They were perhaps twenty paces away, and getting closer.

'Fill 'em full of bolts,' growled Howle. 'You lot, with me. We'll finish 'em off.'

A trio of leather-jerkined Excelsians crept forward, aiming heavy repeaters at the oncoming orruks. Others lifted bows, throwing axes and javelins. They waited until the creatures were only a dozen yards distant, still growling and spitting at each other. Howle swung his hand down sharply, like an executioner's axe.

There was a chorus of clicks, then thrumming strings as the archers released. Perhaps a score of bolts and missiles thudded into the greenskins. They grunted as the deadly torrent struck home, pitching them backwards. One twitched briefly, then lay still. The other roared in confused anger and staggered upright. Riddled with bolts, he brandished his spear. Howle was already moving, along with five other killers. They leapt on the remaining orruk, bearing him to the ground under sheer weight of numbers, though the bulky creature did not go down easily. One great hand snapped out to close around the throat of a sellsword even as the others drove knives and axes into the orruk's torso, again and again. The creature's crude spear jerked out, and Shev saw it punch right through the unfortunate man's chest and through his thin chain surcoat. He gurgled and spat blood, and his two daggers clattered to the floor. But the orruk's fury and impressive constitution could not save it. Howle rammed his saw-toothed blade under the beast's chin, and its bloodshot eyes rolled up in its head. With a gurgling spasm, the creature finally became still.

They all tensed, waiting for the inevitable shouted alarms. The killing had been quick, but hardly quiet. Shev tensed, ready to flee into the darkness. But no cry of warning was heard, no sounds of running feet. She breathed a sigh of relief.

Howle and his surviving sellswords dragged the bodies behind a pile of rubble, including that of the unfortunate sellsword. Shev watched the killer with disdain as he rifled through the slain man's clothes, pocketing a few copper coins and trinkets.

Their bloody task complete, they moved on, breaking across open ground and racing up the steps to the ruined building, ducking into the safety of its shadowed hall.

'Torches,' hissed the Golden Lord. A flickering orange glow lit up the hall as several sellswords lit pitch-soaked brands or activated flare-stones. It revealed an utterly ruined chamber, blackened by fires and covered in scattered debris. Once, white-marble statuary and great, spherical glass cases had filled this entrance hall, populated with all manner of tomes and artefacts. Those relics had been smashed and torn apart, hurled across the room or burned. Holes were smashed in the walls and in the arched ceiling high above. Spears of twilight illuminated gleaming shards of broken glass and crystal. Red-brown stains, perhaps dried blood or something even more repulsive, were smeared across every surface along with crude, scrawled depictions of slaughter and bloodshed, watched over by the greenskins' savage gods. Shev's heart sank to see such thoughtless, pointless destruction. How many secrets were once contained within these walls, echoes of civilisation and culture now lost forever?

Two great antechambers branched off from this great hall, both of which were in the same sorry state. In the corner of one was a pile of fractured skulls and skeletons. Shev knelt down to examine them. They were mostly human, but there were some aelves and duardin bones too. There were scraps of fabric, decayed and faded by time, but with a hint of elaborate embroidery. These, she presumed, had once been the guardians or resident scholars of this place, trapped and slaughtered by the orruks or some other intruder many centuries ago.

'No tombs here,' came Howle's voice, echoing despite his hushed tones. 'And no treasures, either. Damned orruks have had their fun, and there ain't nothing left for us.'

The Golden Lord turned to gaze at Shev. She shook her head.

'I'm telling you, Occlesius is here somewhere,' she said. 'We're missing something.'

'If you've led us all out here for nothing, I'll gut you myself,' hissed a grey-haired woman wielding a wide-bladed khopis. 'Leave you to the greenskins' mercy.'

'Silence,' barked the Golden Lord. 'Spread out and check every inch of this place. Every wall, every corner. Go.'

The sellswords filtered off into the gloom, leaving Shev and the masked man behind. His blank mask was still fixed upon her.

'Madame Arclis,' he said, 'I hope you realise the gravity of the situation. I promised these men and women great rewards for accompanying me here, under your guidance. Should we emerge empty-handed they will desire retribution, and I will be unable to sway them from that purpose.'

'Occlesius rests here,' she said firmly, before striding away.

It had taken years for her to pin down the location of

Quatzhymos, from fragments of ancient texts, maps and spoken legends. Trying to piece together the history of the Mortal Realms was like grasping at smoke. So much had been lost in the horror of the Great Darkness, when daemon-kind had rampaged across the lands, slaughtering and despoiling all in their path. Entire cultures and continent-spanning empires had been brought to their knees, their monuments torn down and their great works of art and literature destroyed or consumed by fire. Little oral history remained, for the citizens of these once-proud kingdoms were either butchered or forced to join the Dark Gods' mortal legions, devolving into little more than sadistic killers.

Only amidst the ruins of murdered civilisations could scraps of the truth be found. Shev had travelled far and wide across the Beastlands, seeking out forgotten tombs, lost cities and hidden repositories, piecing together a fractured history of this dangerous land. She had walked within the Prism-City of Ghlour, waded through the flooded catacombs of Michramicae and breached the sky-vaults of the Cloud Kingdoms. In all those places she had found traces of the great Occlesius, traveller and statesman, inventor and philosopher. He had been welcomed as a hero wherever he roamed, granted the greatest honours and showered with gifts and accolades. Quatzhymos had been his home, and it seemed as though the ancient city had maintained strong trade routes and alliances with almost every major kingdom in this region. Experts from the city were valued as greatly as the mightiest warriors, depicted in great murals leading the construction of wondrous monuments and monolithic statues in honour of the gods. And then, in the blink of an eye, all that grandeur had been torn down, trampled and burned.

As she crept through the dusty halls, the light from her torch illuminated ancient frescoes and murals, most of which had been smashed or scarred so badly they were no longer decipherable. She entered the great hall and gazed up at the ceiling, barely visible in the gloom. There was something up there, poking out of the darkness. A great hanging ornament trailed by cobwebs and ghostly-white with dust, but unlike everything else in this place it was largely intact. From a central disc of dull metal, broad enough for a person to walk along its length with ease, dangled six globes. Now she looked closer, she could see flickers of colour beneath the patina of dust. Clambering up a nearby column, she leapt across and grasped a handhold on a cluster of burned bookcases that were leaning against one another precariously. From there, she could reach a thin ledge that ran around the edge of the chamber. She hoisted herself up, and turned to face the device.

'What are you up to now?' shouted Kurdh from below.

She grinned down at him. 'Exploring,' she said, and jumped from the ledge across to the hanging ornament. The entire thing groaned, swaying under her weight. For a moment she wondered if she had misjudged this horribly. A cloud of dust erupted from the hanging globes, drifting out over the chamber like a miniature sandstorm. She climbed onto the central disc and examined the structure. A track wound its way around the ornament in concentric loops. Each of the hanging orbs was attached to one of these tracks. She felt a tremor of excitement. She heard footsteps below, and saw the Golden Lord and several other sellswords approach.

'The Liber Celestium tells us that there are eight spheres of creation,' she told her audience, gesturing to the hanging ornament. 'Aqshy, Realm of Fire.'

She pointed to a red-gold orb, covered with rivulets of red crystal that shimmered like trails of lava.

'Ghyran, Realm of Life.'

The jade orb, bright and vigorous even in the gloom of the chamber. 'Hysh, Realm of Light and Ulgu, Realm of Shadows. Diametrically opposed yet inextricably linked, they orbit one another, unable to escape each other's pull.'

She reached down, tugged at the chains that connected these two spheres. She rotated them to the right, so that they nestled next to one another. As she did so, they began to glow with a faint light.

'Ghur, Realm of Beasts. Chamon, Realm of Metal,' whispered the Golden Lord, shaking his head. 'To think I missed this.'

'You said eight spheres,' said Howle. 'There's only six.'

Shev laughed, and pointed a finger at the ceiling.

'Holy Azyr, domain of the God-King,' she said. 'It sits at the apex of the firmament. Watching over all.' A column of luminescence rose from the twin orbs of light and shadow. It bathed the walls of the structure in soft, golden light. Above, in the angular recess of the building's roof, loomed an engraving of a flaming comet. As the light found it, it gleamed white-hot, so bright it almost hurt to look upon.

'And below it all, Shyish,' said the Golden Lord. 'The Realm of Death. The land of endings.'

He rapped his stave on the floor of the sanctuary, which began to glow with amethyst light.

The floor creaked, and several startled sellswords leapt out of the way as a great aperture yawned open beneath them. An avalanche of dust toppled away into the darkness, and by the flickering torchlight they could see a stairway spiralling down. The steps were exquisitely carved from obsidian, through which ran veins of gleaming azure. Shev punched the air, unable to help herself. She felt that familiar shiver of anticipation run down her spine, and suddenly all the slog and toil of the past few years faded into insignificance. Before her companions could even react, she was bounding down the stairs, an eager grin on her face.

Chapter Five

The stairway wound down perhaps a couple of hundred paces, before ending at an archway of white marble. She wondered at the stonework. Images and icons had been worked into the structure and inlaid with gold and silver: soaring sail-arks drifting over a jagged mountain range; a city built within a molten waterfall; primordial monuments of forgotten gods beneath the waves; a clockwork metropolis populated by masked, robed figures. Places and realms that Occlesius had visited, perhaps? Scattered memories from an extraordinary life.

The room beyond the archway was a circular chamber, lit by several braziers that still smouldered with a pale blue light. Every inch of the room was covered in yet more frescoes, so many wondrous sights and images that she barely knew where to look. Three mirrors were placed at equal distances around the edges of the chamber, reaching almost to the ceiling. In the centre of the room, on a raised dais, was a large block of grey-white stone. Resting atop this oblong was a golden statue, laid lengthwise. It was a man, dressed in long robes and wearing a skullcap, his eyes closed in repose, his hands crossed over his chest. In one hand, he carried a small, circular device, a globe criss-crossed by bands of silver. In the other, he clutched an eyeglass.

After all these years, she had found it. The last resting place of Occlesius the Realms-Walker. She thought of her father, the mortal who had adopted her, and felt a stab of sadness that she could not share this wondrous discovery with him. An explorer and cartographer of no small renown, Dedrick Reynheim had passed near half a century ago, yet the wound was still raw.

Footsteps echoed behind her. She turned to see the Golden Lord enter the chamber, flanked by a dozen mercenaries. He barely stopped to look at the wondrous carvings, but instead simply marched across the room to the coffin.

'You cannot know how long I have striven to find this place,' he muttered. 'So much I have sacrificed to be here now. So much I have lost.'

With a triumphant growl, he raised his staff and brought it crashing down upon the lid of the coffin. There was a resounding crack, and the marble splintered and came apart.

'What are you doing?' gasped Shev, appalled at such carelessness. Not that she was averse to rooting through the treasures of the long-dead, but she believed you were supposed to do it with at least a certain amount of finesse.

He ignored her. Several of his hirelings approached, and together they hauled the heavy marble lid of the coffin loose. It fell to the floor of the chamber with a crash, releasing a cloud of dust. Shev moved closer and peered into the sarcophagus, her heart thumping.

There lay Occlesius. She thought, for a queasy moment, that he was alive. Though the corpse's skin was pale and stretched, his hair frayed and his teeth yellowed, the preservation of the body was remarkable. Even his eyes remained intact, piercing blue orbs that gazed contentedly off into nothing. In repose he was a nondescript man, quite unlike the illustrations and depictions that she had seen of the great Realms-Walker. He was small and shaven-headed, with a wispy little beard and a weak chin. Time had worn his skin to a grey sheen; his bald pate was heavily liver-spotted, indicating a life spent out under the sun. His clothes were fine silk of a vibrant turquoise, and he wore several rings and bracelets of impressive craftsmanship, bejewelled and gleaming. Around his neck was a chain of silver, from which hung an amber claw sigil.

It was decidedly odd, looking into the face of someone you had spent years studying and researching. For all that time the Realms-Walker had been little more than a name on a page, a thread connecting her to the mysteries of the past. Looking into that coffin was like gazing upon history itself.

Clutched in the arms of the corpse was a silver-bound tome, its surface filigreed with runes and markings she could not decipher. The Golden Lord wrenched the tome from the dead man's grasp.

'The collected writings and memories of Occlesius of Asciltane, the Realms-Walker,' the Golden Lord whispered. 'At long last.'

Shev gazed into the eyes of the dead man. She frowned. There was something strange about the man's crystal blue orbs. The right was milky and glazed, while the left seemed sharper, glimmering in the torchlight. She reached out and tapped it with her finger. It was hard, clicking at the touch of her fingernail. She glanced around. The Golden Lord was engrossed in the tome, not even looking in her direction.

'It must be here,' he muttered. 'It must.'

43

She had no idea what he was talking about. The sellswords were eyeing the frescoes and golden filigrees of the tomb, no doubt wondering if anything in here could be easily looted. Fishing a small knife from her belt, Shev delicately pried the orb out of its socket. It popped out easily, and she palmed it. It was indeed a crystal, fashioned in the image of an eyeball. Upon further inspection, she could see small trails of silver light whirling and coalescing within the iris, casting a faint light across her palm. Odd.

As she watched, the streams of light grew brighter and more insistent, the crystal flaring in her hand like the thorax of a glowfly. She stared into its depths, almost hypnotised by the mesmerising patterns. There was something there, in the depths. She peered closer.

You know, in many cultures it is considered the height of rudeness to break into a man's tomb and start digging the eyes from his sockets.

Shev gave a startled yelp and dropped the crystal, which bounced hard on the edge of the coffin and rolled across the floor.

Will you please be more careful with that? said the voice in her head, with an air of extreme irritation. *It was incredibly difficult to attain, and if it breaks, there is no telling what will happen to me.*

The Golden Lord rapped his staff upon the floor. He was staring at her from across the chamber.

'What did you do?' he said. His voice was ice-cold.

Shev struggled for words.

'I...' she began.

I do not like this one's tone, said the voice in her head.

'What?' she gasped.

He's trouble. Believe me. At my age, you get a sixth sense for these kind of things.

'Stop it!' she shouted, clutching her head as if she could squeeze the unwelcome intrusion out of her skull. 'What in the name of Sigmar is going on?'

'Tell me. Now,' growled the Golden Lord.

Oh, how rude of me. Allow me to introduce myself. Occlesius of Asciltane, at your service, my lady, said the voice. *Or at least as much as a disembodied consciousness can be. I am sorry, I have had precious few intelligent conversations in the past few hundred years. I fear I am going somewhat peculiar.*

'Peculiar?' she spluttered.

'Who are you speaking to?' snapped the Golden Lord. 'Answer me.'

She backed away, but someone grabbed her from behind. She smelt that familiar pungent stench and knew it was Howle. She struggled, but he twisted her arm painfully, locked her in place.

The Golden Lord strode over to her, his staff grasped in two hands.

'You will tell me what happened, now,' he growled. 'Or I will allow Howle here to begin his work. I have witnessed the results of his art, Madame Arclis, and I have no wish to see them practised upon you. So speak.'

'There was a voice… in my head,' she gasped, nodding to the crystal that lay dormant on the floor. 'That thing, it was speaking to me.'

The Golden Lord strode over to the orb. He knelt down to inspect it, then reached out a hand, slowly, to grasp it.

'Could it be?' he muttered to himself. 'Shadeglass, taken from the haunted City of Mirrors. Now I understand. Our great thinker could not bear to enter the lands of the dead, not with so many sights left to see. No, he sought to exist beyond the grasp of the Tyrant of Bones.'

The Golden Lord stood, grasping the orb tightly in one fist.

'Listen to me, Occlesius,' he said. 'Do not address the girl, but speak to me alone. How long have you dwelt here, amidst the rubble of your life's work? Hundreds of years at the very least. I can help you, Realms-Walker. I can take you from this place, free you from the prison you have made for yourself. There are ways, my friend. Ways to restore you to life. All I ask in return is this – tell me where to find the Silver Shard.'

There was a rustling sound, like the brushing of a soft hand over silk. Shev thought she saw a flicker of movement within the mirror to her left.

The Silver Shard, said the voice of the Realms-Walker. By the way the Golden Lord's head twitched and the mercenaries jumped in shock, Shev was sure they all had heard it too this time. He sounded cautious, perhaps even afraid. *How do you know of that name?*

'My reasons are my own,' the Golden Lord continued. 'I know you travelled to the Lost City of Xoantica, Occlesius. I know that you alone returned, from an expedition of five hundred souls. Tell me where it lies.'

I know not, said the voice. *I cannot tell you, for the memories are lost to me. Only a shadow remains, the echo of a nightmare I cannot recall.*

'Try,' said the masked man. 'There are worse fates than death, Realms-Walker, and I will subject you to them all if you do not tell me what I wish to know.'

All I know is that death surrounds this Silver Shard. Abandon your quest, masked one.

'I tire of this,' said the Golden Lord. He hurled the orb to the floor, and it skittered across the stones. Then he raised his staff, which crackled and spat arcs of lightning.

What are you doing? cried the voice of Occlesius.

'If you do not tell me how to find Xoantica, I will shatter

this crystal. What will happen to your spirit, I wonder, when I break the cage that holds it? Perhaps you will travel to the underworld, and the Great Necromancer will finally get his due. Let us find out.'

He aimed the tip of the staff at the crystal, and unleashed a stream of crackling energy. Green smoke began to rise from the sparking orb.

No! You cannot do this.

'Of course I can,' said the Golden Lord, continuing to pour lightning into the relic. There was a high-pitched shriek that echoed around the chamber, a disembodied sound of pure agony.

If you destroy me, I cannot give you the answers you seek!

'Then I will find them another way. I am a patient man, Realms-Walker. I have nothing but time. You, on the other hand, are swiftly running out.'

The screams continued. Shev twisted free of Howle's grip.

'Stop,' she said, moving to the Golden Lord and reaching out a hand to grab his arm. He pushed her away indifferently. The lightning was blinding now. It rippled across the roof of the chamber, and a cascade of dust poured down from the shuddering roof of the tomb.

I will tell you nothing! came the voice, sounding pained and thin.

'You will tell me everything,' snarled the masked man. He touched the tip of his staff to the crystal. There was another burst of electricity, and Shev heard a crack, like splintering stone.

Far to the north! Please, I am not ready for death. There is so much yet to learn. Travel to the farthest reaches of the Talon-coast, where the mountains drift far above the earth.

'The Fatescar Mountains,' the Golden Lord said. 'I know of this place. Continue.'

47

Hidden in the highest peaks is a city named Xoantica. It is shielded from mortal eyes by illusion and magic. That is all I can remember. Only death lies within that place, I promise you that. If you enter, you will not leave.

The Golden Lord's spell ended abruptly. The floor was charred and smoking, and the crystal orb glowed bright, like a hot ember.

'Allow me to worry about that,' he said. He bent and picked up the blazing crystal in one gauntleted hand. 'You merely have to worry about guiding me there.'

I am speaking to you alone now, aelf, came the Realms-Walker's voice, low and urgent and pained. *This man will lead you to your death. You must escape, as soon as you can, and take me with you. This man cannot be allowed to find Xoantica. Please.*

'Madame Arclis,' said the Golden Lord, turning to her. 'I want to thank you for taking me this far. Without your assistance I may never have found this tomb. And yet, I am now faced with a dilemma. You are in the unfortunate position of knowing too much about my intended destination. I wonder, can I trust you to keep my secrets? I am not a trusting man by nature.'

Someone stepped in close and grabbed her by the arm. She felt the edge of a blade in the small of her back. She could tell by the rush of stale breath that it was Howle. Shev's eyes darted to the stairs. Two sellswords, Kurdh and a lean spearwoman, stood guard there.

The Golden Lord sighed, and held up a hand.

'Please, do not be foolish,' he said. 'Even without the ministrations of Mister Howle, you would not make it more than twenty paces. Honestly, I am not some mindless savage. I do genuinely appreciate your skills and your knowledge of the Taloncoast. You are a uniquely gifted woman, Shevanya.'

'You lied to me,' she said. 'All this time, all the nonsense you spouted, and you're nothing but a petty thief after some magical trinket.'

'You knew I was no historian, no scholar. I never even played the part with any relish. I happen to be very skilled at deception, but the truth is that with you it was never called for. Don't lie to yourself, Shevanya. You are not in this trade for anything but your own sense of adventure. Tell me, how many great discoveries have you presented to the Colleges of Azyr? How many of your expeditions have been authorised and funded by the proper authorities? The truth is that you are a tomb robber, and an exceptionally gifted one. Embrace that. I could use your skills.'

Shev said nothing. His words were close – so close – to those her father had spoken the last time they had argued. Before he had died and left her alone in that silent house, alone with her memories and her regret.

The masked man sighed, and waved Howle back with an impatient gesture. The old killer loosened his grip, but she could feel him poised, waiting for an excuse to strike.

'I am sorry I led you here under false pretences. I would rather keep you at my side than have to resort to a more… unpleasant option. I believe that we can achieve great things together.'

It might have been the unsubtle threat that finally made up her mind. Perhaps it was the way that the Golden Lord's men slowly moved to block the exits. Either way, she decided it was time for her to dissolve this partnership. She had one chance, maybe, to take them by surprise. Her hand went to her pocket, and closed around a flat disc of cold metal. A trinket of duardin manufacture that she had reserved especially for moments of great need such as this.

'Very well,' she said, stepping forward with one hand out-stretched, the other clenched in a fist at her side. 'Let's find this Silver Shard of yours. Together.'

The Golden Lord reached out his hand to shake hers.

She hurled the metal disc to the floor, raising an arm to shield her eyes.

The chamber exploded with light and noise, a thunder-ous crack of silver-blue lightning that blasted them all from their feet and left a vicious ringing in their ears. The three mirrors shattered as one, sending shards of glass whipping across the chamber. Howle released his grip on her arm, and Shev snapped an elbow back into his nose, feeling a satisfying crunch as it struck home. She was on her feet in a moment. Around her, the Golden Lord's sellswords rolled and cursed in a daze. The Golden Lord was on his knees, hands cover-ing his face. His mask lay scarred and smoking on the floor. He glanced towards her, and beneath the web of his fingers she saw something writhe and blink. Not human eyes. Not eyes at all, in fact.

If there were any lingering doubts about abandoning this expedition, they evaporated in an instant.

He turned away, grabbing for his mask. The crystal spilled from his grasp and skittered across the floor towards her, and she bent and scooped it up.

Miss... Arclis, is it? came the voice in her head again. *May I suggest a swift egress?*

Shev spun on her heel towards the entrance to the tomb. There was Kurdh, staggering to his feet, sword in hand. She bounded over to him, dodging around his clumsy attempt to grab her and sank her knee into his groin. He folded with a groan, and she pushed him aside, feeling only the slightest hint of guilt. Compared to the rest of them, Kurdh really wasn't such a bad sort. And then she was free, bursting up the stairs into the gloom of the cathedral.

Chapter Six

As she emerged from the tomb and started forwards, two sellswords came around the corner to bar her path, weapons raised, staring in confusion. The sound of clattering footsteps echoed up from below. She spun on her heels and ran in the other direction, darting off into the darkness, her former companions close behind. She pounded through a door at the far side of the hall, entering a corridor lined with shattered marble busts. After several yards, the corridor opened out into a vast hall, filled with looming statues and row upon row of stacked tomes, stretching up into the gloom of the arched ceiling. As Shev darted between the closest opening there was a deafening blast, and a stack of yellowed, curling scrolls to her left exploded in a cloud of choking dust. She could hear muttered curses behind her, echoing across the open chamber.

'No guns, fool! You'll bring the whole cursed place down on us,' someone barked. Howle, perhaps.

Well, that was something, Shev thought.

Her relief lasted a scant few moments. Crossbow bolts slammed into the bookcases and display cases around her as she wheeled around a tight corner. Loud, but nowhere near as deafening as the gunshot. Glass shattered and another cloud of dust erupted into the air. Someone had themselves a repeater bow.

Left! The path to your left, said the voice of Occlesius.

More and more voices echoed around the great hall now, as Howle's sellswords filtered into the maze of bookshelves, hoping to cut off her escape. She had to get out of here before they surrounded her. As she pelted down another long corridor, more bolts skipped and deflected off the stone floor. Something whipped past her cheek, close enough to singe her hair. Two figures stepped out ahead of her at the end of the channel – a burly woman armed with a wicked silversteel mace, and a sallow man wielding a hooked dagger. Shev kept running, and they rushed to meet her.

At the last moment, Shev shifted her momentum, leapt out to the right and caught a foothold on the nearest shelf. As the woman swung her mace diagonally across, missing her by several blessed inches, Shev planted her other boot on the sellsword's face, feeling a satisfying crunch as her heel squashed the woman's nose flat. She kicked off, launching herself high over the remaining mercenary's trailing dagger, landing cat-like high up on the far bookcase, scrambling and hauling herself up as more bolts thudded around her.

She was just hauling herself over the lip of the case when something slammed into her shoulder, pitching her forward. Agony rippled down her left arm, and she lost her grip and tumbled over the far side of the rack, grabbing futilely at anything within reach as she went. Her fingers closed around a cluster of books, but the paper tore at her touch, and she only succeeded in pulling them down with her. She struck the stone floor with enough force to blast the breath from her body, and her jaw bounced hard, sending her head spinning. Spitting blood, she hauled herself to her knees. Despite the chaos and shouting around her, she spared a moment to collate her various agonies. Jaw possibly broken. Ankle little more than a ball of pain. At least two ribs fractured, and a headache like she'd spent the last fortnight swigging duardin fyrewhiskey. Oh, and the crossbow bolt buried in her shoulder. She reached back and tugged out the barb, which took a chunk of flesh with it. The pain almost dropped her to her knees again. What a joyous day this was turning out to be.

'Where now?' she said, throwing the bloody shard away.

The statue, said the voice in her head. *Climb the statue at the end of the hall. There is a window there at the very top, which should take you safely outside.*

'Should?' she said.

Well, it's been quite some time, but as far as I can remember the fall should not be lethal.

She sighed and glanced around, blurrily. There was thick stone at her back, the outer wall of the reliquary. To her left and right, more bookcases, and ahead a statue of a winged creature in flight, half-draconic, half-leonine. Above this marble sculpture was a small arc of violet stained glass, bathing the nearby walls and floor in a haze of purple. More voices reverberated around her. It was hard to pick them out above the ringing in her ears, but it sounded like they were getting closer with every moment. Shev rushed forward, staggered on her injured ankle but hobbled on, making for the statue.

Howle stepped out in front of the statue. He had a loaded hand crossbow aimed at her in one hand, and carried his saw-bladed cleaver in the other. His injured shoulder was bound with dirty bandages.

'No sneakin' away this time, girl,' he said, shaking his head.

She lowered one hand to her belt.

'Ah, ah, ah,' he said, brandishing the alley-piece, barbed bolt nestled in the groove.

She sighed, and raised her hands.

He came closer, within a few feet. With a smile, he slowly lowered the hand bow, and spun his blade in one hand.

'I'm going to enjoy this,' he hissed, raising the blade.

Shev stepped forward and blew a handful of gleaming powder into his face.

Howle cursed and screeched, swinging the knife blindly with one hand, clawing at his eyes with the other. Shev let the blade whistle past her neck, then stepped in close and brought her knee up between Howle's legs. He groaned, then slumped to the floor, twitching, with drool spilling from his mouth.

Shev grabbed the hand bow from his belt, and pressed it to the back of Howle's head, into his greasy mop of grey-black hair.

'I should put a bolt in your head, but I'd hate to rob you of the nightmare you're about to experience over the next few days,' she whispered into his ear. 'That's pure brachitor poison burning its way into your eyeballs right now.'

Howle groaned in horror, and began to claw and rub at his eyes in panic.

'Don't worry, it's actually not lethal, but you'll wish it was. It causes an intense fever and incredibly lifelike hallucinations. It's going to bring all your greatest terrors to life, Howle. Consider this a parting gift.'

With that, she was off, sprinting towards the statue, Howle's gibbering screams echoing in her ears. She clambered up onto the marble creature's wings, hauled herself up and onto its leonine skull. The window was there, barely large enough for her to squeeze through. She hesitated.

Trust me, Miss Arclis! Go now!

She heard shouts behind her, and more bolts skipped and whickered around her. Not much choice but to heed the man's words.

Ignoring the agony in her foot, she stood, ran along the length of the statue's head and hurled herself like an arrow towards the stained glass aperture, hands covering her head. She felt the glass give way, and then she was falling into empty space, tucking her body tight as the ground rushed up to strike her. She hit mossy earth and rolled, crashing through a thicket of thorns that scratched and tore at her skin. Toppling out of control, she bounced painfully down a muddy slope and prayed to all the gods that there wasn't a cliff waiting at the foot of her descent. The world was a multi-coloured blur, then she was falling free again, and with a bone-jarring thud she finally came to a halt. She spent a blissful few moments just lying there, panting and trying to catch her breath as her head spun. Then she felt a hand grasp her arm and pull her to her feet. Through her pirouetting vision, she glimpsed a face staring into her own. A man's face. He appeared to be shouting at her.

She snapped her head forwards into his nose.

Chapter Seven

Armand Callis was helping the aelf to her feet when she head-butted him.

His nose exploded with pain, and he staggered backwards, tripped over a clump of vines and landed on his back-side. His assailant was already running, stumbling like she was half-drunk, clearly still dazed from falling down what amounted to a small cliff, which was understandable.

Another figure stepped out of the undergrowth, slender and tall, dressed in a long leather greatcoat. The aelf woman swung a punch at the newcomer, who simply swayed lazily to the side, caught her arm in a firm grip and twisted, neatly flip-ping the aelf onto her back. Captain Arika Zenthe placed a foot in between the stricken aelf's shoulder blades, and shot Callis a grin.

'You really do have a way with the ladies, don't you, Cal-lis?' she said.

Callis sighed and hauled himself to his feet. Blood seeped

down his face, trickling into his beard. He tenderly prodded his aching nose. Broken, of course. Perfect.

'Usually they leave it a little longer before resorting to physical violence, Zenthe,' he replied.

He leaned over the prone woman, who was struggling and kicking to no avail beneath Zenthe's sharkskin boot. The captive twisted her head to the side, and peered up at him. Her face was thin and angular in the way of aelf-kind, but not so sharply defined as Zenthe's. Her skin was fair, darkened by the sun, and her hair a vibrant russet. One side of her face was webbed by burn marks, reaching from her chin to just below her striking green eyes.

'We have to move,' she said. 'We've got to get out of here, now.'

'Apology accepted,' he replied, nursing his injury. 'Now, what exactly are you doing here?'

'There's no time!' the captive hissed.

Behind him, twigs crunched underfoot, and Callis turned to see Hanniver Toll emerging from the trees, accompanied by several of Zenthe's retinue. The aelven corsairs had already drawn steel, a variety of rapiers, daggers and heavy-bladed cutlasses. Toll was wielding his four-barrelled pistol. The man's eyes were bright with eagerness. It had been a long hunt, and the witch hunter was sensing the kill. He knelt beside the prone aelf and removed his wide-brimmed hat, running a hand through thinning hair.

'Your name?' Toll said.

'It doesn't matter,' she grunted. 'They're coming for me.'

'Good,' said the witch hunter. 'Because the man you came here with is a killer and a heretic, and I am here to see him dead. My name is Hanniver Toll, of the most holy Order of Azyr, and you are my prisoner until such time your own complicity in the traitor's crimes can be determined.'

It was then that they heard the sound of bellowing voices. Deep and guttural, accompanied by the beating of drums and the stamping of feet.

Callis caught Toll's eye.

'Orruks,' he spat. He would recognise that brutish tongue anywhere.

A gunshot cracked out across the darkening sky, and flocks of startled creatures fled into the air, hooting in panicked indignation.

Toll nodded to Zenthe, who hauled the prisoner to her feet.

'Quickly,' he growled, and began to climb the steep slope towards the ruined city.

Callis darted after him, drawing his own blade. He still carried his Freeguild steel, a span and a half of tempered metal with a basket handle. He drew his pistol, a duardin wheel-lock piece, heavy and reassuring in his grasp. The aelves of Zenthe's crew filtered after their captain, bounding up the steep ascent with graceful ease, eager for the killing to start. Even after months of sailing with these rogues Callis still felt uneasy in their presence. Like a brayhorn amidst a pack of wolves.

Zenthe had handed her prisoner over to one of her crew and was now bounding ahead of the others, her long hair whipping in the breeze, twin blades held low at her side.

Ahead, the ragged slope levelled off and Callis could see lit torches and the glimmer of blades. There was a band of perhaps twenty humans, holding a set of stairs against a mob of onrushing greenskins. The steps were slick with blood, and Callis could see broken bodies piled about, forming a barrier over which the whooping orruks clambered eagerly. The night was split by a flash of light and a loud crack as one of the men fired a scattergun into the midst of the advancing mob. Several toppled back in an explosion of pink mist.

Behind the struggling warriors, in the doorway of the shattered building, stood a golden-masked figure, wrapped in black robes and carrying a staff. As they broke from cover, running towards the melee, the figure turned its head to them.

Callis glanced across and saw Toll staring at the figure, his mouth set in a grim line, his fingers bone-white where they gripped his gun.

'Vermyre!' he shouted, and even over the din of battle his voice rang clear.

Then the witch hunter was running again, levelling his pistol. More orruks bounded from the ruins to their left, their voices raised in a single, bestial howl of battle-lust. Without even stopping, Toll aimed his gun to the side and fired. One of the onrushing creatures slumped bonelessly, a bloody hole in its skull. Callis aimed at a second figure and fired, but his shot failed to put the beast down. He had fought these brutes before, and knew well how difficult it was to kill the damned things.

Suddenly, they were close enough to see the creatures' blood-shot eyes, to smell their rancid sweat. Captain Zenthe ducked the clumsy swing of a broadaxe and spun, whipping her blade through the neck of her assailant. The orruk dropped to its knees and she reversed her grip on the blade and brought it stabbing down through the thing's neck. It gurgled and fell to the ground and she twisted her sword and pulled it free. Another greenskin barrelled across Callis' vision and bore an aelf to the ground, smashing the unfortunate soul's face into a bloody ruin with a succession of heavy punches. Callis stepped up behind the orruk and fired a bullet into its skull, and it slumped over its victim, twitching. He turned to see another aelf cut down. Hot blood splattered across his face, and he stumbled backwards, cursing.

More gunshots, and a piercing, haunted scream above the

carnage. He blinked gore from his eyes and sought his bearings. Bodies writhed and killed and staggered in the near-darkness. Toll was several paces ahead of him, hacking and weaving through the melee, fighting with a desperate frenzy quite at odds with his typical, measured swordplay. A trail of bodies lay scattered behind the witch hunter, wisps of smoke rising from gaping bullet holes. But more and more orruks were splitting off to race towards him, and Toll could not carve his way through so many.

'Hanniver!' shouted Callis. 'Fall back, you madman. You'll get yourself killed!'

If Toll heard him, he showed no sign of it.

Toll ducked back from the clumsy swing of an orruk's stone adze and thrust his blade forward, through the beast's ribcage and into its chest. The creature coughed foul-smelling blood which splattered across his face, and without even thinking, he raised his pistol and fired point-blank into its head. He twisted his blade free and continued forward. His chest was heaving, and his breath ragged. It had been a long time since he had put his body through such punishment, but his quarry was here, and this might be his only chance to serve Sigmar's justice. To see his butchered corpse strung about the city gates of Excelsis, a warning to anyone who sought to conspire against their own.

Ortam Vermyre. The Golden Lord. Betrayer of Excelsis, and butcher of the innocent.

Once, Toll had counted him a friend. Vermyre had used that misplaced trust and his own lofty position as High Arbiter of the city of Excelsis to condemn thousands to death in the name of the Dark Gods. The judgment for that crime had been too long in coming.

Another howling face loomed out of the darkness, and he

swept his sabre across to carve a red line across its eyes, never slowing his momentum. Ahead, the orruks were hacking their way through Vermyre's men, overwhelming them with sheer strength and numbers. Still the masked figure watched Toll advance, seemingly oblivious to the death and bloodshed all around him. The witch hunter was close now, perhaps a hundred paces from the melee. He had no idea where the others were, but it did not matter. This was his task alone, and if he died here to end Vermyre's stain on the realms, he would do so content. Time seemed to slow. He lifted his pistol, put the traitor's head in the sight.

Something struck him in the side, a dead weight that smashed him off his feet just as he pulled the trigger. His gun bucked in his hand, firing high and wide. He hit the ground hard alongside his assailant, where they rolled in a tangle of thrashing limbs. He punched out with the butt of his pistol, unable to free his sword hand for a killing strike, and felt it connect. There was a pained groan, and the grip on his waist loosened. He snarled and rolled his dazed opponent over, grabbed his blade and raised it high, ready to drive it through the traitor's heart.

A beam of flickering torchlight washed across the face of Armand Callis, his eyes bulging and his face bloody. Toll's hand was around the man's throat, and he was gasping for breath.

'Toll,' Callis gurgled. 'It's me!'

There was a flare of blue-green light, and Toll loosened his grip on the man's throat and staggered to his feet. The golden-masked Vermyre rose over the mob of orruks as they tore and hacked his band apart. He was borne aloft on a disc of gleaming metal, which rippled with azure flames. Arrows whickered up at him, some missing entirely while others skipped off the floating shield, disappearing into the night. There were screams of outrage from Vermyre's remaining henchmen, as they realised they were being abandoned to their fate.

'Not today, old friend,' shouted Vermyre. There wasn't even any gloating in his words. He simply sounded old, and tired. Toll even imagined he heard a hint of regret. Then the man was drifting away, rising off towards the clustered rocks of the crater rim, out and away from the ruined city.

'No!' shouted Toll. Rage and frustration welled up in him like bile, and he raised his gun once more and fired. Nothing but a dry click. Empty. He cursed, fumbling at his belt for a fresh cartridge, but it was too late. Vermyre was gone. Callis was coughing and spluttering, climbing to his knees. Toll turned and grabbed the man by his leather jerkin, slammed him against the nearest wall.

'I had him!' he snarled. 'I was about to put a bullet through that bastard's skull!'

'You were about to get your guts ripped out by an orruk axe,' spat Callis. 'And you're welcome, by the way. Next time I'll not waste my effort. Now get your hands off me.'

'Fools, if you're not too busy throttling each other we need to disappear,' came a voice from behind. It was Zenthe. Both her curved swords and her clothes were splattered with orruk blood. Her crew were falling back, loosing bolts as they retreated. Behind Zenthe was their prisoner.

'I can get us out of here,' said the aelf girl. 'I know a path out of this crater.'

'Your quarry's gone, Toll,' said Zenthe. 'Now let's move, before the orruks tire of hacking his hired fools into chum and come for us.'

She turned and sprinted after the retreating aelves. The smoke was thick around them now. Callis turned to follow

Zenthe, shooting Toll a dark look as he went. With one last glance towards the skies, the witch hunter followed.

Chapter Eight

Shev ran, slipping and sliding across moss-slick rocks and through dense tangles of barbed vines. She could hear bestial howls as the orruks gave chase. Arrows skipped around them. Ahead, a burbling channel of clear water trickled down a rise of shattered columns.

Ahead, said the voice in her mind, startling her so badly that she almost tripped and fell flat on her face. *Climb. We are close.*

'Here,' she shouted to the others, and leapt up to the first cluster of stones.

'They're closing on us,' shouted the man called Callis. He turned, standing ankle-deep in the running water and raised his pistol. He fired, and a green-skinned figure in the distance crumpled, then lay still. Callis stowed his gun, and Shev stretched out a hand to help him clamber up beside them. The corsair aelves skipped over the rough ground with impressive ease, barely slowing. Ahead was the portico of a great hall, slanted and broken, looming out of the gloom.

It was built from blue-white marble, turned a dirty grey by layers of dust.

There, declared Occlesius, triumphantly. *Your escape route.*

It would be a hard climb, but not an impossible one. Zenthe and her corsairs were already sprinting across the cracked flagstones of the plaza towards the tower of clustering creeper-vines.

How did he know about this place, she wondered? You would have thought that being bound to a coffin for several hundred years would limit one's knowledge of the surrounding area.

Oh, I was not bound to anything, said Occlesius. She was sure she could hear an element of smug satisfaction in the echo that rippled through her mind. *You recall that gem you plucked from my tomb with such quick-fingered grace? That wondrous little device is called a thoughtstone, or a soulstone, and it was fashioned in the arcane forges of Shadespire, greatest city of Shyish. It is crafted from shadeglass.*

'Shadeglass?' Shev muttered. She had come across that word before, somewhere in her father's notebooks.

It captures one's soul upon death. It allowed my consciousness to live on beyond the time of my passing, to drift and travel amidst the walls of this city to certain similar artefacts, to converse with my fellow academicians. There was so much to do, you understand? So much to contemplate. Of course, I had not anticipated sharing the last several hundred years of my existence with only witless orruks for company. Dreadful conversationalists, those creatures. Not to mention their questionable hygiene. They used my herb gardens as a latrine, can you even imagine?

'Could you do me a personal favour?' Shev growled, as she grasped a length of thick, mossy vine and began to climb. 'Shut up!'

She realised Callis was hauling himself alongside her, and she tried to ignore the look of bafflement upon his face. More arrows slammed and whickered around them as they climbed. An aelf to her left gurgled, spat blood, and tumbled away, three shafts protruding from her back. Shev glanced down. A score of orruks knelt at the base of the columns, loosing from crude bone and hide shortbows. Dozens more were leaping onto the vines, climbing with jagged blackstone knives clamped between oversized fangs. Toll paused his climb, reached into his jacket and produced a small, bronze sphere. He pressed a shallow depression on the device with one thumb, and then tossed it down amongst the gathering throng of orruks. It exploded with a snap-hiss, gushing foul-smelling black smoke. She could hear the beasts retching and hacking, bellowing in outrage. Soon the orruks were enveloped in the stinking cloud, and the arrows they launched were hopelessly inaccurate.

They were close now. She risked a glance back down. The orruks were gaining on them with terrifying speed, their thick forelimbs dragging them closer and closer, their small, cruel eyes ablaze with killing rage. Another aelf fell, dragged down by grasping hands. He coughed, then screamed as the creatures fell upon him with stabbing blades. Shev's arms were aching terribly, but fear gave her motion. One grip after another, inch by exhausting inch, she hauled herself higher. The rim of the crater was so close now. Zenthe reached it first, leapt free and caught hold of the opening with both hands, dragging her body over the edge. More aelves made the opening. One turned to pull a fellow corsair out into the moonlight, but three thick shafts of black wood slammed into his chest. He swayed, collapsed to his knees and tumbled back into the rising smoke, forcing Shev to duck to the side to avoid the corpse. Then she was close, and an arm grabbed her firmly by the shoulder and dragged her into fresh air.

They had emerged onto a steep hillside. All around them

was the swaying sea of the jungle canopy, bathed in turquoise starlight. Below, the ground sloped away sharply for several hundred paces, leading to a tangle of thorny bushes and blessed solid ground.

Callis ran forward and began pouring a flask of clear liquid over the web of vines that protruded from the hole.

'Someone get me a torch,' he yelled, throwing the empty container aside. A dark-skinned aelf woman ran forward, clutching a blazing limb of dried wood. She hurled it down into the darkness and lunged aside as a gout of flame exploded out of the gap. Shev heard deep, guttural bellows of agony, and smoke scoured her eyes. A hulking form hauled itself out of the earth, swinging wildly, wreathed in flames. Toll stepped forward, ducked under the beast's swipe, and smashed the pommel of his sword into its snout. It toppled backwards, screaming, and disappeared into the rising flames.

'The fires won't stop them for long,' said Toll. 'Let's go.'

They finally stopped running when the thump of orruk war drums had faded away. They had entered a patch of sparse ground, by the shore of a pool of murky water that shimmered faintly in the moonlight. Clouds of luminescent moths fluttered across the surface, the glow from their wings bathing the ground in a faint green light. Callis leaned against the curve of a tree, panting and coughing, holding the stitch in his side. The aelves took up position around the clearing, aiming their repeater bows out into the encroaching darkness.

'We've lost them,' said Toll, stowing his pistol. He marched over to the aelf girl.

'You will tell us everything you know,' he said, in that low, measured voice that he liked to use for scaring the wits out of people. Callis recognised it well, for it had not been long ago that Toll had turned it upon him. 'From the moment you met Vermyre, to the moment you ran. Leave nothing out. If you lie, I will know.'

The aelf sighed.

'We met in Sayron, perhaps seven months past. At the time, I was cataloguing treasures for some thick-headed noble named Razzicelli, a would-be collector of exotic artefacts with more coin than sense. The pay was good, but the work was dull. Razzicelli had no eye for history or quality. He'd buy anything that sparkled, and hang the price. Still, he had a vault filled with tomes and maps that was larger than the house I grew up in, a library's worth of priceless documents that he was content to let rot away while he chased worthless baubles.'

Zenthe snorted with amusement. 'Sounds like half the nobles in Excelsis.'

'The man you call Vermyre introduced himself as a trader of rare goods,' the aelf went on. 'I guessed he was from old Azyrite stock, because he had plenty of coin. He wasn't interested in Razzicelli's goods, though. Only his library. He was looking for a map to Quatzhymos, and he found it. With my help.'

'Did he tell you what drove him to find this place?' asked Toll.

'It was the resting place of Occlesius the Realms-Walker.'

'A traveller and explorer from many hundreds of years ago,' said Toll, answering Callis' confused expression. 'Before the fall. His writings survive in the great libraries of Azyrheim, but the location of his tomb has long been a mystery.'

'No longer,' said the aelf. 'I had been searching the Talon-coast for a sign of its location for over a decade. I'd found a few clues within Razzicelli's archives. Historical accounts of a city of scholars and learned souls, a place where the high-minded could study and converse in solitude. But it was only when the Golden... when *Vermyre* and I shared our findings that we finally discovered the location of Quatzhymos. He hired the sellswords, and I was the guide.'

Callis studied the aelf as she talked. She seemed admirably unruffled under the circumstances, but there was something strange about the way she spoke. Halting, as if her mind kept slipping from the subject. It was odd. Callis had seen enough terrible liars in his time as a guardsman to recognise the common tics, but this was different somehow.

'What does Vermyre seek?' asked Toll.

'I...' the woman began, then frowned and shook her head.

'He came there for a reason. Think,' barked the witch hunter.

'It's called the Silver Shard,' the aelf said at last. Her eyebrows were furrowed in confusion, as if she didn't quite understand the words she was speaking. 'It's an artefact from a time long ago. Before the tempest of Sigmar. Before the fall. Before the first tribes of mortalkind.'

'What does he want with it?' asked Callis. 'Vermyre's no fool. If he's after some kind of relic, you can bet he has a mind to use it, and I'm betting whatever he's planning is nothing good.'

The aelf shook her head, staring blankly into the distance.

'This thing, it has great power,' she said. 'Power to shape reality. To unmake mountains and to boil the seas. But that's not why he seeks it. At least, that's not the only reason.'

'Why then?' asked Toll. The question seemed to shake the aelf out of her stupor.

'He wants to fix himself...' she said.

'He's been injured?'

'No,' she shuddered. 'Or at least, not exactly. He's been... changed. His face. Whatever it was, it wasn't human. It was writhing, like a pit of vipers.'

Her skin turned pale, and her eyes became wide. She turned and stared at Toll, as if seeing him for the first time.

'He's *broken*,' she whispered. 'And he'll do anything to fix himself. *Anything*. This device, he believes it's what he's been looking for, but he's wrong.'

'This artefact you speak of,' said Zenthe, wiping orruk blood off her blade with the tail of her longcoat. 'Where does it lie?'

'The Fatescar Mountains. There is a city there, lost to time, hidden by illusions.'

Callis frowned. The Fatescar range dominated the northern edge of the Taloncoast, a colossal, hook-shaped expanse of strange, geometric mountains that drifted in the air above a sprawling expanse of thick jungle. What magic kept the immense rocks afloat, no one could say. He knew of several expeditions that had been launched into the area, but none had ever returned. On its own, that was not entirely surprising. There was no corner of the Taloncoast that was safe for travellers to walk. These lands were so wild that he doubted they could ever be truly tamed, even by the might of Sigmar's heaven-forged armies.

'I've heard strange tales about the Fatescars,' said Zenthe, thoughtfully. 'Entire fleets of privateer ships disappearing into nothing. Ships being raised high into the air upon winds of magic. Tribes of faceless serpent people. Of course, there's a thousand tales like that from all across the Taloncoast, and most of them are bilge made up by drunkards or liars.'

'There was once a city in those mountains,' said Arclis. Again, she had that strange expression, like she was reading the words from a tome that only she could see. 'From there, powerful mages ruled over the Taloncoast... and beyond. Shaping the world to their liking. It was they who discovered, or perhaps crafted, the Silver Shard, a weapon of such power that it could undo reality itself. With it they mastered the magicks of illusion and transmutation.'

Callis frowned. 'I've never heard word of this empire you speak of.'

'This was long, long ago,' Shev said. 'Before the God-King returned to the realms. A rival power sought to steal the source of their strength away. There was a great battle... Many deaths. The bearers of the Shard were destroyed. Utterly. Completely.'

'Who ended them?' asked Toll.

'No one remembers.'

She blinked and flinched slightly, as if she had been splashed with cold water, then fell silent. Toll was watching her like a hawk, as was Zenthe. There was something strange about this one.

'This is where Vermyre is headed?' said Toll. 'You are certain?'

'Yes,' the aelf replied. 'He heads to Xoantica.'

'We shall see,' the witch hunter said. 'Bind the aelf's hands,' he barked to Callis. 'She comes with us. I have more questions for her.'

The aelf raised her chin. 'My name is Shev Arclis, and it would do you well to use it.'

Chapter Nine

It took several long, miserable days for them to trek back through the jungle. Early on the first day, it began to rain so thick and fierce that you could barely see more than a few paces ahead. The sweltering heat went nowhere, and so they had the unique pleasure of being roasted alive and soaked to the skin at the same time. Zenthe's aelves hacked their way through thick vines and boughs with their long blades, cursing to each other in guttural aelfish. To Shev's relief, they seemed to know this land well. They deftly avoided clusters of spore-spewing mushrooms and predatory strangler vines, and worked with a quiet efficiency that was a world apart from her former companions. She studied them as they worked. Their skin was brown and sun-beaten, and marked everywhere with tattoos in black ink. They were lithe, but well-muscled, especially in the arms, and almost all of them bore nasty scars, gouges and burns – the life of a corsair in the Beastlands was rarely short of dangers.

For the first couple of days, Occlesius barely stayed quiet for more than a few minutes at a time, peppering her with questions about the wider world. It was when she told him of the rise of Chaos, the butchery and horror that had over-run the realms, that he withdrew, remaining quiet and pensive for the rest of the journey. When she did speak to him, she made sure to keep her voice to a whisper. She kept the shade-glass stone close, palming it when a grim-faced aelf corsair searched her for weapons, never revealing it when in eyeshot of her new companions. It was best, in her experience, to keep hold of whatever advantage you had for as long as possible.

Captain Zenthe never strayed far from Shev's side. The aelf, unlike her human companions, seemed in oddly high spir-its. She seemed particularly interested in her new prisoner, quizzing Shev each night when they finally sat down to rest about her past and her knowledge of the region. Every time Shev spoke of the ruins and wonders she had seen in her trav-els, Zenthe's eyes sparkled like those of a hunting cat before it pounced. It was a look that Shev was entirely familiar with. She'd seen it in the eyes of countless avaricious 'collectors', explorers and sellswords in her time.

Watch that woman closely, said Occlesius, after one such ses-sion. *She is the most dangerous creature amongst this band.*

The humans, Callis and Toll, remained something of a mys-tery. The witch hunter was hardly what she had expected from the stories she had heard of the most feared Order of Azyr. He was quiet, unassuming, allowing Zenthe to command the expedition and bark out orders while he followed on behind in brooding silence. Occasionally, however, she felt his eyes on her, and when she turned, his gaze sent a faint shiver of unease rippling down her spine. That was another look she had seen before, in the eyes of the Golden Lord. Cold, calculating. She had no doubt that if he deemed it necessary, this man would snuff out her life without hesitation.

Callis was another oddity. He was no sellsword, that was clear. His posture was too stiff, his weapons and gear too well-oiled and expensive. He had a soldier's bearing, alert and precise in his movement, his hand never straying from the hilt of his blade. She could hear an almost constant stream of curses coming from the man as he strode after Zenthe's aelves, wiping sweat from his grimy brow and swatting at the finger-sized insects that buzzed and hovered around their party, waiting for their moment to dart forward and partake in a feast of drained blood. He was a city boy, not an explorer. His dark hair was cut neatly in a military style, and his neat beard and moustache had grown bushy and wiry from days out in the wilderness. His skin was dark and sun-beaten, and his unremarkable yet rugged clothes – a dark poncho over a loose cotton tunic, with simple brown breeches tucked into abhor-hide boots – suggested to her he was one of the reclaimed, a descendent of mortal tribesman, rather than a citizen of Arnhem. She wondered how it was that a simple Freeguild footslogger had ended up in the employ of the Order.

Eventually, blissfully, the jungle – and the deluge – began to recede, and they could glimpse the glimmering, azure sea in the distance, through the scraps of withered mangroves. Ahead, she saw cliffs of jagged granite curving around to form a shadowed inlet. There was no beach. The overgrown thickets of the Fatescars reached out over the water, as if outraged at this intruder into their domain. Looming in the centre of the bay was a sleek, black vessel, perhaps two hundred paces from stern to keel. It hung low to the water, almost as if it could slip into the surf like some great aquatic beast to hunt the ocean depths. Its sails were pitch black, angular like barbed daggers, and on each flank it bore a score of wicked-looking ballistae.

'The *Thrice Lucky*,' said Captain Zenthe, as they looked down upon the wolf-ship. 'Have you ever sailed on an aelven wave-cutter, girl?'

'No,' she replied. 'She's a beauty.'

'That she is,' said Zenthe, sounding like a doting parent discussing her favourite child. 'Black-oak hull from the Septillion Forest, can stop a duardin cannon from a dozen paces. Two-score Azyr-forged grand arbalests, strong enough to punch through an Ur-kraken's hide. She's fast as a zephyr and will kill you with a look.'

'Sigmar spare us this speech again,' muttered Callis as he brushed past.

Zenthe gave Shev a smirk. 'The human has no appreciation for the finer things in life.'

They picked their way gingerly down towards the bay, hauling themselves through the thick foliage. Shev's feet ached terribly, and her wet clothes had rubbed her skin raw. She would trade a hundred gold pieces for a minute's rest. Not that she had such money, or was within a thousand leagues of anywhere to spend it.

As they splashed into the shallow waters of the bay, heading towards the ship, a figure appeared on the deck, leaning nonchalantly against the guardrail.

It was an aelf, dressed in the same black leathers as the rest of Zenthe's crew, and similarly swathed in ink and piercings. His angular head was bald, and he wore a violet bandana stained almost black with sweat.

'Captain,' he shouted, and gestured back over his shoulder. Several more of the crew approached and dangled a rope ladder over the side. Callis gestured Shev forward, and she began to climb. Zenthe didn't bother with the aid, instead nimbly scaling the hull, somehow finding foot and handholds in the smooth black surface and leaping gracefully onto the deck.

Shev hauled herself over the side, and found herself face to face with two-score hard-eyed corsairs.

'Lock her in the brig,' said Toll, clambering onto the deck behind her. Zenthe nodded to two burly shiphands, who grabbed Shev none-too-gently by the shoulders and marched her towards a covered hatchway in the deck, down a flight of rough, stained stairs and into the guts of the ship. It smelled of oil, salt and blood down here, though it was a far cry from the stinking galley she and the Golden Lord had hired to transport them. The woodwork was sleek, intricate, polished. Well maintained, without a sign of rootworm infestation or other damage. More crewmembers were oiling the huge spring mechanisms of the great ballistae she had seen from afar, placing barbed spears of black iron in metal containers next to the artillery weapons. A barrel marked with a crimson skull was positioned next to each weapon, tied firmly in place and secured with an iron cap. Tracks of dull iron were embedded in the floor beneath each ballista, so that the weapons could be retracted and brought forward to the firing ports. Shev noticed the floor here was noticeably darker, chipped and stained with patches of reddish-brown.

They strode through another deck, this one filled with rows of silken hammocks, faintly luminescent in the gloom. An aelf knelt nearby, an open box at his feet. She noticed, with a slight shiver of revulsion, that he was watching several large, pale spiders crawl over the bedding, diligently stitching up holes and weaving new strands. The aelf glanced lazily in their direction, and gazed at her with disinterest as he snatched one of the wriggling arachnids and placed it back in its container.

Finally, on the next floor, they came to the brig: a small, cramped chamber at the rear of the ship. One of the aelves pushed her roughly into the cell and swung a latticed door closed. As it slammed shut, a series of interlocking spars clicked into place.

'Could I get some water?' she shouted, as the aelves turned to leave. 'I'm parched.'

They ignored her. She sighed, slumped to the hard floor and tried to sleep.

Chapter Ten

'Tell me again,' said Toll. 'All of it. Everything you can remember about him, anything he said to you, any detail that you can recall.'

Shev sighed, and raised her eyes to the ceiling of her cell.

'I've told you over and over,' she said. 'What more can I say?'

The witch hunter got up from his chair facing her cell, and paced the room, spinning his wide-brimmed hat in his hands. She watched him, eyes heavy with fatigue. His questioning had not been exactly what she expected. When he had first appeared, emerging from the darkness bearing a single candle, one hand on his sword hilt, she had feared the worst.

She had heard the stories. Everyone had. When agents of the Order of Azyr roamed the streets, people vanished. As a child growing up in Excelsis, she remembered one occasion when she had passed the Halls of Questioning with her father and they had heard the faint sound of screams on the wind. His face had gone very pale, and he had ushered her away, answering her intrigued questions with only stern silence.

But there had been no sharp instruments, no hot pokers or thumbscrews.

'Torture is a blunt weapon,' Toll had said, interpreting her surprise. 'It has its uses. But I find it unreliable. Cut a man enough and he'll tell you everything you want to hear, and nothing you can trust. Besides, I take no pleasure in pain for the sake of pain, unlike many of my colleagues. I prefer to utilise leverage.'

'Leverage?'

'You are alone, hundreds of miles from any port of safe haven. For the moment, I deem you to be useful. You know of Vermyre's activities, you know more than most regarding his state of mind, his physical condition. That information is of value to me. It would benefit you to continue to prove useful, Miss Arclis.'

And so she had talked until her throat was sore, at great length, recalling every conversation, every thought she had ever had concerning the man she had known as the Golden Lord, this Ortam Vermyre. Toll listened intently, interrupting her every now and then with urgent questions, sometimes entirely unexpected queries that threw her off guard. Had she ever seen him consume food or water? Did he walk with a limp? When did she meet with him, at what times and in which locations?

This had continued for hours, and she was thoroughly exhausted. She had not slept more than an hour or two in the last few days. The fug of tiredness was causing her to repeat herself, or confuse dates and times.

Now she could hear the tramp of feet on the decks above, and the distant echo of bellowed orders. It was sometime near dawn, and the ship was stirring. They had been going all night. Toll stopped his pacing and placed his hat back on his head. If he was as shattered as she was, he didn't show it. He nodded to her.

'You're of no use to me half-asleep,' he said. 'Rest. We will continue this later.'

With that, the man headed for the stairs, leaving her alone in the gloom once more. She reached for the shadeglass gem, concealed in a hidden pocket built in the sole of her right boot. They'd searched her thoroughly, but not well enough to discover all of her tricks.

The witch hunter is persistent, Occlesius mused. *And he wishes this Vermyre dead. Fiercely.*

'I've no argument with that,' muttered Shev.

Hmm. I must say, I'll be rather annoyed if I've finally escaped from my tedious imprisonment in Quatzhymos only to spend the rest of my days in some dank dungeon.

'So what do you think?' asked Callis, feeling almost human again after a night's sleep, a wash and a change of clothing. He leaned on the rail of the ship alongside Toll, watching as the *Thrice Lucky* drifted out of the bay and into open water. He would not miss this godsforsaken place, that was certain.

'About the girl's story?' said the witch hunter. 'She doesn't strike me as a cutthroat. Nor a thief, in all honesty. I don't think she was misleading about Vermyre, at least. But she's hiding something. I've been doing this long enough to recognise the signs. There's more to her than meets the eye.'

Callis nodded. 'I was thinking much the same.'

There was an awkward silence, broken only by the roar of waves crashing against the hull. Callis glanced at Toll out of the corner of his eye. The witch hunter stared expressionlessly towards the departing coast. He looked old. Tired.

'Speak, if you have something to say,' Toll said at last. 'But for Sigmar's sake stop staring at me like that.'

Callis shook his head.

'You almost got yourself killed back there,' he said.

'I almost get myself killed every other day,' Toll replied. 'It is an unfortunate but necessary part of my profession.'

'Don't do that. Don't brush this off. I've never seen you charge into battle like that, without any regard for your life. You've made this personal.'

Toll turned sharply and met his gaze.

'Of course it's personal,' he growled. 'This is not some simple criminal we're chasing, one of thousands I've put down over the years. This man, I knew him. I called him *friend*. For years, Callis. *For decades*, and I never saw it. Not once. He made a fool of me, and he killed the best, most loyal duardin I ever knew. And you wonder why I want to see him dead, at any cost?'

'At the cost of your own life?'

'Of course. Vermyre cannot be allowed to live, Callis. He almost brought a city of the God-King to its knees. Can you even comprehend what would have happened, had his plans reached fruition? The lives that would have been lost? The slaughter, the horror?'

Toll suddenly reached out and grasped Callis by the shoulder, his fingers digging in painfully. He leaned in, his teeth gritted and his eyes narrowed.

'Don't get in my way again, Armand. If I have to give my life to see that man dead, it's a price I will pay gladly. If you cannot understand that, then you have no place at my side.'

Callis shrugged him off.

'Not interrupting anything, am I?' came a cheerful voice. Captain Zenthe came over, trailed by her first mate, Oscus. The dark-skinned aelf commanded the *Thrice Lucky* when Zenthe was ashore, which Callis took to be a mark of how firmly she trusted him.

'Nothing that concerns you,' said Toll.

'On my ship, everything concerns me, Hanniver,' the aelf replied. 'But suit yourself. There's a strong wind up, and the seas are calm. We'll make good speed.'

'Not quickly enough,' muttered the witch hunter. 'Vermyre's already on the move. Every second we delay gives him the chance to reach the Fatescars before us.'

'He won't arrive before us. We're making for Bilgeport,' said Captain Zenthe. 'The corsair city. It's a pit of scum, but the sky-traders do good business there. We can hire an airship, book passage to the mountains.'

'It means dealing with the Kharadron,' said Oscus. 'They'll bleed us for this. For certain, if they know there's a prize waiting at the end of the journey.'

Zenthe waved a hand dismissively.

'I've negotiated with the sky runts before. They bluster and bellow, but they're a practical enough bunch where money is concerned. I'll get us passage.'

Callis had never had any dealings with the duardin sky-sailors, but he knew their reputation. Avaricious, insular, easy riled and not to be crossed. Few knew the hidden places of the realms better, it was said, though they did not share their knowledge or expertise without exacting a hefty fee in return. It hardly surprised him that they frequented the corsair city of Bilgeport.

'The High Captains of Bilgeport have haunted the trade-lanes for a dozen years,' Toll said. 'I trust them less than I'd trust a crystal-viper. They're bold these days. They know our armies are overstretched, and they bleed our trade fleets dry and sell us back our own goods at twice the price, blaming their attacks on barbarians or sea monsters.'

Zenthe grinned.

'My type of vermin. Don't worry yourself, witch hunter. The

moment they see the shadow of the *Thrice Lucky* drift into port they'll be grovelling at my feet.'

'They're killers and thieves.'

'Yes they are. And if you want to track your man down, you'll have to learn to bear it. At least for now. This is the wilds, Hanniver. We're far away from the Coast of Tusks and from your precious city. You're only one man, and your reputation means less than nothing out here.'

The witch hunter assented with a nod, but Callis was fairly sure that was not his last word on the subject.

'It's a long journey to Bilgeport,' said Zenthe, fetching a black leather flask from her belt and ripping free the stopper with her teeth. She took a long draught and offered it to Callis, who shook his head.

'Suit yourself. Anyway, we'll soon be heading into dangerous waters. You keep your eyes open and act as we say, and you might just make it through alive.'

Callis felt his stomach sink. During the voyage from Excelsis, they had found themselves within an inch of a bloody death on several occasions. Pods of leathery behemoths that hurtled through the waves at frightening speed, and unleashed tidal waves large enough to drown an entire town every time they breached the surface. Gales of razor-sharp teeth that had whipped and shredded at the hull as they huddled below decks. Translucent, glowing pseudopods that wrapped around the hull in the depths of night, searching for flesh to drain dry. With these memories fresh in his mind, he wondered exactly what constituted dangerous waters to the aelf captain.

Chapter Eleven

Shev spent two days swaying between sheer boredom and extreme discomfort. The hardwood planks of her cell made her bones ache terribly, and when she tried to snatch a few hours of precious sleep, the rolling and yawing of the ship sent her tumbling painfully back and forth. Thankfully, Occlesius seemed just as sick of the situation as she did, and rarely emerged to pester her with his endless questions. He seemed rather sullen, as if he resented her short temper and rudeness. She could not care less for that, as long as he stayed out of her head. Every now and then, aelven corsairs wandered through the hold on some errand or another, but despite her best efforts they paid her no attention beyond fetching her stale, maggot-ridden bread, oversalted meat and water every morning.

On the third day she was woken from a fitful slumber by a rapping at her cell. She blinked, bleary-eyed, and saw Captain Zenthe leaning against the bars, dragging the hilt of her sword along the wood.

'Well rested?' asked the corsair.

'Obviously not,' muttered Shev, rubbing at her sore back. 'So you finally remembered about me then.'

'How could I forget,' said Zenthe, with a grin. 'It's not every day you come across an aelf treasure-seeker who consorts with the most wanted heretic on the Taloncoast.'

'Historian,' said Shev. 'Not a treasure hunter.'

Zenthe shrugged. 'As you like. Point is, you've got plenty of secrets tucked in that brain of yours. Plenty of knowledge that might benefit an intrepid ship's captain such as yours truly. Get up.'

Interesting, said Occlesius. *I wonder if our witch hunter friend is aware of this little chat.*

Zenthe rapped her knuckles on the hardwood cell door, which swung open. Cautiously, Shev clambered to her feet.

'Are you hungry?' asked the captain. 'Come with me.'

Zenthe's cabin looked more like the shop of an obsessive antiquarian than a ship captain's home. She could barely move for trinkets, gew-gaws, mementos and trophies. Yellow, curling maps were piled high on a bleached wooden desk, scattered with compasses, quills and all manner of nautical implements, the function of which escaped Shev. Dangling from the ceiling, gently swaying, was a globe of turquoise glass, home to a cephalopodic form that peered at her through one ink-black orb with an air of intense irritation. A row of blades of all different shapes and sizes covered the rear wall, from fine Excelsian steel sabres to strange, vicious-looking duelling hooks attached to spiked gauntlets. There was a strong smell of oil and rich wood, with a hint of spices.

A truly fascinating collection, mused Occlesius. *Clearly this aelf has done a fair bit of travelling herself. Pray ask her what that squid creature up there is, I've never seen one of those before.*

'No,' hissed Shev under her breath.

'Sit,' said Zenthe, gesturing to a stool piled high with detritus. Shev brushed it aside as carefully as she could manage. Something darted out from under the pile of leather-bound tomes and scattered trinkets. A golden scarab: no living creature, but a ticking, whirring automaton. It settled on Zenthe's desk, until the aelf captain brushed it away with an irritated swipe and put her boots up on the hardwood surface. She stared at Shev with narrowed eyes, rapping one finger on the side of the desk. There was a rather long silence.

'So,' said Zenthe, finally. 'How does someone like you end up in league with a traitor like Vermyre?'

'I told you before, I had no idea who he was.'

'You must have heard of the battle of Excelsis. Towers in the sky, daemons on the streets. The purges. The burnings. It's not only Hanniver Toll who hunts the man. I've never seen so many bounty-seekers and findsmen on the prowl. His face is on the wall of every outpost from here to Hammerhal.'

'He doesn't look like that anymore,' muttered Shev, suppressing a shudder as she recalled the things that writhed within the Golden Lord's face.

Zenthe frowned at the remark, but didn't press further.

'I had no idea who he was,' Shev continued. 'He was just someone with resources. Someone who seemed to share the same interests as me. He was clever. Careful. He knew his work, and he knew when to let me take the lead.'

There was a knock on the door, and an aelf entered. He hobbled across to Zenthe's desk, bearing two plates. His left leg tap-tapped on the floor as he walked. It was made of dully gleaming steel, thin with sharp, splayed claws. The smell of smoke-cured fish caught Shev's nostrils and her stomach groaned with longing.

Zenthe nodded at the cook and pushed a plate across to her guest.

'Eat,' she said.

She needed no urging, and fell upon the meal like a starving wolf at a carcass.

'How did you get into all this?' asked the captain. 'Raiding ruins is not exactly common work.'

'My father raised me out here,' said Shev through a mouthful of food. 'In the wilds, on endless journeys, excavations. He was Azyr-born. Fascinated by what lay beyond the gates of the celestial city, out in the realms. He was searching for answers as to what the world was like before the fall. How people lived. How they died. He never stopped travelling, and I went with him. Eventually age caught up with him, and he couldn't do it anymore.'

'He aged? So he was not an aelf, then? Not your real father?'

'As real as any,' snapped Shev. 'He never abandoned me on some street corner like my own flesh and blood did. He raised me, taught me.'

Zenthe held up her hands.

'Aye, I understand. The man was a saint. Good for him. So you've travelled far, then? You've visited many ruins and tombs that happen to be stuffed with priceless valuables ripe for the taking?'

'I told you, I'm no grave-robber.'

The captain waved that off, as if it were of no consequence at all.

'Do you have any idea how much a woman can make from the black market sale of old world relics?' she said. 'There are so many fat, rich fools from Azyr looking to spend their coin on useless trinkets from one dead kingdom or another. I could use your knowledge, girl. This is the way fortunes are made.'

Shev wasn't about to say that coin didn't mean a thing to her, but the idea of helping rich Azyrites loot all the priceless artefacts they desired and haul them off back to their palatial residences and private collections was not exactly appealing.

'I keep telling you,' she said. 'I'm not interested.'

'Well, that's a shame,' sighed Zenthe. 'I was hoping that if we were to work together I might be able to persuade Toll not to put a bullet in your head once he's done with you, but it seems it isn't to be.'

'He's a witch hunter. He speaks with the authority of Sigmar himself. How could you stop him, even if you wanted to?'

The captain's eyes narrowed, and she snarled, revealing sharp white teeth.

'The only word that matters on the *Thrice Lucky* is my own. Toll is a guest on my ship, only for as long as I allow it. He's already stretching my patience thin by dragging me on this fool's endeavour. You know, there will already be some upstart fool back in Excelsis laying their plans for usurping my territory. Do you know how many souls I'll have to send back to the deep when I return?'

'Why come out here at all?'

'Because being at the top of the food chain becomes dull after a while.'

Zenthe speared a chunk of smoked fish with her knife and devoured it, never taking her eyes from Shev. She lowered the knife slowly, until it pointed at Shev's coat pocket.

'So,' the captain said. 'Are you going to tell me about that shiny trinket you've been cradling?'

Shev froze.

Careful, said Occlesius. *I warned you that this one was dangerous.*

'This,' she said, reflexively grasping one hand to the shadeglass orb. 'It's just an heirloom. From my mother's family. I keep it close.'

'Hmm,' said Zenthe. 'Let me see it, just to be sure.'

She stretched one hand out, twirling her knife in the other.

Hesitantly, Shev fished the orb from her pocket and handed it to the aelf. Zenthe closed one eye and held the crystal up to the light. She rolled it in her hand, and tapped it with her blade. Then she leaned back, tossing it up into the air deftly, eyeing Shev. Catching it, she wrapped the stone in her palm, slammed her hand on the desk and raised it again, fingers splayed, to show that the orb had disappeared.

'Looks valuable. Maybe I should take care of it for you,' she said. 'How would you feel about that?'

'I told you,' said Shev, leaning forward and meeting the captain's eye. 'It was my mother's jewel. I'd like it back.'

The captain's hand shot out, so fast that Shev barely saw it move. It stopped an inch before Shev's eyes, the jewel once again clutched between the captain's fingers.

'I can appreciate a clever liar, but I don't like being taken for a fool,' Zenthe whispered. 'Think carefully about your place on this ship, girl. You have few enough allies as it is.'

She opened her hand and let the shadeglass gem fall into Shev's lap. Rummaging around in her desk, she brought out a silver chain with an empty locket. She flicked it with her knife, and Shev caught it. The locket was just large enough to house the crystal.

'If that's such a treasured heirloom of yours, it seems a good idea to keep it safe and in plain sight, no? Consider this a gift.'

There was a frantic knocking on the door, and the first mate, Oscus, bounded through. He wore a devilish grin.

'Fin on the horizon,' he said. 'Thirty-pointer, at least.'

Zenthe practically jumped over the desk.

'Beat to quarters,' she shouted. 'Ready the arbalests. I don't care if it takes us off course, I'm not letting a beast that size escape us.'

She turned to Shev, fire in her eyes, all the tension that had filled the room dispersed in a moment.

'Want to see the *Thrice Lucky* in action?'

Oh yes indeed, said an excited Occlesius.

Shev shrugged, not sharing his enthusiasm.

Chapter Twelve

The deck was a maelstrom of activity. Corsairs rushed to and fro, dragging great barrels marked with blood-red runes to areas on the foredeck, and lashing them in place with thick chains. The sails were at full mast, billowing forwards with the wind behind them. Shev blinked and winced at the blazing sunlight, unprepared for its intensity after several days locked up in near-darkness. They were out on the open ocean now, a churning expanse of green-tinged waters below, a cirrus-streaked desert of azure above. The seas were calm, by the standards of the Taloncoast. The *Thrice Lucky* rose and yawed beneath them, carving through rushing wave-walls with ease, sending up a shower of bracing mist. Shev took a deep gulp of fresh air. It certainly felt good to be outside again. She rushed alongside the captain to the fore rail. Scanning the line where sea met sky, she could see nothing. Zenthe had a golden eyeglass raised, ornately crafted to resemble the questing tentacles of some deep-sea creature.

'Sight me,' she bellowed.

'Two leagues off the starboard bow, captain,' shouted a look-out nestled in the rigging over their heads. 'We're closing. Blood of Khaine, it's a big beast.'

'I see it,' hissed Zenthe. 'A ghyreshark. It's our lucky day. Oscus, I have the wheel.'

She tossed the eyeglass to Shev and darted over to the prow, and the great wheel. It was carved from the same black wood as the vessel, but wrapped in leathery hide. An aelf abandoned the device as the captain approached, handing her control of the *Thrice Lucky*.

Shev raised the eyeglass and gazed over in the direction that Zenthe had indicated. At first the violent motion of the ship made it almost impossible for her to sight in, but after a few moments she steadied herself, and managed to scan the horizon. Nothing. She moved along, searching for something. There. She frowned. That was no fin. It was a mast, sticking out of the water, almost as tall as the *Thrice Lucky* itself. She looked again, and her heart froze in her chest. It was a creature, all right. She could see the black immensity of it just below the waves. The fin was immense, barbed and serrated like a saw blade. It was hard to gauge exact distances from here, but it looked like it could easily fill the deck of the *Thrice Lucky*.

That is indeed a ghyreshark. A species well-known for its vicious hunting patterns. It kills far more than it can consume. Many scholars contend that it possesses a daemonic taint, which would account for its legendary ferocity.

'We are going to die,' she whispered. Oscus heard her, and gave a malicious bark of laughter.

'Maybe we will,' he said, and flashed her a grin. 'Or maybe we'll earn enough from the kill to make this entire voyage worthwhile.'

Hanniver Toll emerged on deck, his companion, Callis, in tow. The ex-soldier looked ever so slightly green. He was clearly not a nautical man, then.

'Are we under attack?' shouted the witch hunter, rushing to the rail and peering off at the horizon.

'Not yet,' laughed Zenthe, pulling the wheel far to starboard, angling the *Thrice Lucky* in towards the looming monstrosity. 'But I'd recommend holding onto your hat, witch hunter. This may get a little rough.'

Toll turned, and saw Shev. She backed off a little, raising her hands. He strode over to her, and for a moment she thought he was going to grab her and drag her back down to the brig. Instead, he held a hand out for the eyeglass. She handed it over. The witch hunter raised it to his eye.

'Sigmar's blood,' he cursed.

He handed the eyeglass back and marched over to Zenthe.

'This was not the deal, Arika,' he growled. 'You were handsomely paid for this journey, and I bled myself dry getting you what you wanted. Our target is Vermyre. We are not here to go... fishing.'

'We're six months past the deadline you gave me, witch hunter,' Zenthe replied, not even turning to meet the man's gaze. 'Six months. And have I complained? Have I threatened to abandon you here and return to Excelsis?'

'Yes. Every day. In fact, you threatened that exact thing this morning, not four hours ago.'

Zenthe laughed. 'Perhaps you're right about that.'

She turned, and slapped Toll affectionately on the shoulder.

'Don't look so worried, Hanniver,' she said in a cheerful voice. 'This will be a morning's work, at that. The beast's close, and there's nothing on these seas that can outrun the *Thrice Lucky* when her blood is up. We'll have the thing gutted and skinned before you can blink.'

'Or it will eat this ship whole, and we'll all die out here for nothing.'

'Or that might happen, yes. But there's no use complaining, as you so rightfully pointed out to me. Just make yourself useful and do as I say, and we'll be back on the trail of your traitorous friend in no time.'

Shev held the glass out for Callis, who stood at her side looking very far from comfortable.

'You want to look?' she asked.

'No thanks. I think I'll save the soul-rending terror until the sea monster's a bit closer, if it's all the same to you.'

Shev laughed.

'The captain knows what she's about,' she said. 'This is what they do for a living, after all. I'm sure we'll be fine.'

That unearned confidence faded, flickered and died over the following minutes, as the *Thrice Lucky* drew closer to their quarry, and the true scale of the ghyreshark became clear.

Shev clambered midway up the mainmast for a better view, grasping a firm hold of the sinew ropes that bound the *Thrice Lucky*'s sails in place. She looked ahead, and could see the great fin sending streams of water surging in its wake. The creature was vast. One could see the shimmering silhouette of it a few feet beneath the waves, enormous and streamlined, carving through the water like a bullet. Its great tail flicked from side to side, large enough to crush a dozen warriors with a single swipe. How could they even begin to hurt such a monster? Its angular head was large enough to engulf the prow of their ship. As she watched, the creature rose, letting its snout break the surface. One enormous eye gazed sidelong at them, a huge, pitch-black orb nestled above a maw crammed with fangs the size of greatswords.

That is… rather larger than I had been led to believe. Mhyroone's

Scourges of the Beast-sea contends that the ghyreshark can grow no larger than two-hundred spans, but that seems markedly larger.

'Maybe they've grown up a bit while you've been trapped in that amulet,' she said.

It would appear so.

There was something primal and terrifying about the sleek, blunt ferocity of that body, colossal even in such a vast expanse of open water. All she could think of was how easy it would be to tumble overboard into that bottomless abyss, and how helpless you would feel splashing around and choking on water while that enormous shadow circled closer and closer. She gripped the guide-rope so hard it hurt.

They should not be standing open on the deck, said Occlesius. Shev glanced below, and saw the aelves rushing to and fro with barbed harpoons in hand. She could see Callis, struggling to maintain his footing on the yawing deck.

'Why?' she said.

Those great jaws are not a ghyreshark's only weapon.

Callis had long ago decided that the open sea was not for him. The jungles of the Taloncoast might be filled with slavering monsters, flesh-eating insect swarms and all manner of other horrors, but at least there you could run. Or stand and fight. Or hide. Out here, you were so awfully exposed, with only a few-score lengths of solid wood between you and the great, bottomless nothing of the ocean. Which was filled with creatures like the one currently eyeing them like they were a floating dinner table piled high with its favourite treats. He wanted to throw up, and only refrained from hurling his meagre breakfast over the side of the ship because he didn't want to give Zenthe's crew another reason to despise him.

'Arika Zenthe,' muttered Toll, striding over and shaking his head. 'She'll be the death of me, I swear it.'

He glanced at Callis and winced.

'Throne of Azyr,' he said, 'you look awful.'

'If it matters, I feel even worse,' he snapped. 'Look at the size of that thing. How are we going to do anything but scratch its hide with these glorified crossbows? You need cannon to take something that size down. Lots of them.'

The witch hunter squinted out towards the great shadow of the beast. It was close now, within the range of an arbalest volley. As they watched, it sank out of sight, its great fin dipping below the waves. Zenthe hauled on the ship's wheel, and the *Thrice Lucky* turned sharply to port, leaning so hard that the two men had to shuffle and stagger to regain their balance.

'She's circling for a strike,' yelled the captain. 'Give her a volley as soon as she breaches.'

Toll grabbed Callis by the shoulders.

'Trust me, the *Thrice Lucky* is built for this work,' he shouted, over the groaning of timbers and the roar of the flapping sails above them. 'Do as they say, and for Sigmar's sake don't fall over the side.'

Comforting. And with that he was gone, racing down towards the access hatch that led to the gunnery deck.

'You,' shouted Oscus, sprinting over to Callis with an armful of vicious-looking barbed spears. 'You know how to hurl a javelin?'

'I do.'

'Then grab one of these, and wait for my signal.'

Toll cursed as he bounded down the stairs into the gloom of the gunnery deck. This was a pointless, foolish endeavour. If it had been anyone but Zenthe ordering it, he would have simply put a gun to their head and ordered them not to be so godsdamned stupid. Pulling that trick on the *Thrice Lucky*, however, would be a sure way to him and Callis being thrown overboard. He would have to simply hope they scraped through this intact, and remonstrate with the stubborn aelf afterwards.

The aelven corsairs were hunched in teams behind their wicked arbalests. One sat at the firing level, squinting through the porthole across the raging sea. Another two would hand-crank the arms of the weapon back once a round had been loosed, and a third stood by a rack of black-iron shafts, cruelly barbed with razor-sharp hooks that would ensure that once the missile had sunk into flesh, there would be no tearing it out. A great barrel had been lashed beneath each ammunition rack, all marked with an angular rune in blood-red paint. Or possibly just blood.

'Ready yourselves,' bellowed the gunnery chief, a tall, broad-shouldered aelf missing the lower half of his right arm and one of his ears. He gave Toll a gap-toothed grin and nodded to the rearmost port-side arbalest.

'Crewman down over there,' he said. 'Got himself killed by an orruk, to our shame as much as his. You think you can handle this?'

'I should imagine so,' muttered Toll. He rushed over to the arbalest, kneeled in place beside the great, recurved limb. Close up, it smelled of oil and dried blood, and a deeper, acrider stench he couldn't identify.

'Here she comes,' shouted the aelf manning the firing lever.

Toll gazed out of the sighting aperture, a wide, circular port-hole that looked out across the open ocean. There was a tidal wave rushing towards them. A great maw rose from the water, a broad, heavy snout some fifty yards across, its surface scarred and lined with jagged quills that rose above two pitiless orbs of obsidian. It was moving at a fierce speed, aiming amidships. It was, it seemed to Toll, set on him in particular. Displaced water arced over the behemoth's head, and it opened its maw wide to reveal a thick forest of curving yellow teeth, descending away into the blackness of its gullet. Toll had never seen such an immense beast, in all his years on the Taloncoast. It looked as though it could capsize the *Thrice Lucky* by simply crashing its angular tail against the hull.

'Take aim,' roared the chief. 'Eyes and throat. Even you sorry fools should be able to hit a target that size. Let's kill this creature and earn ourselves a fine bounty.'

Toll's gunner raised the arc of the ballista a few inches, muttering over and over to himself in aelfish, one eye closed and beads of sweat pouring from his brow.

The ghyreshark was only fifty paces away.

'Loose!' came the roar.

Twenty harpoons soared out over the water, streaks of black lightning that riddled the monster's head, some sticking deep into its barbed hide, other skipping off and splashing into the waves. Not enough. Not nearly enough.

At the very last moment the beast submerged again, swerving to the side and striking the *Thrice Lucky* with the force of a thousand battering rams as it dipped beneath the waves. The deck beneath them rose, it seemed almost vertically, and Toll was sent flying back, head over heels, by a wall of water that struck him in the face with stinging force. The vessel groaned in protest, swaying and rolling, and Toll's head struck a beam, knocking him face down in the swirling flood, lights exploding behind his eyes. He gasped reflexively, and swallowed a mouthful of acrid water. Someone grabbed him under the arms, hauled him free.

'Get back on that ballista, or I'll gut you myself and hurl

your worthless corpse overboard,' screamed his saviour, before shoving Toll towards the crew who were already struggling to load a new harpoon.

The witch hunter made a mental note to track down the owner of that voice after this was done.

Someone was screaming. He glanced to the side and saw an aelf lying in a foaming pool of blood, his leg crushed underneath one of the arbalests. The artillery piece had been torn off its moorings with the force of the impact. He almost tripped over another body, sightless eyes staring at the ceiling of the gunnery deck, a splinter of wood the size of a dagger embedded in his neck. A great rent had been torn in the ship's hull, lengthwise across the chamber, and water gushed in every time the *Thrice Lucky* rose on a cresting wave.

Toll splashed over to the limb of the arbalest, and began furiously winding the hand-crank, readying for another volley. Their loader grabbed another bolt, opened the lid of the blood-marked barrel and sank the missile's tip into a bubbling, hissing pool of bile-green liquid. There was an acrid stench that sank to the back of Toll's throat, causing him to cough and retch. The aelves, he noticed, had donned silk masks that covered their mouths and noses. He had no such luxury.

'Let's see how she likes a taste of althasca venom,' shouted the chief.

Callis picked himself up off the deck, his head spinning, spitting water.

'Ready yourselves,' shouted Oscus, who was somehow on his feet, holding another javelin. 'She's coming around.'

Callis staggered over to a rack full of the black-iron missiles, and grasped one. The cold metal was reassuring in his hand. The corsairs were dipping their projectiles in a steaming barrel of bubbling liquid. He followed suit. The vicious barbs at the tip of the weapon began to hiss and smoke, and where the substance – whatever the hells it was – dripped onto the soaking deck, it left wisps of steam and pockmarks of blackened wood.

Captain Zenthe was wrenching the *Thrice Lucky* around, and the deck swayed beneath Callis, almost sending him tumbling. He had no idea what the substance on the end of his javelin was, but he was fairly certain that accidentally sticking himself with it would not be wise. A score of aelves lined the rail, each hefting a missile. At least three had been swept overboard, and he could see them writhing and splashing in the foaming spray, screaming for help that he knew they could not provide.

A living missile exploded from the depths. The full weight of the ghyreshark's barbed upper body broke clear of the waves, and two of the stranded aelves were swept into its gaping jaws. They hurled their missiles. Callis bent his body, added all his weight to the throw. Even so, his was the shortest throw by far. The aelves' missiles clattered into the creature's head, while his sank into the grey-white flesh above its gills and stuck firm. He saw a gout of blood spurt free, and the surf turned foamy reddish-brown. As the beast crashed back into the waves, it sent up an enormous geyser of bloody water, covering them all. It sank below the *Thrice Lucky*, blessedly not striking the ship this time. Callis and the crew grabbed more javelins, and raced to the far side. Nothing. There was a long, horrible silence, broken only by the clatter of waves against the ship's hull.

'Do you see it?' shouted Zenthe, holding the vessel in a straight line.

'Nothing,' came a voice above Callis. He looked up to see Shev, their prisoner, up in the crow's nest. She was scanning the waters around them. 'Maybe it dived?'

Oscus laughed.

'We've barely scratched its hide. And ghyresharks do not abandon a kill. She's coming back, mark my words.'

Seconds stretched on into minutes. The tension was worse, if anything, than fighting the damned thing. They nervously hefted their javelins, every muscle poised for action.

One of the aelves inched over to the rail, peering over the side into the murky depths.

'I think it's gone,' he said. 'I can't–'

There was a deafening smash of timbers. The *Thrice Lucky* was lifted almost vertically by the impact, sending them rolling and tumbling across the deck. Callis struck the aft cabin wall with bone-jarring force, and something heavy slammed into him. A groaning corsair writhed with one arm twisted at a sickening, unnatural angle. Then, with awful inevitability, the front of the vessel dropped, slamming into the water, which rushed up eagerly to swamp the deck. A flailing, screaming body was sent hurtling over the port rail, grasping helplessly for a handhold. Callis staggered upright amidst the chaos and, with a score of remaining aelves, staggered to the side of the ship. There was the monster, sweeping around the *Thrice Lucky*, its barbed hide bristled with harpoons and javelins, pouring black-brown blood into the foaming surge. Its great eye was fixed on them, a hate-filled gaze that seemed almost human in its intensity. It pulled alongside them, its great bulk parallel to the *Thrice Lucky*.

'Down!' yelled Oscus. Callis was too slow, still dazed from the fall. Someone barrelled into him from the side, and sent him tumbling to the floor. He saw a tangle of auburn hair, and realised it was the Arclis girl who had pushed him to the deck.

In that same moment, the monster's hide undulated strangely before it spat forth a hail of barbs, each as long as a spear. They whickered across the water and slammed into the hull of the

Thrice Lucky with a rhythmic series of thuds, digging deep into the wood. An aelf next to Callis was struck through the eye by a shaft. More went down as those too slow to react were riddled like pincushions. Oscus stood, sighted and hurled his javelin. It soared out and struck the beast in the eye. The creature thrashed, unleashing a horrible, gurgling groan, driven to a mindless frenzy by the agonising wound. Callis hurled his own javelin, which fell just short, sinking into the depths.

The *Thrice Lucky* cut sharply ahead of the floundering ghyre-shark, circling its great bulk as it drifted and thrashed in the bloody waters. Its enormous head was covered in lacerations and seeping gashes, and the eye that Oscus had pierced was little more than a ruptured crater. As they came around to face the beast broadside on, Callis found himself staring into the creature's one undamaged, hate-filled orb.

'Loose!' came the command from the gunnery deck. A dozen missiles whipped out across the churning sea, each striking home across its ruined maw. With one last, shuddering twitch, the beast rolled over, exposing a grey-white belly riddled with ancient scars.

The cheering only grew louder. Someone clapped Callis on the back. He leaned against the gunwale, and let out a heavy sigh.

Chapter Thirteen

Shev staggered to her feet. Her head was bleeding. She'd struck it painfully on the deck while pushing Callis out of the path of the ghyreshark's razor-barbs. The organic missiles were buried all about the deck, or sunk deep into the corpses of nearby corsairs. The surviving crew seemed to pay little mind to their fallen kin. More aelves were swarming onto the deck, wielding an intimidating array of cleavers, long, hooked poles and other instruments of butchery.

And so the butchery begins, said Occlesius. *It's remarkable, Miss Arclis, how little the practice has changed in all the years since my demise.*

'You don't strike me as the type who did a lot of privateering,' she muttered under her breath.

Indeed, no, but I was given the rare honour of accompanying the King of Carsinnian upon one of his famous scythagor hunts, on the occasion of his forty-first marriage. I do believe that he died on that very trip, eaten by the very creatures he sought to bring back to his feast tables. A tragic case.

She rolled her eyes.

Several of the landing craft that were stowed on the deck of the ship had been smashed to kindling, but the remainder were being attached to thick ropes and lowered overboard. Captain Zenthe's voice rang out over them, loud and clear.

'We move fast,' she bellowed. 'There's an open banquet out there, inviting every ur-kraken, gavrocha and razorjaw shoal from here to Excelsis to fill their guts, and I've no wish to be stuck in the heart of a feeding frenzy. We take the teeth, the liver, the eye, and as much hide as you can peel. Go earn our coin.'

The crew roared in triumph, and as many as could fit packed themselves into the shore boats. Shev went over to the rail, where a thoroughly soaked and blooded Callis was leaning, panting heavily.

'Hell of a catch,' he muttered weakly.

The sea was already churning with hundreds of ravenous predators, from swarms of diamond-shaped fish with vicious-looking fangs, to many-tentacled jellyfish that wrapped barbed tendrils around the corpse of the great beast, flensing flesh and feasting on the black blood that poured free.

'Not going out there to claim a trophy yourself?' Shev asked Callis, flashing the soldier a grin.

'I'd rather not, if it's all the same to you,' he replied. 'I value all my limbs. Thanks for… what you did.'

Shev shrugged, meeting the human's gaze for a moment before looking away.

'They start stripping this creature before even checking their fallen,' Callis said, and there was a clear tone of disapproval in his voice.

'There's no time for sentimentality out on the high seas,' Shev replied. 'In minutes, every beast within a dozen leagues will descend upon this carcass. Trust me, I've seen a dying deepstalker stripped of flesh within a few moments, and those things are larger than even this monster.'

The butchery that followed was indeed fascinating, if more than a touch disgusting. The aelves latched grapples to the mountain of dead flesh and swarmed across the corpse like insects, hacking and tearing, stripping skin and digging deep into the beast's cavernous innards. Long, forked poles were inserted into the gory cavern, and an enormous purple and black muscle was extracted. Aelves armed with saw-bladed halberds hacked and carved at thick strands of sinew and muscle until the organ came free. Then they bound it in leather and rope, poured a clear white liquid over it, and massaged the substance deep into the flesh.

Some sort of preservative, mused Occlesius. The battle against the creature had fascinated the Realms-Walker. *I believe in my day the sea-hunters used a blend of stalk-crystal sap and great-whale tallow. I still recall the stench. Horrible stuff, but it keeps the rot away for many months.*

Callis had turned a rich sea-green, and was leaning even more heavily against the rail, shaking his head.

'I thought you were a Freeguild man,' said Shev, enjoying his obvious discomfort. 'Aren't you soldiers meant to be well-versed in spilling blood?'

'Don't worry yourself with me,' he snapped, before staggering over to the rail and vomiting loudly and repeatedly into the ocean.

Seasickness is one aspect of mortality that I do not miss at all, said Occlesius, with a hint of pity in his voice.

'Fourteen souls back to the deep,' said Oscus. 'Four arbalests damaged beyond repair, at least until we make port, and several

breaches in the hull, thankfully above the water line. I've got a
crew working on it, but we need to find calmer waters.'

'All in all, a profitable venture,' said Captain Zenthe, cheer-
fully. 'When we're done here we'll make for the Singing Isles,
find a quiet bay and make repairs before we head to Bilgeport.'

'Another delay,' said Toll. 'I believe you said that we would
be finished here and back on our way within a day.'

'Oh lighten up, Toll,' sighed Zenthe. 'It's a half day's sail to
the Isles, at most.'

'And another day at least to fix up the *Thrice Lucky*,' said Toll,
not in any mood to be patronised. 'Don't take me for a fool.
We're damned lucky the hull wasn't breached. You were reckless, and we very nearly paid for it with our lives. No more,
you understand?'

Zenthe's eyes narrowed, and she stepped towards Toll. She
loomed over him, all the humour drained from her face in an
instant. His hand twitched towards his blade instinctively, but
he held firm, meeting her gaze.

'Don't second guess me, Toll,' she said, softly, every syllable
dripping with menace. 'Not ever. I alone command the *Thrice
Lucky*. Your Order means nothing to me. Less than nothing.
I am not some weak-hearted human for you to order around.
I've been hunting on the open sea since before you were born.'

'We had a deal,' said Toll. He was uncomfortably aware of
Oscus circling calmly behind his back, no doubt ready to sink
a blade between his shoulder blades the moment Zenthe gave
him a signal. 'Once Vermyre is dead I'll be gone from your
sight. Until then I expect you to honour your word.'

Zenthe's eyes were more pitiless and threatening than the
ghyreshark's.

'Do you know what I did to the last fool who questioned my
honour?' she whispered.

'Something creatively appalling, no doubt. Would you kindly tell your first mate that if he takes one step closer to me it will be his last?'

Zenthe's expression remained stony for a few tense moments, but then her thin lips creased into a smile, showing her brilliant white teeth.

'That's what I like about you, Toll,' she said, suddenly full of cheer. 'You're a stubborn one.'

She clapped him on the shoulder, and Oscus stepped back, leaning casually against the rail, his eyes still fixed on Toll. The tension had not entirely broken.

'Don't worry,' said Zenthe. 'We'll be back on the trail in no time. And look on the bright side. We made enough on this kill to hire the sky runts to take us all the way to Azyr itself, if we please.'

With that, the captain was away, bellowing orders at the aelven crewmembers who were hauling the stripped trophies from the ghyreshark carcass up onto the deck.

Oscus stared at him for a while, expressionless, then returned to cleaning grime from beneath his nails with his flensing knife. Toll met his gaze for a few moments and then walked away. His heart was thumping in his chest. That had almost been the moment, he was sure. Ever since he had met Zenthe, a confrontation with the mercurial corsair had seemed inevitable. She was beyond doubt a useful ally, who had saved his life more than once. But he could never trust her, and today was a firm reminder of that. She cared for nothing beyond her own desires. He had been foolish to question her command so openly, he knew. To the corsairs, that was little short of mutiny. He'd heard of Fleetmasters who had flayed their lieutenants alive for less. He had let his frustration get the better of him, and not for the first time in recent days. Picking a fight with

NICK HORTH

Zenthe aboard her own ship was akin to slicing your arms bloody and leaping into shark infested waters.

'What was all that about?' said Callis, approaching, his clothes soaked in blood and grime. He looked as battered as Toll felt, but his eyes were furrowed in concern.

'Nothing,' Toll said, not feeling in the mood to elaborate. 'Where's the girl?'

'She's helping them carve up the prize,' said Callis, smirking and shaking his head. 'She's only been out of her cage a half day, and already the crew's got more respect for her than either of us.'

'They don't trust my kind,' said Toll. 'And they care even less for Freeguild soldiers. You can bet Zenthe's mixed up in a dozen rackets for which I'd be obligated to summarily execute her and her entire crew, and they know it.'

'Well that's comforting,' said Callis. 'I'll expect a knife in the back any day now.'

'There's no danger as long as Zenthe's kept happy,' said Toll. 'I've already paid her a lord's ransom to take us after Vermyre, as well as a dozen other favours that damned near drained every resource and contact I have in Excelsis.'

'All that for one man...' muttered Callis.

'A price I pay gladly,' snapped Toll. 'I would think that having yourself witnessed what that man is capable of, you would agree.'

'I want him dead, sure enough. I'd just rather not sell my own life in the process.'

'Then perhaps you are not cut out for this line of work after all,' said Toll, and strode away towards his cabin.

Chapter Fourteen

He was close. He could feel it. Magic had seeped into this place like spilled oil, saturating every inch of it. The ancient trees had curled and warped into impossible shapes, binding themselves around one another like the coils of some great serpentine beast. Time stalled. He walked for an hour, only to glance behind and see the same cluster of calcified wood spearing up from the forest floor. He tripped and lost his footing, tumbling down a steep slope of crooked deadwood branches that tore at his robes and scratched bloody lines across his flesh. When he stood, he was in a place he did not recognise at all, a shallow grotto filled with pools of bubbling quicksilver. Looking up, he saw bodies nailed to the trees around him. Gleaming skeletons, encased in metal, leered down at him. He fell to his knees, and a ragged, joyless laugh escaped his parched-dry lips. It turned into another coughing fit. Lightning bolts of agony wracked his malformed face, and he felt something writhe and hiss beneath his mask. Caustic black bile seeped out from under the golden rim, dribbling down his chin. That only made him laugh harder.

Ortam Vermyre, former High Arbiter of Excelsis and loyal servant of Tzeentch, reduced to this.

Seeing Hanniver Toll again had brought many unpleasant memories rushing back. The day the conquest of Excelsis, planned since before the city's birth, had failed. The day *he* had failed. His transformation had started soon after. At first, it was an itch beneath his skin, one that could not be satisfied. Then, he had awoken amongst bloody sheets and scraps of skin in some lice-infested hellhole, and he could not feel his face at all. He remembered the purity of horror he had experienced as he raised one trembling finger to his cheek, and felt...

To know that you had disappointed a god. It was quite the humbling feeling.

Vermyre had exhausted his vast reserves of money and influence in the search for some way to fix his malformed body. He had trawled through libraries full of ancient lore. He had spoken to wise men and healers, wizards of the Celestial College and agents of the Dark Gods. He had known, of course, that it was useless. No mortal could cure the corruption seeping into his body. He had seen the same thing happen to others many times, when he served the will of the God of Sorcery. But the certainty of his damnation only made his search for absolution more frantic. With no more resources to call upon, he had turned to desperate measures. Like a creature of the night, he had slipped back into the city of Excelsis.

Where once he had ruled this city – perhaps its most powerful and influential figure – now he was reduced to a misshapen shadow, crawling through sewers and alleyways, terrified of showing his face. He had broken into the city's College of Magic, travelling via secret passages he had been shown by the traitorous former Archmage, Velorius Kryn. The man had been slain in the battle for the city, but the Order of Azyr had not found all of Kryn's hidden repositories of forbidden texts. It was in the pages of the old mage's journals that Vermyre had first learned of the Silver Shard, an item that Kryn had researched in great detail. Indeed, the wizard had been laying the groundwork for an expedition to Quatzhymos before his death.

This was his chance to be rid of the curse that afflicted him, and to take his revenge upon the city that had defied his will. And once Ortam Vermyre had a goal, there was nothing in the realms that could bar his path.

The undergrowth rustled, very slightly. Vermyre staggered to his feet, and stared off into the surrounding gloom. He knew when he was being watched.

'Come out,' he hissed, in a language older than time. 'I command you.'

'You command?' came a voice from the shadows. 'You are weak. Dying. A pitiful human. You command nothing from us.'

'Come out of the shadows!' he bellowed. His words reverberated strangely in the claustrophobic confines of the grotto.

For a moment, nothing moved. There was no birdsong, no hiss or click of insects. This place was deathly quiet. He could hear nothing but the arrhythmic beating of his own heart.

Then they came, drifting out of the gloom like whispers of smoke. Tall figures on bent-back legs, their skin a pale azure. They were bedecked with gems, tattoos and all manner of gewgaws, and each carried a gleaming spear of silver. Tzaangors. The smallest stepped in front of him. Its avian face was concealed by a silver mask shaped in the image of a roaring drake. Twin horns curled back from its skull, and in one hand it grasped a bleached wood staff tipped by a giant, blinking eye.

'This is a forbidden place, human,' it said in its strange, lilting voice. There seemed no way that such a bestial creature could speak so softly. 'We would have taken your flesh long past, but I smell the touch of the Changemaker on you. Speak. Why do you come to the Shal'kol'ma?'

'In search of allies,' Vermyre hissed. There was only silence in return. 'I seek an artefact of formidable power. The Silver Shard. It lies in a hidden city, far to the north. I would claim it in the name of great Tzeentch. But there are others–'

'The hunter. The soldier. The corsair. The seeker,' said the creature. 'We know of them. We saw them in your dreams.'

'Then you know they are enemies,' Vermyre hissed. 'They would claim this artefact for themselves. For their God-King.'

'We do not follow the weak,' said the beastman. The eye on his staff pulsed, flicked from side to side. The creatures stepped back as one, and the shaman followed. Vermyre ground his teeth together so hard he tasted blood. Not like this. It could not end like this.

'Do not turn your back on me!' he screamed. 'I command you.'

They stopped. Turned as one. Gazed at him, with pitiless eyes.

'We do not follow the weak,' the shaman-creature repeated. 'Only the strong. The worthy.'

Then he heard the tread of heavy feet, crashing through the undergrowth. The tzaangors began to chant, a high-pitched sound that made his gorge rise. An enormous form burst into the clearing. It was tzaangor, but a true monster of its kind. Where its kin were lithe, this thing was huge and musclebound, clutching a great two-handed club, dotted with vicious shards of green-black stone. Above its thick, corded neck the creature's head split, as if it had been cleaved in two by an axe swing. Two malformed half-skulls emerged from the torn flesh, filled with misshapen needles of yellow-brown teeth. The thing howled, a sound of fury, pain and sorrow. Vermyre felt an unexpected twinge of sympathy, and almost laughed at the inappropriateness of it. The creature stalked towards him, spinning that great club around as if it weighed nothing at all.

The creature roared, and spittle flew from its twisted horror show of a face. Vermyre's staff was a dead weight in his hands, but he grasped it close. The monstrosity began to stalk forward. He backed off, forming the shape of a spell in his mind.

It moved astonishingly fast. Before he could even mutter the arcane phrase that would have sent a spear of force tearing through its chest, the creature leapt forward, bringing the club around in an arcing swing towards Vermyre's shoulder. He ducked, hearing the rush of air as the weapon whipped past. He was rising to his feet when something struck him in the chest, sending him flying through the air. He landed hard on his stomach and the air was blasted from his lungs. Through bleary eyes, he saw the trunk-like legs of the creature striding relentlessly after him. He tried once more to shape a spell, but the pain was too much and the power slipped away from his fingers. Suddenly, the beast was upon him again. He ducked an overhead swing that would have crushed him into bloody paste, rolled aside and scrambled away on all fours. His audience hissed and jeered. One leaned close, jabbering in what he assumed was laughter. He struck it in the face with his staff, wrapped his arms around its neck and hauled it down, twisted and sent it staggering into the path of the oncoming monster. The startled tzaangor cried in outrage, and then the great club came down and split its skull, splattering the ground with brains and purplish blood. The creature tossed the carcass aside, still coming for Vermyre relentlessly.

He muttered an arcane phrase and the tip of his staff blazed with purple flame. He lashed it across at chest height, unleashing a wave of fire that rushed out to envelop the creature. It shrieked in pain, its flesh bubbling and scarring, its limbs twitching in agony.

Laughing, he came forward to strike the burning tzaangor hard between the eyes, spilling its blood.

'Worthless, wretched creatures,' he snarled. 'I should destroy you all.'

He summoned another gout of flame and sent it whipping out towards the watching beastmen. It enveloped three of the brutes, and to Vermyre their screams were the most exquisite symphony. If the tzaangor's kin were enraged by this callous murder, they did not show it. The leader, the shaman-beast carrying the eye-tipped staff, simply gazed at Vermyre through expressionless eyes.

Beneath him, the smoking flesh of the monstrous champion was stirring. Though he had scorched the creature to the bone, it somehow managed to drag itself upright. He struck it hard in the chest, battering with the heavy metal of his staff and feeling bone give way. The creature did not seem to notice. Its eyes were frenzied, maddened, its awful cloven skull now marked by patches of raw flesh. Even as he shattered part of the thing's beak with a two-handed blow, it rose and slammed the tip of its club into Vermyre's chest, bowling him over.

The blow was as powerful as a close-range volley of scatter-shot. Vermyre's head spun.

Breathing was agony. He could feel the grinding of smashed bones in his chest, each rise and fall sending barbs of white-hot pain knifing through him. He got the staff up and somehow deflected another blow, but then the creature slugged him hard with its meaty fist, catching him in the neck and spinning him to the floor. He choked on a mouthful of dust and crawled away with a whimper. He felt a vice-like grip around his nape, and then he was being lifted into the air. The beast whipped him around and sent him flying through the air. He lost his grip on the staff, and crunched into something hard and unyielding. He felt more bones give way. His arm was twisted unnaturally, and blood poured from smashed teeth and torn gums. The tzaangors had fallen silent. They knew it was the end. As did he. The sad end of Ortam Vermyre. Butchered in the darkness before an audience of savages. He staggered to his feet, refusing to die on his back like some mewling coward.

The beast charged forward, and again it grasped him around the throat. It lifted him into the air. His vision swam as the thing squeezed, and he spluttered and gurgled. The light faded. He felt a peace fall over him, for the first time in many seasons. Even the pain of his shattered bones seemed to fade.

And then, he saw it. The sea of twisted blasphemies, the endless nightmare that awaited his soul. He saw figures screaming in unknowable agony as they burned for an eternity in the fires of change. He saw fields of silvered skulls, fields of writhing flesh. The sky was a bleeding wound, from which emerged a tower of crystal, impossible in dimension. Within that ancient fortress dwelt something ancient and eternal, something beyond the comprehension of mortalkind. And he could feel the heat of its fury from here, melting his skin, which ran from his bones in seeping torrents. That unconscionable horror had come for him and him alone, so badly had he failed. He felt a terror such as he had never known, almost agonising in its intensity.

'No!' he screamed. 'Not that. *Anything* but that.'

He tore at his face, yanking the cool metal mask loose. Suddenly, he was staring into the misshapen faces of the hulking avian beast. Its eyes widened in shock. He felt the writhing beneath his bones, and the cracking and popping as his true face emerged. He started to laugh. Great, choking gasps of laughter in a voice that was not his own. He pressed his head against the creature's, and he felt the thing beneath his skin reach forth and wrap its barbed tendrils around the beast's twin skulls. It loosened its grip on his neck and desperately scratched at his skin, hammered at his ribs, but to no avail. He could hear the tearing of flesh, and hot blood poured into his mouth. He chortled wetly as he bore the creature to the ground, tendrils dug deep into its brain, sucking greedily. The creature kicked and struggled, but eventually it lay still. He rolled free, slipping in a pool of spreading gore. He noticed with interest that his broken arm supported his weight with no pain. In fact, he felt no pain at all. He glanced at the mangled corpse of his enemy. There was nothing but crushed bone and meat where its two heads used to be. Around him was silence. He rose to his knees, and stared around the circle at the watching tzaan-gors, smiling broadly. Showing them the truth of what he was. What he had become.

'The Conduit,' hissed the shaman. 'Blessed of the Changemaker.'

'Blessed?' said Vermyre disbelievingly. *'Blessed?'*

'We follow the Conduit,' said the creature, bowing before him. Its brethren followed suit, as one.

Vermyre's body shook. He could not keep it in. He burst into wracking laughter, clutching his belly and sprawling onto the floor, roaring so hard that it hurt. He could not breathe. It was too perfect.

Chapter Fifteen

The Singing Isles were well-named. Even from a distance, Callis could hear a mournful, lilting sound drifting over the crashing of the waves and the roar of the wind. As the *Thrice Lucky* drew closer, he could see purplish, rolling beaches and twisting coils of bleached coral. There were dozens of these rocky outcroppings protruding from the waves, some barely larger than a house, others far larger and dotted with clusters of swaying trees. The water here was so clear they could see right down to the sea bed, a carpet of shimmering colours and darting fish.

'What's making that sound?' he asked.

'The trees,' said Shev, pointing to the nearest cluster. The trunks were all encrusted with a glittering substance which cast a prismatic glimmer across the water. The leaves were similarly iridescent, and chimed gently as the breeze sent them tumbling against one another.

Now that Callis looked, that pearly, glimmering dust was everywhere. Trails of it ran across the ocean floor beneath them, and the beaches they passed were not made of grains of sand, but of multi-coloured motes of the same substance.

The *Thrice Lucky* drifted gently through this strange landscape, the corsairs running a line of chain over the side to measure the distance to the bottom, making sure they did not stray into the shallows and find themselves stranded.

There was a stillness in the air that sat uneasily with Callis. After months on the trail, he was used to shrieking jungles and treacherous seas, to always being on edge. This place was so still it felt unnatural to him, a mirage of peace in a wilderness of rage and motion.

'I don't like this place,' he said. 'It's too calm. Something doesn't feel right.'

'Captain Zenthe says this is as safe a haven as you'll find on the Taloncoast,' said Shev. 'Something here keeps the beasts of the sea at bay, she says.'

'Does she now?' said Callis. 'You're developing quite the rapport with our noble captain.'

'Right now I'm short of allies,' Shev replied, shrugging. 'I'll take those I can find.'

'Arika Zenthe is no one's ally but her own,' said Callis. 'Trust me. If she values you, it's because she thinks you could be useful to her. Just watch yourself. This woman rules the waters within a hundred leagues of Excelsis, and you don't climb that high without leaving a mountain of bodies beneath you.'

'I've heard the stories.'

'And I've seen her work,' said Callis sharply. 'I'm just saying, watch yourself.'

The aelf smirked, and leaned out over the rail, letting the wind rush through her outstretched fingers. They were sailing into a wide, semi-circular atoll, hidden from sight by a wall of dead coral that wound along the island ahead like a ridged backbone. A long strip of beach reached out into the bay, and beyond that was a tangle of woodland, filled by yet more of those strange, crystal-lined trees.

'Sigmar's teeth, I can't wait to set foot on dry land,' sighed Callis. Doubtless there would be all manner of blood-sucking beasts hiding in the vegetation just waiting to sink their teeth into him as soon as he hopped ashore, but right now he hardly cared.

They anchored a few dozen paces from the beach, and lowered one of the shore boats into the water. Callis immediately clambered in, much to the grumbling annoyance of the corsairs. He checked his pistol to make sure it was primed, and took a bench next to the first mate, Oscus. The aelf eyed him blankly, but didn't speak. There were nine other aelves in the boat, all armed. They would be the scouting party.

There was a great splash, and a spray of water cascaded over them.

Shev Arclis emerged from the water, spitting and grinning.

'Oh gods, that's the first time I've felt clean for weeks,' she laughed, and flicked a handful of water at Callis, striking him in the face. He snorted with laughter and jabbed out with the tip of an oar, pushing her under.

'Enough,' grunted Oscus. The aelves began to row them in, and Shev swam alongside on her back, kicking her long legs in exaggerated arcs. Her hair swirled around her scarred face in an auburn halo. She flashed him a wide grin. Callis realised he was staring, and looked away.

The beach drew nearer, and they hopped over the side, weapons drawn, splashing through the shallows and onto dry ground. It was quiet. The undergrowth barely stirred. A few long-plumed avian creatures trilled from the tops of the gleaming trees. A faint, pungent smell met Callis' nostrils, like rotting meat. Shev emerged from the water, shaking her hair dry, leaving gleaming footprints as she strode up the beach towards them.

'We are alone,' said Oscus, waving to the *Thrice Lucky*. More boats were lowered in the water, and several aelves began to dive into the water to examine the wolf-ship's many abrasions. From the shore Callis could get a better look at the damage. She had held up surprisingly well against the ghyreshark's battering strikes, but had not escaped unharmed. There was a gaping hole that ran across a section of the middle deck, and the ship was listing badly, which suggested a breach on the lower hull.

'It'll take a good few hours to get her sea-ready,' said Oscus grimly. 'I do not like being out here, exposed. Reavers hunt these waters, and worse things will come drifting out from the abyss come nightfall.'

Toll followed Zenthe down into the depths of the *Thrice Lucky*. They could hear the moans and shrieks of injured crew echoing from the gunnery deck. Toll had seen the wounded, and had no illusions about the likelihood of many survivors. The barbs that the ghyreshark had expelled were lined with small coarse growths, like thorns, that snapped away when you tried to pull them free, scattering into flesh. If that happened it was as good as a death sentence, he knew. They would quickly turn septic and poisonous, like a bullet fragment, and you'd slip into an agonising fever and eventually blissful oblivion. Another piercing scream cut through the gloom. His own scars ached in sympathy. The cross-shaped wound on his back, where a bullet had ricocheted deep and his old friend Kazrug had set to work digging it out with a fire-heated blade, while he writhed and screamed. The great gouge on his thigh, where he'd been forced to perform the same operation with trembling fingers, removing the splintered fragments of an arrowhead while ravenous hounds howled in the distance, coming closer with every moment.

He banished the unpleasant memories. They descended into the lowest deck, the bilge. It reeked. Even Toll, who had been around death, disease and war for all of his adult life, was taken aback by the smell. It was a piquant blend of week-old corpses, filth and decay, backed by the sickly-sweet aroma of rotting fish. Brown-green water lapped around the length of the hull, thigh-deep, dotted with the floating corpses of various vermin. He could see the ridge of the keel running down the far end of the chamber. Thank Sigmar, it looked to be undamaged. By the soft glow of lambent sconces that dotted the wall – filled with some kind of luminescent shell-dwelling creatures – Toll could see scores of pale, long-legged arachnids skittering across the ceiling of the chamber.

Four aelves were wading through the foetid murk, inspecting a large wound in the side of the *Thrice Lucky*. Wedges of dark wood had been hammered into the breach, and the makeshift repairs smothered with a stained strip of sail. Yet, even now, a torrent of water was spilling through holes in the blockage. Toll was astonished that they were still afloat.

'It's bad, captain,' said one of the crew, a heavily scarred aelf with a shock of white hair wrapped up in a tail on the top of his skull, his face smeared with sweat and grime. 'But not fatal. It can be patched with a little effort, but we'll have to sail easy until we reach Bilgeport and make more extensive repairs. She'll handle the journey, but another bad hit and she could splinter along the length of the hull. If that happens, we're all heading to the deep within moments.'

Zenthe let loose an impressive stream of curses that went on for some time.

'Arkir,' she said, at last. 'You're in charge of the repairs. Get it done. We're a day and a half's sail from port. We'll make it.'

She turned and pushed past Toll, heading back up the stairs. He said nothing. There was little point. He knew Zenthe well enough not to press her when she was in a foul mood, and the joy of the ghyreshark kill had swiftly worn off. He supposed that the damage was worse than she had thought.

'Don't utter a word, Toll,' she said, as if reading his mind. 'The catch will more than make up for the damages. I could buy a whole new ship for what we'll make from the liver alone. There's always some damn-fool alchemist with more money than sense who's willing to trade a fortune for new ingredients.'

'This is your ship,' said Toll, and when she turned to glare at him he simply shrugged. 'I've no interest in going over the same territory again. Just get me to Bilgeport, and I'll be on my way. Our partnership is over.'

'You still owe me,' she said. 'And I mean to collect what is due.'

'I'm a man of my word, Arika. You'll get what you seek when we return to Excelsis.'

The tension hung in the air between them for several long moments. Finally, the captain turned and headed up the stairs to the main deck, saying not a word.

A chill breeze was beginning to blow by the time the work teams had hacked down a supply of timber for repairs, a refreshing zephyr that was a welcome change after several days of unrelenting heat. The aelves had stripped to the waist and fashioned makeshift lifts out of the ballista tracks, winching piles of thick timber to the main deck. Callis watched them work, enjoying the sensation of the sand trickling between his toes, the slight chill of the lapping waves. He closed his eyes, and sighed. What he would not give now for a pint of amber mead, a bustling tavern. Street cobbles under his feet. He heard the scuffed footsteps of someone approaching, and reluctantly climbed to his feet. Oscus appeared, his shirt drenched in sweat, sleeves rolled up to expose well-muscled, tattooed arms.

'We will the survey the island,' said the first mate. 'To make sure we are alone. We don't want to be surprised while *Thrice Lucky* is vulnerable like this. You're coming with us, guilder. Fetch your blade and follow me.'

Callis was surprised at that. Was it progress, he wondered? Or were they simply planning to stick a knife in him and leave him out there to rot?

He nodded, and joined Oscus and six other crew members. They had ditched most of their armour and gear, and carried machetes to hack away the undergrowth. They stared at him expressionlessly. One spat a mouthful of black phlegm onto the sand. Callis returned the insult with an obscene gesture he had learned from one of the duardin gunsmiths back when he was in the Coldguard. That earned a snort of laughter from the others.

'I'll come too,' said Shev, to his surprise. She was unarmed. Callis offered her his backup pistol, a snub-nosed little two-barrel piece he kept tucked in his belt, but she shook her head.

'Guns are more trouble than they're worth, in my experience. I'll stick with my knife.'

'Suit yourself. But stay close.'

Sarcasm dripped from Shev's tongue. 'I feel safer already.'

They filtered into the treeline, slow and careful. They walked for several minutes, padding through waist-high clumps of purple grass, crunching over scattered shards of coral as quietly as they could manage.

'Your companion and Captain Zenthe have blades at each other's throats again,' said Shev, as they walked. 'That's going to come to a head, sooner or later.'

'Zenthe's losing interest in the chase,' said Callis. 'She never gave a damn for capturing Vermyre. What Toll promised her – beyond coin – I've no idea. But whatever it was, it's not enough to keep her out here forever.'

'I always imagined that a witch hunter would rely more on threats and brute force than bribery.'

'I've never had dealings with any other agent of the Order,' said Callis. 'But Toll's not the kind to throw his weight around unless the situation calls for it. He plays a long game, one that involves keeping our mercurial corsair content. Besides, there's few who know the sea lanes better than Zenthe.'

'Stop your mouths,' hissed Oscus.

The noxious smell was slowly getting worse. Callis had an unpleasant feeling that he knew the source of it. He had been around enough battlefields to know the scent of flesh left to rot in the sun. Eventually, they began to see flickers of blue through the trees, and a few minutes later they emerged on the far side of the island. Callis cursed softly.

Ahead of them was a wide, rough expanse of dead coral, far larger than the beach on the opposite side of the island. It was littered with dead things. Mounds of skeletons and enormous, spiral shells as tall as the *Thrice Lucky*. Thin, cartilaginous racks of bone piled over thick slabs of rancid hide. A shapeless mass of flesh, long trails of winding tentacles rotting in the sun. There were more familiar corpses, too. Humanoid, lying shattered and broken, skulls removed. This close, the smell was overpowering. Emerging from amidst this carnage was a crude obelisk of piled stones lashed together with sinew. A single, sickening totem rested at its apex. Callis moved closer.

Bile rose in his throat. The totem had been delicately carved from the splayed ribcage of a human. Atop this macabre sculpture sat the victim's skull, mouth open in a silent scream. More skulls were piled high around the obelisk, which was stained a deep brown. The bones had been picked clean by scavengers, but they were still smeared with blood and patches of sticky brown gore.

'Flesh Reavers,' said Oscus. 'Mortal tribes who hunt the seas,' he added, noticing Callis' blank expression.

'Are they here? On the island?' asked Shev.

'I do not think so,' said Oscus. 'They raise these shrines to their sea gods across the Taloncoast. They hunt beasts, burn ships, raid the coasts. Then they bring their bounty of flesh to the nearest totem, offer the skulls to their gods. The rest they devour.'

'If you knew about these savages, why did you bring us out here?' said Callis.

'We did not think they dwelled within these islands,' Oscus replied. 'Their home is north, beyond the Sea of Spines. But more of them come, with every passing season. As the God-King's cities grow and grow, they sense fresh prey.'

The aelf strode to the totem, stepping over picked-clean carcasses. Several long-tailed crustaceans that had been swarming over the yellowing bones scattered as he passed. He smashed the bone effigy with his blade, knocking it to the floor.

'These kills were recent,' he said, disgust clear in his voice. 'Perhaps ten days old. Maybe less. They may still be close. We must not linger here.'

Chapter Sixteen

Zollech sat alone in the dim light of his war tent, running the whetstone down the edge of his axe. The blade was already sharp enough to split skin at the merest touch, but the repetitive motion soothed him, quieted the throbbing in his skull, and so he continued.

The tent parted, and Krom entered. The blood priest had to stoop, so tall and thin was he. His pale skin was smeared blue with dye made from crushed coral, and he had slicked his hair with blood. He carried his own weapon, a long-handled mace with a head fashioned from chipped obsidian.

'It is time,' said Krom.

Zollech rose without a word and secured his horned barbute in place. It sat tightly over his skull, the long cheekguards cold against his skin. He hefted his axe, twirled it in his hands, feeling the reassuring weight and balance. It was a strong weapon, forged by city dwellers from good iron. He had claimed it long ago, on only his third raid. Zollech had killed many people, so many that he remembered few of their faces. But the old soldier whom he had taken this weapon from – he could picture every line of that one's face. The weathered skin. The sad eyes, widening in pain and shock as the spear had slipped into his guts.

'The clouds gather,' said Krom. 'And the seas churn red. Do not fail, my chieftain. Send him worthy souls, for it has been far too long since we honoured him, and his anger is rising like the tide.'

Together, they strode out into the light. Zollech glanced out across the endless expanse of the ocean. The priest was right. Swirls of red trailed through the water, which churned and foamed with gore. A killing frenzy. The beasts of the sea were devouring each other. He could see arcing fins tearing through the chaos, bursts of bloody spray jetting into the air.

'The Blood Kraken watches,' said the priest.

They walked along the jagged shoreline of broken, dead coral. Zollech's men were crouched or slumped across the rocky outcroppings, their eyes fixed on their chieftain. Ahead, the dusty trail emerged in a great, wide circle, marked out with spears, swords and axes thrust into the ground. The dead reef formed a wall around the killing circle, and scores of warriors lined its length, bare flesh marked with war paint and old wounds. He could feel their eagerness, their longing to see spilled blood. They would not have to wait long. Three men waited in the arena. Two were small, lithe, armed respectively with serrated blades and barbed hooks. They were almost mirror images of one another. Zollech recognised them instantly as the twins, Foreg and Margos. The third was a giant of a man, taller even than Zollech. His skin was as white as the belly of a shark, and his body was a wall of muscle and scarred skin. He clutched a great glaive with a blade the length of his forearm. He smiled as they entered the circle, exposing a row of teeth filed to needle-sharp points. Dried blood stained the man's throat and neck where fangs had pierced his own flesh.

'We stand beneath the eye of the Blood Kraken,' roared Krom, raising his hands above his head, brandishing his mace. 'Witness to this offering. Too long has it been since we offered tribute. Since we sent an offering of worthy skulls down to his eternal throne beneath the waves. He is angered, my children. Greatly so. Eight daemon-ships have we lost since the last crimson moon. One hundred souls taken, and still his wrath is not satisfied.'

There was a chorus of jeers from the crowd.

Zollech grinned beneath his helm. A burst of harsh laughter escaped his lips, aching his throat where he had caught a bullet from a duardin's fire-pike many years past. He savoured the pain like an old friend, channelled it into anger. All would soon know what it was to challenge Zollech, captain of the *Skull Taker*.

Krom waited, let the shouting die down. Then, he raised a hand.

'Only those who prove worthy may claim the skull of a chieftain,' he said, and though he spoke softly, his voice carried far upon the wind. 'And so these warriors challenge for the right to lead us. Blood will be spilled today, worthy blood, for each man here has claimed a thousand skulls and more for the Blood Kraken.'

He gestured to the twin warriors.

'Foreg and Margos, of the *Flayed Throat*.'

There was a roar from the twins' crew, and a hail of javelins and thrown axes crashed to earth. Foreg and Margos neither spoke nor reacted to the shouts and bellowed oaths. Their eyes were on Zollech. He gave them a smile. They were nothing.

Meat for his axe. It was solely for his other opponent that the chieftain cared.

'And Muul, captain of the *Zanthacra*,' shouted Krom. The response was greater by far than for the twin reavers as the pale giant stepped forward. Fully half of the gathered crowd howled the name.

'Muul! Muul! Muul!'

A fight broke out in the highest spires of the dead reef. A blade flashed in the sunlight, and there was an arc of crimson. A dead body toppled bonelessly down the mound of bleached coral, leaving a trail of smeared gore in its wake. Zollech could smell the iron tang of the blood. It soothed the throbbing in his skull.

Muul stepped forward, eyes locked on Zollech. He was grinding his teeth, a sound like bones crunching under the weight of an axe. He had ever been an ambitious one. It was said he heard the words of the Blood Kraken in his skull when the red rage was upon him. He was the only warrior here whose tributes to the Blood Kraken rivalled Zollech's own. He was also younger, stronger. Taller by far. Muul's glaive was dripping with blood. It had already tasted death, this day. He paced back and forth, his face twitching, his eyes bloodshot.

'The Blood Kraken must be appeased,' said Krom. 'And so these three warriors are chosen, the greatest amongst our number. They face Zollech of the *Skull Taker*!'

Many voices rose to support their chieftain, though far fewer than there once would have been, even a few spans past. They had been too long without glory. A debt was due.

Zollech stepped forward, not taking his eyes from Muul. As chieftain, it was his right to speak. He stood, still as a statue, and waited. Then he hefted his axe, and pointed it directly at the younger warrior silently. Words meant nothing, in the end.

He'd heard every threat and hollow boast. No amount of bold talk had ever saved his foes from a bloody death.

Muul laughed, a gurgling, bubbling sound, and began to circle him. That surprised Zollech. He had expected the rage-filled warrior to charge him with everything he had. Foreg and Margos approached, spinning their dual weapons with practised ease.

Margos was small, compared to Zollech and Muul, but no less scarred by battle. One ear was little more than a ragged strip of flesh, and a red line carved down his face diagonally, turning his face into a permanent leer. In one hand he carried a barbed hook, with a handle grip that enclosed his fist. He raised the weapon and pointed at Zollech.

'You have failed us, old man,' he rasped. 'Now it is–'

Foreg's sword hacked into his twin brother's skull. Margos' eyes rolled back in his head, and he fell to his knees. Foreg wrenched the blade free, and the dead man toppled forward bonelessly and lay still.

Their audience brayed with laughter, pleased with this ruthless act. There were no rules in the circle. No bonds of honour or blood. Only one would emerge alive. Foreg's cruel, pinched face was locked in a triumphant smirk.

The throbbing in Zollech's head turned his vision crimson, as crimson as the blood that spurted from the twitching corpse of Margos. He started to laugh, as he always did when the killing joy came upon him. Muul made his move, swiping forward with his glaive, using his formidable reach. Zollech smashed that blade aside contemptuously, following with a wide swipe of his axe that sent the gigantic man stumbling back. He recovered fast. As Zollech reversed the swing, hoping to club his foe's brains out with the iron-wrapped haft of his axe, Muul snapped out a punch that connected with his nose, squashing it flat. He felt blood pouring from the wound, and reached his tongue out to taste the sweet-metal flavour. Foreg rushed in, hacking and thrusting at Muul. His blade tore a gash down the big man's arm, but it was not deep enough. Muul smashed Foreg in the ribs with the haft of his glaive in return, and when the smaller man crumpled, he lashed out at his throat. Foreg only just scrambled out of the way, though his foe's glaive carved a crimson arc across his back as he retreated.

They were all bloodied now. There was the briefest moment of respite as they circled one another, searching for an opening.

Muul ran a long, pink tongue down the side of his blade, savouring the gore that was smeared across it. Zollech had heard the stories. The master of the *Zanthacra* liked to consume raw flesh. Living flesh.

Foreg struck at the pale giant's ribs, but Muul was unthinkably fast, catching the blow on the haft of his glaive. The two exchanged a flurry of strikes. Foreg's sword hacked deep into Muul's shoulder, and the smaller warrior bellowed in triumph. Muul didn't even scream. Instead he caught his opponent's hand in one meaty fist, held it tight. Foreg slashed at the man's side with his blade, but the pale man seemed oblivious. His head snapped forward, and Foreg screamed. Muul ripped a chunk of bloody meat from the man's neck. His following roared in triumph. The giant chewed on the mouthful of gore a moment, then swallowed it whole. Foreg was gurgling on the floor, trying futilely to stem the torrents of blood gushing from his wound. Muul smiled a red smile.

'I will taste your flesh, chieftain,' he promised. 'You have strong blood in you.'

The smell, the scent of blood was overpowering. The rhythmic drumbeat in Zollech's head was almost deafening, calling him to abandon his wits and surrender to the rising tide, to drown in carnage and gore, even if it was his own.

He let himself fall into the crimson current.

They rushed each other, caution abandoned in favour of the white-hot joy of battle. Their blades clashed. Zollech punched out, struck Muul's jaw and felt teeth shatter. He received a head-butt in return, and his already broken nose crumpled with the sound of grinding cartilage. Muul's arms were wrapped around him, tighter than a kraken's embrace. He gasped for air, spat bloody drool into the pale giant's eyes. Muul's teeth snapped forward, bit into his cheek and tore a strip of flesh free. He could hear the man's gurgling laughter, high-pitched, almost like that of a child. His vision swam as Muul rained punches into his side. A rib cracked. With all his strength, he dragged his axe free, tore a great gash across Muul's belly. The giant stumbled back a step, and his iron grip relaxed for just a moment. Zollech's body was a bloody ruin, but he felt no pain. He stepped forward and brought his axe down with a scream that tore at his throat. It split Muul's glaive in two at the haft.

Shrieking in outrage, Muul raised the jagged spike of the haft in two hands and drove it into Zollech's shoulder. It struck deep, and ground on bone. The white-skinned giant slammed punches into his face, great hammer-blows that rattled his skull. Again and again his head shook, rattled by the ferocious assault. Somewhere he lost his grip on his axe, and sank to one knee. Still Muul continued to pound his heavy fists into Zollech's face. He couldn't see. He couldn't hear. But he could smell the big man's rancid, rotten breath. His hand scrabbled around in the dry earth, and his fingers closed on a hard shard of coral. In a single swift move, he rose and struck out with the makeshift weapon, trusting to the Blood Kraken to guide his arm. It struck home with a wet, tearing sound, and there was a choking gasp.

Through a bleary storm of blood and black lights, Zollech glimpsed his foe. The shard had pierced through Muul's throat. The giant staggered, eyes rolling back into his head. Zollech fell upon him, bearing him to the floor. He tore the coral shard free, and stabbed it down again and again. The spatter of blood that trailed through the air in front of him became the coils of the Blood Kraken. In each razor-bladed limb, it grasped a single skull, and within its immense form there gazed a single, furious eye, a cyclopean orb of blazing yellow fire that seared through his very being.

The Blood Kraken had witnessed his bloody work, and it was content.

When the haze began to clear, Zollech realised that he was hacking away at little more than a pulped and shapeless mound of flesh. His hearing returned with a painful ringing sound, and he heard the thunder of the watching warriors. He felt a hand on his shoulder.

'It is done,' said Krom, the blood priest.

Zollech staggered to his feet. He was caked in gore from head to toe, but his wounds caused him no pain at all. Rain began to drizzle down, and he raised his head and let it clear the blood from his eyes.

'None can deny that the Blood Kraken has chosen this man to lead us,' Krom screamed. 'Now we hunt, for flesh and for glory! We churn the seas red with the blood of our enemies, and make tribute of their skulls to the dweller in the deep. We sail!'

The response was deafening. Even dead Muul's crew joined the chorus, bellowing Zollech's name.

Through the noise cut another voice, an urgent call.

'A sail! A black sail!' shouted a warrior perched on the highest strata of the dead reef.

Zollech bent to grasp his fallen axe and began to climb, hauling his battered body up the face of the cliff. Making it to the summit, he stared out over the wide expanse of the Singing Isles. The skies overhead were darkening, and the mist of rain made it hard to pick out the silhouette of a ship at first. Then he saw it, drifting out from the bay of a half-moon shaped island. A sleek three-master, gagger-like black sails and an angular hull that sat low to the water. A ship built for speed on the open ocean. Aelven, so he guessed. A gift from the Blood Kraken for their bloody sacrifice.

'To the waves,' he bellowed, brandishing his axe high. 'Tonight, we feast!'

Chapter Seventeen

'Sails on the horizon!' came the call.

'Raiders? How many do you see?' shouted Zenthe, rushing to the fore guardrail.

'A dozen sails, half a league distant and closing,' shouted the lookout, pointing out beyond the curve of the nearest reef wall. 'War galleys. Reaver ships, captain. They've sighted us.'

Toll swore. He was no expert sailor, but even he knew that in shallow, coastal waters, galleys had the edge over a wolf-ship like the *Thrice Lucky*. Without the need for wind or currents, they could rely on the strength of a few score well-trained oarsmen to outmanoeuvre larger ships.

'Raise anchor,' shouted the captain. 'Ready the ballistae. We make for the open seas, and hope we can catch a strong wind.'

The crew rushed to their positions, some aelves shimmying up the mast guide-ropes to unfurl the sails, others heading down below to man the artillery.

'This will be a damn-near thing, either way,' muttered Zenthe, scanning the horizon. 'The tribes that raid the seas out here, they know their seamanship well. We're a wounded giant, ripe for the kill.'

'We can't outrun them?' asked Callis. 'Was I mishearing all those times you boasted about the speed of this boat?'

'You heard me well enough,' Arika Zenthe snapped. 'She can outrun anyone on the seas with a decent head of wind, but it's as still as death out here. Even if we could set full sail, these channels are too tight. We'd strike a reef or a cluster of rocks and we'd be stuck floundering while they swarmed all over us.'

The *Thrice Lucky* groaned as they swept around a forked spear of lichen-covered rock and entered a narrow pass between two jaws of jagged stone. Toll saw the truth of Zenthe's words. Their hull might be strong enough to fend off a ghyreshark's strikes, but one wrong turn and they would find themselves aground, trapped on those outcroppings.

Even at the speed they were cutting through the clear waters, Toll's heart leapt into his mouth when he glanced over the side. The water was shallow here, startlingly so. It seemed impossible that the keel wasn't already being scraped to splinters across the sea bed. They had only just cleared the channel when the shout went up from the rear of the *Thrice Lucky*.

'Sails!'

Toll turned, and sighted the oncoming ships through his eyeglass. They were sleek, narrow vessels, cutting like daggers through the water. Upon the prow of each was fashioned a dae-monic visage, roughly but imposingly carved, leering hungrily at their prey. Horned, fanged faces, splattered with blood-red dye. Some had yellowed skulls stuffed into their mouths. He could see figures on the deck; brawny, pale-skinned humans, flesh marked with smears of crimson war-paint. The men had long beards, forked and slickened, while the women had short, spiked hair, shaved to form a ridge down the centre of their skulls. A number wore scraps of armour or helmets, but most went unarmoured. Twenty or so manned the oars on each galley, while half a dozen strode along the deck or stood upon the fore rail, brandishing axes, spears and boarding hooks. He could see their lips move, and knew they were chanting. He glanced above, at the galley's triangular sails. They were black, marked with the image of an eight-tentacled sea beast with gaping jaws, each limb grasping a grinning skull.

'Heathens,' he spat. 'Not mere looters. There will be no bargaining. No taking of prisoners. If they board us, they will slaughter us all.'

'Heathens I know how to fight,' snarled Callis. 'Let them come.'

'These are hardened killers,' said Toll. 'They have raided the Taloncoast for centuries, surviving this beast-haunted wilderness against all odds. They will not die easily.'

'I'd like to see them survive a bullet in the skull,' Callis replied.

'Toll's right,' said Shev, frowning at the oncoming reaver ships. 'I've encountered their kind before, and I've no wish to repeat the experience. If we've any luck left, we'll reach the open sea and outrun them. If not...'

She left the thought unspoken.

The swirling clouds overhead began to spit a torrent of lashing rain. Ahead, Toll could glimpse the glowing line of the horizon, appearing through gaps in the web of rocky spears. They were close to the open sea. The wind was picking up, but hardly filling the sails. They hung, flapping lazily in the breeze. With every second their pursuers came closer, spreading out as they advanced like wolves on the hunt, looking to surround their quarry. The rear arbalests, a pair mounted on the aft rail, began to load shafts, harpoons tipped with a strange shape, like a blunt-nosed arrowhead.

'It's too far,' frowned Callis. 'They'll never score a hit from here.'

'Just watch,' said Toll.

The corsair gunner sighted and loosed one of the missiles. It arced up and out over the water. It was obvious from the second it was launched that there was no way it would strike one of the vessels. Instead, it struck the water, perhaps forty paces short of the leftmost reaver ship. No sooner had it struck the water than it exploded in a sheet of purplish flame that spread across the surface like spilled wine on parchment. Yet it did not burn out, nor did the lapping waves or pouring rain extinguish it. An entire section of the channel was now aflame, tongues of searing fire forking up in search of something to devour, hissing and spitting in the downpour. As they watched, one of the ships, unable to manoeuvre clear in the cramped confines, barrelled through the patch of burning sea. The boat went up like a pitch-soaked torch. A hulking figure on the prow staggered to and fro, engulfed in fire. They could hear his ragged shrieks over the wind. More blazing figures leapt into the water, trying to escape the rising inferno, which now spread out on all sides of the doomed vessel. There was no relief from the hungering fires. The reavers splashed and burned and screamed, and thick black smoke rose into the air above the remaining ships.

The aelf corsairs laughed, and slapped each other on the back.

'Rotten way to go,' muttered Callis.

'Save your pity,' said Toll. 'And pray that more burn before they reach us.'

The rear arbalests opened up again, and yet more eruptions of flame spread out across the channel. More ships were lit ablaze and the smell of burning flesh met their nostrils. The *Thrice Lucky* yawed to the right, cutting clear of the channel. There was open ocean ahead. The rain was pouring so hard that it hurt, thick bullets of freezing sleet that hammered the deck with a staccato rhythm. Finally, there was a wind. The sails opened and filled, and immediately they could feel the rush of speed.

Too little, too late, Toll was sure. The aelves' purple fire had accounted for perhaps four or five of the twenty vessels in pursuit, but the arbalests were out of the incendiary rounds.

The reavers were close now. Toll could hear their guttural chanting, a bellowed sound in some ancient island tongue that sent a chill down his spine. The daemon-headed prows were mere yards behind them, charred black by the aelven fire. The lead vessel was lined with flayed skins and blackened skulls, larger than the other reaver ships by some measure. Along its flank were mounted several rotting torsos, impaled to the deck by long spears. A giant of a man stood tall on the prow, holding a heavy broadaxe easily in one hand. His face was mostly covered by a blood-smeared barbute, topped by two curling horns. His muscular body was riven by multiple slashes, deep cuts that seeped bright red gore. The man seemed to pay his wounds no mind. The witch hunter raised his weapon and sighted the man, but thought better of the shot.

Let them come a little closer, he thought. Let me make every shot a killing shot.

One of the rear arbalests loosed a missile, which sailed past the huge warrior and scythed through a row of oar-bearers, pinning several to the deck. The aelves were loosing their repeater bows now, sending a hail of bolts whickering into the reavers. In return, the barbarians hurled javelins and throwing axes. The range was extreme, but even so the well-aimed missiles struck the deck of the *Thrice Lucky*. An aelf caught a thrown axe in the foot and fell to the deck, shrieking and clutching at the severed stumps of his toes. Larger warriors came forward, hurling grapples. Some fell away into the surging waters, but others stuck fast, carving gouges out of the hull as their barbed hooks dug deep into the wood. More slammed home on the far side of the *Thrice Lucky*. Toll sprinted forward. Drawing his blade, he hacked at the rope that dangled from the nearest boarding claw. His rapier was a fencing blade, ill-suited to such crude work, but it was Marchiana steel, forged by the undisputed master bladesmith of Excelsis. It made short work of the thick hemp, which sprang away into the water. The crew of the *Thrice Lucky* was hacking as many grapples away as they could, but more reaver ships were pulling alongside, and with every passing moment more missiles clawed into the hull. Toll saw one grapple strike an aelf, digging into his neck and releasing a spurt of crimson. The sailor was yanked off his feet, striking a dizzying blow against the guard rail before spinning off into the waves.

'Prepare for boarders!' yelled Oscus.

The first head emerged over the lip of the port rail, a bald, snarling face, eyes wide and bloodshot, deep in the battle-frenzy. Oscus stepped forwards and rammed a dagger deep into the warrior's eye socket. The man's corpse tumbled away. Two ships were racing parallel to the *Thrice Lucky*, latched tight by multiple grapples. Warriors were hauling themselves up the ropes, leaping and grasping hold of the portholes on the gunnery deck below, before dragging themselves over the side and onto the deck. One unfortunate boarder grasped a handhold just as an arbalest loosed its lethal missile. It impaled the warrior through the guts, hurling him twenty paces to crash against the rough hull of his own vessel, and splash away into the depths. Yet, as many reavers as they butchered, more clambered up towards them, axes strapped to their backs or clamped between yellowed fangs filed to needle points.

'Steady yourselves,' roared Zenthe, and as Toll glanced to the wheel he saw her yank it sharply to the left. The port side of the *Thrice Lucky* struck the nearest reaver ship, and the bulkier vessel crumpled the oars of the war galley like kindling, smearing several boarders into bloody paste as they were ground between the two ships. The enemy vessel spun, hopelessly unbalanced with one row of oars gone, and was leaning lengthwise when a pursuing vessel rammed it amidships. The stricken galley came apart in an explosion of wood splinters, upending its crew into the waters. The ship that had struck it fared little better, breaching the water as it smashed into its ally, before turning over in the crashing surf, its prow crumpled.

The stunt had bought them some time, but the impact had slowed the *Thrice Lucky* badly, and more ships were drawing alongside, readying grapples of their own. Toll heard commotion behind and spun to see half a dozen burly beserkers crash to the deck, wielding vicious axes and serrated blades. They swept their weapons around in wide, careless arcs, cleaving aelves in two or hacking off heads with every swing. Toll watched Callis step up and blast one of the boarders in the chest with his pistol, unleashing a gout of white smoke. The man staggered a few steps, but came on at the former Freeguild soldier. Callis fired again, emptying a second barrel, and the man's skull came apart in a wet eruption of blood and brains.

The deck was a chaotic melee, a cramped and brutal brawl in which the heavy-bladed humans had the advantage. Toll knew their attackers lacked the skill and precision that marked the corsairs' deft swordplay, but it seemed to take a dozen lethal wounds to drop any of them, and all the while they swept those vicious axes around in great scything arcs. He stepped in behind one and locked an arm around the man's throat, pressed his own four-barrelled pistol into the small of his opponent's back and fired, emptying every chamber at once. The man's chest simply exploded, showering the deck with intestines and fragments of bone. In response, aelves began to fight in packs, bearing the reavers down in numbers, and stabbing them over and over and over again until they ceased to move. The deck was slick with gore. It was all Toll could do to keep his feet, as it swayed and rolled beneath him.

A warrior charged at him, near seven feet of corded muscles and shark-hide leather, swinging a wide-bladed cleaver. Toll staggered backwards, not even bothering to deflect the man's blows, instead ducking and swaying aside. The man over-extended, slipped just slightly, and Toll thrust out with the tip of his blade, scoring a hit across the man's ribs. It barely seemed to slow the reaver. He snarled, drooling bloody spittle, bellowing nonsensical, animal sounds. A backhand swing just missed Toll's leg and then the man barrelled forward, shaggy head down, aiming at the witch hunter's chest like a charging bull. Toll let the reaver's momentum carry him onto the point of his rapier, which slid through flesh with sickening ease, sliding deep into the man's clavicle.

It should have been a kill. Instead, the man kept rushing forwards and struck Toll in the chest. They sprawled across the deck. Something hit Toll in the face, hard. A fist, or a boot, he wasn't sure. The reaver had lost his weapon, but he straddled Toll's chest, hands locking around the witch hunter's throat. The man's veins stood out like thick ropes. His eyes rolled predatorily back into his head as the blood frenzy overcame him. Toll choked, trying to wrench himself free. Having lost his pistol in the fall, he rammed the pommel of his blade into the reaver's temple, over and over until his hands were slick with blood. Unable to quite angle his blade for a killing blow, his vision began to cloud over as he gasped for breath.

'Agh'rakh t'or,' barked his assailant. 'Maskga ran vem'tra, tu va Khorne! Tu va Khorne!'

The man's back arched, and his vice-like grip loosened. He spat blood, which dribbled into his matted beard. Then his head lolled, and he slumped over, dead. Toll dragged in a painful lungful of air, gasping and coughing. He shoved the corpse away. There were three black-shafted bolts riddling the man's spine. He looked up and saw Shev stationed up in the mainmast, wielding a repeater bow. She gave him the briefest nod, and raised the weapon to her chin, loosing another volley. Another reaver went down, a bolt protruding from his eye.

Chapter Eighteen

The woman drove Callis back, tirelessly swinging her glaive, never giving him a moment to strike back. Her face was a twisted mask of hatred, her yellow teeth filed to killing points. A strip of orange hair ran down the centre of her narrow skull, spattered with blood. He gave ground, stumbling over moaning bodies and sliding in pools of blood, trying to work some space between them. The woman spat blood in his eyes, and he cursed and slipped to one knee. He raised his sword, intercepting her descending glaive, but she rushed in behind the strike and drove her knee up under his jaw, snapping his head back.

He sprawled against something hard and unyielding that blasted the air from his lungs.

The reaver raised her glaive high.

Arika Zenthe leapt from the forecastle above, soaring above the swirling melee, twin swords whirling. As she fell she twisted in mid-air like a carnival performer, bringing the arcing blades down in a cross cut that carved a bloody cross into the scar-faced woman's back. The reaver toppled with a rattling moan. Zenthe rolled as she landed, coming into a spinning kick that sent another reaver stumbling away. Axes and cleavers swept out at her, but she flowed like quicksilver, ever out of their reach. Another reaver went down, clutching an opened stomach. Another grabbed at the crimson ruin where his eyes had been only moments before, grunting in agony. A fork-bearded reaver raced towards the captain, arms outstretched to grasp her in a crushing embrace. She turned, and whipped her blades back and forth. Fingers rained to the deck, and the man stumbled to his knees. She reversed her grip on one sword and brought it down, sinking into the reaver's neck. He gurgled and rolled over.

The aelves of the *Thrice Lucky* cheered their captain wildly.

'Enough!' roared Zenthe, flicking blood from her blades. 'Get back on those arbalests, fools.'

Callis reloaded his pistol, searching for targets. They had cleared the deck for now, but more grappling hooks were flying in.

Zenthe raced past, bounding back up the steps of the forecastle to the wheel. He followed her. The rain was so thick they could barely see more than a few hundred paces ahead. The skies rumbled, and a flash of lightning revealed more reaver ships closing in on all sides.

'They have us,' growled Zenthe. 'They'll wear us down, bleed us until we're dry and feed on our carcass.'

'Captain!' came a shout from the crow's nest, up on the main mast. There were several aelves up there, the finest shots in the crew, wielding repeaters. 'Storm off the starboard bow, a league and a half away.'

Zenthe raced to the rail, and peered off into the distance. Callis approached. At first he could see nothing but driving sleet, heavy black clouds overhead, and the knife-like shapes of the reaver ships cutting alongside them. The sea was a rain-shrouded valley of churning grey, against which the *Thrice Lucky* seemed laughably, pitifully small, little more than a child's toy. The waves were growing fiercer with every passing moment. Then he saw it. Far off, a cluster of spiralling, black tempests reaching down from the darkening clouds, each large enough to swallow the *Thrice Lucky* whole. Spirals of lightning flickered and sparked around the whirling vortexes.

'There,' said Zenthe, 'that's a ship-killer if ever I saw one.'

Oscus was at the wheel, bleeding from a dozen wounds, teeth gritted in pain.

'I can take us around it,' he growled.

'No,' said Zenthe. 'We're going straight in, right down the throat of the storm.'

She took the wheel from the first mate, dragging it to starboard, angling them towards the looming maelstrom.

'Let them follow us, if they dare. If we die, they die with us.'

'You're out of your damned mind,' whispered Callis.

Zenthe's laughter was harsh and bitter.

'It's taken you this long to notice?'

Shev could see far from her perch, and she did not like the look of the waters ahead one bit.

They were sailing to their deaths.

My gods, whispered Occlesius, and she shared his awe. A spear of lightning arced down from the heavens, illuminating perhaps a dozen whirling tempests that whipped the seas to a frothing maw of white foam. Enormous funnels of water formed, dragged up from the ocean by the unthinkable power of the storm. At the base of each, the water was churned into a swirling vortex. She could see dark shapes flittering in and out of the raging waterspouts, beasts of the sea torn from their lairs, helpless in the face of this unnatural calamity. For a moment, she thought she saw a bestial face form in the clouds above; a body of striated clouds, eyes of crackling lightning. Then the *Thrice Lucky* dipped to crest the bow of a wave, and she had to lean out to grab hold of the rigging, her stomach lurching at the sudden change of momentum.

I had forgotten, so long have I slept. There is truly no limit to the wonders of the Eight Realms. Have you ever seen a more majestic example of the ferocity of nature?

'We're going to die here,' she muttered.

Perhaps. But if that is so, you have to admit it's a spectacular last image to take with us to the Realm of Endings. Who knows, I may simply sink like a stone to the bottom of the ocean, where no mortal being has ever strayed before. What beings slumber down there, I wonder? What ancient gods dwell at the foot of the abyss?

'There are some mysteries I have no interest in solving.'

Below, the deck was littered with corpses, both reaver and aelf. More of the daemon-headed ships were slicing through the waves towards them, sensing the kill. If they were aware of the nightmare they were about to enter, they showed no sign of it. Their angular prows carved through the waves with ease, a sure sign that while the raiders might appear like little more than savage killers, they knew their seamanship well. The *Thrice Lucky* – scourge of the seas – was being outmanoeuvred by another predator. The reaver longships sailed high in the water, and their rows of oars afforded them formidable agility and speed even in the midst of the thrashing waves.

They are too swift, said Occlesius. *We'll not outrun them in these waters.*

Staring out at the hunting ships, Shev didn't doubt the man's words. If the storm didn't consume them, the killers in those vessels soon would.

Chapter Nineteen

Toll could see the scale of the calamity they were headed towards, and his jaw locked firm as he understood the inevitability of their fate. It was one thing to face impossible odds with your feet planted and a blade in your hand, but it was quite another to plummet into the heart of a disaster, your life and your mission entirely in the hands of another.

It was an unpleasant sensation, and one that Toll had not experienced in some time. Zenthe was perhaps the finest shipmaster in these seas, but surely this task was beyond even her skills.

'Can you get us through that?' he shouted, staring at the mountain-sized column of water that was rapidly approaching, and the gaping hole in the ocean beneath.

Zenthe gritted her teeth as she hauled the *Thrice Lucky* around in a tight turn, taking them over the crest of a wave and angling them out past the monstrous tempest. 'That is a foolish damned question. Just keep those blood-hungry dogs off my deck and leave the sailing to me.'

It was impossible, Toll knew. No one could sail through that maze of death in one piece. They were already doomed, and it was too late to choose another path now. The thought that he would perish without passing justice upon the traitor Vermyre was too sickening to bear. How many lives would be lost because of his failure, he wondered? How many cities would burn?

And worst of all, Toll's greatest error, his failure to recognise the evil brewing within his old friend, would never be redeemed.

Callis approached, black hair slicked to his skull, his cheek marked by a nasty cut that ran from his brow to the edge of his jaw. He had stowed his pistol. Guns were temperamental at best in such torrential downpours, even master-crafted duardin firing pieces.

'They're still coming,' he shouted over the crashing of the waves. 'They're following us right on into that insanity.'

'Trust Arika,' said Toll. His fingers closed tight around the hilt of his sword. The freezing rain was chafing his hand raw. 'She will take us through.'

He didn't believe it, of course, but what else could they do?

Zollech stared at the wrath of the Blood Kraken, the storm that his vengeful god had loosed upon them. Ever was the dweller in the deeps a mercurial master, bestowing great gifts and terrible punishments on his faithful, often in the span of only a few moments. He had thought that his blood offering in the circle had been enough to gain the war-like deity's favour, but that had been a foolish hope. Such meagre death could never appease the Great Hungerer. It required a far greater tribute.

Their failure to stop the aelven wave-cutter had been their doom. Now they would die along with their intended prey, dragged down by the storm into the depths of the many-limbed god's lightless realm. So be it.

'We are bound for the bottomless deep, our souls claimed by the Blood Kraken,' he roared, turning to the ranks of oarsmen still drawing them through the waves with fearsome speed. 'But before we die, let us claim one more tribute for his lightless halls!'

They shouted their assent as one, and redoubled their efforts. Zollech had never seen the *Skull Taker* carve its way through the waves with such speed and purpose. Around him, angling in on the fleeing corsair vessel, were a dozen remaining war galleys. The foe's steersmen knew their trade well. By all rights they should have overrun the ship and taken the deck already. Each time they drew close the aelf wave-cutter arced away, riding the waves with astonishing grace for its size. If this was to be their last hunt, then it would be a worthy kill indeed.

Armand Callis had never lived through anything like it. As a child growing up in Excelsis he had watched the storms rage off the coast, out beyond the sea wall around the forest of swaying masts that was the city docks. He had watched the skies alive with light and noise, and stared, open-mouthed at the spectacle. His mother had threatened him with all manner of punishments one night when he had loosed the latch on his window and climbed upon the roof of their house to watch one such tempest, the fiercest he had ever seen. He remembered the smell of lightning on the wind, the arcing crescents that reached out like fingers of fire across the bay. He remembered, vividly, the dreams that had followed that night. In them he was lost out amidst that raging, elemental chaos, adrift and terrified. Helpless against the unimaginable power of nature.

That potent terror came rushing back now, though this time

it would not vanish with the dawn. The *Thrice Lucky* tossed, yawed and spun, seemingly out of control, its masts and sails protesting with creaking roars as the winds whipped them to and fro. It was almost impossible to keep one's footing, like trying to balance upright on a galloping steed. The aelves moved with impossible grace across the deck, while he staggered, then fell. The wind and rain were torrential, so thick and violent that he could barely see ten paces in front of himself. He teetered as the bow of the ship rose high into the air and struck against the ship's rail. He gasped in terror as the churning ocean rose to slam into his face, toppled backwards and sprawled on the deck.

He felt hands around his shoulders, helping him upright. He turned, and stared into the face of Shev Arclis. She was yelling something, but he could not make it out in the thunderous noise of the storm. She leaned in, bellowed in his ear.

'We have to get below!'

Arms wrapped around each other's shoulders, they stumbled across the deck, skidding on the sheets of water that gushed across the surface. Bodies slid and rolled, splashed overboard or struck the rail with bone-crunching force. Callis looked around for Toll, but the witch hunter was nowhere to be seen. There was the hatch to the lower decks, shut tight and barred with heavy pull-locks. Callis knelt, yanked at the metal latch and tugged one free.

There was a burst of lightning and an almighty crack, the sound of a hundred cannons discharged at once. Splinters rained down, and a shadow loomed over them. Callis blinked through the rain, and saw the rear mast toppling towards him, trailing smoke and flame.

Shev battered into him from the side, and they rolled clear. The heavy timber slammed onto the deck, crushing an unfortunate crewman beneath it. It had fallen on the deck hatch, barring access below. Ropes whipped across the deck, and one hooked Callis by the ankle. He was dragged on his front across the splintered wood, yelling and flailing, entirely helpless. He caught hold of something, the leg of an arbalest, smashed apart by falling beams. Splinters of wood dug into his fingers, but he dared not let go of his lifeline. He kicked frantically at the loop of thick rope around his boot. It was attached to a flap of sail, which was fluttering and whipping back and forth over the edge of the ship. Slowly, inexorably, he was being dragged into the ocean. His foot was agony, twisted badly in the fall. He had no idea where his blade was. He scrabbled at his belt and grabbed a thin-bladed dirk, tried to hack his foot free.

The ship yawed again, and his bloody fingers slipped and lost purchase on the arbalest. He skidded across the hardwood, smashed his head against something hard, then tumbled into empty air.

Chapter Twenty

Toll stood hunched by Arika Zenthe's side, grasping hold of the forecastle and staring at a sight he knew he would never forget. They circled the edge of an abyss. The *Thrice Lucky* leaned agonisingly, a scant few hundred paces away from tumbling into that gaping void of swirling water a dozen boat-lengths across. Captain Zenthe's teeth were gritted, her eyes narrowed and veins bulged from her thin neck.

He could have sworn she was smiling.

The vortex of water rose up into the clouds in the centre of the maelstrom, a spiralling column large enough to devour a fleet whole, one end vanishing down into the depths. And still the reaver ships came on. They were close now, gaining ground with the loss of the rear mast. Their own sails were filled with the howling wind, stitched with the same bloody image of the kraken. As Toll watched them bearing down, one vessel strayed too close to the whirlpool's edge. Rather than tumbling down into nothing, it was dragged into the air by the cyclonic winds that whipped about the vortex. Tiny figures, screaming men and women, were plucked from the deck and sent spinning through the air, sucked into the enormous waterspout. The mast and its sails were torn from the spinning vessel, and then the entire hull came apart in a shower of splinters. The shattered fragments of the ship circled the tempest like a swarm of insects, before disappearing into the jet-black clouds above.

Something struck the *Thrice Lucky* hard on the port side. The ship groaned beneath them, and they drifted closer to the abyss, Zenthe screaming in rage as she hauled the wheel in the opposite direction.

'Get them off our flank,' she yelled. 'Or they'll drive us over the edge.'

Oscus ran with Toll, making for the far side of the ship, where a group of corsairs were raining down javelins on to a reaver galley which was angled into the prow of the *Thrice Lucky*. The oarsmen were not abandoning their posts to leap aboard their quarry. They were no longer trying to take the *Thrice Lucky* alive. They were out for the kill, and they were willing to throw away their lives to ensure their prey's destruction.

Toll grabbed Oscus' arm.

'How do we drive them back?' he shouted. 'The arbalests are shattered, and there's no route to the lower decks.'

'Follow,' the aelf shouted back, and hauled himself over the side of the rail.

Toll cursed, and rushed forward. Oscus was clambering down the hull, agile as a spider, missiles slamming into the wood around him. With one hand he reached down and prised open one of the gunnery deck portholes, and with serpent-like grace he slipped his body through the gap, disappearing into the hull.

Toll sheathed his blade and lowered himself over the edge of the rail, following the first mate. Below, he could see the oars of the reaver galley, and the storm-lashed ranks of barbarian raiders, still bellowing their battle-hymns as they drove their vessel against the *Thrice Lucky* with suicidal determination. One of the figures gestured up at him, and axes and spears began to clatter and bounce off the hull around him. He lacked Oscus' dextrous grace, and it was all he could do to stop himself from falling. Whether he hit the ocean or struck the deck of the reaver ship, that would be the end of him. He strained for the open porthole with one hand, gritting his teeth and clinging to a tear in the hull with the other. It was too far. A flash of silver rushed past his eye as another missile clattered from the wood, mere inches from his face. Sooner or later a lucky throw would strike him.

He let himself fall, scrabbling across the slick wood, desperately reaching for the lip of the porthole. He grasped it, and his feet skidded across the wood as he hung there. Strong hands grabbed him and hauled him through the portal, and he splashed into ankle-high water.

He spat out a mouthful of the rancid liquid and looked around. The gunnery deck was a charnel pit, littered with dead aelves and the bodies of human raiders who had tried to enter the same way as Oscus and Toll had just done. Only a couple of the arbalests were still in shooting position. The others had been torn from their moorings, and now lay in a shattered heap at the far end of the chamber.

'Come on,' snarled Oscus, gesturing him further into the depths of the ship. They ran as fast as they could, splashing through filthy brown water and scattered debris.

Even Toll, no man of the seas, could tell that the *Thrice Lucky* was dying. She was a tough ship, no doubt, but she was taking on water now from a hundred different wounds.

'How long do we have?' he said. Oscus turned, and fixed him with a sad look. It was the first time he had seen any emotion from the taciturn first mate.

'She could go at any moment,' the aelf said, running one hand along a great crack in the hull. 'She is made from strong, solid oak, but even she cannot take this punishment. Even if the maelstrom does not take us, it will be a miracle if we make port.'

'Then let's make sure we take as many of those savages with us as we can,' Toll snarled.

Oscus nodded, and ducked through into a low chamber, behind the stairs to the lower deck. This was the armoury. It was dank and lightless, for no flames could be risked so close to their black powder supplies. After a moment his eyes adjusted to the light, and he saw rows of dully gleaming repeater bows, swords and boarding axes set around the walls of the chamber. At the rear were piled crates, and Oscus was levering one such container open. Toll grabbed a sword from the rack and used its blade to help pry the lid. It snapped open, and dropped to splash in the water pooling around their boots.

'Careful with these,' hissed the first mate, gently removing a large, glass container filled with an opaque liquid. Toll frowned, unsure of exactly what he was dealing with. 'You spill one in here, and we're dead in moments.'

'What am I holding?' asked Toll.

'One of the captain's rarer finds,' said Oscus. 'One that cost many lives to obtain. We will only need the one, trust me on this.'

Something within the jar snapped against the glass with surprising force, and Toll almost dropped the entire case. He peered closer, but could see nothing through the milky liquid.

With both of them steadying the jar, Oscus led the way back to the secondary deck.

'Help me with this,' he said, hefting the heavy container up and leaning it against the edge of the porthole. 'When it breaks, it must not be in contact with the *Thrice Lucky*. We must make sure it lands right on their deck. Ready?'

Toll nodded. On the first mate's mark, he thrust the container out into the empty air, and watched it sail through the rain and crash onto the deck of the reaver vessel, amongst the crew. At first, nothing seemed to happen.

'Wait,' said Oscus, watching the ship intently, a sinister smile on his sharp features.

Something began to swell amidst the rain-splashed deck of the enemy ship. At first it was formless, bulging, like an amniotic sac. With every passing moment it grew, forming pseudopods of transparent matter, which whipped and searched about like questing tendrils. One wrapped around the flesh of an oarsman, and the man arched his back and screamed, steam rising from a burning lash where the strange creature had touched him. Another pseudopod wrapped around his throat, and the man's cries became little more than a choking gurgle. Even through the lashing rain Toll could smell the scent of burning flesh. The formless shape grew larger and larger, and more reavers began to thrash as the searing tentacles lashed and grabbed at them, burning through hide wraps and metal armour with shocking ease, sending up wisps of smoke whenever they met exposed flesh. The reavers had abandoned their oars now, and were hacking at the amorphous blob with axes and blades, but to their horror even their weapons smoked and crumbled as they contacted the bizarre creature.

The war galley lagged and scraped against the side of the *Thrice Lucky*, its momentum lost as more and more reavers scrambled to take up weapons against the thing growing from the deck of their ship. As Toll watched, he could see the thing begin to smoke and burn at the very deck beneath it, the wood crumbling away under its gelid bulk. Something resembling a head was forming amidst the mass, with malformed, primitive eyes like pale yolks. The thing was large now, filling the entire centre of the ship and growing with every second. He could see bodies writhing within its translucent form, dissolving and burning even as they struggled to break free. With a chorus of screams, the ship broke free of the *Thrice Lucky*, disappearing into the gloom. The last thing Toll saw was several translucent limbs reaching around to envelop the dying ship, contracting with enough strength to tear the timbers of the galley apart.

'What in Sigmar's name was that thing?' he said, shocked at the swiftness and horror of the reaver ship's demise.

'The spawn of something that lives deep, deep below, in lightless realms that no mortal can ever reach,' said Oscus, still wearing that vicious grin as he savoured the screams that rippled across the water. 'Something for which there is no name.'

Chapter Twenty-One

'Armand!' yelled Shev, as she watched the man get swept overboard, dragged by the rope that had entangled him. She raced across the deck, and peered out over the rail. There was a terrifyingly small amount of ocean between them and the edge of the maelstrom, and between that and the *Thrice Lucky* was the largest of the reaver ships, close enough to touch the hull. Warriors were hurling more grappling claws, and she ducked aside as one slammed into the deck at her feet. Callis lay sprawled on the prow deck of the daemon-headed ship, half-dazed, while a giant of a man advanced on him wielding an axe as tall as Shev herself.

Desperately, she looked around for something to use, something to distract the hulking killer. She had no weapon. Nothing.

He is a dead man, said Occlesius sadly. *You cannot save him. Do not watch this, Miss Arclis.*

* * *

Callis snorted with helpless laughter, shaking his head. Against all the odds he had somehow managed to survive being thrown over the side of the *Thrice Lucky*, only to find himself crashing to the deck of the very killers hunting them across the seas. He had to see the funny side, even in situations like this, with his impending death at hand. A scarred brute of a man advanced on him, carrying a vicious broadaxe as if it weighed less than a blade of grass.

Callis reached to his belt and drew his dirk. Melt about seventeen similarly sized weapons down and re-forge them, and you'd have almost enough metal to make the hilt of his opponent's axe. He was too tired and bruised to let the fear overcome him. Better this way. Better to die under the strike of a longaxe than plunge into the seas and be dragged down into the inky blackness.

'What are you waiting for?' he laughed, flipping the blade into a backhand grip, as he had learned to fight on the streets of Excelsis. 'I've killed half a dozen of your gutless kin today. It's about time one of you gave me a proper fight.'

His opponent's mouth twitched just slightly, perhaps revealing a flicker of amusement.

Callis barely even saw the strike coming. Like a striking spider the savage snapped forwards, bringing his axe down to carve Callis neck to waist. It was only a fortuitous roll of the waves that sent him stumbling back out of the big man's reach, splashing in a great puddle of bloody water that had gathered in the prow of the reaver ship. Callis rolled, and the axe crunched into the deck, sending water splashing into the air. He kicked out and connected with the brute's jaw, but the man didn't even seem to register the blow. He grabbed Callis by the front of his shirt and lifted him into the air. His face was older than Callis had expected, lined and weathered, with a covering of grey-white stubble. The man slammed a fist into his side. Dizzy, and sputtering for air, he stabbed out with his dagger. The blade pierced the man's hide wraps, and he felt it scrape across bone. The savage growled, hurled him against the totem at the front of the ship. He slammed into the unyielding surface and slid to the floor, losing his grip on the dagger.

The man stalked purposefully after him, hefting his axe. The longboat heaved to the side, and Callis gazed up blearily to see the towering whirlwind of the waterspout, no more than five hundred paces from the ship. This close, the sound was apocalyptic, a rushing roar of wind and hammering rain. The timbers beneath him groaned and creaked, and he felt the back half of the ship sway to port, drawn inexorably towards the approaching catastrophe.

The reaver lord stepped close and smashed a fist into his face. His vision went black for a moment, and when he came to he was being lifted into the air, and he was staring into the man's bloodshot eyes. His breath smelled like smoke and dried blood.

'Weak,' he growled, and his vice-like grip tightened around Callis' throat.

The boat swayed again, and the reaver stumbled, his foot slipping just slightly on the rain-swept deck. His grip slackened just a fraction, and Callis made a spear of the two forefingers of his right hand and thrust them into his assailant's eye. The man grunted in pain, and Callis followed with a knee to the groin. Not a technique they taught you in the Freeguild drill schools, that one. More fool them. The big man's grasp weakened just slightly, and Callis twisted and wriggled free. He crashed to the deck, rolled and snatched up his knife. As he turned, he just barely ducked aside from a swipe of the reaver's axe. His opponent's eye was pouring blood, and the man's posture had changed. Gone was the slow, assured menace, replaced by a killing fury.

Callis rose, exhausted. He clutched his pitiful blade in shivering fingers. The meagre weapon was not going to be nearly enough. The reaver was too big, too strong. Sooner or later, no matter how much he skirted around, that axe was going to crash into him, tear him in two. He glanced around desperately for something he could use, some way to escape the drifting vessel, but saw nothing. To his horror, the *Thrice Lucky* was slowly pulling away from the longship, away from the raging waterspout that threatened to grasp him up in its raging mouth.

The man stalked closer, raising his axe. A strobing flash of lightning illuminated the drops of blood that slid along its surface, and the raging fires in the reaver's eyes.

Something sailed in over the water, arching gracefully over the waves, and struck the advancing warrior in the side with both feet. It was Shev Arclis, a thick rope secured around her waist. As her momentum was suddenly reversed, she swung back out over the water.

The savage barely even staggered under the blow, but it stopped him in his tracks. He stared up at the dangling aelf, and as she began to swing back towards him once more, he swept his axe back, ready to strike her in two. Callis surged to his feet, leaping up and wrapping his arms and legs around the barbarian's sturdy frame, locking his hands tight around his foe's throat so that the man could not bring his axe to bear.

Shev crashed in again, and all three went down in a tangle of limbs. Callis clung on like a gryph-hound with its beak locked around an intruder's leg, knowing that if he released his grip they were both dead. The big man slammed elbows into his side, and bucked and rocked with furious strength, but still he would not let go, even through the haze of pain.

Shev darted in with a blade, seeking to sink it between the struggling warrior's ribs. A kick sent her flying backwards, almost disappearing over the gunwale. From the rear of the ship a burly figure dressed in rain-swept rags rushed forward, attempting to tackle her, but she slipped out from under his searching hands with easy grace, planting a boot in his back and sending him tumbling into the waves.

She bellowed something at him that was lost in the storm, face pale with terror as she stared up at the approaching whirl-wind. Forking tendrils of lightning were reflected in her eyes. Beneath Callis, the towering warrior finally found his feet, and began to rise. With an animal howl he bent his body forwards, bucking and sending Callis somersaulting into the air. He lost his grip around the man's throat and landed in a shuffling roll, staggering towards Shev, who was entranced by the catastrophe about to swallow them. The silksteel rope was fastened tight around her waist, and he prayed that it would hold. He grasped the rope and wound it around his wrist, and turned to see the warrior leaping towards them, murder in his eyes.

Callis stepped up onto the gunwale, dragging Shev along with him, and let himself fall backwards into the sea. The waves rose up to claim them with a stinging slap, and he could not help but gasp, and therefore swallow a mouthful of bitter, ice-cold seawater that burned his throat. Shev was clutching his arm so hard it hurt, her fingers digging into his flesh like claws, but he welcomed the pain. It was the only thing he could focus on in the swirling, pummelling madness that enveloped him. An undercurrent caught them, lifted them high, and for a moment his head broke the surface of the water. His arm was almost yanked out of its socket by the force of the tightening rope, but still he held on.

He saw the horn-helmed warrior, standing upon the prow of

his ship, eyes fixed upon his own. The man's colossal, muscled form was shaking, and Callis realised that his foe was laughing. He thought he could even hear the booming sound for a moment, above the churning waves. Like the great head of a sea-serpent, the tempest rose behind the laughing man, a monster with a body formed of whirling corpses and whipped-up shards of flotsam. As if he weighed no less than a feather, the man was lifted up into the air, and sent whirling into the heart of the beast, and Callis saw a bright spray of blood as rushing knives of wood and bone flayed the flesh from his body. Then he was lost in the whirlwind, absorbed by the ravenous monster.

Callis felt, almost imperceptibly, a slight tug upon the rope he clutched in bleeding, scraped-raw fingers, and then a wave rose up and crashed down upon him, driving him deep beneath the waves into a world of swirling bubbles and inky blackness. His head struck something solid with enough force to snap his jaw shut, splintering teeth, and he knew no more.

'Stronger than he looks, this one,' was the first thing Callis heard. He recognised that voice, harsh and dismissive, but not the faint undercurrent of grudging respect that it carried. Light speared into his skull and lit a thousand painful fires behind his eyes, but he forced them open anyway. Oscus loomed over him, his angular face spattered with blood and marked with several ugly bruises.

'Oh gods,' muttered Callis, as he hauled his aching body upright. 'Where is the aelf? Where's Shev?'

'Here,' came a voice from beside him. The aelf lay on the deck of the *Thrice Lucky*, nursing an ugly scrape on her forehead, but otherwise looking largely unharmed. She flashed him a pained grin.

He stood, and felt a firm hand take him by the shoulder and steady his feet. It was Toll, and though the man's face was lined and his eyes baggy with tiredness, Callis felt he saw a flicker of concern cross those pale, grey eyes.

'We dragged you out of the water,' said Toll. 'Thought you were dead, at first. Both of you.'

'The reavers?' Callis asked.

'Dead,' said Arika Zenthe. She was leaning on the fore gunwale, staring out across the oceans. 'All of them. The storm took them.'

For the first time, Callis noticed how quiet it was. Warm light filtered down from above, bathing the deck of the *Thrice Lucky* in soft amber. There was a light, refreshing breeze that felt like cooling water on his skin. It seemed like they had entered another world entirely in the time he had lain unconscious. He could not reconcile this sunny, calm place with the raging violence of the tempest that had so nearly devoured them. Toll released Callis' shoulder, allowing him to find his own feet. The deck beneath him was stained a dark brown. Against the forecastle, he could see a pile of torn bodies. From a glance, it looked to be at least thirty or so. More than a quarter of the ship's crew.

He glanced up, and saw the splintered lance of the mainmast. It had been shorn free, along with the mizzen and a great chunk of the bowsprit. Jagged lumps of torn wood and coils of sea-soaked sails were piled across the deck. A kneeling workband was pulling one of the fallen sails taut against the hull on the starboard side, nailing the fabric into the deck with heavy wooden stakes. Callis was no expert on sailing ships, but even he could see that the *Thrice Lucky* was limping like a wounded auroch. If another daemon-headed longship appeared on the horizon, they would have not a hope of outrunning it.

'We're half a day out from Bilgeport,' said Oscus. 'We'll make it, if the weather holds.'

Callis walked over to Shev. With a wince, he knelt down beside her.

'Thank you,' he said simply. He'd have liked to be more eloquent in his gratitude, but right now the words just wouldn't reach his lips. She smiled and shrugged.

'Forget it,' she said. 'At least, until I get myself into trouble. Then return the favour.'

Chapter Twenty-Two

The first they saw of Bilgeport was the curving arc of a shell, reaching over the horizon like a crashing wave frozen in time. Beneath that enormous mass lay a mountain of bone, painted green-grey with weed and algae. As they drew closer, Callis could see five immense ribs, carved open and filled with ballistae and cannon – organic watchtowers facing out over a great harbour of swaying sails. The head of the dead beast lay perpendicular to the rocky shore. It had been hollowed out and carved to form a bizarre dock, sheltered by the strange, crested skull. Two rows of razor-sharp teeth, each stained by age and the size of a ship's mast, formed a formidable defensive wall around a series of jetties, upon which they could see the hustle and bustle of movement: ships unloading and stowing their sails, and bare-chested figures of all descriptions hauling crates and barrels up a gentle slope and into the darkness of the main body.

'There she is,' said Zenthe. 'The reaver port. You get used to the smell. Eventually.'

'Certainly hope so,' said Callis. It was a unique aroma. Fish oil and urine, mixed with smoke, tallow and rot. There was also the slightest hint of fragrant spices and perfume trying vainly to mask the stench.

'Take us in,' Zenthe said to Oscus. 'And handle the docking fees. We're the *Black Dragon*, out of Sayron. You're Captain Duventhe, and you're here to trade ghreshark skins.'

At Callis' questioning glance, she explained.

'We're limping into port half-dead. I'd rather not draw any unwanted attention, if possible. I know this place. We're sailing into a den of hungry sharks while seeping blood. Maybe we stay out of sight and mind until we've got ourselves a ride out of here.'

'We?' said Toll. 'There is no "we". We're done, Arika. You can find your own passage. I thought I had made that perfectly clear.'

There was a tense silence as the two glowered at each other.

'As you like,' said the captain at last, with a cold smile.

They'd changed sails on the approach to Bilgeport, exchanging the *Thrice Lucky*'s familiar black and yellow array for dull, grey leathers. There was little they could do about masking the ship's sleek, obviously well-crafted hull, beyond patching up the gunnery ports. Still, the vessel hardly looked like a Fleetmaster's flagship with half its hull shattered, its mainmast lost and blackened fire damage across the deck. They passed ships of all shapes and sizes as they drifted between the great jaws of the harbour. War-galleys gilded with silver and gold, bearing great palanquins upon the forecastle from which fat, powdered merchants sprawled, attended to by dozens of scrawny slaves. A duardin cog-hauler chugged past, thick smoke billowing from its three chimneys. Upon the jaws, which had been widened and abutted with stone walkways, sailors, servants and merchants lay sprawled in the sun. At the eastern edge of the port a tower rose, crafted from pink stone, with its own secluded harbour amidst the chaos. It reared into the sky, protruding from a wide, circular socket of the dead behemoth. A perimeter wall enclosed a harbour in which bobbed a great, three-masted vessel, its sails blood-red and white, marked with a winged serpent in flight. Gold-barrelled cannon rippled along its length, gleaming in the sunlight.

'That's the *Blood Drake*,' said Zenthe. 'High Captain Kaskin's ship. It's said she's the deadliest vessel on the Taloncoast. It might be true, as of now.'

'This thing,' said Callis, gesturing to the carcass that housed the reaver city. 'What in Sigmar's name was it?'

'They say it was one of the spawn of Nharvolak, the dweller beneath the waves,' said Oscus. 'Every five hundred years the great beast would rise from the deeps, destroying cities and civilisations, unleashing its spawn upon the oceans to devour all life. Less a creature than a god of beasts, a deity of ruinous power created to destroy those who dared attempt to conquer the majesty of nature.'

'So what happened to it?' said Callis.

'The God-King drove his hammer into the great beast's eye, or so the legend goes,' said the first mate. 'Blinding it, and sending it back down into the depths, back to its lair. Its spawn were slaughtered. Most sank along with their progenitor, but this one was beached upon the shore and expired. Carrion-beasts and savages picked the flesh from its bones, and finally something even worse happened upon its remains. The High Captains.'

'Their kind has lurked here since the founding of Excelsis,' said Toll. 'Picking off the bones of the dead. They range south as far as the Coast of Tusks, preying upon merchants, travellers and whoever else strays into their path.'

'Why are they still here?' asked Callis. 'Why have the freeguilds not been sent to wipe them out?'

'Because they're clever,' said Zenthe. 'They steal and kill only when they know they can get away with it, and they leave no witnesses. And they know when not to let their greed get the better of them. The Stormcasts, the guilds, they've too many foes on all sides as it is. They can't spare the ships or the troops. Anyway, the High Captains make sure the right palms in Excelsis are greased. As long as they're careful, they stay outside of the law.'

'For now,' said Toll, eyeing the ships lazily drifting out of the bay.

They slid into a berth alongside a barnacled wooden pier, upon which stood a small, yellow-toothed man surrounded by a gang of burly-looking fellows armed with spiked clubs. The small man was carrying a slate and a quill, and peered at them through his crab-like eyes as they drifted past.

'Name and cargo,' he yelled, in a high-pitched, raspy little voice.

'*Black Dragon*, out of Sayron,' Oscus shouted back, leaning against the rail and raising a hand to cover his eyes from the sun. 'We're carrying hides and oils, for market.'

The dockmaster nodded to the gouged holes in the side of the ship.

'Looks like you've taken a pounding,' he said.

'Raiders,' said Oscus. As he spoke, several of the crew lowered the gangplank, and the dockmaster hobbled along to meet them, his henchmen following lazily behind.

'Surprised you're alive,' he said, spitting a mouthful of black slime onto the pier. 'They send us a few gifts, every now and then. Ghost ships, the crew flayed and stuck to the masts. Just to remind us they're out there waiting. More and more of them every season.'

'Some less now,' said Oscus. 'You can arrange our repairs?'

The dockmaster nodded.

'If you have the coin, I'd say we can.' He scratched his wispy beard. 'But repairs like this, it'll cost you. If you can't pay the docking fees, we'll take it out of her hull, and you'll pay the rest in blood to the High Captains.'

Callis saw Zenthe's hand twitch to her sword hilt. She had her hood up and was standing amongst the rest of the crew.

'We've got your coin,' said Oscus, his voice deadly even. He gestured, and several aelves hauled a sheet of skinned ghyre-shark hide forward. The quills had been plucked out and the skin cured, leaving a thick, oily-looking leather covered with circular pockmarks. It didn't look all that appealing, in Callis' opinion, but Shev had explained that when properly treated and worked, it could stop a crossbow bolt or a sword blow. It was also light and supple, which suited sailors well – you did not want to be fighting at sea in heavy plate or chain. The dockmaster whistled as he hobbled up the gangplank towards them. He knelt by the thick, barbed leather and ran a hand along the hide. He yanked his fingers back with a hiss, and Callis saw a thin line of bright red blood.

'You were lucky, it seems,' he said, sucking the blood from his gashed hand. 'There's always a market for good shark-hide, and this looks like a fresh kill. We'll take it all.'

There was an uncomfortable silence. Oscus let it hang long enough for Captain Zenthe to sound an objection, but she said nothing. Eventually, the first mate nodded, and gestured for the crew to bring up the rest of the shark hide. The dockmaster gave a black-toothed grin.

'We'll arrange a repair crew,' he said. 'There's ale pits and bawdy houses aplenty, should you need to avail yourself.'

'You bring us the supplies, we'll make the repairs,' said Oscus.

'No one steps on this ship but my own crew. Are we clear about that?'

'As you like,' shrugged the small man, wiping sweat from his greasy brow. He hobbled away down the ramp, muttering to his attendants. Oscus turned to Zenthe.

'That's our prize gone,' he said. His eyes were narrowed, fixed upon the retreating dockmaster. 'We should have opened that wretch's belly. This is robbery, plain as the rising sun.'

'Of course it was,' said Zenthe. 'This is Bilgeport. It was built by thieves. But we must play this carefully, for now. We're short-handed and under-gunned, and we're resting in a pit of vipers. As much as I'd like to nail that stinking rat to my prow, we need to keep our heads beneath the surface.'

She turned to Toll.

'You'll find the duardin at the sky-dock,' she said. 'Port side.'

'What will you do?' asked Callis.

'Repairs to the *Thrice Lucky* will take some time,' said Oscus. 'Several days at least, if we can even trust that stunted wretch to deliver us the materials we need.'

'Then we sail back to Excelsis,' said Zenthe. 'I'm done with this fool's errand.'

Chapter Twenty-Three

'That's the *Thrice Lucky*?' Captain Kaskin snorted, dabbing at his great, sweaty mass of a forehead with a silk handkerchief. 'The Wolf of Excelsis? The ship that broke the Tenth Kerran Blockade? That half-wrecked piece of flotsam is the flagship of the famed Fleetmaster Arika Zenthe?'

He giggled, a childlike, nasal sound.

'They've seen hard fighting,' said Captain Lorse. Where Kaskin was a painted walrus of a man, dressed in garish greens and golds, Lorse was wiry and weathered, with the scars and burns of a life spent fighting and killing on the open seas. 'They've masked it well enough, but that's a vicious wound in the lower hull. They're lucky they made it to port.'

'Not so lucky,' said Captain Azrekh. The duardin leaned against the far wall, his muscled arms folded, stubby fingers covered almost entirely with gleaming rings.

Ortam Vermyre moved to the balcony of the High Captains' Lodge, leaning against the rail and looking out over the harbour. He could see the tiny figures upon the deck of the *Thrice Lucky*, to-ing and fro-ing as they hauled crates of cargo onto the pier. He had arrived here a half day before Toll and his band. The witch hunter had made better progress than Vermyre had expected, though it seemed they had suffered for their haste.

'They've lost half their crew,' he said. 'They're weak and exhausted. You'll never have a better chance to end Captain Arika Zenthe. And with her dead, her crew slaughtered, that leaves the Excelsis harbour without an overlord. And you three gentlemen with an intriguing opportunity.'

'To control the docks of the City of Secrets,' muttered Lorse. 'That's real power. Real coin.'

Vermyre smiled beneath his mask. He had considered passing by Bilgeport and heading straight for the Fatescars. His tzaangor allies had their own, unique methods of transport, and so there was no need to buy passage upon an air-vessel. But Vermyre had known that Toll would travel here eventually, and had sensed a chance to spring a trap upon his pursuer, and retrieve something of value in the process.

Vermyre could feel Azrekh's eyes boring into him, and turned to meet the duardin's gaze.

'What do you get out of this, masked one?' Azrekh said, narrowing his slate-grey eyes. A vicious, skull-shaped brand covered the left side of the duardin's face, turning his frown into an ugly leer. A former slave, this one, so the stories said. Of course, that painful history hadn't stopped the good captain dabbling in the trade himself. In fact, he was an infamously cruel and ruthless master.

Vermyre had dealt with the High Captains many times before, though always through intermediaries. It was amusing to think that these three men were standing next to one of their greatest benefactors, completely oblivious as to his true identity. They had been useful privateers, allowing him to direct Bilgeport's raider fleets to targets that would most benefit Ortam Vermyre; the trade convoys of his rivals, for instance.

They were the perfect tools for his current needs. A simple play upon their greed and their envy of Arika Zenthe had opened the door, and it had been a simple thing to open their eyes to the many possibilities of a world without the aelven corsair.

'I desire only one thing in exchange for the information I have just given you,' Vermyre said. 'There is an aelf girl aboard that ship. With scars upon her face. I require you to hand her over to me. Unharmed and untouched. That is the only payment I require. A simple reward for alerting you to Captain Zenthe's presence, no?'

The duardin snorted.

'Believe that I have a vested interest in eliminating Zenthe and her crew,' Vermyre continued. 'She travels with two humans. An old man and a former Freeguild soldier. They die alongside the good captain.'

Kaskin waddled over to a large, cushioned curule and heaved his great bulk into it. The seat groaned like a dying man. Like everything else in this building, the curule was a riot of violent colour, a pink silk cushion propped up by golden limbs fashioned in the shape of a hunting cat's claws. Gems were studded into the arms and down the length of the beams. Vermyre, who'd long lived amongst the high classes of Excelsis, took in the rest of the chamber, with its eclectic styles and shades, its serving staff dressed in long, violet togas, skin painted light blue and mouths hidden behind gauze cloths. It was a poor man's idea of a rich man's luxury, and all the oils and expensive perfumes in the world could not erase the stench of fish guts drifting in through the open window. Captain Kaskin snapped his fingers, and a slave girl emerged with a cold towel and began to mop Kaskin's brow. He stared at Vermyre through piggy eyes.

'One would be forgiven for thinking that the reason you wish Zenthe slain is because she comes here looking for you,' he said. 'One might wonder exactly why the Fleetmaster of Excelsis might be out here on the hunt. I'd wager that stone-hearted creature wouldn't leave her lair unless she was chasing coin. Or something else... valuable.'

A shrewd man who hides behind the illusion of a fat fool. One does not become a High Captain unless one is both clever and ruthless, thought Vermyre. Yet his greed makes him predictable.

'Perhaps we should take off that mask,' said Azrekh. A knife had appeared as if by magic in his hands. He spun it around with quick-fingered grace. 'Prise it off your face, and see what lies beneath.'

Vermyre's mouth filled with hot bile. A voice was telling him to do just as the duardin had said, to tear the golden mask free and unveil his true shape. He bit his lip so hard that he tasted the sweet-metal tang of blood.

'That would be unpleasant,' he said. His voice was even and calm, betraying nothing of the storm within. 'For both of us.'

'You threaten me here?' snarled Azrekh. 'In my own chambers? I could have you flayed alive.'

'That was not a threat, High Captain. This is.' Vermyre rapped his staff hard upon the floor. There was a sickening thud from outside the room, and then a high-pitched scream that was abruptly cut off. The doors swung open, and two of Vermyre's tzaangors strode through, their mottled blue feathers splattered with gore. One of them was holding up the bloodied corpse of a guard, his throat slashed open. The creature cocked its head, wiped its silver dagger on the dead man's nape, and let the corpse fall to the ground with a sickening thud.

'Do not bother calling for aid, Azrekh,' Vermyre said, leaning upon his stave and enjoying the duardin's look of outrage. 'It would only result in more dead.'

'You bring these… *beasts* into our city?' gasped Lorse, hand hovering above his pistol.

'To prove a point. If I wished you three dead, I would have my allies here slit your throats while you slept. Be assured, I have no interest in removing you from power.'

There was a long silence. Captain Azrekh stared at him, unflinching. Eventually, Kaskin broke the tension with another high-pitched giggle.

'Gentlemen, please,' said the large man, waving a hand to dismiss the now terrified serving girl, and taking a deep swig from a goblet of crystal wine. 'Captain Azrekh, Captain Lorse. I assume that you, like me, recognise that the ship indicated to us by our masked friend here is indeed the *Thrice Lucky*?'

Azrekh said nothing. Lorse approached cautiously, one hand resting upon the pearl-handled pistol on his hip. Vermyre could hear the sound of rushing blood, and the colour seemed to fade from the garishly decorated chamber. It would be such a simple thing, to reach out and crush the throats of these arrogant fools, to put out their eyes and hurl them from the tower. To hunt down Toll and show him the truth of what he was, to see the fear and horror in his eyes before he…

No. He would not give in to that. Loss of control was loss of power, and he would not allow himself to suffer such indignity. He took a deep breath, and squeezed his eyes shut. When he opened them again, Azrekh had taken a seat and tucked the knife back in his belt.

'Suppose it doesn't matter who you are,' said the duardin. 'For now.'

'Exactly,' said Kaskin. 'We capture Zenthe and her crew, and we put them to death. Publicly and messily. We show the captains of this port that we bow down to the aelves no longer. We will take what is ours by right.'

Vermyre frowned.

'Do not toy with these people,' he said. 'Kill them, quickly and definitively. As long as they are alive, they are dangerous.'

'No,' said Kaskin, shaking his head. 'We have to send a message. We have to let the crews know that Zenthe's power is crushed. Completely and irrevocably.'

'Then show them her severed head.'

'Zenthe's shadow has loomed over Bilgeport for years,' said Azrekh. 'Her ships have sunk our fleets, stolen our booty and butchered our people. Her name is spoken with reverence and dread within these walls. Death alone won't banish that fear.'

Vermyre sighed. So be it. Let these fools play out their little farce. As long as Zenthe and her crew were delayed and thrown off the hunt, it mattered little to him. By the time they recovered, it would be too late.

'You let us worry about the how of it,' the duardin continued. 'They're in our court now, alone and vulnerable. Let us see how the legendary Captain Zenthe manages without her lackeys around.'

'Very well,' said Vermyre. 'I leave the means of their destruction to you. Your men will deliver the girl to me exactly as you find her – untouched and unharmed. Tell them to take her to the Jade Golem. I have quartered there. Then, our business will be done, and I shall take my leave of your fine city.'

He stood and gave a cursory bow, then marched out of the chamber and down a wide, curving staircase with an ornately carved ivory rail. Statues and busts of the current High Captains were ensconced upon the walls, alongside their predecessors. Trophies of all descriptions were mounted alongside: guns, swords and weapons from a hundred different cultures, stuffed animal heads and the skeletal remains of slain creatures.

He would need to be wary of these men. They may be thugs, but they were no fools. During his time as High Arbiter of Excelsis, Vermyre had become very well acquainted with the brutality of the High Captains. He had even called upon their services, from time to time, through an intermediary. He had carefully ensured that they stayed out of the sights of the Order of Azyr's hounds, as well as the city's regiments. Bilgeport had prospered under his stewardship, and it appeared – judging by the number of sails and corsair ships in the reaver city's harbour – that his successor had not decided to clamp down on their activities, at least for the moment. No doubt the captains were continuing to pour coin into the pockets of the Excelsis establishment. If they garnered enough support, they could even gain the leeway to pursue their foolish war against Zenthe's privateers. It mattered little. They needed only to do their part this day, and he could put them out of mind.

This is a delightfully colourful place, said Occlesius. *How charmingly ramshackle everything all is. And I don't think I've ever witnessed such a gathering of ne'er-do-wells and cut-throats.*

'Yes, well, you can't smell it,' muttered Shev, wrinkling her nose. 'So I hardly feel you're getting the true picture.'

The docks were busy and swelteringly hot. She saw a wide variety of illicit goods being bartered and sold right off the deck of moored vessels. Much of it was rare skins and other items stripped from the area's diverse wildlife. One wide-decked galley was almost entirely covered by mottled sea-serpent hides of various hues. Others were stuffed with cages from which trapped animals were issuing outraged hisses and squawks. A man brushed past Shev with a cage slung over one shoulder, containing a spider-like creature with garish purple bands upon its segmented limbs. It slammed its many-eyed head against the bars to no avail before its bearer disappeared into the crowd.

So much life, sighed Occlesius. He was clearly in his element. *You don't know how much it means, Miss Arclis, after so long alone. I must thank you for bringing me out into the world.*

'Don't get too comfortable yet,' she warned. 'Vermyre's out there somewhere, and I'm sure he'd love to get his hands on you again.'

Yes, well. Our witch hunter accomplice seems a capable man. I am sure he will get his man. And then, perhaps we can look to the future.

'Excuse me?'

You and I are kindred spirits, Miss Arclis. We are both explorers, intrepid souls who brave the unknown in search of secrets that none have unearthed in thousands of years. Granted, I am somewhat less mobile than I used to be, but think of the partnership we could form! I simply must see more of this new world that has spread out before me. Excelsis, this City of Secrets, for one. I hear that the entire city is powered by prophecy. Remarkable.

'You mean you want me to take you sightseeing?'

Pray do not be so dismissive, the Realms-Walker said, with a hint of reproachfulness. *My knowledge of these lands is extensive. Imagine how useful my expertise could be to you on your next expedition.*

'Let's try and survive this one first,' she said, though in truth his offer intrigued her. To have someone at her side who had truly lived through the days of the Age of Myth. A renowned explorer, no less.

Please, at least consider my offer. Think upon it.

The docks gave way to a sprawling shanty-town of tumble-down shacks, built from bone and driftwood and covered with hides and leathers. Callis followed Toll through the heaving mass of bodies, hand placed carefully over his coin purse, although the paltry offering within would hardly set a thief's heart aflame with greed. He scanned the local populace as he walked, taking in an eclectic blend of cultures and cloth-ing styles. Here and there strode silk-smothered popinjays, faces powdered and heavy cutlasses slung rakishly upon their belts. These were privateers who thought themselves gentle-men, and delighted in aping the trends of Azyrite high society, even as their teeth rotted away from swigging rancid grog and smoking hasca-weed. Their brightly coloured tunics and ruffs stood out amidst the swirling mass of bare-chested, tattooed sailors, hard-weathered men and women who bore all the hall-marks of a hard life spent out on the open ocean. A duardin missing both his legs spat something unpleasant-sounding as Callis strode in front of his path. The amputee was dragging himself along in a wheeled cart fashioned from the shell of a crustacean, which also housed a number of bottles of brown-ish alcohol and a crude yet vicious-looking blunderbuss. There were fat merchants wrapped in exotic drapes, holding their noses as they were carried through the grime-encrusted streets on creaking palanquins.

It reminded Callis a lot of the Excelsis docks, though some-how the place managed to be even less reputable. With no Freeguild patrols to keep even a cursory watch over the mar-ketplace, the cutthroats and belt-cutters roamed freely, drifting through the river of people like sharks on the trail of spilled blood.

'Charming place,' said Shev, following behind.

'I've got earth beneath my feet and the promise of liquor. As far as I'm concerned this might well be paradise.'

Several skinny, dirty street kids skittered past, and Callis felt a hand brush against his belt, searching for something to prise free. He grinned.

'Not bad,' he yelled after the retreating children. 'But I'm afraid I'm a poor mark.'

The lead urchin, a small, freckled redhead girl with matted hair, turned and flicked him an obscene gesture, following up with several crude suggestions as to his possible ancestry. He gave her a wave, and she ran off through the crowd.

'I knew you were a city boy,' said Shev. 'But I didn't figure you as a guttersnipe.'

'Benefits of a criminal youth,' said Callis, with a grin. 'I mixed with a bad crowd, so my mother used to say. Believe me, it came in pretty handy when I was in the city guard.'

'You don't have to tell me,' Shev said, flashing him a wide grin of her own. She raised one hand, with a flat, round coin pinched between her thumb and forefinger. His last glimmering.

He gave her a mock bow, genuinely impressed.

'The Square of Prophets was my domain,' she said. 'Plenty of old, fat merchants and priests wandering through, their pockets filled with all manner of interesting things.'

'I had no idea I was speaking to a master of the craft,' said Callis, as they walked on. 'You grew up on the streets?'

'I did,' she replied. 'Learned a few tricks from the best pickpockets and second-storey artists in Excelsis. That was a long time ago.'

'You're full of surprises,' he said.

They trudged up a rickety, curving ramp that led them to another level of the port, a bazaar filled with stalls and great, circular tents. The crowds here were even thicker than in the hovels below, though it was clear that this was a place of business. Offers and counter-offers of merchants rang out over the general din of noise and hissing cook-pots, hawking all manner of illicit goods. Callis saw Excelsis-forged steels, barrels filled with wriggling, fork-tongued amphibians, and bales of sirigrash, a sickle-shaped plant harvested from the seafloor that the Excelsis city guard had long ago banned due to its occasional side effect of causing delusional madness in those who sampled it. In fact, as he glanced at the bewildering variety of produce on display, Callis noted a score of shipments and substances for which you'd earn a lengthy spell in the dungeons if you tried to flog them on the streets of Excelsis.

'There,' said Toll, as they reached the far end of the marketplace and emerged onto a wide, flat balcony that overlooked the greater city. Far in the distance, built upon a rising spire of bone and rusted metal, they could see the sky port. Four duardin vessels rested there in great berths, lit by sunlight that poured through holes in the shell of the dead behemoth. They were squat, powerful-looking airships, rippling with cannon and reinforced steel. From the deck of each protruded great, metal spheres, covered with vents and rivets. It seemed impossible that such a heavy vessel could ever stay in the air, but Callis had seen the skymasters of the Kharadron in battle before, and knew well just how agile and deadly their craft could be.

The lift that took them up to the sky port was a worryingly ramshackle construction of rusted cables, cogs and tow-ropes, manned by a surly gang of humans and duardin who lounged, drinking and playing cards. As Toll approached, they stopped their game, eyeing him curiously.

'I would speak with the captain of those airships,' he said, gesturing to the platform far above their heads. 'Take us up.'

'Want to speak to the cloud-beards, do you?' snorted an old, grey-haired duardin with a metal hook on one stubby arm. 'Hope you've brought plenty of coin, boy. They'll have the shirt off your back before you can blink.'

'You let me worry about that,' said Toll.

The old duardin shrugged, and snapped his fingers. Two of his crew rose grumbling from their seats and made their way over to a great, barrel-like device covered in soot and grime. The greybeard gestured for them to stand upon the platform, and they obliged. One man hauled upon a great, brass lever built into the strange device, and it began to cough and smoke. Slowly, the great cogs next to the platform began to creak and rotate, with a grinding, squealing sound.

'This does not look safe,' said Callis, gazing up at the lip of the sky port above.

'Calm yourself,' said the old duardin. 'We ain't had an accident in at least a couple o' days.'

His cackles were drowned out by the roar of the engine and the clattering of gears, and the platform began to rise. Callis badly wanted to hold on to something, but there were no rails. He watched with a distinct sense of unease as Shev ambled right to the edge of the platform and peered out over the side as the ground fell away underneath them.

With only a few heart-rending stalls and stutters, they finally made it to the edge of the sky port. Ahead was a veritable minefield of crates, barrels, containers, scattered tools and ropes. Working their way through this maze of detritus, hauling and stacking the cargo upon the decks of the docked sky-ships, were dozens of duardin dressed in black and red leathers. Even in the heat, Callis could see not a scrap of flesh beneath their heavy suits, and each wore an intimidating metal mask shaped in the image of a scowling duardin face. Ridged silver plates formed a beard, and across the eyes and mouth were perforated vents and lenses that resembled the scopes of Ironweld firing pieces. One of the duardin spotted them and made his way over, a hand resting upon the golden handle of a many-barrelled scattergun wedged into his belt.

'Those lackwits below were very clearly instructed to ring the damned bell before they sent anyone up,' he snarled. His mask turned his words into a metallic growl, but his accent was surprisingly clipped compared to most of the duardin that Callis had encountered.

Toll approached, hands raised.

'I'm here to speak with Captain Bengtsson,' he said.

'Admiral,' said the duardin. 'Admiral Bengtsson, and he is disinclined to receive visitors while he is preparing for the fleet's departure. In short, we are busy, and we have no time for any more "honest, above-board dealings" from smooth-talking conmen.'

'He'll want to speak to me,' said Toll. 'I represent the Order of Azyr, blessed seekers of his divine majesty the God-King. And I have an offer for your admiral that he will want to hear.'

The duardin eyed them for a long moment, then nodded.

'Wait here,' he said, and headed off towards the largest of the three airships. Up close they could see the magnificent craftsmanship of the vessel, the gilded panelling that formed the broad, deep hull, and the gleaming barrels of swivel-guns and rotary cannons that lined the gunwale. Callis whistled.

'Serious firepower,' he said.

'The Kharadron do not believe in moderation in warfare,'

said Toll. 'I've witnessed the results of an airship bombing run. Only rubble, fire and ashes left behind.'

Callis had spent his life around the guns and siege engines of the Ironweld engineers, and he had thought their weapon-smiths amongst the finest in all the realms. Yet these vessels made the inventions of the cogheads seem almost primitive. The largest was a broad, deep-hulled monster of riveted iron plates and layered panels of gold, marked by duardin runes and bearing the enormous sculpture of a stern longbeard god upon its prow. Its surface bristled with bombs and cannon of every conceivable variety. There was more firepower there than in an entire artillery detachment. A great engine-sphere rested on top of a squat cabin that ran along the rear of the ship. The enormous metal orb was lined with vents and beaten panels of corrugated iron, and dotted here and there were opaque port-holes that glowed with a faint, blue light.

'Sigmar's teeth, I can't wait to fly on one of those,' he muttered.

Shev raised an eyebrow. 'So hurtling through the air on a lump of metal is fine, but a bit of sailing gives you the jitters?'

'At least I know if I fall overboard I'll be dead as soon as I hit the ground. Not splashing around in the dark with a thousand unspeakable horrors drifting ever closer.'

'Unless you land in the water, of course.'

Callis shrugged, conceding the point.

The duardin who had addressed them strode up to a bolted door built into the side of the airship, and rapped on the metal with his gauntleted fingers. After a few seconds, the hatch opened, and the crewman hopped up a short flight of steps and disappeared into the vessel.

'I wonder how it all works,' said Shev, raising one hand to her brow as she squinted up at the enormous vessel. 'How do you keep something so heavy in the air?'

'I've heard Ironweld folk ask the same questions and get nothing but frosty glares in reply,' said Callis. 'They keep to themselves, do the sky-folk. Don't appreciate people poking their nose into their affairs. I'm sure they'll just love you.'

As they watched, a duardin in a bulky, armoured suit, much heavier than the ones his fellows wore, emerged on the deck of the rightmost ship. A metal sphere not unlike those mounted upon the airships ascended from the shoulders of the rig, attached to a large fin of corrugated steel. They looked on, astonished, as the duardin rose into the air, moving with unbelievable deftness and agility despite the bulkiness of his equipment. He came to rest upon the very top of the engine-sphere of the nearest vessel, one of the smaller gunships, and they saw the flare of a handheld torch as he began to hover over the superstructure of the vessel, welding and hammering panels.

'If it's not magic, I've got no idea how it's possible,' said Callis, shaking his head.

After several minutes, the hatch of the flagship creaked open, and the duardin re-emerged. He strode over to them, pausing every now and then to bellow instructions to his crewmates.

'Admiral Bengtsson will speak with you,' said the duardin, gesturing to Toll. 'Alone. Stow your weapons. I'll search your pockets, too. Never can be too careful where business is concerned.'

To Callis' surprise, Toll nodded and removed his coat, handing it to the armoured duardin. The Kharadron whistled and two of his crew approached, patting the witch hunter down efficiently and with no thought for comfort. They removed his shoulder holster and the two pocket-guns he kept tucked in the metal cap of his belt, as well as a small armoury of blades and unidentifiable paraphernalia. Toll bore the thorough patting-down without complaint, safe in the knowledge that they missed several of his most subtle and lethal devices.

The Kharadron snorted with amusement as he rolled a small sphere of bronze in his hands.

'You've no shortage of interesting toys, human,' he said. 'Impressive.'

'I would be very careful with that, friend,' said Toll, as one of the duardin passed his jacket back to him.

'Gunnery Sergeant Drock,' the leader said. 'Grundcorps. Follow me.'

Callis and Shev made to follow, but Drock held up a hand.

'Just him,' he said. 'You two wait here.'

'This might take a while,' said Toll. 'Head back to the alehouse we passed, beyond the free market. The Drowned Rat.'

'Appealing in name as it was in appearance,' muttered Callis.

'Just keep to yourselves and wait for me,' said Toll, before turning to follow Drock towards the enormous skyship.

Chapter Twenty-Four

The great door groaned open, and Toll followed Drock into the depths of the ironclad. It was gloomy inside, a cramped tube of looming bulkheads and corrugated walls lit by foul-smelling lamps that cast a hazy orange light across the walls.

Toll passed chambers stuffed to the ceiling with crates, barrels, cages and other paraphernalia, lashed together with leather bindings and overseen by yet more masked duardin. They gazed impassively at him as he passed. It might simply be an illusion of the mind, but the interior of the vessel seemed far larger than he had expected. Everything was functional, utilitarian; there was not a stretch of wall or floor given over to aesthetics rather than practicality. Its smell was sharp and bitter, but not entirely unpleasant; the chemical tang of oils and work-leathers, sweat and hard labour.

Drock tramped up a short flight of corrugated stairs and came to another bulkhead, secured by a heavy door upon which was marked a series of runes that Toll could not understand. His knowledge of the skyfolk's language was passable, but each of the Kharadron skyports had their own cultural subtleties and linguistic quirks. From the markings he had seen upon the vessel's hull, Bengtsson's crew hailed from Barak Zilfin, one of the largest of the skyfolk's enclaves.

The gunnery sergeant rapped sharply on the door, and there was a barely audible grunt from within. Drock heaved the door open, revealing a small, dimly lit chamber dominated by a huge ironwood desk. Surrounding this ornately carved piece was a thick jungle of towering paperwork – scrolls, tomes and charts of all description, stacked together in piles so immense it seemed they would crush a person if they were to fall. In the midst of this forest of fading yellow papyrus sat another armoured duardin, hunched over a desktop scattered with maps and aethermatic gadgetry, lit by an egg-shaped lamp of polished bronze that dangled from the ceiling on a copper cord.

Just as the rest of his crew, Admiral Bengtsson was clad in a full-body leather oversuit and a mask that entirely covered his face. His mask was by far the most ornate that Toll had seen, however. It was fashioned from gleaming gold, the lower portion forming a great, wedge-like beard and sweeping moustache, the upper half an imposing duardin frown. The eyes were sky-blue sapphires, the brow ridged with rivets of silver. It was an imposing visage, to be sure.

'Well?' barked Bengtsson. His voice was harsh and deep, with a faint lilting quality to the accent. 'Time's wasting, sir. I believe you had a proposition to bring before me?'

Toll removed his hat and stepped before the admiral's desk. There was no seat. Bengtsson was clearly not a duardin who relished company.

'Hanniver Toll, agent of the Order of Azyr,' he said. 'I am

in pursuit of an individual who has committed untold crimes against the free city of Excelsis. I arrived here by sail, but I fear my quarry further eludes me with every passing moment. I require swifter passage.'

Bengtsson leaned back in his chair, making a steeple of his gloved fingers.

'The *Indefatigable* is no passenger ship,' he said. 'Tell me, why should I interrupt a profitable trading mission for your convenience?'

'As I said, I represent the Order–'

'If the next words out of your mouth are an attempt to threaten me into compliance, I should warn you that the last human to offer me an ultimatum fell for hours before he struck solid earth,' said Bengtsson.

Toll raised his hand in acknowledgement, and shook his head.

'Not at all, admiral,' he said. 'My position affords me no jurisdiction over the skyfleets of Barak Zilfin. I am well aware of this. But I am in a position to greatly reward those who assist me in my attempts to bring this fugitive to justice. The Order does not forget its allies, admiral.'

'Indeed?' said Bengtsson. 'Tell me, who is this fugitive you seek? Who is so important that an agent of Sigmar is sent so far out of his domain to see justice served?'

'His name is Ortam Vermyre. Recently, he has gone by the title of the Golden Lord.'

'Subtle fellow.'

'He can be when the occasion calls for it. For decades, Vermyre was the High Arbiter of Excelsis. There was no more important mortal soul in the City of Secrets.'

'Until he opened its gates to a daemonic invasion,' said Bengtsson. 'I've heard tell of the sacking of Excelsis, Mister

Toll, and of your traitor lord. I am aware of the sizeable bounty
on that one's head. But tracking criminals is not my business.'

'Make it your business, and I can offer you more than coin,'
said Toll.

Bengtsson leaned forward. It was damned strange, dealing
with someone without being able to look into their eyes. Perhaps that was why the Kharadron were such renowned masters
of the mercantile arts. Still, Toll fancied that he could sense
the duardin's curiosity.

'You know of Excelsis' greatest export?' he said.

Bengtsson waved a dismissive hand. 'Of course. Secrets and
lies, mined from the Spear of Mallus – a relic of the old world,
if the legends are true. Slivers of the future, from which a man
can make his fortune. Tell me, if the city is so rich in prophecy, then how is it that it contains such a multitude of beggars,
drunks and liars? I've travelled to your City of Secrets, witchfinder, and I've no burning desire to return.'

'The auguries are real,' said Toll. 'Some are little more than
whispers, faint inklings of potential. These we allow the populace to trade and barter as they see fit, for alone they are all but
meaningless. But there are greater truths that are mined from
the Spear, admiral. Kept under lock and key at the behest of
the Collegiate. Some are nothing that mortal souls could possibly contemplate, secrets of such shattering power that only
the greatest minds of the age could hope to interpret them.
Others are simply too valuable to be made public knowledge.'

'Get to the point,' said Bengtsson, though there was an edge
to his voice that betrayed his growing interest.

'I know what the skyfarers treasure above all else,' said Toll.
'The breath of Grugni. The fuel that powers your fleets and
your cities. Aether-gold. If you agree to give me passage, I can
grant to you an augury of incomparable value, one that would

make you the richest sky-captain on the Taloncoast. Perhaps in all the realms.'

There was silence, for a long while. Bengtsson's crystal eyes never left the witch hunter's.

'And the Collegiate, they would agree to this?' he asked at last.

'Of course not,' said Toll. 'But I've no intention of asking for their permission. I mean to see Ortam Vermyre dead, admiral, and I will pay any price to see that happen.'

Bengtsson leaned back in his chair, steepling his fingers and studying the witch hunter.

'I'm listening,' he said.

Chapter Twenty-Five

In Callis' long and varied experience, The Drowned Rat was perhaps the most depressing establishment he'd ever had the misfortune of visiting. It was a squat, cramped hovel carved out of clay and propped up with mortared bone. The only light sources were a couple of half-heartedly excavated holes in the slanted roof that bled a thin trickle of light across several hide-wrapped stools and tables. The apparent proprietor was a leathery, ancient duardin with a missing eye and a mouthful of broken teeth, who peered at Callis as if he were a particularly low species of vermin that had crept into his establishment.

'Two ales,' attempted Callis.

'Ales?' spat the duardin, turning up his considerable nose.

'Forgive my ignorance. What's the typical delicacy you serve around these parts?'

'Guama,' grunted the barkeep, and proceeded to pour a thick, greenish-brown liquid into two clay cups. There was a strong, altogether unpleasant smell, somewhere between damp wood and sewer runoff. Callis offered a thin smile, slotted his last glimmering across the counter, and warily carried the two cups of unspeakable liquid over to where Shev was waiting in one dank corner.

He slid the aelf her drink across the table. To his surprise, she took up the cup and took a great swig of the stuff. Her face went through several stages of grief, and ended somewhere near capitulation.

'Gods, that's rough,' she groaned.

Callis took a sip of his own, and immediately regretted it. The substance tasted even worse than it smelled, but it did at least leave a satisfying fire in his stomach.

'I hope your man can find us passage,' said Shev. 'Bilgeport is short of charms, and you can bet our quarry is already nearing his prize.'

'Toll can be very persuasive when the need arises,' he said. 'And he won't allow Vermyre to slip away from him. Not again.'

Shev frowned, and her lips twitched, as if she was about to say something.

'Speak whatever's on your mind,' he said.

'It doesn't worry you?' she replied. 'The intensity with which he hates this man? I've known men lost to revenge before. It never leads to anything good, Armand.'

'Vermyre's betrayal left a scar, that's true,' Callis nodded. 'But I put my trust in him. He's not led me astray before.'

She leaned back in her chair, peering at him through those hazel eyes.

'Why are you out here, Armand?' she asked. 'You're no true believer, that's for certain. A man like you, who made his name in the battle for Excelsis – even a Reclaimed – I'd have thought you set up for life.'

He sighed and shrugged. Even that small motion sent a

shiver of pain through his chest. If he was honest with himself, he hadn't truly given much thought to why he'd accepted Toll's offer of employment. It was hardly as if the witch hunter had lied about how hard and thankless the work would be.

'For most of my life, I thought the army was my calling,' he said, choosing his words carefully. 'I was a good soldier. My comrades respected me, I think. It was a tough life, but it gave me structure. Purpose. And then, in a moment, I lost it all.'

'Vermyre's betrayal?'

'Yes, but that was only a part of it. Everything I had ever known. All the assumptions I had made, the foundations of what I believed in, they were shattered. Suddenly, the world became an infinitely larger and more terrifying place. But, somehow...'

'You found your place in it?'

He nodded. 'I can't really explain it. My life was unmoored, and exposed for the lie it had always been. There were daemons amongst us, all along. But rather than the fear I expected, I only felt a calm assurance. As if my entire life had been leading up to this moment of realisation, and now I was truly free.'

'Maybe I was wrong,' she murmured. 'Maybe you are a true believer after all.'

He laughed and raised his cup. She clinked it with her own, spilling a few drops of its foul-smelling contents. He realised he was staring. She was beautiful. The scars were nothing, really.

The door of the tavern swung open with a creak.

Captain Arika Zenthe – or whomever she was currently pretending to be – strode in, accompanied by Oscus and four other aelf corsairs. Zenthe still had her hair covered by a scarlet wrap, and she had ditched her twin swords in favour of a pair of ruby-hilted daggers that were secured crosswise upon her leather armour. The duardin barkeep shrank back just a bit behind his counter. Obviously the aelves of the Scourge were considered no less enigmatic figures in Bilgeport than they were along the dock districts of Excelsis.

'Save the bilgewater,' Zenthe said as she entered, waving a dismissive hand at the nervous duardin. 'I've brought something that's less likely to rot my guts from the inside.'

The captain drew a decanter of amber liquid from within her coat, and pried loose the stopper with her teeth. She caught sight of Callis and Shev in their dimly lit corner.

'Well, if it isn't Arclis the tomb-thief and the indomitable guilder,' she said, spitting out the cork and taking a deep draught of the decanter's contents. As she approached their table, her angular nose crinkled in disgust. 'By the deep, you were actually foolish enough to drink their local fish-piss? Gods help you, both of you. Pour that trash out, and let's have a proper drink.'

Callis sighed, and tipped his drink out onto the floor. A small, six-limbed, purple-shelled crustacean that had been nestling between the dusty cobbles gave an indignant shriek as it was doused in the sour guama, and scuttled away into the shadows.

Zenthe poured him a slug of the amber liquid. Her men took tables around the bar. Callis noted that they were far from relaxed. They all carried weapons, and had chosen positions which gave them a good view of each entrance.

'Expecting trouble?' he said, and took a swig. Fiery, but with a pleasant honey-like aftertaste.

'Always,' she replied, lowering her voice just a fraction. 'Arika Zenthe is not a name that's praised to the topsails in these seas. I've made fools of the High Captains far too many times.'

'Well, as long as they don't know we're here,' said Shev.

Zenthe fixed her with an almost pitying stare. 'Of course

they do. Or, if they don't yet, they soon will. You can't just disguise a ship like the *Thrice Lucky*, girl. We might have bought some time, but nothing more. We're in the bloody water, and there's sharks circling. Probably the only thing that's holding them back is they expect me to have something up my sleeve.'

'And do you?' asked Callis.

'No,' said Zenthe cheerily.

He sighed, and drained the last of his liquor. Zenthe refilled his cup.

'Don't worry your precious heads, young ones,' she said. The good captain was grinning honestly for the first time in days. Callis realised that she was genuinely enjoying herself. 'I've been in far worse scrapes than this. And I know the High Captains better than they know themselves. Azrekh, the runaway slave. Lorse, who'd gut his own mother for a glimmering. That fat slug Kaskin, cleverer than you'd give him credit, despite his bluster.'

'If what you say is true then might it not be a good idea to lie low somewhere?' whispered Shev. 'Maybe head back to the ship, or book passage to Excelsis.'

Zenthe sighed.

'The *Thrice Lucky* is probably the least safe place in all Bilgeport,' she said, then took a long, slow draught of liquor. 'She's made her last kill. Hull breach like that, you'd need a team of shipwrights working on her day and night for the next span to get her back cutting the waves. She's served me well, but like all old wolves, there comes a time when you can't lead the hunt any more. Here's to her memory.'

Callis was surprised how sad he was to hear her say those words. He'd hardly enjoyed a moment of his time on the *Thrice Lucky*, but the wolf-ship had cut a path through the worst the

Taloncoast could throw at her, and brought them out alive. Well, most of them anyway.

'We're here until we can find safe passage back to Excelsis,' said Zenthe. 'With a captain we can trust to keep their mouth shut. Not an easy find.'

'Or until we find a ship worth stealing,' muttered Oscus.

'My hopes on that end aren't high,' said Zenthe. 'The state of most of those half-rotted cogs out there in the bay, I'd give it a league at most before they went under. If a shipmaster in my fleet dared let their vessel decay to such a state, I'd have them flayed to the bone.'

She drained the last of the amber spirit. Callis and Shev raised their own cups and drank along.

Chapter Twenty-Six

The light was dimming now as Toll made his way back from the skyport. In the distance, he could hear the holler of drunken voices and a clatter that was clearly intended to be musical, but fell some way short. Here, though, it was quiet. Disturbingly so.

Footsteps. Soft, careful, but unmistakeable. He was being followed.

Toll took a sudden turn, passing into a narrow alley that ran between two rows of cramped, clay huts. Shell fragments mixed with broken glass on the floor, and he had to skip awkwardly between patches of dry earth in order to mask his path. He turned again, and on his right there was an open hole, a make-shift window that led inside one of the crude yurts. With a smooth, practised grace he grasped hold of the sill and levered his body into the structure, pressing flat against the far wall. Two shadows drifted past the opening. They stopped, briefly, and he heard the hush of whispering voices, though he could not make out the words. The sentiment, however, was easier to grasp – they were confused and angry. After a moment, they continued on, following the path ahead.

Toll stepped cautiously forward. Something draped in hides and net wrappings lay in the corner of the hovel, and it groaned and muttered something as he passed.

There was another opening at the front of the shack, and he passed through, turning to place his feet upon the sill and jumping to catch a hold on the rough timber roof. He pulled himself up as quietly as possible, and then dropped low as he saw movement across the way, on the roof opposite his own. A human form, wrapped in a black cloak, wielding an alley-bow. The cross-shaped head of the weapon drifted across the streets below as the sniper sought his target.

Me, no doubt, thought Toll. He had hoped that their presence would go unnoticed for at least another few hours, long enough for him, Callis and the aelf girl to depart upon the Kharadron vessel. As always, however, his best laid plans appeared to have gone awry.

The sniper offered a muttered curse, and moved closer. He was now no more than ten feet away, and his back was turned.

Toll rose, push dagger clenched between the first two fingers of his right hand. He ran, put his foot on the lip of the roof and hurled himself across the gap. The crossbowman was just turning when Toll struck him, bearing him to the floor. The man fired, and the bolt shot out from under Toll's arm and disappeared into the night. Barring one hand across the man's throat, throttling his startled grunts, Toll struck out with the dagger, sinking it into the sniper's chest. The man gurgled and spat hot blood onto the side of the witch hunter's face. Toll did not relent, striking until the man's ragged breathing finally cut off.

He heard movement below, and a soft, low whistle coming from the alley running off to the west, towards the market square. He grasped the alley-bow, its hardwood grip slick with spilled blood, and raised it to his chest. It would be best to keep this quiet.

Bracing one foot back, he leaned over the edge of the roof, leading with the muzzle of the weapon. He saw a flicker of motion, little more than a brush of shadow. He fired, and heard a gratifying howl of pain in response. He put two more bolts into the inky darkness where the sound had come from, and then rolled backwards as a corresponding scatter of bolts whickered off the roof by his feet, tearing up a cloud of dust and splintered wood.

'Jed! Jed!' he heard, a panicked hiss.

Toll slipped off the roof on the right hand side, furthest away from the voice and the low moaning of the cutthroat he'd snagged with that last bolt. More footsteps, rushing closer, and the flicker of torches at the far end of the alley. This wasn't good. They could easily box him in here, trap him and run him to ground. Whoever had made their play, they were taking no chances. He rummaged in his coat, fished out the bronze sphere that had so interested Gunnery Sergeant Drock earlier. It vibrated a little, and he gripped each half and rotated his hands. With a satisfying click the two ends split apart, revealing a thin band of perforated holes along the circumference of the orb. He waited two breaths, then rolled the sphere down the end of the alleyway, where a huddle of figures was just hoving into view.

The sphere spat thick, green smoke which rolled up the red-clay walls of the alleyway, smothering the advancing figures in a choking fog. Toll heard coughing and retching as the acrid gas did its work. Then, raising the collar of his coat to cover his mouth, he ducked low and advanced forward, right into the cloud. A figure stumbled out of the haze, holding

one gloved hand to its eyes and spluttering. He saw the out-line of a broad, well-muscled body, clutching a vicious-looking axe. The man looked up from his retching fit as Toll's pistol butt descended towards his face. He managed a startled yelp before the club hit him on the base of the neck, driving him to his knees. Toll swung again and again, until he felt the body go limp. Then, just as more figures began to stumble out of the smoke, he rolled the body into a break in the alley to his right, and tugged off its black cloak. Sweeping the garment around his shoulders, he grabbed the man's boarding axe – a thick-hafted weapon with a double-edged blade – and brought up the cloak's hood.

'Nagash's rotting bones,' spat the nearest figure, leaning against the far side of the alley. Toll emerged from his hiding space, making a show of rubbing at his own eyes – it wasn't hard, as the choking gas was biting deep into his skin, sting-ing like daemon-blood.

'Jed and Hogrim are bleeding out,' came another voice. 'He's a slippery one.'

'The High Captain warned us no less,' whispered the first figure.

'I saw him run that way,' Toll grunted, making his voice a low growl. Whether it was the sting of the smoke or the dim light, the band of cutthroats seemed not to notice that one of their number had been replaced. Muttering curses and threat-ening bloody vengeance upon their quarry, they began to file past Toll. One of them stretched out a hand to help him along, but he shook his head and pretended to dry heave, waving the man on.

As soon as they had filed off into the shadows, Toll's coughing fit miraculously ceased, and he slipped away into the darkness, moving as fast as he dared towards the Drowned Rat. He only hoped he could reach his companions in time. He was crossing a grimy square littered with broken glass when he saw the silhouettes of figures rise from the low buildings ahead, the gleam of metal in their hands. A hail of bolts slammed into the earth all about him, kicking up a cloud of foul-tasting dust. He froze, knowing that he was marked on all sides.

'You're a talented man,' came a gruff voice from his left. Sauntering out of the darkness came a duardin wielding a saw-toothed blade, flanked by two burly henchmen. Toll recognised the burn-mark of an escaped slave upon the newcomer's brow, and marked him as High Captain Azrekh. This one had a reputation for sadism and brutality that echoed even on the streets of Excelsis.

'Give it up now,' grunted the duardin. 'No way out of this, witchfinder.'

Cursing his ill fortune, Toll raised his hands, letting his stolen crossbow clatter to the floor.

A figure stepped out from the shadows across the square. As it crossed into the flickering moonlight, Toll saw a featureless golden mask, and long, flowing robes of black.

'Ortam,' sighed Toll. 'I should have known you'd wish to gloat before you finish me. You always did find the sound of your own voice the sweetest symphony.'

Vermyre laughed. There was a gurgling wetness to the sound. Following behind the former High Arbiter came a thin, sallow man that Toll recognised as High Captain Lorse. Where Azrekh and Kaskin flaunted their ambition and indulged in the embellishment of their legend, Lorse remained a rarely-seen, enigmatic figure. Toll had long marked him as the most dangerous of the three.

'This is foolish,' muttered Lorse, his voice gravelly and strained. The tales said that a former rival had taken a knife to Lorse's throat in a drunken brawl. 'You never told us he was a witch hunter. We drain a little blood from Excelsis every now and then and no one notices. We start butchering members of the Order, we'll have the damned storm-bringers at our docks before we know it.'

Vermyre rested a hand on the man's shoulder. Lorse flinched, perceptibly, and adopted the expression of a man who had a live blade-spider crawling across his face.

'No one will ever know what happened here, if you are diligent,' he said. 'Hanniver is a secretive man, who operates for months, sometimes years without contact or support from Arnhem. By the time the Order notes his disappearance, if indeed they ever do, they will have a thousand other crises to occupy their time. We live in a time of great opportunity, High Captain, if we only have the wit and the boldness to seize it. You think that Arnhem will mark the disappearance of one man, while across the far realms their cities are besieged?'

'We exist out here only by the barest of threads,' said Lorse, shrugging Vermyre's hand free. 'I'm not fool enough to think we'd last a day if the Scourge fleets sailed upon Bilgeport. Kaskin, Azrekh, they see the Sigmar-worshippers' indifference to us, and they mistake it as fear. We overreach ourselves.'

'Only by risking the unthinkable do we forge our destinies,' said Vermyre.

'You can stow that mealy-mouthed trash,' sneered Lorse.

Vermyre was not a tall man. Yet he seemed to loom over the High Captain. The air in the vicinity turned thick and oppressive, and Toll imagined that he felt a low, rumbling sound like rushing blood.

'You may leave,' said the masked man. 'See to your prisoners.'

Lorse, his face pale and hand twitching towards his gun-belt but never truly threatening to reach it, shook his head and began to stride away, a mob of burly cut-throats forming up around him. Toll heard his boots crunching across the shattered glass of the square as he retreated.

'You need me here for this,' said Azrekh, running his finger along the flat of his flensing knife. 'If there's something you need from this wretch, I'm the man to get it… Always wondered how a witchfinder would fare under the blade.'

'That will not be necessary, High Captain. Our business will shortly be concluded.'

Vermyre turned his gaze to Toll.

'Here we are then,' he said. 'Reunited at long last.'

Toll thought of a thousand threats and curses he wished to hurl at the traitor, but gave voice to none of them. He locked his gaze with that impassive mask.

'Nothing to say? You've pursued me across the vast ocean, worked your old bones to dust in order to see me dead, and when you finally catch up with me you stand sullen and silent?'

Toll's eyes flickered around the square, searching for some form of escape route. Ahead, a hundred yards or so to the north-west, he could hear the sound of running water. One of the filth-encrusted canals that sluiced down towards the harbour, carrying the detritus of the city's population. If he could reach it…

'I did truly regard you as a friend, Hanniver,' said Vermyre.

Toll let out a bark of bitter laughter. 'Don't speak to me of friendship. You betrayed me, Ortam. You made a fool of me for years. Decades. You set my city aflame, and you allied yourself with daemons and witchkin.'

'I did as I–'

'And for what?' Toll hissed. 'For power? For your wretched faith? Look what that has brought you. You wear that mask to hide your face, not because you fear Azyr's hunters, but because you fear what you are becoming. Arclis told me what is happening to you, old friend, and why you seek this Silver Shard.'

Vermyre's hand twitched, as if he would reach to unclasp his false face. Then he lowered his hand, and gave a soft, sad chuckle.

'You know, there are those who believe I am blessed,' he said. 'That the reshaping of my flesh is some form of gift from the Changemaker.'

'And this is the master to whom you swore your soul?' asked Toll, shaking his head. 'You're an intelligent man, Ortam. A cultured, educated man. You must know what awaits those who worship the Lord of Lies.'

'I am no priest of the gods, Hanniver. I never was. I seek only an escape. Freedom from the doomed cause to which the God-King has bound us. Strife and endless war, against a foe we can never defeat. You of all people should know the futility of this struggle. You have glimpsed the true scale of the powers arrayed against mortalkind. We cannot triumph.'

'It doesn't matter,' Toll said, shaking his head. 'Better death. Better oblivion than whatever has happened to you.'

'In that we at last find agreement,' said Vermyre. 'I am done serving the will of gods and monsters, Toll. I will find this Silver Shard, and I will use its power to remake my flesh. Then, I will drive you Sigmarites and your hypocrisy from these lands one city at a time. I will start with Excelsis. Let that wretched place burn first, and let the gods bicker over its ashes.'

'That's all you can think of?' Toll said, shaking his head in disgust. 'All this scheming, and the best you can do is to attempt an atrocity you failed at once before?'

'That will serve for now. And it will hurt you, Toll. *You* reduced me to my current state. It is only fair I destroy your world in turn.'

'You'll never stop being a tool of the Dark Gods, Ortam. Even now, you're dancing to their tune. They own your soul and your fate, and there's no cure that can save you.'

Vermyre was silent for a long while. 'I should kill you,' he said at last.

'If you leave me alive, I'll come for you. They won't hold me here, not forever. I won't stop hunting you.'

Vermyre approached. He clutched his staff tightly, raising it across his chest in two hands. Again, Toll could hear that strange pulsing sound, growing ever louder and more resonant.

'I should,' he muttered.

'Why don't you have your slave do it for you?' said Toll, gesturing to High Captain Azrekh. 'This one professes such a love of knifework. I wonder, if the High Captain here is such a terrifying scourge of the seas, why is he rotting out here in this wretched hive, surrounded by drunken sots and fools? Could it be that you're just a thug with a blade, Azrekh, and there are more terrifying things festering at the bottom of the city's midden-pits?'

Azrekh's eye glazed over with fury.

'Oh, I'm going to enjoy skinning the flesh from your bones, boy,' said the duardin, starting forwards with his blade twirling in his hands.

'Azrekh, stand back,' snapped Vermyre. 'This is my business.'

The High Captain raised a hand, and the crossbows swung away from Toll, and levelled at the masked figure.

Vermyre hissed in anger. 'Don't be a fool,' he snapped.

'You don't ought to talk down to me, masked one,' said the duardin. He was only a few yards from Toll now, his two bodyguards keeping pace. 'This is my city. *Mine*! I will show you what happens to those who insult me in my own hall.'

Using the distraction, Toll clenched his wrist and snapped

NICK HORTH

his hand out to the side. The sleeve-gun clicked and whirred as the clockwork mechanisms sent it nestling into his palm. He turned, and fired at the man on his left. There was a small, sharp crack, and a dark stain spread across the man's shirt. With a small cough, he tumbled backwards into the dirt.

The witch hunter was already moving, stepping within the reach of the stunned Azrekh and locking his arms around the duardin's thick neck, driving a knee into the man's leg and knocking him down. Someone loosed their repeater in panic, and the other bodyguard let out a pained shriek as the bolt took him in the leg.

Toll saw Vermyre making a shape with his fingers, and threw himself aside. A bolt of searing fire flashed past him, engulfing a wooden shack in purple flames. Suddenly, the night was alive with dancing trails of light. Crossbow bolts skittered and slammed into the wall behind Toll as he ran, hands covering his face from the scorching heat of the blaze. He saw Vermyre weave another bolt of fire, but then he was barrelling through a decaying gate of mildewed driftwood, which burst apart in a hail of wet shards. He disturbed a colony of yellow-fanged bilge-rats as big as hounds, and they scattered, screeching and shrieking in indignation as they flooded around his legs.

Something slammed hard into his shoulder blade, tearing through flesh and striking bone, but he did not stop for he knew that to do so would be to die.

Ahead, he could see the curving wall of the canal, and beyond that the crude, square-shaped line of a sewer outflow, gushing a stream of thick, soup-like brown-grey into the river.

He slipped on the cobbles, reaching down to steady himself, and a hail of bolts slammed into the wall where his head been just seconds ago. Then he was running again, and the backstreet trailed off into a dirty slope piled with filth, broken bottles and picked-clean bones. He skidded down this foul-smelling hill, and threw himself into a dive, the oil-sheen surface of the foul canal water reaching up to envelop him with a freezing embrace.

'Slippery bastard,' cursed Azrekh, as he strode along the shoreline searching for Toll's body. They'd found only his wide-brimmed hat, the torn impact of a crossbow bolt gouged along the left side. But there was no blood, even though the High Captain swore that he'd caught the fleeing man with a thrown blade.

Vermyre considered burning the impulsive duardin alive. His blood was thundering in his veins, and the dark presence that had nestled in his soul demanded a blood sacrifice for this failure. He could – *should* – have killed the witch hunter outright, but now he was loose, and Vermyre knew Hanniver well enough to know that a few wounds would not stay him for long.

He cursed.

Azrekh stared back at him, his expression daring Vermyre to open his mouth. It would be so sweet to peel this arrogant wretch's flesh back from his face, to feast upon his brain-matter in full view of his minions, to hear them scream and run in terror.

No.

Not here.

Not now.

Such reckless displays of his power would only draw further attention. Toll was unlikely to be the only agent of Azyr operating in these waters. It would be a fine thing indeed to outsmart his nemesis, only to blunder into the gun sights of another bounty hunter or hired killer.

'You should find him,' he said, instead. 'You do not want Hanniver Toll loose in your city, believe me. He has a way of upsetting things.'

'He won't. He'll be dead before the opportunity presents itself,' snapped Azrekh.

'I suggest you simply kill your remaining prisoners, rather than allowing them to escape also. Or else you can be assured that your reign as High Captain will be even shorter than most.'

He scanned the bubbling waters of the canal one last time, but saw nothing. As he turned to leave, Azrekh's men leapt aside to clear his way.

This had been a setback, but he was still ahead of schedule, and his pursuers had been dealt a heavy blow. It was time to move. The lost city of Xoantica awaited.

Chapter Twenty-Seven

The door of the Drowned Rat exploded inwards, slamming into the far wall with a sound like a gunshot. As the first cloaked figures began to charge through, Zenthe's crew were already on their feet, drawing blades, handbows and pistols. The first man to enter, a shaven-headed brute wielding a heavy mace, fell riddled with bolts. There was the crack of a pistol, deafening in the cramped confines of the tavern, and one of the *Thrice Lucky* aelves went down with a gargling scream. The duardin bartender howled, lying flat on the floor with his hands over his head. Callis rose, kicked the table over to free himself and drew his own weapon.

'The back door,' shouted Shev, huddled in the corner. 'More of them.'

Callis swivelled and fired. Splinters flew up as his shot smashed through the shell-covered doorway. He heard a muffled groan on the other side, but it burst open a mere moment later, and more figures poured in. He hurriedly fished a fresh cartridge out of his belt pouch, and as he did so he saw that Captain Zenthe was sitting idly on her chair amidst the carnage, with an expression of bored indifference upon her face.

A bullet ripped past and shattered the glass decanter she held, sending glittering shards of crystal scattering across the floor.

'Oh, enough,' Zenthe shouted, a look of irritation breaking out across her face at last. 'Enough.'

To Callis' astonishment, the shooting ceased. The newcomers, whoever they were, filtered into the tavern, which was now filled with the bitter tang of gunshots and the smell of freshly spilled blood. Over to Callis' left, someone let out a long, drawn-out moan of agony, soundly ignored by everybody in the room.

'Which of you is it then?' Zenthe continued, pacing up and down in the middle of the chaos. 'High Captain Kaskin, do I smell your particular stench wafting in through the door? Or is it the noble Azrekh I should be conversing with?'

There was a long silence, broken only by the sound of the barkeep's whimpering. As Captain Zenthe passed his prone form, she aimed a swift kick at his buttocks. He fell silent.

'Arika, my dear,' came a high-pitched, nasal voice, which was oddly childlike. 'It is a pleasure as always. I would ask you and your crew to drop your weapons, if you would be so kind. Otherwise I'm afraid we may have to resort to knifework, and you know how much I despise needless bloodshed.'

Zenthe snorted. 'Oh, you're a saint amongst cutthroats, Kaskin, the gods know it.'

The captain gave a curt nod to Oscus, and the brawny aelf let his handbow fall to the floor. Zenthe's crewmates did the same, muttering and cursing as they did so, and – with no little reluctance – so did Callis. The High Captain's men scooped up the fallen arsenal, and went through the routine of patting down their captives, searching for hidden weapons. They found a not insignificant arsenal – a vicious collection of punching daggers, knuckle-bars, coshes and razor-wire garrottes.

'Is it clear?' came that childlike voice again.

'Aye, sir,' said the largest of the thugs, a split-nosed brute swinging a heavy two-handed club.

A huge man stepped through the door. He was enormously fat, and swathed in a crimson silk shirt and bright blue pantaloons, with a ridiculously colossal hat perched jauntily upon his big, square head. His arms and hands were bedecked with gleaming jewellery and chunky golden rings, and his broad, youthful face was split in a delighted grin.

'Arika, Arika,' he crooned, dipping into an elaborate bow. 'It is a wondrous pleasure as always, my dear. Tell me, how have the seasons been treating you?'

Zenthe took a step closer to Kaskin, and the High Captain's guards immediately closed around him, weapons raised. Kaskin waved them down.

'Rough seas out there, as you know,' said Zenthe.

'Oh, as always. I was appalled to hear of the state of the *Thrice Lucky*, my dear. Such a shame, to see a ship that conjures such a ferocious reputation limping into port like a wounded beast. My commiserations, Arika.'

He bent his head and clasped his hands as if in prayer, a gesture that dripped with naked insincerity.

'Gods below, spare me the theatrics, you beached whale,' sighed Captain Zenthe. 'I assume those other two deviants are nearby? There's no chance you'd have the spine to orchestrate this without them.'

'Just so,' came a voice from the rear entrance. There stood a duardin bearing a vicious skull-mark tattoo on the left side of his face, idly spinning a flensing knife in his hand. He was slighter than most duardin Callis had known, but there was a whip-like tension to his stance that spoke of swift and lethal grace. He frowned as he noticed the duardin's face was smeared with blood, and flecked with ashes. His jaw was clenched shut, and his eyes were dark slits of malice. He looked like a man ready to kill.

'And Captain Azrekh joins our little gathering,' laughed Zenthe. 'Tell me, Oddo, how did the wound I left you at our last meeting heal up? Did I leave a scar?'

The duardin's face didn't move, but his eyes glinted. Another figure slipped in behind him, entering the tavern cautiously.

'And here's the last of your wretched little triumvirate,' said Zenthe. 'High Captain Lorse.'

'Zenthe,' nodded the newcomer. He scanned the room, eyes passing briefly over Callis and resting on Shev. He clicked his fingers, and two of his men moved forward and grabbed the aelf by the arms, hauling her towards the door as she kicked and struggled.

Callis took a step forward and immediately drew the aim of several pistols and crossbows.

'What do you want with her?' he said.

Lorse raised an eyebrow. '*We* don't want a thing. She's just a part of the deal. Sit down.'

Callis' eyes darted about the room, searching for anything he could use to his advantage. Lorse had a pistol tucked loosely into his belt, and two knives sheathed on a leather strap across his chest. The nearest guard was bleary-eyed, rubbing his temple with the haggard look of someone who had whiled the night away drinking. If Callis could get hold of the High Captain's blade, kill him quick and hurl his body into the guard…

He would never make it. Too many pistols drawn, and too great a distance.

Shev's eyes met his own, and she gave a slight shake of her head. He took a deep breath. She was right. Now was not the time for ill-advised heroics. Then the aelf was gone, dragged out into the cloaking darkness.

'I've waited a long time for this,' growled Azrekh. 'And there's no getting away, Zenthe. No one's going to pull you out of the fire this time.'

Zenthe simply fixed the duardin with a cold smile.

'I'm telling you, we should just kill them all now,' muttered Lorse. 'Put an end to it.'

'No,' said Kaskin. 'Bilgeport has to see her die at our hands. They have to know who rules these seas now, from here to Excelsis. That's the only way.'

Azrekh nodded. 'Death's one thing. Humiliation's another. They're going in the Pit. We're going to host a spectacle the likes of which the scum of this city have never seen before.'

Rough hands grabbed Callis and the others, and dragged them towards the door.

Shev tried to keep her footing as they half-carried, half-dragged her down alley after alley. She thought, perhaps, they were heading towards the harbour. She saw the rising silhouette of the High Captains' Tower looming ever closer. It was almost pitch black now, but she could see pale, hostile faces peering out at their party with predatory interest, like carrion birds waiting for their turn at the corpses.

Keep calm, Miss Arclis, said Occlesius, and for perhaps the first time she was grateful for the calming sound of his voice echoing in her head. *Be ready. I will watch for the right moment, and as soon as I tell you to run, you must make good your escape. We'll get out of this, I assure you. No one can keep Occlesius the Realms-Walker contained for long.*

'Here,' growled the heavyset man who had her by the arm. She looked up to see an unremarkable two-storey building overlooking the harbour bay. She could see the water from here, dark and glinting in the light of a yellow moon. They pushed her inside, where a single brazier lit a featureless room of red clay, casting flickering shadows across the wall.

'Our bargain is concluded,' came a familiar voice, and her blood froze in her veins. 'You may leave.'

The High Captains' cutthroats filed out, leaving Shev sprawled in the middle of the room. Darkness loomed in the doorway to her right, seeming to shift and swirl with life. A figure stepped through the portal, a figure she recognised instantly. The expressionless mask of gold shimmered dully in the torchlight, and she thought she could see a faint gleam of silver light deep in its sunken eyeholes.

'Hello, Madame Arclis,' said Ortam Vermyre.

Oh no, said Occlesius.

He crossed over the room towards her, and she thought she caught the spectre of a limp in his stride, a slight spasmodic twitch. There was movement behind the masked man, and in the shadow of the doorway she briefly saw a flash of bright colour, and the shimmering orb of an avian eye, lurid yellow and burning like wildfire. She snapped her hand away, suddenly filled with an intense revulsion.

If Vermyre noticed her unease, he did not let it show.

'My dear Shevanya,' he said, and though he spoke softly, those words sent a shiver of caution through her. 'I always knew we would meet again. Please, do not be alarmed. I hold no grudge regarding the ill-favoured nature of our last meeting. I hold myself responsible for the misunderstanding. Of course you ran from me, I accept full responsibility.'

The masked lord leaned close. The stench of ash and

quicksilver burned her nostrils. She backed away, desperate to put as much distance between her and this creature as possible.

'I told you once that you and I were destined for great things, Shevanya. I still believe that is true. For now, however, I require two things. The first is your cooperation for the next few days. Second...'

Vermyre stretched out a hand, fingers curling upwards like claws.

You must, said Occlesius. *He will take me from you regardless.*

Slowly, regretfully, she unhooked her necklace, and passed him the crystal. As soon as she removed it from her neck, it was as if she knew true silence for the first time in weeks, like a layer of her subconscious mind had been stripped away. The sensation was unsettling, and not entirely pleasant. She had got used to having the Realms-Walker's voice around.

Vermyre held the orb a moment, staring into its roiling depths. Then he swept it into the pocket of his robes, and gestured for her to follow him. She did not want to. Whatever lurked in that shadowy doorway, she was sure it desired nothing less than to feast on her soul. Vermyre chuckled beneath his mask, a horrid wet sound.

'You have nothing to fear from them,' he said. 'Now follow me, Madame Arclis. We have business to attend to.'

She got to her feet and followed Vermyre out into the night. He led her along the right-hand side of the harbour, lined with shanty-houses and crumbling stone walls. Perched upon these crumbling structures were thin, horned figures with jagged beaks and curving horns. Their eyes burned like coals in the darkness, and she shivered as they peered down at her malevolently.

'Pay them no attention,' said Vermyre. 'They will not lay a claw on anyone unless I desire it.'

'You've certainly improved the quality of your associates,' she replied.

He laughed.

'You may not believe this, Shevanya, but I've genuinely missed your company.'

'Where are you taking me?'

He stopped and turned, raising his staff in one hand. The dark, glittering waters of the harbour began to churn and boil.

'We're going for a ride upon this. A gift from my new allies.'

A shape emerged from the water, shining in the moonlight. It was a length of red-tinged crystal, perhaps half as long as the *Thrice Lucky*, fashioned in the rough shape of an arrow-head. At the edges, the crystal folded back to form jagged walls, and a fan of spear-length spines jutted out from the sides of the bizarre vessel, like the fins of a deep-sea creature. Shev noticed that the underside of the craft was lined with strangely organic-looking hook shapes, like curved teeth. At the centre of the vessel rested a pulsing core of purplish light, and when Shev made the mistake of gazing at the emanation, she felt her head spinning and her stomach turn.

There was a sense of utter wrongness about this ship, about these creatures.

Vermyre stepped aboard the crystal ship as it emerged onto the dockside, and held out his hand for her to follow. She did not deign to take it, instead grudgingly making her own way aboard. Though the surface was slick with water and smooth as ice, she found that she could easily keep her balance. The vessel radiated a strange heat. The avian creatures moved to join them, not taking their eyes from her. They muttered and clicked in their own strange tongue as they boarded. Others, she saw, had mounts of their own. Ugly, disc-shaped creations, similarly organic in appearance, and lined with razor-sharp blades and serrated teeth. As they stepped aboard these bizarre devices, they began to lift into the air with a droning hum.

Vermyre intoned an arcane phrase, and the crystal ship followed suit, rising swiftly and gracefully into the night sky. It made not a sound as it rose into the air, but soon the shimmering bay of Bilgeport spread out before them, and they could see the light of the corsair port twinkling and fluttering beneath.

Somewhere down there were Toll, Callis and the others, at the mercy of the High Captains. Shev was not much for praying, but she beseeched any gods that were listening to help her friends survive what was coming.

Chapter Twenty-Eight

Callis and the others spent the rest of the night in a lightless, stinking dungeon somewhere near to the dock district, listening to the shouts and drunken chanting of Bilgeport's noble populace. Huge, evil-eyed rats scurried across the rough stone of Callis' cell, and he whiled away the few hours until dawn by pinging rocks at them. Zenthe's snores reached him from the opposite cell, and he shook his head in baffled astonishment. How could she sleep so easily at a time like this? They needed to get out of here, they needed to pick the lock, or bribe the guard or… something. *Anything.* In a mad rush of fury, he stood and crossed the chamber to rattle the rusted iron bars.

'Hey!' he shouted, hoping to draw someone near. 'Hey, you out there!'

There was no response. Gods, but his head was throbbing. Whatever Zenthe had given him to drink had skipped straight to the hangover.

'Rest your bones, guilder,' came Oscus' soft, calm voice.

He was leaning against the bars of the cell next to Zenthe's, studying his fellow captive with calm amusement. Callis felt a powerful desire to punch him in the jaw.

'What's your plan then, exactly?' he snapped. 'Wait until dawn to get ourselves drawn and quartered?'

Oscus yawned.

'There's naught to be done,' he said, with an unspeakably irritating lack of concern. 'Not yet. You see those bars, there's no give there. There's no locks to pick, or secret tunnels to escape by. So yes, we wait. They've already made their mistake by not killing us outright when they had the chance. We'll find our moment, and we'll make them pay. Or we'll all die. Painfully.'

'Oh, that's brilliant,' sighed Callis, slumping down to the floor and aiming a kick at a particularly ugly grey-white rat that had ventured too close. 'Not for the first time I count myself fortunate to serve as acting crewman on the good ship *Thrice Lucky*. Long may she sail.'

'Careful, boy,' said the first mate, softly.

Callis ignored him. His thoughts drifted to Toll. Where was the witch hunter? Had he been captured too? Maybe he was lying dead in a gutter somewhere, killed by the very man he had sought to bring to justice. And Shev... She was at the mercy of the maniac Vermyre, and there was nothing he could do about it.

Purplish light began to seep through the cracks in the ceiling, drawing vertical streaks across Callis' cell. Dawn was fast approaching. He curled up in the corner of his cell, as far away from the skittering rats as possible, and tried to sleep.

He had only snatched a few precious minutes of sleep when the clatter of boots and a chorus of shouts forced him awake. He dragged himself to his feet. His head throbbed painfully, and his mouth was bone dry. Down the corridor came a score of armed men and women, rattling clubs and blades against the cells as they approached, making a din that did Callis' tender head no favours.

'Up you get, scum,' barked the leading figure, a huge brute of a woman with one side of her head shaved, wielding a vicious barbed whip. She stepped up to Callis' cell and unlocked the door, and two of her burly associates rushed in to drag him out with little regard for care or restraint.

'It's time for you to put on a show,' said the woman, with a black-toothed grin. 'Don't disappoint me now, you're to give the audience good sport before you croak it.'

'That will certainly be the first thing on my mind,' said Callis, earning himself a painful clout from one of his captors.

Zenthe and her crew were bundled out of their cells alongside Callis, though he noted that the guards were rather reluctant to lay hands upon the aelf corsair or her accomplices. For her part, Arika Zenthe was the picture of indifference. She stifled a yawn as they strode up the steps of the dungeon and out into bright sunlight, and the hoots and jeers of a gathering crowd. They were in a plaza of sorts, dominated by a gaudy, bronze statue of a buxom mermaid carrying an amphora, from which she poured a torrent of water into a hexagonal marble-tiled pool. Disreputable types were sprawled across the fountain like beached seals, all of them bearing the look of people who'd not yet quite recovered from the previous night's festivities. The rest of the square was taken up by mobs of curious onlookers, sailors and capering street urchins, along with several entrepreneurial types who'd erected stalls selling dubious-looking roasted flesh or jugs of ale.

Beyond the crowd, Callis could see that the ground fell away in a series of switchback staircases, revealing a sunken, stone-walled arena surrounded by a rickety wooden amphitheatre. At one

end of this ragged-looking coliseum there was a covered platform from which soared three garish flags. One bore the image
of two blood-smeared knives, another a leaping spinefang
drake, and the last a phoenix in flight, its heart pierced by an
arrow.

'The flags of the High Captains,' said Zenthe, following his
gaze. 'They're going to treat their loyal subjects to a live exe-
cution, then drink in the applause like fine wine.'

They reached the first stair, and Callis caught a proper look
at the arena for the first time. Sleek, stone walls covered in
dripping lichen dropped down twenty feet to a surface of slick
rocks, dead coral and scattered detritus. It looked like a rough
beach at low tide, and he could smell the slightly unpleasant
tang of rot and brine as he drew closer. Scattered about the
arena floor, which was perhaps three hundred paces across,
were deep, dark pools of green-black water that glimmered
like the eyes of a ghyreshark in the early morning sun.

The sound of the crowd reached fever pitch as the con-
demned were led down to a great iron gate at the rear of the
arena. One by one they were taken out to this gate, stripped
of their manacles and thrust through the entrance. It came to
Callis, and he stood and waited for the gaoler to unlock his
bindings.

'What am I going to find in there?' he said.

The woman smiled widely, and launched a glob of black spu-
tum into his face.

'Right then,' he said, wiping it away.

The gaoler and her accomplices grabbed his arms and forced
him stumbling through the door. He almost lost his footing on
the seaweed-covered floor. From here, he could see four great
sluice-gates built into the walls of the chamber, and a series
of smaller openings dotted high up on the wall. Brown stains

poured from the entrance of these channels, like vomit down a drunkard's shirt.

Zenthe and her crew stood on the largest stretch of solid ground, a flat shield of sun-baked rock around which bubbled a stream of clear water. Oscus had gathered up a fist-sized rock with a flat, sharp edge. As Callis approached, Zenthe bent and grasped the rusted hilt of a sword that lay abandoned at her feet. The blade was broken about two hand spans from the crosspiece, but the remaining edge was sharp enough.

'Welcome, welcome all,' came a booming voice from above. High Captain Kaskin sat sprawled high above on the covered dais, reclining on an enormous cupola while servants and slaves dashed forward with plates of food and immense amphoras filled with wine and spirits.

The crowd now packed the looming amphitheatre. Callis could see row upon row of faces, cackling and whooping at the carnage yet to come. Bottles rained down upon them, along with a variety of less pleasant objects. As Kaskin spoke, the audience began to chant his name. He drew in their worship for a few moments, then held his hand up for calm.

'Before you stands the legendary Captain Arika Zenthe,' he bellowed at last, gesturing at the arena. 'Scourge of the Talon-coast. Raider of the Coast of Tusks. She-wolf of the waves. How many of you here have suffered at her vile whims? How many honest sailors have been forced at sword point to relieve their ships of priceless cargo, or else be butchered and cast to the depths?'

There was a deafening roar, at which Zenthe began to grin delightedly. Callis wondered if there was anyone here she hadn't made an enemy of.

Kaskin gestured for calm again.

'Long has the noble haven of Bilgeport suffered at her hand, accused of deviancy and buccaneering by those thin blooded fops of Excelsis, those cowardly hypocrites, while all along they harbour the most infamous rogue of all within their very port!'

Another round of bellowing, and another hail of bottles, rotting food and assorted waste.

'No longer, I think!' roared Kaskin, raising his hands to the heavens, then taking a great swig from his wine cup, splashing purplish liquid across his slab of a face. The crowd's howls bordered on the exultant. Callis never ceased to be amazed at the manner in which a gathering of mortals could indulge themselves with a display of communal hypocrisy. Looking up at those in attendance this morning, he wondered if a man or woman amongst them was even passingly familiar with the concept of honour or decency. The chances were stacked against it.

'Enough talk,' growled High Captain Azrekh, and though he barely raised his voice, it still carried clear across the arena. 'Give us good sport before you die, Zenthe.'

He raised a hand and dropped it sharply, like the fall of a guillotine blade.

At that signal there was a low rumble of grinding chains as the sluice gates slowly wound open. A torrent of foetid water spilled forth from four quarters, splashing out across the rocky ground of the arena. After several moments the openings higher up on the stone walls followed suit. The water level was rising quickly. The crowd began to chant and howl like rabid wolves. Callis fell into a combat-ready crouch, preparing himself for the bloodshed to come.

'Rally to me,' said Zenthe, twirling her half-sword with easy grace.

Shapes began to emerge within the rushing water. Lithe, serpentine forms, covered with row upon row of hooked spines.

Long, forked tongues licked and tasted the earth, as sightless eyes gazed ominously about the coliseum, and a low, hissing whisper reached Callis' ears.

'Voridons,' muttered Oscus, who still had his rock clenched in his fist. 'Beware their bite, or you'll find your joints locked solid while they start to eat you.'

Half a dozen of the eel-like creatures crept closer and closer, sliding in and out of the swirling eddies. Callis and the others gave ground, retreating to dry earth. One of the aelves hurled a stone, striking the nearest serpent in the jaw, smashing loose a scatter of curving teeth. It reared and hissed, its long tongue waving back and forth like it was brandishing a blade. Another darted forward and struck out, sending Oscus scampering backwards. They were blind, these creatures, Callis realised, but they could somehow sense that there was prey close at hand. With an unsettling, quiet coordination they spread out to surround their quarry.

A small, wiry aelf called Huvon, who Callis recalled had manned the quartermaster's chamber on the *Thrice Lucky*, darted out to strike one of the serpents with a chunk of rock. It seemed to anticipate the attack, and as his hand came in it contorted its body and whipped forward, wrapping itself around the unfortunate corsair's arm. He howled in agony, and the crowd roared their bloodthirsty approval. Callis felt his stomach turn as he saw the serpent's spined hide contract and twist, forming a grinding maw that stripped flesh from bone with sickening ease. The beast tried to snap its jaws out and bite Huvon in the neck, but before it could strike, Zenthe rushed forward and hacked off its upper jaw. There was an awful, hissing screech, and the serpent released its death-hold, falling away to splash and writhe in the steadily rising water, releasing a cloud of blue-black blood.

Two more of Zenthe's crew rushed forward to haul Huvon back. The tough old corsair was hissing through gritted teeth, staring up hatefully at the crowd who mocked and jeered his injury. The water was lapping around their ankles now, and rising faster with every passing moment.

Callis estimated they had perhaps another ten minutes before they were treading water. He shuddered to think of those barbed horrors slithering towards him from below, wrapping themselves around him and dragging him down to be torn apart.

Zenthe splashed forward, stowing her weapon and raising up a flat disc of smooth rock from the shallows. She hefted the weight and brought it crashing down upon another of the beasts, crushing it in place. Its tail whipped and lashed the air in helpless protest. Oscus knelt by its head and brought his rock down once, twice, three times. Sickly pink matter spilled from the thing's shattered skull.

Two down, thought Callis.

He heard the chortling, nasal laughter of Kaskin above the crowd.

'Good show,' giggled the High Captain. 'A good show indeed!'

Working in pairs, cautious and lethal, the aelves isolated and carved up three more of the serpents, hacking them into pieces or bludgeoning them to death with whatever came to hand. As Oscus struggled against the last remaining beast, Callis pried the rock from his ally's grasp and drove the crude weapon under the creature's chin, slitting its throat. The water had now risen to their knees, and two-thirds of the arena was now submerged. Only a few scattered islands of shale and stacked rocks remained above the water line. No aelf had yet fallen, though Huvon had lost much blood and looked pale and haggard. Callis had seen similar wounds before, and guessed that the corsair would soon bleed out. The aching certainty of their demise was a greater horror than any deep-spawned thing that could spill out of those sluice gates. One by one they would be dragged down, torn apart and devoured, all to the sound of ringing laughter. He looked up to the stands, saw the bared teeth and sweat-soaked faces of the frenzied crowd.

Was this it, Callis wondered? Had he abandoned a promising career in the Freeguild to die for the entertainment of these wretches? He prayed for a glimpse of Hanniver Toll's weather-worn face amidst that crowd, but saw nothing. It was a fool's hope, he knew. Most likely the witch hunter was already dead.

'That was just a taster,' bellowed High Captain Azrekh. 'Let them test themselves against Old Skinshear.'

The roar from the audience became, if possible, even more raucous. They began to chant as one.

'Skinshear! Skinshear! Skinshear!'

At the far end of the arena, another gate slid open, three times the size of the first. From within, Callis heard a skittering, scratching sound. An enormous sabre-like limb emerged from the darkness, tapping on the floor with a strangely sickening precision. Its rough, calloused surface shone in the sunlight, and it widened at the bottom, forming a spade-shaped blade. Another limb followed the first, along with a wiry frond of antennae, curling and twitching as they tasted the air.

Crawling from the darkness came a shape from Callis' darkest nightmares. Arachnoid in form, slender and thickly plated with chitin, it advanced on eight skittering legs, the front two armoured and thick, the rear ones bunched, stubbier. It was the size of a small house, yet it scuttled across the rushing streams of seawater with horrid swiftness and grace. In the midst of its sclerotised head were buried a dozen pitch-black, shining eyes, above a mouth stuffed with dripping fangs. Callis felt a rush of terror and revulsion that threatened to steal the strength from his bones.

'That's an abyssal flayer,' said Oscus, and Callis registered the fear in the usually unflappable aelf's voice. 'By the deep, how did they capture one of those?'

Chapter Twenty-Nine

Callis leapt aside as the monster's armoured forelimb crashed down, shattering the rock he had been perched on into pieces. He landed in cold seawater, kicking his legs frantically as he sought to escape the thing's reach. A corpse bobbed in front of him, torn nearly in half, seeping bright blood into the frothing surf. He saw a pale, aelven face, eyes lifeless, features twisted in horror. An arm grasped him by the shoulder, and aided him out of the water onto a shelf of rock covered with spined barnacles.

It was Oscus. His teeth were gritted, and he clutched his arm, but other than that he seemed unscathed.

'How in Sigmar's name do we kill that thing?' Callis gasped, staring at the chitinous horror as it circled them, twitching and clicking its great limbs together with an awful snapping sound. Two aelves were dead already, ripped apart with sickening ease, their ruptured remains hurled aside or stuffed into the monster's maw. Blood and saliva drooled from the thing's hooked fangs, and its eyes were fixed on the survivors.

'Distract it,' said Zenthe. She had somehow got hold of another blade to match her rusted half-sword, this one a saw-bladed dagger she had pried from the hands of a floating corpse.

'What are you going to do?' said Callis, but before the captain could answer, Oscus was dragging him away, rushing and splashing through the knee-deep water towards the south-eastern edge of the arena. The creature known as Skinshear tracked them with beady eyes, scuttling its great body across to face them.

Oscus hefted a good-sized rock and sent it whipping out towards the abyssal flayer's head. It flicked a leg out and blocked the blow, and its multiple orbs seemed to lock onto the first mate with alien malice.

Callis, for his part, really had no idea what he should do about the hideous thing bearing down upon him. He opted to scramble up onto the nearest formation of rock, a narrow ridge of coral-encrusted stone that ran alongside the eastern wall for a dozen paces. A glass bottle hurled from the crowd glinted at his feet, and he reached into the bloody water and grasped it. Arching his back, he hurled the missile at Skinshear. It struck the creature on the back, shattering into a thousand glinting shards as it broke upon its hardened armour shell.

The monster flicked its gaze between its two assailants, no doubt judging which one it should dismember first. Its eyes settled upon Oscus, and Callis felt a surge of relief accompanied by only the slightest twinge of guilt.

Skinshear skittered forward, its forelimbs jabbing out at the first mate. Oscus ducked under one and hurled himself out of the way of the other, landing nimbly upon a protruding rock, then skipping to another, somehow weaving his way through the wall of slashing limbs. The crowd groaned and howled at each near miss. The first mate was scampering with light-footed grace beneath the beast's armoured torso, while Skinshear shrieked, then circled, trying to split the aelf with its blade-limbs.

Callis kept up a rain of missiles – rocks, plates of coral and whatever else was near at hand. He'd lost sight of Zenthe, but if she didn't act soon, Oscus was dead. He couldn't keep this up much longer.

Then the creature did something that took Callis entirely by surprise. It ignored the troublesome aelf dashing beneath it, and dashed towards the other visible prey instead. The movement was sudden, terrifyingly so. One enormous, stabbing forelimb was mere inches from his face when his frozen body snapped into motion, and staggered aside. Replaying that same moment in his mind later, Callis would wonder how Skinshear could possibly have missed its strike. All he would remember was that limb arcing down to splinter rock into scattered shards, and the sudden sensation of flight as the creature whipped its leg back swiftly, catching him in the chest with the broad flat of the claw and sending him hurtling backwards through the air, his arms windmilling crazily.

He struck the wall of the arena hard, enough to blast the breath from his lungs and briefly darken his vision, but blessedly not enough to shatter bone. He slithered down and splashed face first into the water, and in his delirium he swallowed a huge mouthful of bitter brine, and began to choke and thrash. In his punch-drunk daze he staggered upright, gagging and spluttering, to see the beast rise up above him. He could see the glistening streams of water cascading down its armoured form, and those awful, piercing orbs gazing down upon him with alien hunger.

There was a peal of insane laughter, and he looked to his

right to see Arika Zenthe dashing along the crest of rock, twin blades raised above her head, wild delight in her eyes. She leapt, impossibly high, and sailed beneath Skinshear's flailing arms straight towards its ugly face. It managed a hiss-shriek of fury before both weapons sank deep into the pitch-black orbs of its eyes.

Skinshear rocked back, armoured thorax twisting as it turned circles in maddened pain. Zenthe tucked her legs and hit the water in a graceful dive, somehow angling her body so that she missed the teeth of the rocks below.

The roar of the crowd choked, then died.

As the monster writhed, Oscus approached it steadily. He held a jagged harpoon of rusted iron scavenged from the arena floor. Hefting the weapon, he whipped his arm forwards, hurling the missile with unerring accuracy. It struck the abyssal flayer in the mouth, sinking deep and sending up a gout of thick, black blood. There was a horrid, wet rattle, and Skinshear collapsed on its back, its limbs whipping about spasmodically. After a few moments, the movement ceased.

Zenthe pulled herself out of the water alongside Callis.

'How many playthings do you think they have left?' she said, casually wiping spatters of black ichor from her forearms.

'Enough to keep us going for a while yet,' muttered Callis, groaning as he massaged his aching head. 'Throne of Azyr, this hangover is murder.'

Zenthe chuckled at that, and clapped him on the back.

Then she strode forward along the shelf of rock, which was by now almost submerged by the rising tide. She raised her hands, waved and then gave an elaborate bow pretending to take in applause that was certainly not forthcoming.

'So,' she shouted, gesturing up at the High Captains, who were staring down at her with ill-disguised fury and hatred.

'What else do you have for me to kill? Perhaps one of you might like to come down here and challenge me yourself? How about you, Azrekh? Maybe I'll cut that slave-mark off your face, sell you on as damaged goods.'

There was a faint but unmistakable ripple of disbelieving laughter amongst the crowd.

Azrekh started forwards, hands grasping the rail at the edge of the stand as if he meant to leap down upon the aelf. Kaskin rose to his feet, surprisingly swiftly for such an enormous man, and placed a hand on the duardin's shoulder.

'You hear me now,' shouted Zenthe, circling with her finger raised at the now quiet crowd. 'My words are for all of you. None of your pitiful pets can slay me. I've hunted deep-drakes in the mists of the Shadow Sea. I slaughtered the Abyssal Queen and took her skull for my drinking cup. I duelled the Lord Rukhar amidst the crystal-reefs of the Ten Thousand Eyes, and sent his flagship to the depths. I will escape this cage. I will kill everything you send at me, and I'll build a mountain of their torn corpses and scale these walls.'

Perhaps it was Callis' imagination, but he swore that at least a dozen onlookers began to back away from the stands as the captain finished her speech.

'All of you, ask yourselves now, do you wish to be here when I do so? When your mothers told you tales of the corsair queen Arika Zenthe, did they say that she was a merciful woman? Or did they warn you that if you crossed her, she would flay the skin from your bones and use it to patch her sails? Ask yourselves that.'

'Very amusing, Arika,' Kaskin crooned, and doffed his ludicrous hat in mock praise. 'Very impressive. But I think it is time that the day's entertainments came to a close. Release the cages. All of them.'

The ogors grunted and resumed turning the enormous levers, and there was a rumbling, clanking sound. The gushing streams of water became even more violent, and at the far end of the arena they heard the sound of rusting bars creaking open.

Oscus had retrieved his harpoon, and now made his way over to Callis and Zenthe. There was now no part of the arena that was not submerged. They were standing on the tallest shelf of rock, but even there the tide reached up to their knees. Callis' feet had gone numb, frozen by the cold water.

Serrated, blade-like fins cut through the gushing channel at the far end of the arena, scything through the water with lazy menace. Silhouettes rippled just below the surface, large and sleek-bodied.

Oscus, Zenthe and Callis moved back to back, blades drawn. As the creatures came close, Callis saw the glint of needle-sharp teeth, and a flash of luminescent scales shining beneath the waves.

Chapter Thirty

As the underwater beasts drew closer and closer, Callis heard a new sound. It was a low, rolling hum, something like the accumulated noise of a swarm of insects. It set his teeth on edge. Looking up, he saw people in the crowd begin to point and shout. Confusion, then worry became evident on their faces even at this distance. Up in their podium, the High Captains were standing, staring up past the far wall of the arena and into the bright early morning sky.

A shadow fell across the arena. Looking up, Callis saw the enormous wedge-like shape of a ship's hull drift overhead, iron-riveted plates bristling with shaped charges, vicious-looking harpoons and gas-powered cannons. A fleet's worth of firepower crammed into one ship. Admiral Bengtsson's flagship, the *Indefatigable*.

'I'll be damned,' chuckled Zenthe, shaking her head.

Flying alongside the enormous vessel like pilot fish were stocky, armoured figures strapped to floating spheres of metal, longrifles and barbed boarding spears clutched in their hands. These figures descended with surprising grace, and as they came close Callis saw the gleam of their metal face-masks. The Kharadron opened fire, flares of bright light erupting from the barrels of their firing pieces. Bullets fizzed and splashed through the water all around the exhausted survivors. Blood sprayed, and tails thrashed and writhed in the surf as the sky duardins' shots blasted apart beast after beast. One of the descending duardin hurled a harpoon, and Callis gave a startled cry as it missed him by mere inches, whipping past his shoulder. He spun, and found himself gazing into the jagged-toothed maw of one of the sharks, split by a length of polished metal. The harpoon had gone straight through the creature's ugly, hammer-shaped head.

The Kharadrons reached out, grasping Callis, Zenthe and Oscus with steady hands, two duardin taking a firm hold of each while the others formed a shield of guns and blades. Callis found himself hauled bodily out of the water, gasping and laughing as the duardin's back-mounted engines fired and lifted them into the air towards the hovering sky-ship. Up, up they went, and Callis could see the pale, scared faces of the crowd staring up at them in astonishment. Kaskin and Azrekh were on their feet, the former backing away towards a narrow, rising staircase that led from the High Captains' seats to the upper level of the city.

'Remain where you are, Kaskin,' bellowed a familiar voice. 'You all stay exactly where you are. Nobody take a single step, or this ship will unload with every ounce of ammunition it has.'

Through his fug of pain and exhaustion, Callis felt a surge of blessed relief. His carriers soared up past the gunwale of the duardin vessel and landed on the deck, depositing their living cargo none too gently. Callis smacked the corrugated metal hard, and rolled. He felt rough hands hauling him to his feet. There stood Toll, bruised and bloodied but otherwise intact, standing next to an imposing duardin clad in metal plate armour and strapped into an enormous, vented back-pack. Tubes and piping connected this bizarre device to the duardin's ornate, golden chestplate, and to the brace of pistols he wore at his belt. Like all of the duardin on deck, this fellow went fully masked, but it was clear to Callis immediately that this one gave the commands on this vessel.

'Welcome to the *Indefatigable*,' grunted the duardin.

Toll gave Callis a brief nod, and his top lip raised just slightly in an almost imperceptible smile. Zenthe was deposited by another pair of engine-clad duardin, and landed gracefully on her haunches, followed swiftly by the wounded Oscus.

'Toll, my old friend,' said Captain Zenthe, with an approving nod. 'I must say that you certainly know how to make an entrance.'

'Arika,' said the witch hunter.

Callis turned back to the gunwale. Below, the High Captains' bodyguards had formed a circle around their masters, but even at this distance Callis could see they were nervous, and on the verge of fleeing. After all, what possible use could their match-locks and cutlasses be against the metal behemoth that had its cannons levelled squarely in their direction?

'We had a deal, Bengtsson,' Azrekh roared. 'A duardin, even one of your kind, keeps his word. No actions, covert or other-wise, against the city of Bilgeport while you trade at our docks, that was the agreement. Signed by your own hand. You're going to break your oaths? Is Radrick Bengtsson nothing more than a backstabbing coward?'

The heavily armoured duardin – Bengtsson, Callis pre-sumed – unfurled a waxen scroll from a pocket on his belt.

The document was almost as long as the captain was tall, every inch of its surface covered in a precise, even script.

'You did, of course, review the contract we agreed upon?' said the admiral, his rumbling burr of a voice strangely modulated by his mask. 'In particular, sub-clause two hundred and sixteen?'

Azrekh's face contorted with irritated confusion.

'What in the hells are you prattling about?' he snarled.

'I'll spare you the exact details, but suffice to say that after an initial period of three seasons has passed, the agreement offering my trade convoy exclusive buying and selling rights within your borders – along with the corresponding pledge on my part to withhold force of arms while my ships are berthed within the vicinity – may be annulled at any time by the delivery of a notice of cessation. I trust you received my missive in the early hours of the morning?'

'Your... missive?' stammered Kaskin.

'I fulfilled all the requirements we agreed upon during our initial negotiations,' continued Bengtsson, in a matter of fact and slightly stern tone, as if he was a disappointed father addressing his lackadaisical son. 'Our business is concluded, and as is written in artycle three, point twenty-nine of the Kharadron Code, I am free to negotiate a new trading charter with any party that I choose. And, as a subsequent result, I am no longer bound by pledge of neutrality.'

'You thrice-cursed son of a pox-ridden–' howled Azrekh.

'Please, let us maintain a professional demeanour,' snapped Bengtsson, cutting the duardin captain off. 'I can hardly be blamed for your failure to review our contract in even the most cursory fashion.'

'The prisoners you took from the *Thrice Lucky*,' growled Toll. 'Where are they?'

Azrekh stared back at the witch hunter. 'Dead, mostly. The rest are chained up in the dungeons, below the salt-warrens. So what happens now, witch hunter?'

Toll stared down upon the High Captains for a long moment. Nothing could be heard but the actinic hum of the sky-ship's great spherical engine.

'All of you stand accused of heresy and sedition, of piracy and the pillaging of supply routes to the God-King's free cities. In doing so you endangered the lives of innocent citizens and loyal soldiers of Azyr alike. There is only one punishment fitting for your crimes.'

Toll turned to Bengtsson, eyes as hard and pitiless as the deep ocean.

'Bring it down,' he said.

Zenthe began to laugh as the duardin gunners hauled the deck guns round to target the far wall of the arena, where torrents of water still poured through the giant sluices, filling the stone bowl beneath them. Callis could see corpses bobbing in that foaming pool, both aelf and beast.

Then the guns opened up.

The sound was deafening. Callis covered his ears as the enormous, six-barrelled volley gun mounted on the fore of the vessel stitched a line of thudding explosions across the sluice-gates. Swivel guns below the rim of the gunwale added their formidable firepower to the barrage, aiming at the wooden stands, which came apart as easily as wet parchment as high-explosive shells detonated and shredded the huge supports resting beneath the seats. Once again the screams of the audience rang out, but now they were filled not with bloodlust but with terror. Dozens of bodies tumbled out into empty space as the stands began to come apart under the barrage, striking the stone floor below with bone-cracking force. The High

Captains' box was bracketed by blossoming gouts of flame as more rounds slammed home. The flags of the pirate leaders swirled and rocked in the firestorm, catching alight and raining down into the churning waters of the arena.

Kaskin turned to run, but his immense body only made it a few paces before a cannon round blasted apart the archway beneath him. The High Captain waved his hand desperately, almost comically, before the ground beneath his feet betrayed him, and with an ear-splitting scream he fell away into a cloud of smoke and rising dust. Callis saw Azrekh, not running but firing a pistol and screaming in defiance, yellowed teeth bared like those of a mad beast. There was a bursting cloud of blood and the High Captain was hurled back, head over heels, his chest a ragged ruin.

Callis watched the devastation, feeling slightly sick. This was not a pinpoint, surgical cannonade, but a barrage designed to spread fear and destruction as far as possible. He gripped Toll's arm, meaning to ask the witch hunter to stop the carnage, but Toll simply met his gaze and gave a slow shake of his head. Zenthe's laughter echoed over the symphony of rattling volley-gun fire and the rising crescendo of detonating cannon round. The stands were now a crumbling inferno. With an awful groan, the far wall of the arena gave way, and a great tidal wave of unleashed water poured free, smashing open the gate at the opposite side of the circle, surging out into the city streets. An ogor, riddled by bullets, lay slumped over the great gate-wheel.

The *Indefatigable* began to rise away from the carnage, soaring over the city. The rising flood spread out amongst the narrow streets with the vengeful rage of a beast unleashed from a cage, smashing down makeshift hovels and clay-walled buildings, devouring all in its path. When the entire lower level of Bilgeport was flooded with filthy mud-brown water, the guns finally ceased firing.

According to Bengtsson's calculations it would take two to three days to reach the Fatescar Mountains, if the weather held to its current maudlin haze.

'Always avoid those skies if we can help it,' said the admiral, as he spread out a chart across his desk, indicating a strangely geometric formation of mountains marked to the far north-east of the Taloncoast. 'The winds will change upon you in a moment, and we've had more than one sky-ship disappear out here, without a trace.'

'We know the rumours,' said Zenthe. The corsair was leaning against the far wall, eyeing the cluttered contents of the admiral's chamber with interest.

'Indeed,' muttered the duardin irritably. 'No doubt you've extensive experience of sailing these sky-lanes. Perhaps I should hand my commission and my share of this journey's galkhron over to you?'

Zenthe held up her hands in a gesture of appeasement.

'Take pity upon a captain without a ship or crew of her own,' she said.

'As I recall, you do have a crew,' Callis pointed out. 'Still locked up in the Bilgeport dungeons.'

'And before we departed I sent Oscus to see to their release,' said Zenthe, shrugging. 'By the time we return, I expect they'll have looted everything of value in that cesspit of a city. For now, I'm nothing more than your humble passenger.'

Seemingly satisfied with Zenthe's answer, Bengtsson turned to Toll. 'Do you even know what you're looking for? If there truly is some lost city out there, no one's seen it and lived to tell the tale. We might be chasing a ghost.'

'Vermyre knows where it is,' said Toll. 'If he's willing to risk everything he has to get there, you can be sure that Xoantica is real. And every moment we waste, he draws closer to his prize. This Silver Shard, whatever it is, cannot be allowed to fall into his hands.'

Bengtsson shrugged. 'As long as you pay what was promised, I'll sail you to the jaws of Ignax herself.'

'And what exactly did you promise the good admiral here?' asked Zenthe, studying Toll through narrowed eyes.

'You'll both get what is due,' snapped Toll, with an uncharacteristic outburst of irritation. Callis studied the witch hunter's drawn, pale face. 'Until then, you both work for me. Get me to the Fatescars, admiral.'

With that Toll left, leaving Zenthe and Bengtsson to an uneasy silence. Callis trailed after the witch hunter as he strode out of the cramped corridor of the *Indefatigable* and into the glaring light of the midday sun. They were far out over the ocean now, and the wind was whipping past them at a fearsome pace. Far below was the sea, a shimmering carpet of azure, and above, the clouds whirled and spun in an endless, maddening dance. Above, far to the left and right, Callis could see the two other vessels in Bengtsson's fleet, ranging slightly ahead of the ironclad.

Toll leaned against the gunwale, hand clutching his ribs. They'd stopped a few short hours to heal and resupply their vessels, but it was hardly the long recuperation they needed. None of Toll's wounds were serious, but they were certainly taking a cumulative cost upon the man. Every step appeared to hurt.

'You should go below and rest,' said Callis.

'Later,' said Toll. They shared an uncomfortable silence for several minutes, simply staring at the clouds rushing past and shoals of skimmerfish jumping and whirling in the seas below.

'I thought, when I first met you, that you were nothing like the stories of the witch hunters that I had heard as a boy,' said Callis. 'Ruthless, cruel fellows, who would kill anyone they suspected of heresy without question or hesitation. I thought you were different. But then I saw what you did today.'

'Did it disappoint you?' asked Toll.

'You know for certain that everyone we killed today was guilty? That no innocent person got caught up in the carnage, or drowned when we flooded the city streets?'

'The innocent do not flock to a place like Bilgeport, Armand. These people have existed out here for too long, leeching off the lifeblood of the free cities. Enough is enough. They required an example of what happens when you defy the will of Azyr.'

'Firing into crowds is not what I signed up for, Toll.'

'That same crowd was more than happy to watch you, Zenthe and the others torn to shreds in that arena. That same crowd was filled with killers, pillagers and other scum. Shed no tears for them, Callis.'

'I don't. That's not my point.'

'Many of my kin would have set this whole port alight. They would have slaughtered every man, woman and child that draws breath within these walls, and they would have done so without qualms. I do not share that ruthlessness, but I am also not a man who suffers sedition and acts of treachery against the rightful rule of order.'

Callis shook his head. 'There's right and wrong, Hanniver. Even in this trade.'

'Tell that to the thousands of loyal Sigmarites that the High Captains robbed and killed over the course of their rule. Enough of this navel-gazing, Armand. We have a task to see through. If you care so much for innocents, think of the thousands dead at Vermyre's hand. For their sake, at least, I need you focused on the mission ahead.'

Chapter Thirty-One

Despite her current predicament, Shev could not help gasping aloud in wonder as she looked upon the Fatescar Mountains.

The first she saw of them was an immense, polyhedral mountain ridge looming out of the mist, impossibly smooth and angular, floating in mid-air several thousand leagues above rolling forest hills. As far as she could tell, the mountain itself was formed from natural stone. It was worn, weathered and covered in thick vegetation. As they drew nearer, she saw a crystal-clear waterfall spilling over the nearest face of the immense structure, raining down upon the canopy far below.

Gradually, more of the floating rocks began to appear. Some were flat shelves of stone, others had a more rounded, organic shape. In one, she thought she recognised the profile of a human face, thick and overgrown with a beard of evergreen trees. In another, a sun-dial. There, the hilt of a titanic dagger. More geometric shapes, endlessly varied in size and form. Smaller islands of stone orbited those immense mountains, half-shaped and crumpled, as if they were the abandoned projects of a bored deity, left scattered upon his workbench.

'My gods,' she whispered. It was so beautiful, yet somehow terrifying at the same time. To know that mortalkind had once wielded such incredible power. The power to create a world, or destroy one.

The crystal ship rocked and yawed beneath them, causing them to stumble a few steps. Vermyre laid a hand on Shev's shoulder to steady her. She flinched, aware the man was trying to restore the easy camaraderie they had shared when they first began their search for Occlesius. It was a futile effort, now that she knew what lurked beneath that golden mask. Just being near Vermyre made her skin crawl.

'Incredible, is it not?' said Vermyre, with a note of awe in his voice. 'I have heard the tales, of course. I have even seen the sketches of explorers who have ventured here, but to see it in person…'

'They were building something that they never finished,' said Shev, indicating the bizarre arrangement of shapes. 'I wonder if we'll ever know what they were creating.'

Momentarily forgetting her situation, she found herself lost in thought. Civilisations did not create wonders like this for no reason. Maybe there was a theological component here, a relic of old gods worshipped long before the peoples of this region turned to the worship of Sigmar. Yet the more she looked, the less likely that seemed. There was a lack of uniformity to the shapes that was somehow unnerving.

'Perhaps we shall discover the truth behind this place very soon. Perhaps a remnant of their ancient empire yet lives, within these very mountains. We will discover the truth together, Shevanya.'

One of the avian creatures approached, and trilled something in a language she could not understand, but still made goosebumps rise on her flesh. Vermyre nodded, and waved a hand to dismiss the beast. She noticed that the beastmen had drawn and nocked arrows upon their bows, and there was a definite sense of unease in the air.

'Something is trying to draw us away,' Vermyre muttered. 'There is an illusion hanging over this place, I can smell it. Something dwells within these mountains, and it does not care for intruders.'

Shev frowned. Now that she looked closer at the wondrous view before her, she realised that there was something strange about this place. There was a stillness to it, a silent tension that seemed quite out of place in the otherwise raucous wilds of the Taloncoast.

'There's no birdsong,' she muttered.

'What?' asked Vermyre.

'There are no sounds of any kind,' she said. 'Listen. Surely you'd expect birds to roost up on these mountains, far away from danger. Can you see any signs of life down there?'

They circled the hexagonal mountain slowly, listening to the roar of the waterfall as it arced over the lip of the floating rock and poured away into nothingness. Now that Shev looked closer, the treeline seemed unnaturally orderly, arranged in neat, strict rows like those of a plantation. She peered into the gloomy, overhanging canopy, searching for a hint of movement, but found nothing. Not a creature stirred amidst the mountains.

'Curious,' whispered Vermyre.

Shev's sense of unease only grew as they sailed further into the mountains. It was hard to put her finger on, exactly. She felt like someone who had just awoken, and was trying desperately to sort the illusions of a dream from the hazy, unreal world she had been born into.

They drifted through a swirl of mist that left dew-drops across their skin, and rose over the crest of a wide, flat disc whose scattering of trees were arranged in a strange spiral pattern. Beyond rose the largest island yet. It was shaped in the image of a human face, strangely featureless and mono-lithic. There were no eyes, nor ears; simply the smooth, mannequin-like shape of the face, blackened and weathered. Across its great, stern brow ran a crown of mountainous peaks, capped with scatterings of foliage. Water trickled down the face of the titan in great gushing falls, pouring from its open mouth, which had been worn away over the centuries so that it gave the impression that the great head had its mouth opened in a scream.

The largest of Vermyre's beastmen came forward, striding across the crystal ship in that odd, jerking gait. The other tzaan-gors looked upon it with reverence, and it was not hard to see why. Clearly this was some form of high priest or shaman. It stood a head taller than Shev, its piercing gaze burning from beneath a plated war-mask that ran the length of its beak, and shimmered with a faint luminescence. Two great, curved horns rose back from its brow, bedecked with silver chains and marked with runes that turned Shev's stomach. Its chest was bare, but below a belt of gold it wore a half-robe of bright orange. Dangling crystal chimes tinkled as it walked. Its staff was silver, capped with a swirling eye of jade, and it carried a ritual dagger at its belt.

As it neared, she smelled a sweet yet sour stench, sweat mixed with sour-smelling unguents. It stared at her and cocked its head slightly, and she felt a shiver run through her body as she looked into its pitiless eyes.

'We are close,' it hissed, surprising her by speaking the com-mon tongue in a voice that was strangely human, considering

CALLIS & TOLL: THE SILVER SHARD

its hideous appearance. 'This isle, I sense a great enchantment upon it. Something powerful resides within those peaks.'

'Then that's where we go, Yha'ri'lk,' said Vermyre. 'Let us descend.'

The crystal ship yawed and dipped its nose, and they sailed through the mists towards the titanic head. Great trails of vines drooped from its empty eye sockets, and as they soared over its brow they caught their first glimpse of the forgotten city of Xoantica.

Shev's breath caught in her throat. She saw spires of white marble hidden between mountain peaks that rose on both sides: a city of pure white arranged in concentric circles around a central tower that stretched high into the skies, its arrow-head tip almost brushing the low-hanging clouds. The body of the spiral tower was worked in gold, and glimmered in the hazy mid-morning light.

Below, she could see abandoned arterial thoroughfares that stretched throughout the city, lined by solemn statues of robed figures whose features she could not make out from this distance. There was no sign of damage, that she could see, but a tangible sense of doom hung heavily over the place. It felt like nothing more than an enormous graveyard, each white-marble structure a monument to the dead.

'Many people died here,' said Vermyre. 'I can feel it. The place is rife with death.'

He turned to Yha'ri'lk.

'Take us down,' he said.

They came to rest on a plateau of smooth ground overlooking the northern edge of the city. The air was still, and without even the sound of the wind rushing past them the silence was even more unnerving. Vermyre's beastmen clutched their silver spears nervously, their avian heads snapping this way and that as if they smelled predators drawing close. On the ground there were perhaps fifty of the creatures, though she saw more circling overhead on their bizarre, half-organic flying discs. The ones above carried ornate bows, strung with crystal shafts.

Vermyre was studying the shadeglass gem with a look of intense concentration. Shev dreaded to think what priceless information he was garnering from its helpless occupant. Quite apart from getting his hands upon the Silver Shard, the damage Vermyre could reap if he was armed with the sheer amount of knowledge that Occlesius possessed did not bear thinking about.

'We move,' he said at last, and they began to make their way down the bluff towards the empty city.

A great arch loomed ahead, its wrought-iron gate ajar. The gatehouse was ornamented with two sweeping statues which leaned out from the central columns: smooth, faceless figures wielding staves of gold, holding their weapons crosswise over the entrance to Xoantica. The gateway was wide enough to admit dozens of carts, and the road was paved with flat, square stones of pure white, marvellously shaped. Somehow, the surface was as smooth as if it had been laid yesterday, with none of the wear and tear one might expect from a busy thoroughfare. Shev took in the gatehouse, which was supported by a thick white marble wall and a row of granite columns threaded with trails of gold. There was almost no depth to the carvings, no sign of ostentation beyond the obviously expensive materials. It was a grandiose piece of architecture, but it felt strangely sterile, almost funereal.

They entered, passing through onto what Shev assumed was the arterial highway. It was wider than the buildings on either side were tall, and like the entranceway it was almost impossibly smooth and well-aligned. She thought of Excelsis, with its rough-cut cobbles and haphazard arrangement of slums and way-houses. Judging by the size of the city as they descended, she guessed Xoantica had once housed more than fifty thousand souls, but there was not a single sign of habitation anywhere. No abandoned carts, no slumped skeletons. The sheer lifelessness of the place made her shiver. She felt as if the shadows were watching her, as if the spirits of the dead were all about, unseen yet undeniably present. It was like walking through a graveyard in the early hours of the morning.

Vermyre's tzaangors filtered out across the open street, weapons raised.

'Do you feel it?' asked the masked figure. 'This place is heavy with enchantments. It has been ripped out of time, smothered by obfuscating magic.'

Far ahead they could see the gold spiral tower, rising up from a huge, domed hall that rested upon a rise in the centre of the city. The path they now walked led pretty much directly to that central building, whatever it was.

'A temple?' wondered Shev. 'Or a palace, perhaps.'

'In all likelihood home to whoever those fellows were,' said Vermyre, gesturing ahead.

Lining the thoroughfare were immense statues of gold. They depicted stern, robed figures, heads bowed in solemn thought, staffs raised and forming an archway across the curving road. Again, the statues were oddly minimalist in design, with wide, curving outlines and featureless faces. But they were clearly figures of grave importance.

'They bear the trappings of priests, or magi,' said Vermrye. 'I think it is safe to assume that these figures, whoever they are, once ruled over this city. Or at least served those who did.'

Shev's head was beginning to throb. There was something

deeply strange about the arrangement of these streets. Though the thoroughfare remained more or less stable, the side-streets – filled with rows of colonnaded halls, soaring spiral domes and grand, marbled porticos – seemed to sway and shift on the very edges of her vision, their dimension shifting slyly each time she turned her head away. The effect was nauseating and dizzying. Once, she could have sworn the ground before her appeared to slope away, and stumbled awkwardly when she stepped forward and realised that was not the case. They had walked for many hours, it seemed, when she glanced to her left. With a lurch of dismay, she saw the very gatehouse they had entered, at the far end of the street to her right, distorted strangely like an uneven reflection.

'What?' she breathed, shaking her head in confused disbelief.

'Ignore it all, save this road we walk,' said Vermyre, clasping her firmly by the forearm and dragging her onwards. 'A spell of concealment and disorientation, nothing more. The weak-minded would eventually walk right out of the city, and forget they had ever been here. Or they might wander these roads, lost for an eternity, and simply drop down dead from exhaustion or hunger. Small wonder that none have ever visited this place and returned. Save our precious Realms-Walker, of course.'

Vermyre clutched the shadeglass gem in his fist. The light within the crystal danced madly between his gloved fingers, like a flame buffeted by the wind.

'What are you doing to him?' she said.

'This place is guarded against the mortal mind,' Vermyre replied, gesturing at the silent halls around them. 'Old and powerful magic, beyond even my ability to decipher.'

He raised the gem high. 'But the Realms-Walker knows the correct path, even after all these years. I know not how or why the knowledge remains with him, but it is in here. And while this stone is in my possession, Occlesius can keep nothing from me.'

Dread rose within Shev like a tide. How many other dangerous secrets and deadly artefacts did the Realms-Walker have knowledge of? She needed to get the crystal, and Occlesius, back from Vermyre.

'How far are we from the tower?' she said. 'We don't seem to be getting any closer.'

'Oh, we are. As much as this city wishes otherwise. We are drawing near. Move.'

The *Indefatigable* drifted through the serene mists of the Fatescar Mountains, through the floating islands of stone that hung impossibly above the sprawling sea of woodland. Callis had never seen anything like it. It was a vision from some naptha-smoke summoned dreamscape. They descended underneath an inverted pyramid of bleached-white stone, a single white-wood tree dangling upside down from its nadir.

Callis raised the looking-glass to his eye and searched the skies for signs of another vessel. He had no idea how Vermyre intended to reach these mountains, but he would have required aerial transport of some sort. Yet no sky-ship drifted out of the clouds. Perhaps they had outpaced the traitor. More likely, he was already at his destination.

'It's too quiet out here,' said Toll, pacing the deck alongside Callis. The man was like a wound spring, now they were so close to their quarry.

'Where are we headed?' asked Bengtsson. The admiral, it turned out, did none of the flying aboard a Kharadron ship. His role was far more logistical. Business-minded, if you will. As far as Callis could make out, Bengtsson called the shots when it came to the crew's endless search for aether-gold, the gaseous substance that powered both their vessels and their sprawling sky-ports.

'I'm not sure,' Toll admitted.

'We can't search every one of these islands,' said Zenthe. 'We'll be here forever.'

Toll cursed. Callis knew the corsair was right. They could sail these mountains for days and find no sign of anything. The blurred circle of the looking-glass' viewfinder passed over a detached head of a titan, floating serenely and bizarrely through the mist. Upon its head lay a crown of jagged mountains, and as Callis' eyes passed over them he saw a faint sparkle of light as the sun caught something.

'There,' he said, indicating the strange formation. 'Take us in.'

As they neared the head-shaped mountain, Callis thought he saw a flock of birds rising from the mountaintops, disturbed by the flight of the *Indefatigable*. Then he frowned, re-focusing the looking-glass and noticing the strange flecks were in fact circular shapes that were soaring towards them at great speed. There were roughly forty or so in all, and they flew in arrow formation, knifing towards the oncoming airship. He saw the gleam of silver weapons, and a flash of bright blue flesh. A thin, muscular torso capped by a pair of curving ram horns.

'To arms,' he shouted. 'We're under attack.'

Most of the Kharadron were already in possession of rifles and pistols, and they took up firing positions behind the gun-wale, aiming out towards the oncoming flight of strange discs. Callis knew only too well the creatures that were racing towards them. Tzaangors, twisted beastmen in thrall to the Dark Gods. He had fought them before, during the climactic battle for Excelsis. They were savage, sadistic killers, and they had been a favourite tool of Vermyre's.

'Targets, point four-five mark,' roared Drock, the gunnery officer. 'On my order, bring them down.'

The tzaangors were close enough now that they could see the horrible, half-organic shapes of their disc-shaped mounts, and hear their cawing war-cries carried across the wind. Arrows whickered down from the oncoming flock to slam into the deck of the ironclad, skipping off as they struck hard metal and spinning away into empty air. One pierced a duardin's mask, and the unfortunate victim flopped bonelessly to the ground, twitching. More arrows rained down. The distance was great, but the beastmen loosed with terrible accuracy. Even their missed shots wrought terrible damage. Callis saw one arrow strike the edge of the ship's volley-gun turret before flicking off and taking a kneeling crewman in the throat.

More duardin fell, and though the range was great, their companions responded in anger.

The sound was deafening, as the Kharadron discharged blunderbusses, pistols and long-barrelled carbines, filling the skies with hails of lethal metal. The tzaangors swooped as one, soaring down and over the deck of the *Indefatigable*, still loosing arrows. One of the beastmen recoiled as a flurry of shots slammed into its chest, and it flipped over backwards into empty air, tumbling and spinning helplessly. A duardin wearing a heavy battle-suit stepped up and fired a heavy, egg-shaped projectile from a hand-mounted launcher. Leaving a spiral contrail as it whipped through the air, the missile struck one of the circling discs and detonated, tearing rider and mount apart in a burst of shrapnel.

Callis sighted upon a low-flying beastman and fired. His shot took the creature in the shoulder, and it lost control of its mount. The unfortunate tzaangor slammed face-first into the great engine-sphere of the sky-ship, leaving a crimson smear across the metal surface.

The deck was wet with blood, both duardin and tzaangor. Bengtsson was blasting away with his two heavy pistols, roaring instructions and commands to his crew. The heavy-armoured duardin seemed to be wreaking the most grievous damage, armed as they were with the largest firearms. They seemed akin to the sharpshooter marines that were posted to Freeguild ships of the line – specialised warriors who did the bulk of the fighting while the crew worried about getting to their destination alive.

'They're aiming to bring us down,' Bengtsson bellowed, and Callis looked up to see a trio of beastmen carrying long silver staffs, drifting above the apex curve of the sky-ship's main engine. He could hear their foul chanting from here, and he aimed another bullet in the direction of the closest beastman, but his shot travelled wide.

From the tip of the creatures' staffs spat a silver flame that spread across the metal surface of the sphere. Great clouds of ill-smelling smoke rose from the affected area, along with a deafening rattling sound. The ship's nose dipped alarmingly.

'Kill them,' roared Bengtsson, and the combined firepower of the entire deck turned upon the three tzaangors. The fore mounted volley-cannon turret opened up, spitting staccato bursts of metal that all but disintegrated one of the creatures in a cloud of pink mist. The others attempted to withdraw, their sabotage completed, but a disciplined fusillade of volley gun fire sent them careening and tumbling towards the ground far below.

The Kharadrons' fearsome firepower had driven the remaining tzaangors back, and they flocked down towards the mountain valley below, screeching in triumph. Duardin crewmen rushed to and fro, desperately trying to put out the flames which engulfed a fair portion of the engine-sphere. A winding length of metal-capped hose was deployed, and it spat a stream of water up at the inferno. But these flames were magical in nature, and they would not be quenched so easily. The engine screamed and whined, and a vent-cover detached and went spiralling off in the empty air.

'We need to put her down, admiral,' one of the duardin roared over the noise. 'We need to get that hole capped, and the fires out.'

'There!' bellowed Bengtsson, indicating the mountain valley below, which was already rushing up towards them at a fearsome pace. Callis swore he could see the tops of buildings protruding from within that sheltered gorge, though the smoke that had enveloped the deck made it impossible to say for sure.

'Better grab hold of something,' shouted Zenthe in his ear, and Callis ducked down behind the iron-plated wall of the central cabin, wrapping his arm around the heavy wheel-lock of the door. He felt his stomach lurch as the ship descended, hurtling through the clouds with terrifying speed. The mountains began to rush by on either side, terrifyingly fast, and it still felt as though they were accelerating. Then the hull of the ironclad struck solid ground, and Callis' arm was nearly torn from its socket. They skipped, bounced and struck again, and by some miracle of sailing, the duardin pilot managed to haul the *Indefatigable* into a wide, arcing turn. A torrent of shattered rock and mud was thrown into the air.

Then they were slowing, the momentum of the vessel righting itself, and it came to a halt, leaning precariously to starboard. Callis staggered to his feet and made his way over to the rail. They had come to rest a mere hundred or so yards away from a cliff of unforgiving stone. If their momentum had taken only a few more seconds to play out, they'd have smeared themselves across that shelf of rock.

'That was too bloody close,' said Bengtsson, before turning to bellow more instructions to his crew.

Toll made his way gingerly over to the side of the ship.

'Well,' he said, gesturing towards a gleaming golden tower that rose into the sky to their right, protruding from a sea of white marble halls and soaring colonnades. 'I think we've found our lost city.'

Chapter Thirty-Two

After what seemed like days, the main thoroughfare came to an end at the mouth of a great plaza, surrounded on all sides by an immense curving colonnade of golden columns. Ahead, the central square met a slowly rising series of stairs, separated in the middle by another golden statue, this one far larger than the others. In one arm it grasped a silver blade; the other hand was raised, palm out in a gesture that needed little translation. Beyond the statue was an immense hall, colossal and isoscelic in shape, with a great dome from which the central tower of spiralling gold protruded. Two enormous doors barred the entrance to this building, secured by twisting handles of silver that looped and entwined like writhing snakes.

'We're not alone here,' said Vermyre.

Shev could sense it too. Her head was clearer now, the dream-like sense of muddied confusion lessened. The presence that still dwelt within this city. It was concentrated here. At the eye of the storm.

Cautiously, Vermyre and his tzaangors made their way across the plaza. Shev followed at a short distance, peering into the dark recesses between the forest of marble columns, expecting something horrible to emerge from within at any moment. The great statue loomed overhead, and she noticed that this one, unlike its fellows, was not entirely featureless. It bore a circlet of flame across its brow, and there was a faint line of indentations running down its cheeks, which appeared to be some kind of script, though the work was too fine to pick out at this distance. The colossus' concave eyes were narrowed, and its mouth was a thin, stern line. Whoever this ancient ruler had been, she doubted they were well known for their mercy.

It was then that she noticed the eyes. They blazed in the shadows beyond the golden columns, yellow and piercing in the gloom.

The tzaangors had noticed them too. They screeched and brandished their silver weapons, forming a semi-circle around Vermyre. The shaman, Yha'ri'lk, snapped his fingers, summoning a flickering silver flame, which he touched to the end of his staff, wreathing the tip of the weapon in fire.

Slowly, the eyes began to move, and the watchers emerged from the darkness.

They were scale-skinned and hulking bipedal creatures, their rough flesh crudely daubed in crimson and aquamarine, ridges of bone protruding from their backs. Their snouts were long and filled with sharp fangs, and each carried a club or axe ancient in design, but no less intimidating for that. Jewels, gems and tokens of gold were strung from their necks and pierced through their flesh. Their shields carried lurid, geometric shapes. The saurian creatures radiated a sense of primordial threat. Shev did not see them as predators, exactly.

There was no hunger in their beady yellow eyes – just a cold, alien curiosity.

'I mean to enter this place,' announced Vermyre. 'It would behove you not to stand in my way.'

No answer. The creatures took a step forward, as one, and began to beat their clubs upon their hide-wrapped shields, unleashing a low, rumbling sound.

'I have no interest in killing you,' Vermyre tried again. 'Whatever you are.'

They took another step forward, and the drumbeat grew louder.

Vermyre sighed. 'Very well.'

He raised his staff and unleashed a bolt of night-black energy that speared into the closest beast, blasting it from its feet and sending its body sprawling across the plaza.

The creatures roared in fury, and rushed forward in a scaled tide.

There was something wrong with the world.

The feeling grew ever more certain and more sickeningly tactile with every step Callis and the others took into Xoantica. They had left the majority of Bengtsson's crew behind with the *Indefatigable*, with orders to make the necessary repairs and then regroup in the centre of the lost city. The admiral himself had insisted upon accompanying them, as had Zenthe. The ground seemed to be passing beneath their feet, but the physical distance was disconnected from time itself. Callis concentrated with all his focus, plotted one hundred paces, and looked up to find that he had barely progressed more than a few yards. The alleyways of marble houses that stretched off in all directions ebbed and shifted at the end of his vision. The angles of the city were impossible, and he knew that if he tried to rationalise its insanity, he would lose his mind. After perhaps two hours of walking – or as near as Callis could guess – he made the mistake of looking up into the sky, expecting to see the reassuring span of clear blue.

Instead, he saw more streets, winding away in a ceaseless refraction, curling and twisting in on each other like he was gazing into an immense carnival mirror. He stopped, on the edge of throwing up.

'We can't stop, Armand,' came Toll's voice, and Callis felt a reassuring grip on his shoulder. 'We're too deep. Too far in. There's an enchantment over this place, a powerful spell that's warping time and space. All we can do is continue, and try to find the source of it.'

'I can't… concentrate,' hissed Callis. 'My head is spinning. Every time I open my eyes, the world shifts.'

'This is old magic,' said Zenthe, and her voice echoed as if from far away. 'Older than any of us here. I've never felt anything like it.'

'We continue,' repeated Toll, hefting Callis to his feet. 'We are close, I can feel it.'

And so they walked on. Buildings rose up on all sides, strangely organic shapes carved from pure-white marble, great columned halls and soaring towers that twisted off into the maddening sky. He saw the dark thresholds of their doorways, and it was easy to imagine that alien eyes were peering out from within. But he sensed that there was no life here. Not even the tiniest insect stirred, and the wind itself was non-existent, as if the weather itself dared not tread within these borders.

He did not know how long they walked in silence. At last, they turned a corner and emerged onto an enormous central thoroughfare that stretched on and on towards a domed hall of immense proportions, capped by a spiralling tower of white gold. The road curved away ahead of them, leaving the earth and reaching towards the kaleidoscopic sky, where a dozen identical roads – complete with their own set of identical, haggard travellers – wound towards that same apex.

Across the empty air, far away in the distance, they could hear the sound of clashing blades, and shrill, inhuman screams.

'Vermyre,' spat Toll, drawing his blade. 'He is here. We must hurry.'

Shev watched as the lizards came at Vermyre in their scores. Yet none could lay a hand upon him. He conjured streams of living flame which enveloped the saurian beasts, melting them to ashes in a matter of moments. He turned the ground to liquid silver, and drowned them in molten metal. Others, he simply struck with his staff, sending shattered, broken bodies flying in all directions.

He was laughing as he slew, an unhinged sound. Shev stayed close, because he was the only thing between her and these guardians, whatever they might be, but every inch of her body crawled with horror as she watched Vermyre unleash his monstrous rage. She looked for an escape route, but saw nowhere to run. The tzaangors eagerly indulged their own passion for slaughter alongside their master. The reptilian creatures were tough and strong, but Yha'ri'lk's warriors were many, and they were fighting with an exultant glee that the defenders of this strange city could not match. Their arrows brought down charging foes by the score, and as the saurians died they erupted into searing motes of star-light, evaporating into the aether. Shev felt a great sadness with each fresh kill, one that she could not entirely put her finger on. Despite their savagery, there was a nobility to these creatures, an honest and natural ferocity quite unlike the vicious sadism of her current allies.

'Enough,' said Vermyre, through another burst of wet laughter. 'Let this distraction cease. 'Yha'ri'lk, follow me. The rest of your warriors will hold these steps, and let not a single enemy through.'

The tzaangor shaman screeched a command, and his hundred or so warriors formed up around the entrance of the domed hall. Several of the beasts bent in prayer, and began to chant in a harsh, hideous tongue. The air turned hot and oppressive, but before Shev could witness the results of their sorcery, Vermyre grabbed her and dragged her through the enormous archway and into the domed structure. The sounds of battle abruptly ceased as soon as they crossed the threshold. Looking around, she saw a cavernous entrance hall soar away into darkness far above, and a single, broad stairway spiralling towards that black nothingness. Like everything else in Xoantica, the building was an astonishing piece of architecture, carved flawlessly from the same silver-lined marble, but it was almost entirely free of ornamentation. The walls were edged in gold and gently curved towards the summit of the tower, but there were no epic scenes of battle, no monuments to the glory of those who had once ruled here.

'Come now,' said Vermyre, ushering her towards that winding stair. Yha'ri'lk and a retinue of warriors followed, leaving the majority behind to defend the stairway.

They began to climb.

The entrance to the great, domed hall was the site of furious battle. Bipedal, reptilian creatures swarmed up the central steps towards a barricade manned by tzaangors, with long horns and armour that gleamed bright silver in the hazy light.

'More tzaangors,' hissed Callis. 'Looks like Vermyre has not cut all ties with his former allies.'

'We're walking into quite the melee here,' said Zenthe. 'These other creatures, how do we know they're not going to turn on us the second they see us?'

'We don't,' replied Toll. 'But we're going up there, nonetheless. You and the admiral are welcome to wait for us here, but if Vermyre sets his hands upon the Silver Shard, there's no telling what nightmares he'll unleash. If we have to kill our way through these things, so be it.'

Together, they ran on. As they neared, they saw that the lizard-creatures were not pouring from hidden boltholes or underground lairs. Instead they seemed to materialise out of the very air, summoned into being and given violent purpose by some unknown force. They wielded ancient-looking weapons crafted from gold and obsidian, crude in construction but somehow imposing also, as if they were an echo from an older and more savage age. Their scales were flecked with crimson war-paint, and jewels and necklaces hung from their scaly flesh.

As Callis and the others approached, a score of the beasts detached from the main host and began to encircle them, eyes glassy and unknowable, weapons raised but not yet in a threatening manner. Ahead, the two stairs wound their way around the side of a central bannister of gold, leading up to the gigantic doors of the building, which were strangely featureless and unadorned.

'We seek no quarrel,' said Toll, raising his weapon high and away from the creatures. 'There is a man who has come here, an evil man, twisted by the powers of the Dark Gods. We seek to end him.'

The creatures continued to circle, their obsidian shields lowered towards the newcomers, maces and axes readied. Callis sensed a strange sort of synchronicity to their movement, a faintly unnatural edge that reminded him of the metal automatons he had seen Ironweld engineers put to use. These were not natural creatures, he realised. At least, not entirely. There was some force at play here greater than any of them knew.

The circle tightened as the beasts stepped in as one.

'I don't think our lizard friends here want our help,' whispered Zenthe. 'I think that if we want into that building, we're going to have to blast our way in.'

'Wait,' said Toll.

He stepped forward, and from beneath his robes he produced an amulet fashioned in the shape of Sigmar's hammer.

There was a flicker of something in the lead creature's eye, just for a moment.

'I serve the God-King,' said Toll, brandishing the amulet. 'The Lord of Azyr, bane of Chaos in all its forms. I swear before you now, I come to rid the taint of the Dark Gods from this place.'

The creatures ceased their prowling, and stood stock still. Then, again moving with impossible synchronicity, they peeled off and raced up the steps towards the fray, utterly ignoring Toll and his band.

Bengtsson let out a slow whistle of relief.

'Well, that's a fortunate turn of events,' he said. 'Bad enough just the one army wanting us dead, without those damned things after us too.'

'Well said, duardin,' nodded Zenthe. 'Now, if we're done talking?'

Blades raised, Arika Zenthe bounded up the winding steps towards the sounds of battle.

Chapter Thirty-Three

The staircase wound on and on. Shev was hardly in poor phys-ical shape, but even she had to stop and catch her breath on more than one occasion. It was more than the distance trav-elled. It was the oppressive air in the place that pressed down upon them with crushing force. In her travels, Shev had been to many places which seemed – for want of a better word – cursed. Ruined cities where even centuries after the carnage that had seen them fall, ghosts of the dead still lingered. She had that feeling now, multiplied a hundredfold. It was as if the city of Xoantica itself was enraged by their presence, and had leveraged all of its formidable power towards crushing their will. She was filled with a deep despair, and a growing terror that she would never escape this lost city alive. She would be trapped here, along with all the others, damned to an eternity of wandering these halls.

Vermyre bounded up the stairs like an eager child, full of nervous energy even after his battle with the saurian warriors.

Where, for the others, each step further into this cursed city seemed to sap the strength and will from their bones, the opposite seemed to be true for their leader.

'So close now,' he muttered, over and over.

Shev made the mistake of looking down to see how far they had come. She saw nothing but a pitch-black abyss stretching away into nothingness. Her head spun, and she stumbled, cracking her knees painfully upon the stairs.

Vermyre paused to drag her none too gently to her feet.

'Do not look back,' he hissed. 'Whatever crafted this enchantment, it wants us to give in to doubt and confusion, to turn back in defeat. But if we are strong, we can break through this illusion. Push beyond, to our true destination. Stay with me, girl.'

What was there to do? To retreat now, to trek back all the way across the great expanse of the ruined city seemed a far more harrowing task than to simply push ahead. So Shev gathered her wits, shook the dazed confusion from her mind, and began to walk.

One foot after another, that was the way. Forget everything but the slow, steady advance. Step by step. Shev fell into a kind of hypnosis, and time lost all meaning. And then, like emerging from a strange trance, her boots were once more on level ground.

She found herself looking upon a gateway large enough for a gargant to pass through, lined by statues of gold – looming figures, hooded and robed. Beyond was a narrow hall, leading to a great pair of double doors. The hooded statues were arranged in pairs along the corridor, facing one another with staves raised high to form a solemn salute. A small, circular window high above washed the chamber with a silver glow, revealing images worked into the floor. Stern patriarchs directing hordes of faceless slaves in the construction of a great city. Several robed figures standing upon a crest of rock, hands outstretched as mountains were rent asunder at their command. Amorphous, tentacled creatures descending from a blackened sky. Those same robed figures were depicted in this last image, but Shev could not tell whether they were standing in defiance of the shapeless beasts from above, or whether they were beckoning them down from the skies.

Vermyre looked towards the distant doorway.

'Behind these doors lies the Silver Shard,' he said. He nodded to Yha'ri'lk, who gestured two of his warriors forward. The creatures advanced cautiously, spears levelled, eyes darting across the chamber in search of hidden threats.

The leading creature had reached the mouth of the corridor, where the chamber floor was broken into rows of tiles inlaid with strange, sweeping sigils. It looked like nothing more than a scroll of hieroglyphs writ large across the floor, stretching the length of the adjoining hall. The tzaangor passed beneath the first archway of raised spears, its own weapon raised high as if it expected the statues to strike down at any moment. There was no movement at all. The chamber remained eerily silent.

Emboldened, the second creature moved forward. Its clawed foot pressed down upon the floor, and was instantly engulfed in a roaring column of fire that rose to the ceiling, filling the chamber with heat and light. Shev gasped and staggered backwards, knocking into Vermyre. They tumbled to the floor together, and amidst the tangle of limbs, Shev slid her hand into the man's pocket. Her fingers closed around Occlesius' shadeglass gem.

Vermyre's bloodshot eyes met hers, filled with fury, and she knew instantly he had sensed her theft.

He grasped at her, his hand locking around her arm with

terrifying strength. She could smell the rancid sourness of his breath. She drove the tip of her thumb through the eye socket of his mask, wincing as it sank into something soft and gelid. Vermyre howled with pain, and his grip released just enough for her to squirm free and scramble to her feet.

The columns of flames cleared, leaving nothing of the unfortunate tzaangor behind but a cloud of drifting ashes. Its companion took an ill-judged step backwards and was engulfed in another gout of fire, this time gushing from a hidden aperture in the wall of the corridor.

Shev put her head down and bolted for the hallway. A slim chance at freedom was better than none.

That was very nicely done indeed, came Occlesius' voice in her head. His normally sprightly voice was thin and strained. *We must get out of here. I touched his mind as he invaded my own, Miss Arclis. The man is unravelling, body and soul.*

'I really hope you know how to get us through this,' she said, racing towards the corridor at full speed.

'Stop her,' roared Vermyre, and Yha'ri'lk's warriors moved to cut her off. She ducked around the first beast's searching claws, jumped and tucked into a roll that took her somersaulting past the next creature. Then there was clear space between her and the double doors fifty yards away.

Left, and forward twenty strides.

She twisted her run, and as she did so a bolt of arcane energy soared past her and struck one of the tiles ahead, unleashing another flaming blast. She put her hands up to guard her face and ran on, counting the distance in her head.

Stop! She stuttered to a halt, skidding across the polished floor. Footsteps behind her closed in fast, but there was no time to turn.

Jump to the tile marked with the spiral star. To your right.

She glanced up, saw the tile, tensed her legs and jumped. Something caught her by the ankle and she slammed to the floor with enough force to drive the air from her lungs. Wheezing, she turned to see a tzaangor's face, its cruel eyes gleaming beneath a half-mask of silver. It reached down to grab her by the throat.

She tucked her legs in, planting her boots squarely on the creature's tattooed chest before thrusting out with all her strength. The tzaangor stumbled backwards, landing hard on a tile and unleashing another column of flame that rushed up from below to swallow it whole. Ignoring the dying creature's piercing screams, she rolled upright and jumped for the spiral-marked tile again, tucking into a roll as she landed.

Fifteen paces away now. So very close.

'Where next?' she screamed, her voice ragged as she tried to catch her breath. She heard more blasts of fire, and more screaming. She turned to see three more tzaangors, gaining on her with every moment, cruel blades clutched in their hands and murder in their beady eyes.

I… cannot recall.

'Think, damn you!'

Shouting does not help my powers of recall, the Realms-Walker snapped. *There was a pattern, I recall, a cypher reflected in the path one must follow. A prayer in an ancient tongue. But what was it?*

One of the tzaangors was getting closer by the moment, preparing to leap over to the spiral-marked slab. She unclipped her tool-pack from her belt and hurled it. It landed square in the centre of the adjoining tile, and just as the tzaangor jumped across the five-foot gap, a blast of flame issued forth which sent its body tumbling away, ablaze.

'I'm out of tricks, Realms-Walker,' she hissed. 'What do I do?'

All glory to Nem'k'awet, the Lord of Silver Skies, muttered Occlesius. *He who stands betwixt the pillars of Knowledge and Damnation... what next... what next... Kir'li'sami'yen the... the Herald of Ascension. Ovkoris, the Whispering Blade! That's it, Miss Arclis, the sword, look for a sword!*

Her frantic eyes scoped the room, until finally – there – the tile to her upper left. Etched upon it was a sword, radiating what looked like beams of light.

Shev leapt, landing painfully on her knees and skidding across the final row of tiles. She had made it. Once more the floor was solid marble, and no more statues loomed above her.

'Thank you, my friend,' she said, with a sigh.

Oh, don't mention it. I was actually convinced I had got that last one wrong.

She saw Vermyre staring at her from the far end of the corridor, and she tipped him a salute, tossing the shadeglass gem in her hands. Blood ran freely from the mouth of the man's mask.

'You have made a grave mistake, Shevanya,' he said, his voice even but with an unmistakeable tremor of rage. 'I had every intention of letting you leave this place alive, but now? I think not. You will perish along with all the others.'

'We'll see about that,' she said.

With that, she gave a swift bow, before turning to heave open the doors.

Callis dodged a jabbing spear, and struck at the arm wielding it. He was rewarded by a pained shriek and a spurt of purplish blood. The tzaangor rocked back and was buried under a charging horde of saurians, who hacked and clubbed it to death. He turned, looking for the others. They were hard pressed, facing a wall of beastmen who gibbered with a lunatic glee as they fought, not giving an inch despite the numbers arrayed against them. They had formed their bizarre, disc-shaped mounts into a makeshift barrier that whirled and spun, the razor-sharp teeth of the unsettlingly organic devices shredding the flesh of any creatures that strayed too close.

The lizard warriors continued to hurl themselves selflessly at the intruders from all sides, but they could not dislodge them. Worse, now more tzaangors were flying down from above to join the melee, drawn here by the shrieking calls of their kin.

'We need a way through,' shouted Toll.

'Leave this to me,' growled Bengtsson. He reached to the rear of his war-suit, and detached a black-leather satchel hanging from his belt. He opened it to reveal an egg-shaped device of cold metal that tapered to a blunt point at one end. At the other end was a small brass cog, and Bengtsson gave this a hard twist and hurled the object into the thick of the fighting, with a shout.

For a moment, nothing happened. Then there was an enormous explosion of flame that sent bodies hurtling through the air, both saurian and avian. Chunks of marble were torn free from the doors and sent knifing through the mass of bodies. Callis' ears rang, even though he'd jammed his fingers in them before the blast went off, anticipating what was to come.

'I did warn them,' said Bengtsson, with a hint of irritation, observing the carnage.

'Remind me to pick up a few of those beauties before we part ways,' said Zenthe, clapping the duardin upon the back before sprinting through the gaping breach his bomb had opened in the enemy line. By the time the shaken tzaangors had recovered, Callis and the others were at the foot of the great staircase leading away into the darkness of the dome's central tower. Bodies littered the floor, along with smears of blood and dust. Zenthe smashed a foe in the face with the pommel of her sword, ducked beneath the awkward swing of a silver-tipped spear and thrust a dagger through its wielder's heart. Two more tzaangors, recovering quickly now, tried to pin her against the bannister of the stairway, but Bengtsson drew and fired two pinpoint shots, putting smoking holes through both of the creatures.

Callis and Toll fought back to back, turning with practised ease, unbalancing their foes before passing them on to one another for the swift and easy kill. Callis feinted a high slash, causing a beastman to raise its spear to block the blow. Toll spun and fired beneath the unfortunate beast's guard, blasting it several yards across the chamber. As Callis turned in that same arc, he cut the legs from under a surprised creature, which howled with agony as its ruined limbs spurted dark blood across the shining tiles.

'Too many,' grunted Toll, pausing amidst the carnage to reload his pistol.

'Take the stairs,' said Zenthe. Her blades dripped with blood, and she had that look of sheer joy on her face that always slightly unnerved Callis. 'Myself and the good admiral can deal with things down here, can't we?'

'Don't die up there before you pay me what's due, witch hunter,' growled Bengtsson.

Without another word, Callis and Toll made for the stairs, bounding up them two at a time.

Slamming the doors shut behind her, Shev found herself in a huge, circular chamber, so wide and high that it felt more like a cavernous cathedral than the apex of a tower. Indeed, as she took in the immense dimensions of the place, she knew with queasy certainty that there was no way this chamber matched the size of the tower top she had seen from outside the domed structure. It was far too large, and the shape was all wrong. The walls swooped overhead to form soaring arches, like the ribcage of an enormous skeleton, and far above she could see a great circular window, open to the sky. Hazy light beamed down from this opening, filling the hall with a sickly yellowish glow. Ahead, the ground sloped up slightly, several short stairs leading towards a great dais of smoothly cut obsidian.

Upon this dais rested two things.

The first was a shimmering wound in the world, like a disjointed reflection. Around this breach in reality, time and light flowed strangely, never quite in perfect alignment. She could make out a shape in the midst of that strange breach, a flowing shard of silver that appeared to resemble a molten blade. As she moved closer, however, she thought she might have imagined that it had any physical form at all. One moment it was a sparkling cloud of gold, the next a wave of molten metal. Ever-shifting, and almost painful to look at.

The other thing was even stranger. It sat upon a throne of burnished gold, which hovered serenely above the gleaming floor. It was large and lumpen in form, but despite its unimposing stature it radiated immense power. Its flesh was grey-green, decayed but not rotten – it reminded Shev of the embalmed corpses she had witnessed in the throne tombs of ancient emperors. Somehow she knew, instantly, that this was the being that had laid the illusory curse that had so nearly laid them low. Yet it lay, collapsed and corpse-like, showing no interest at all in her presence.

She had moved to within perhaps fifty yards of the dead thing's throne when a blue light began to shine before the mummified figure, a sheet of sparkling blue motes that coalesced into the form of a small, blue-skinned reptile leaning upon a red-gold staff shaped in the image of a coiled serpent.

The creature wore a startling headdress of yellow and red feathers, and looping necklaces made from precious metals dangled over its narrow chest. It cocked its head, studying her through small, quick-witted eyes.

'You trespass,' it said, its high-pitched voice strangely melodic. 'This is no land for mortalkind. No place for the living. You bring enemies to this grave-city.'

'They brought me here, and not by my will,' gasped Shev, still unsteady on her feet. 'What are you, anyway?'

'Guardians,' the creature chirped. 'Of an ancient evil.'

'The Silver Shard,' she whispered, and the creature's clever eyes bored into hers.

The chamber shook. Shev turned and saw the doorway rattling under intense force. Vermyre was already past the trapped hallway. Somehow the door she had so easily passed through was keeping him at bay, but she was sure that could not last long.

'What is this thing?' Shev whispered, staring at the shifting pattern across the chamber. 'Why does Vermyre want it so?'

'It is a relic of a darker time,' the creature said. 'An abomination that should not exist. It is death, and worse, oblivion. Not for mortal hands, young one.'

I… remember, said Occlesius. *I was not a guest here, but a prisoner. Gods save me, I know what it is, Shevanya. The Silver Shard. I know the truth of it. He cannot have it! He must not have it!*

'The farwalker speaks truth,' said the priest, bobbing its head.

'Wait, you can hear his voice?' Shev said, eyes furrowed in confusion.

'My master can, and so passes his voice to me. Our paths have crossed before, when the farwalker was flesh and blood. He was here at the death of this city.'

At your hands, said Occlesius. *I remember the stars burning, and the screams of the dying. I remember blood staining the streets, and the mad laughter of daemons. I was bound and chained in this very chamber, another sacrifice for…something terrible.*

'A great blow was struck against the Dark Gods that day,' said the creature. 'At great cost.'

Another hammer-blow at the door. The golden surface crumbled under the onslaught, dust and dislodged stone pouring through as the hammering continued.

'And you've waited here, all these years? Just to protect the shard?'

The creature gave a slight chirp, which might have indicated amusement.

'We are not here. We were never *here*, young one.'

'We have to run,' she pleaded. 'Please. The man that searches for this weapon, he is no normal human.'

'He is tainted,' the creature nodded. 'The same darkness that scars his soul also resonates within the Silver Shard. It calls to him, for it longs to be free. This moment, my master has foreseen. No one will leave this place.'

No sooner had the creature spoken than a shockwave smashed the doors from their hinges, sending them sliding across the floor. In the entranceway stood Vermyre, staff raised, madness glinting in the sockets of his golden mask.

He entered the chamber, flanked by the remaining tzaangors.

Vermyre's eyes fixed upon the Silver Shard. It flickered and reformed again, and Shev was sure she saw it take the form of a gleaming longsword, its blade etched with runes, and a single, flawless ruby embedded in its hilt. Then the momentary image was gone.

'Turn back, cursed one,' said the lizard priest. 'This path leads only to your demise.'

Vermyre strode slowly up the steps to the dais, his eyes still fixed upon his prize. Shev backed away slowly, but the man seemed to have forgotten all about her in his obsession. Yha'ri'lk and his retinue loomed over the diminutive creature, but it did not seem in the least intimidated by them. It merely tilted its head, as if passingly curious as to their intentions.

'You break the peace of this chamber, and you awaken my lord,' trilled the reptile. 'Many tasks occupy his sleeping mind, but still he has the power to unmake you all into star-matter.'

'Silence,' spat Vermyre. He thrust his staff forward at the lizard creature, and from its tip burst a trail of blue-white flame. Barely seeming to move, the lizard wove a net of force in the air, and the unnatural fire poured across its invisible surface like water breaking upon rock. There was a blinding flash of light and a loud crack, and suddenly a formation of shield-bearing saurian warriors were arrayed about the priest. They spread out, putting themselves between Vermyre and the Silver Shard, clubs and axes raised to strike.

'Get out of my way!' Vermyre thundered. Flames erupted from the tip of his staff.

Chapter Thirty-Four

Arika Zenthe rolled underneath the clumsy swing of a beast-man's blade and swept her own sword back in a vicious arc, taking the thing's back-jointed leg off at the knee. It collapsed to the floor, shrieking and writhing. She reversed her weapon and stabbed it through the heart.

'Where are these damned things coming from?' roared Bengtsson, who had his back pressed against the far wall, and was blasting away with his two heavy pistols. A pile of ruined corpses lay sprawled at the sky-beard's feet. She had to admit, he had a knack for this kind of work.

More and more of the avian creatures soared down upon those discs of warped metal, hurling themselves into the fray with manic delight. Only the equally deranged bravery of the lizardfolk had kept them at bay. Every time a rank of saurians was brought low by arrows or pierced by the tzaangors' silver spears, more warriors appeared in flashes of searing light, racing into the fray with not a moment's concern for their well-being. Zenthe couldn't care less. If the foolish creatures had such a taste for death, let them do the bloody business of dying while she and the duardin stayed as far out of the fray as possible.

She spun, carving a cross into the chest of another beastman as she brought her weapons down. The dull creature's eyes went wide, and it gargled on its own blood before toppling to the floor.

'As much fun as this is, we can't keep it up forever,' she said, taking a moment to survey the hall. Acrid smoke from Bengtsson's blasting charges lingered in the air, while the dead and the dying littered the floor. Zenthe's ears rang with the sound of the duardin's pistol as it blazed. Hateful weapons, guns. Useful of course, but there was no subtlety to them. In her opinion, they were the mark of a clumsy and unskilled warrior.

'I concur,' Bengtsson grunted as he cracked the heavy metal barrel of his handgun over an assailant's head. 'Unfortunately, it seems our tactical opportunities are limited.'

Zenthe scanned the entrance hall, looking for anything they could use. She frowned as she noticed an antechamber that ran off to the left, opening out into a wide, circular hallway filled with golden statuary.

'Come on,' she said, grabbing the duardin's arm and directing him towards the second doorway. 'I think our scaled friends have got this all secured. Let's see if there's anything in this godsforsaken place that's worth our time.'

Bengtsson snorted. 'Did anything catch your eye while we were walking through this desolate place, aelf? It's abandoned, and it seems to have been designed by a race with no appreciation for artistry or embellishment beyond a few blank-faced statues and a whole lot of marble. We'd be more likely to–'

He fell silent as Zenthe placed a hand over the metal grille of his battle-mask. She pointed a single, slender finger towards the room ahead. It was filled to the brim with blades, staffs and other esoteric items, all suspended from the walls with silver chains. The room seemed to stretch on forever, curving around them for at least five hundred paces. Paintings hung on the walls, and along the centre of the room ran a series of hexagonal display glasses, filled with all manner of arcane devices and shining jewels.

'I stand corrected,' muttered Bengtsson.

'The situation is obvious,' said Zenthe. 'Neither of us have yet received any remuneration from the witch hunter, yes?'

'Correct.'

'In which case, I propose that we abandon our heroic defence of the perimeter against the vile hordes, and commence a thorough inventory of this chamber, to see if there's anything here worth looting. Agreed?'

Bengtsson's nod of approval was the only affirmation she required. At last, she might begin to make some actual coin from this fool's errand.

Shev leapt aside to avoid another torrent of flame and tumbled down the short flight of stairs, landing painfully on her back. The once silent hall had broken into madness, as Vermyre and his tzaangors unleashed their magics against the city's bizarre defenders. The saurian warriors were enveloped by twisting trails of silver fire that wound around them like constricting snakes. One lizard approached the circle of tzaangor elders, its club raised high to crush Yha'ri'lk's head, but before its weapon could descend, a wave of sickening colour enveloped its body, trapping it in place. The creature's scaled flesh began to hiss and bubble, and a moment later it evaporated like boiling water, turning into a gust of superheated steam.

Shev rolled behind the scant cover of the nearby steps, hurled javelins skipping off the polished floor around her. She looked upon the chaos before her, and knew that Vermyre and the tzaangor shamans' combined magic was too much for the defenders. The saurian creatures bravely threw themselves through the bombardment of magical energy, trying to bury their foes under sheer weight of numbers, but it was futile. The chamber reeked of charred meat, and the bittersweet tang of boiling metal.

Vermyre lashed his staff across like a headman's scythe, and a rippling blast of silver-white force erupted out to strike the diminutive reptile priest across the torso, sending his broken body tumbling like a child's toy, bright blood seeping from a diagonal wound across his chest.

The mummified corpse upon the golden throne began to twitch and stir.

Its gem-studded chair rose, soaring above the furious battle, and the creature's eyes opened. They blazed with the fire of stars. It was agony to even match that primordial gaze, which Shev instinctively knew belonged to a being far older than this forgotten city. Far older, perhaps, than the realms themselves.

Lightning rippled along the burnished gold of the mummified creature's throne. The form stretched out a hand and channelled this fulminating power into a blast of lightning that careened across the hall and struck two of the tzaangor shamans. The beastmen shrieked and howled as their bodies were engulfed in crackling fire, their twisted flesh burned and blackened.

Yha'ri'lk and his remaining kindred did not falter under the hail. As one, they stowed their curved ritual blades and each removed a crystal vial filled with shimmering, turquoise liquid from their belts. Chanting a mantra in a tongue that sent shivers of revulsion up Shev's spine, the tzaangor shamans poured the contents of the crystal vials into their mouths. Their eyes began to burn with unearthly light, and their muscles corded and rippled as the sorcerous concoction seeped through their bodies.

Still moving in unnatural synchronicity, the tzaangors raised their staffs and unleashed a tidal wave of silver fire that flooded across the hall, immolating the remaining saurian warriors and engulfing the creature's throne. Shev could see the mummified thing twitching and screaming within the cascade of flame.

Vermyre ran towards the Silver Shard, stretching out one gloved hand.

'No!' gasped the wounded saurian priest, dragging its body towards Vermyre, blood dripping from its tiny, needle-like teeth. 'Mortal hands cannot wield the shard! Its power is too great.'

Vermyre laughed bitterly.

'I fear there is no longer anything mortal about my flesh,' said the masked man, and with that he tore the black glove from his hand. Underneath was no human arm, but a chitinous gauntlet of azure crystal, from which stared several bloodshot eyes, embedded across its length. The tips of the fingers were boneless and shifting, like amorphous tentacles.

The thing that had once been Ortam Vermyre, High Arbiter of Excelsis, thrust its mutated limb through the shifting portal.

Toll staggered out onto a wide platform of obsidian. It was a great, high-ceilinged auditorium, stairs rising towards a great central dais in the distance. He saw the eruption of magic that enveloped the stage, and the strange sight of a floating throne engulfed in fire. He saw Shev Arclis cowering away from the display of ruinous magic.

He saw all that, but his eyes were fixed only upon the sight of Ortam Vermyre, grasping in one malformed hand a sliver of shapeless silver.

The witch hunter ran, his pistol raised high.

'Ortam!' he bellowed, and his nemesis looked up with eyes that reflected silver flame. Vermyre's mask melted from his face as if it had been washed away by rain. In its place, Toll saw the true visage of his old friend and greatest betrayer. The entire left side of the man's face was now a writhing mass of segmented tendrils that looked like nothing less than the twitching legs of a spider. The mouth was dragged down on that same side, half-formed into the circular maw of a carrion-eel. The left-hand eye had split and poured down towards the cheek, and trails of silver blood were dripping from this awful wound into the man's mouth.

'Look upon the face of failure, Hanniver,' spat Vermyre. 'Here is what your great victory at Excelsis brought me. Do not worry, my friend. My companions over there assure me this is in fact a blessing!'

He began to laugh, hacking up more silver liquid.

Despite his hatred for the man, Toll could not help feeling a stab of pity. He could not comprehend what it must have been like, feeling one's body shifting and transforming into something monstrously wrong, the fear and revulsion of one's own flesh. Then he recalled the blood that had flooded the streets of the City of Secrets, and the thousands of honest souls that had burned in witchfire. He remembered his old friend Kazrug, shot down by this very man, and his compassion melted away in an instant.

He fired four blasts.

Toll was stunned when Vermyre did not even raise the staff. Instead of striking their target, the bullets were transformed into four yellow-feathered hawks with needle fangs and long, drooping tail feathers. They swooped into the air, cawing and screeching.

Vermyre laughed. 'I did not even mean to do that. I think that mastering this Silver Shard is going be a most interesting diversion.'

'You're not leaving here alive,' said Toll. He was vaguely aware of Callis rushing past him, helping Shev up from the floor.

'You've already lost, Hanniver. By the Changemaker, this... thing. The sheer power of it, it's incredible.'

Callis felt a wave of relief wash through him when he saw Shev was still alive and apparently unharmed. A dozen yards ahead of her, Vermyre's pet beastmen continued to pour a stream of liquid flame onto the throne of that strange, squat creature, and so involved were they in the spellcraft that they did not seem to notice him at all as he slid into position behind the aelf, nestling his duardin wheel lock against the lip of the shallow staircase.

'By the God-King, it's good to see you're all right,' he said, then pulled his backup pistol from beneath his coat and offered it to her, grip first. 'It's loaded and primed. I know you don't much like these, but...'

She practically tore it from his hand, and leaned over to plant a fierce kiss on his lips.

'Err...' was all he managed as she pulled free.

Shev just laughed, shaking her head. 'I thought you were dead. Gods, I thought I was dead as well.'

'Yes, well,' said Callis, trying to recover his composure. 'Don't give up hope just yet. I assume you've noticed that we very much failed to keep Vermyre away from that thing.'

He raised his head and fired towards the traitor. He'd made

kills at a similar range a hundred times before, but this time nothing happened. He thought he saw a faint ripple of effervescent light, like a miniature rainbow, but Vermyre did not react.

'There's some kind of spell-field around him,' said Shev, after firing her own weapon to no greater effect. 'Our guns are useless.'

There was a sudden rush of air, and Callis was struck with a feeling of intense disorientation, as if he were dangling from the highest mast of the *Thrice Lucky* in a raging storm. The room seemed to vibrate and roll, and he staggered backwards, seeing Shev roll aside with a groan.

The wide chamber rocked with an eruption of immense power. Callis and Shev were sent hurtling backwards, rolling and sliding across the smooth ground. Dust and shattered masonry rained from the ceiling.

Through bleary eyes, Callis looked up to see a radiant light where the flaming throne had been only a moment before. Silhouetted before that blazing light were the thin, bent skeletons of the tzaangor shamans, little more than etchings made from ash. The light dimmed, and Callis saw the throne descend from on high with slow and steady grace. A creature rested upon that conveyance, charred and burned but unbowed. Its rheumy, ancient eyes seemed to bore straight into Callis. It waved a stubby hand in a gesture of utter indifference, and the beastmen's skeletons scattered into nothing. Only the melted husks of their weapons remained, rattling to the floor.

The monster that had once been Vermyre turned, raising the Silver Shard high. Before Callis' eyes, the immense power melted into quicksilver and reformed itself around the shape of his golden staff.

The creature upon the throne said nothing, but it gazed imperiously at the twisted human.

'You want this back, do you not?' said Vermyre. Then he rapped the staff against the chamber floor. A ripple of light ran across the length of his body, and when it receded, that hideous, malformed face was once again the visage of the man who had betrayed Toll and Callis, and had set Excelsis aflame. Round, slightly boyish, with a smile that did not reach his eyes. Though the mutations had disappeared, Callis' sense of revulsion did not subside. He could still smell the corruption upon the man, a sickly-sweet stench like incense mixed with decaying flesh.

'Come and take it, if you can,' Vermyre said.

The lizard-like creature gestured at the sorcerer, and the glass portal high above smashed asunder, raining shards of coloured crystal all around them. A sliver of glass sliced a red furrow down Callis' face, from his temple to his lower chin, and he cursed and covered his head with his hands. Racing through the shattered window came motes of blazing light, each as large as a human head, burning with the fire of stars. They slammed into Vermyre with horrendous force, but he merely staggered back a few steps and shook his head, laughing. Again, the creature swept its hands out and shaped an arrow of energy that slammed into the former High Arbiter. This strike smashed Vermyre to the floor with the power of a hammerblow. Callis heard the distinct crack of shattering bone, and saw a spiderweb of cracks splinter across the obsidian floor.

'That will not do it, creature,' said Vermyre, hauling himself to his feet. Toll ran forward, perhaps hoping to strike at the man with his rapier while the traitor was distracted, but Vermyre absent-mindedly swung his staff out to the side and sent the witch hunter sprawling.

'Let me show you how to dispose of one's enemies,'

Vermyre growled, and thrust the staff out towards the reptile. The ground shattered and erupted in spear-length shards of obsidian, a wall of piercing pikes that slammed through the creature's throne, penetrating stone and flesh alike. The creature hissed in agony and its throne began to soar high towards the ceiling, dripping black blood. Vermyre smiled and gestured again, and this time the very walls of the structure splintered and came apart, forming lashes of stone and crystal which reached out to strike the palanquin. Its occupant wove its arms in desperate patterns, smiting the reaching crystalline whips with blasts of living light332ning, but there were simply too many. Callis watched, appalled, as one of the lashing tendrils pierced the bloated beast, tore it bodily from its throne, and flicked its lifeless corpse aside. The creature struck the wall, rolled and hit the floor of the chamber with hideous force.

'No,' whispered Shev, and Callis shared her despair. They knew nothing about the mysterious beast, but it had been a protector and a guardian, they understood. And it had been perhaps their only chance of defeating the ascendant Vermyre.

The arch-traitor whirled his arms above his head. The cavernous roof of the hall began to come apart, as if caught in the path of a ferocious hurricane. Round and round swirled those tendrils of splintered stone, unmaking the very foundations of the building, tearing open a great, gaping hole in the featureless dome above.

Callis opened fire, as did Toll and Shev, standing amidst the cataclysm and pouring bullet after bullet towards Vermyre. None connected.

From the corner of his eye, Callis saw the shattered body of the guardian twitch. One of its eyes was little more than a shapeless red ruin, but the other still burned with intensity. It raised a single, webbed hand, and the ground disappeared from underneath his feet.

Chapter Thirty-Five

They had been standing, all of them, within the disintegrating temple. Shev was certain of that. And then, with the abruptness of a flash of lightning, they had been sent… elsewhere. They were falling, weightless through a swirling vortex of colours and shapes that made no sound or sense at all. Freed from gravity and reality and anything comprehensible by the mortal mind. Shev looked down at her body, and saw it morph and twist and reshape itself into an impossible fractal collision of bones and skin and clothing. Callis, to her left, was screaming as his body helixed around itself. She was screaming too, she supposed, though her main feeling was a form of detached, maddened curiosity.

Then, as one, they slammed to solid earth. Dense, overgrown earth, wet with dew and thick with sharp thorns.

Shev staggered to her feet and rose to see…

Xoantica. As it had once been. She did not know how she knew that, but gazing down upon the majestic sweep of the city it seemed an undeniable fact. The skies were such a clear, bright blue it was almost painful to look upon. Surrounding them on all sides were thick, lustrous trees with dangling fronds and brightly-coloured fruits hanging from their boughs. Ahead, through the dense vegetation, she could see a clearing, and the looming shape of some kind of structure. The sounds of life were deafening. The hissing chorus of startled insects, and the hoots and shrieks of birds in the trees. Life, where none had stirred before. She heard rustling movement within the tree-line.

'Sigmar's teeth,' spat Callis. He clambered to his feet, looking about as startled and discombobulated as Shev felt. He was waving his pistol around like a drunken man, still clearly disorientated from their bizarre journey.

'Where are we?' said Toll. The witch hunter knelt, running his hand through the wet grass. 'This is the very city we entered, but…'

He did not finish the thought, but he and Shev shared a knowing glance. Both of them could feel that something unutterably strange had happened here.

'We must keep going,' she urged.

They forced their way through the tangle of thick vines, slapping away thumb-sized mosquitoes that buzzed and droned about them. After some effort, they emerged on the crest of a shallow hill, and looked out over the city of white and gold. She saw the full beauty of Xoantica for the first time. Enormous, spiralling ziggurats rose from a network of immaculate roadways, reaching as high as castle towers. The walls of these great structures were lined in gold, bedecked with strange, asymmetrical runes and intricate engravings of stern figures, heads bowed as if in prayer. Amphora-carrying statues lining the avenues of the city poured streams of crystal-clear water into fountains and softly burbling waterways. There were carriages on the streets, elegantly curved traps pulled by giant, long beaked birds with iridescent feathers. Pedestrians too. Humans mostly, robed and cowled, but here and there the slender forms of aelves.

'Where the hells are we now?' whispered Callis.

'Inside the master, Lord Pa'tha'quen'tos, memories,' came a chirping voice from behind them, strangely halting in its speech pattern.

They turned to see the same diminutive lizard-priest that had greeted them in the chamber of Xoantica's great hall. Gone was the ragged tear that Vermyre had opened in the blue-skinned creature's hide. It walked towards them with an odd, hopping gait.

'Xoantica, as it was,' the creature chirped.

'Quite the place,' said Callis.

'A mask. A *golden* mask, to hide the truth,' the creature hissed, waving a dismissive claw.

The image of the city blurred and shifted, and they felt the ground surge beneath their feet. When vision came back to them, they were standing inside what appeared to be a temple, shrouded in shadow. Above, braziers of purple fire cast flickering shadows across rows and rows of hooded figures. Each carried a silver knife, and wore an ornate mask of silver studded with gems and engraved with patterns of pale gold. Some of these masks were fashioned in the shape of prey-birds, hooked and avian. Others were shaped like grinning half-moons, or horned and fanged beasts. The fug of incense and burning oils hung heavy in the air, seeming to blur the motions of the robed figures. They were chanting, low and insistently, in a tongue that sounded like the droning of insects. A column of more than a hundred sorry, stick-thin slaves shuffled down towards the centre of the chamber, where there lay a circular pool surrounded by stone pillars marked with profane symbols and engraved script. Liquid boiled erratically within that enormous well, occasionally spitting upwards. It looked like molten silver, though Shev thought she could see shapes moving in that morass, a nightmarish and unformed mass of organic matter, compound eyes and lashing tongues.

'Sacrifices,' said Toll softly, staring at the victims as they were led forward. All hope and even fear had gone from their eyes. There was only the dull glaze of resignation.

'Once scholars and masters of magic, lured here by false promises,' said their guide, startling Shev. The creature stood only a few yards from her, gazing at the ceremony with narrowed eyes. 'Xoantica professed to be a city of learning. Of reason. All lies, of course. Its rulers cared only for power. Forbidden knowledge. The Changer of the Ways heard their prayers, and was gratified by their duplicity.'

The slaves lined up around the swirling mass of molten metal. A figure stood upon a raised pulpit at the far end of the room, wielding a silver staff flickering with a turquoise flame. A woman, skeletally thin and with long, white hair bound in a knot on the top of her skull. Her mask was smooth and featureless silver, bound so tightly to her face that it almost seemed the gleaming metal was her skin. She wore magnificent purple robes, high collared and embroidered with intricate patterns of gold and silver. The priestess rapped her staff upon the ground. Several hooded figures below raised their curved daggers and stepped forward. Their knives slashed across the throats of their captives. Shev looked away in revulsion. When she glanced back, trails of bright crimson were mixed in with the shimmering silver, and corpses were strewn across the floor.

The quicksilver began to bubble. Mist filled the room as the hooded figures' chanting rose to a demented crescendo.

A great claw reached forth from the metallic pool. Then an immense, bird-like arm, shimmering with iridescent feathers. A jagged beak broke the surface next, a lashing tongue tasting the air with obscene delight. Shev felt a wave of purest terror, such as she had never known before. Beside her, Callis' hand flew to the symbol of the God-King he wore around his neck, his expression panic stricken. The simmering metal and rising steam obscured much, but within the swirling clouds, the shadow of something monstrous, several times the size of a man, could be seen. A hide of iridescent colours, rippling with corded muscle. Coils of night-black scales. An abomination from another realm, forcing its way into reality.

Within the glittering mass, a slimy lens peeled back to reveal a yellow orb that blazed with primordial malevolence. In that gaze was a horrifying madness, a gateway to a trillion nightmarish futures of agony and torment. Shev clutched her chest, staggering backwards.

Time stopped. Around them, the ranks of robed cultists froze in the midst of their exultations, daggers raised high in triumph. The choking fog grew thicker, mercifully masking the horror in the molten pool.

'What in Sigmar's name was that thing?' Callis gasped, wiping blood from a split palm across his coat. Shev realised that he had clutched the God-King's relic so tightly it had pierced his skin.

'A daemon,' Toll answered, suddenly looking very old. 'A powerful, greater daemon.'

The lizard priest bared his needle-like teeth. 'Servant to the Lord of Lies,' it hissed. 'Thank your gods you did not witness its true form, only an echo of the past. A memory.'

Shev wished she had seen nothing at all. When she closed her eyes, she still saw the malignant eye seared upon her brain, the sulphurous stench of its flesh still souring her nostrils.

'Nem'k'awet was the name the daemon gave,' the creature continued. 'The lord of Silver Skies. Not its true name. The mortals' worship drew it forth to ravage the realms once more, and in return it offered them a gift of unimaginable power.'

Their surroundings twisted once more; suddenly they were atop the highest peak of Xoantica's golden tower, an enormous, disc-shaped platform open to the sky. Surrounding the city on all sides were mountain peaks, obscured by rain that lashed down in stinging sheets. The purple-robed figure they had seen in the sacrificial chamber now stood before a pyre of purple flames, within which writhed malformed shapes. Flames lashed out angrily from the pyre, though they could not breach the warding circle that was marked upon the floor, a hexa-grammatic shape formed from bloody corpses. Mortal cultists stood surrounding this hideous scene, divested of robes. Lightning flickered across bare, pale flesh that was marked with tattoos and ritual scars. They were guarding yet more prisoners, these ones shivering and terrified, some lolling and screaming incomprehensibly, clearly driven to madness by their suffering.

The white-haired woman reached a hand into the flames, which coiled around her body to no avail. With a scream of triumph, she drew forth a blade of pure silver. It was almost impossible to fix one's eyes upon that sword, for it seemed to pulse and flicker in and out of reality, changing form with every passing moment.

'Nem'k'awet's gift. A weapon born from the purest insanity of the Chaos realm. Imbued with the stuff of daemonkind,' the lizard priest spat.

Letting out a howl of exultant triumph, the sorceress flicked the blade at the nearest bound prisoners. A beam of sickening un-light washed across them. They screamed helplessly as their bodies melted into a tangle of yellow-banded, triple-headed serpents.

The cultists of Xoantica fell to their knees, raising their hands in worship of their unspeakable master, their voices frenzied as they screamed their praise to the skies. The priestess raised the weapon again, and muttered a profane incantation.

Corposant light enveloped the platform as a beam of crackling energy reached far into the distance, scattering the tenebrous clouds as it roared above the earth. This lance of silver-white energy struck the distant peak of a mist-shrouded mountain, enveloping it in a writhing web of phosphorescence. With a sound like a great dam bursting, the mountainside melted, pouring down the valley like a golden flood, releasing torrents of glittering steam into the sky.

'Its power was terrible, even then,' the creature continued. 'Even from afar my master sensed the violence of its birthing. A blade to cut the strands of fate, to unmake the great tapestry. It could not be.'

Time shifted once more. Night and day whirred past with dizzying speed. They watched as Xoantica grew, greater and grander than ever before. Endless columns of slaves poured into the city, guarded by legions of masked warriors. The city rose, tearing free of the earth, and the Taloncoast fell away beneath them. As if at the hands of a god, the very shape of the Fatescar Mountains began to change, moulded into being by waves of blinding light. Defeated kingdoms were cowed, their masters dragged through Xoantica's streets in chains. Armies of winged creatures, golden-helmed and beautiful, sought to lay the masters of the city low, but they were defeated alongside all the others, their wings broken and their ankles shackled. Shev and the others saw all this in a matter of moments, a dizzying rush of images that seared into their minds and made the stars spin overhead.

And then, with terrible suddenness, the passage of time ceased. Shev collapsed to her knees, gasping for breath, her head spinning. She looked up to see that they were in the grand plaza of Xoantica, which was lined with cowled figures. There was the masked priestess, surrounded by armed thralls and cultists, tracing burning sigils in the air. The woman carried the daemon's gift in steady hands. There was a faint halo of orange flickering above the canopy of the surrounding halls, and Shev smelled smoke upon the air. Screams echoed in the distance. War had come to the streets of Xoantica. The stars overhead burned with blinding light, transforming night to day in an instant. Columns of starlight slammed into the plaza's marbled tiles, coalescing into ranks of saurians and mighty war-beasts. Shev saw lizard warriors mounted upon bipedal reptiles with bone-crushing jaws, lumbering, spiked behemoths with diminutive saurians scampering across howdahs raised on their sturdy backs. There, in the centre of this starhost, was the same bloated creature that had rested upon the dais, though here its flesh was lustrous, and its eyes blazed with the light of the heavens.

The Xoanticans joined their voices in blasphemous communion, and the Silver Shard flared in the darkness. A sickening wound tore open in the sky, vomiting varicoloured light across the forum. From this breach poured a tide of capering, pink-skinned monsters with gangly limbs and wild, brimstone eyes. Something else stirred behind that roiling portal, and insane laughter rolled across the land like thunder. Unperturbed, the reptilian army came on. The mortal cultists leapt towards their enemy with no thought for their own lives, loosing bolts of silver-white energy that blasted apart onrushing saurians. Gangling daemons spat fire, and in turn were crushed or blasted apart by spiked clubs, or pierced by javelins of black stone. Lord Pa'tha'quen'tos soared across the battlefield at the head of his starborne host, straight towards the wielder of the Silver Shard. Lashes of power from the priestess cut down the scaled warriors. The Silver Shard sang shrilly in the heretic's hands as it slew, making Shev's ears ache as though they were bleeding. The masked woman struck the shard against the paving of the plaza, and the ground split open. Waves of magma vomited through the split, drenching cultists and saurians alike, melting them to ash. She flicked the shard and tore gilded columns the size of ongoro-trees free from their roots. They hurtled through the air to crash amongst the invaders, crushing them beneath the weight of the grinding marble.

Lord Pa'tha'quen'tos came on, through the rain of magma, deflecting the sizzling downpour with a dismissive wave. Meteors screamed in his wake towards the priestess. Shev's heart leapt as the priestess barely raised the Silver Shard in time. The flaming missiles disappeared in a burst of light, turning into clouds of many-hued dragonflies which danced in the air.

The battle that followed was almost impossible for Shev to interpret. The storm of magic was blinding, a display of cataclysmic power that filled the air with fire and raining comets. Ruptured bodies littered the ground, and daemonic forms cavorted amongst the smouldering ruins of the once great city. On the steps of the great palace, the battle was won. Opening his stubby arms wide, Pa'tha'quen'tos raised his hands and the tortured night skies flooded with light. Rays of celestial magic speared down to immolate daemons and cultists alike, and where they struck saurian warriors, the scaled ones were enveloped in radiant energy, their wounds fading away and their relentless assault intensified.

The priestess of Xoantica cowered under the sudden blare of light. An enormous, bipedal war-beast barrelled through the press of bodies, bellowing in fury. Its rider, an armoured reptilian warrior, roared in triumph, his spear taking aim at the bearer of the Silver Shard. The war-beast grabbed the priestess in its jaws, and fangs the size of swords crunched down with terrible force. The cursed weapon fell from its wielder's lifeless hands, clattering down the steps of the palace to land before the palanquin of Lord Pa'tha'quen'tos.

Even as it lay untouched, the blade began to shimmer. It twisted and reformed, turning into a flowing lash of quicksilver and then a great, avian talon. Finally, it settled into the image Shev had first laid eyes upon in the grand chamber – a twisting wound in reality, trembling with barely suppressed power.

The tableau froze once more.

'Battle was fierce. The city destroyed, though at great cost to my master,' said the lizard priest, and Shev thought she heard a hint of sadness in its melodic voice. 'The masters of Xoantica were all slain, but the stain of their evil was not swept away.'

'The Silver Shard,' said Toll.

'Could not be destroyed.' The creature bobbed its head. 'Not without great cost. Master's power has kept the sword hidden, safe. Until now.'

'And now Vermyre has it,' said Callis. 'And we're all about to find out just how bad that is.'

'Time is an enemy now,' the creature continued. 'Lord Pa'tha'quen'tos is gravely wounded, and this moment slips away like sand through our claws.'

'Then why are we here? Where have you taken us?' demanded Toll.

'Nowhere. My master plucked this moment in time out of the great tapestry and drew you here. Will not last for long, but it will serve.'

They heard footsteps upon the hard stone of the tower top, and turned to see a figure approaching them. A short, balding man, skin weathered by the sun. He was dressed in the same rags that the sacrificial victims had worn, his body was thin and marked with bruises and cuts. Though his cheeks were gaunt and his eyes sunken, Shev recognised the face of Occlesius the Realms-Walker, the greatest statesman and traveller of his age, from her books. It was the same slight, weak-chinned visage she had seen in the man's tomb, but here. He stared at his hands in wonder, pinching the flesh of one palm and wincing slightly as he did so.

'I live again,' he said. 'Flesh and bone. How is this possible?'

'It is not,' said the creature. 'Only memory. You were here on this day, far traveller. You were here at the fall, at the death of Xoantica. That is how you are present.'

Callis raised his hand, an expression of utter confusion on his face. 'Would someone care to explain who in the Eight Realms this balding fellow is?' he said.

'I am Occlesius the Realms-Walker, scion of Asciltane and–'

'This stone,' Shev explained, cutting Occlesius off and raising the shadeglass gem.

'This man was once a traveller, an explorer who journeyed far across the Eight Realms,' Shev explained to the bewildered looking Callis. 'Upon his death, he had his memories, his soul essence stored inside a shadeglass crystal.'

'To simply fade from the world, all my experiences lost to the ages,' said Occlesius, 'that I could not abide. The great Katophranes of Shadespire demanded a high price indeed for that crystal, but I paid it gladly.'

'So he's been, what, in your head this whole time?' said Callis.

'In a way,' said Shev. 'It's complicated.'

'No time,' hissed the priest. 'No time for this! You were here, far traveller. Amongst thousands, your life alone was spared. We shaped your memories before we released you, so that you could not remember what you saw when Xoantica died.'

Occlesius' eyes furrowed in confusion. 'I remember all of my travels, but I remember nothing of this city beyond a few scattered images. All I know is that I witnessed something terrible here. Why? Why was I not killed when you purged the life from this city?'

'Your fate is bound to the stars. You have been marked in the grand constellation, far traveller.'

The creature looked at them all in turn. 'Same for you, young ones. This moment was mapped in the stars long ago by the Old Ones. This is why your lives have been spared.'

'Enough of this cheap prophecy. Vermyre has the Silver Shard,' Toll continued. 'Every moment we delay, the more damage he can wreak. Take us back. Now.'

The reptile's wide, unblinking orbs fixed upon the witch hunter.

'You cannot win,' it said. It didn't seem possible that the creature's long snout and toothy maw should be able to even pronounce the common tongue, yet it spoke the words with perfect clarity. 'With the Silver Shard – the fang of Nem'k'awet – in his grasp the sorcerer is beyond your powers to slay. There is only one way now to be rid of it.'

'What do you intend?' asked Toll.

'Give the master time, distract the human for but a few moments. Lord Pa'tha'quen'tos can open a breach to the shrieking nothingness. The void between realms. There we will trap the Silver Shard, where none can ever reach it.'

'Why didn't you do this before?' asked Shev. 'Why didn't you get rid of the damned thing while there was still time?'

The creature's gaze turned to her. It cocked its head slightly, staring at the shadeglass amulet around her neck, and despite herself her hands twitched towards the gem.

'Not easily done,' said the creature. 'May kill the master, and he has much still to do. Many tasks to be accomplished, across the star-ways. The stars burn in the fires of war, and my master's kind are few. Each death is a defeat. Yet this mortal must not take the shard. No choice.'

'And you?' she said.

Again, it cocked its head in that curious manner. Shev was sure she caught a flicker of amusement in the creature's expression, although it was almost impossible to tell for certain.

'No more real than this earth,' it trilled, tapping its claws upon the dewy ground. 'Only my master's memory. His last memory. And now our time is almost over. But there is another price. The reason we once spared your life.'

The creature turned to Occlesius.

'The gem of soul-crystal that binds your astral form,' it said. 'We must trap the sorcerer within. In possession of the Silver Shard, he might escape from the Great Nothing, such is its power. *No.* We must trap him as we bound Nem'k'awet.'

'Wait. What will happen to Occlesius?' said Shev.

The creature tilted its head again.

'He will join my master in oblivion,' it said.

Occlesius closed his eyes, and shook his head.

'Not now,' he whispered. 'Not when I am finally free.'

'There has to be some other way,' said Shev softly, knowing as she spoke that her words were meaningless.

'It's a sorry hand you've been dealt,' said Callis, fixing the

Realms-Walker with a sympathetic look. 'But if we don't defeat Vermyre here, we're all doomed regardless.'

'So are thousands more innocent lives. Vermyre means to burn Excelsis to the ground, and that is simply the beginning,' said Toll. 'The power to wreak such damage, in that man's hands? It cannot be allowed, no matter the cost.'

The witch hunter strode over to Occlesius, and looked into his eyes without flinching.

'I'm sorry, but you have already lived your life,' he said. 'If your existence has to end so that others may live on, then so be it.'

'Not your choice,' said the priest, then raised a claw to point at Occlesius. 'His, only. Must not resist when my master draws his spirit from the stone – if he does, then the sorcerer will surely break free. Will not hold for long. But long enough.'

'I… I shall not resist,' said Occlesius. He looked up and met Shev's eye. She saw fear there, but resolve too. 'You are right, master Toll. I have already lived far too long. Perhaps it is time to rest at last.'

Shev stepped forward, and took the old man's hand. He was trembling.

'Thank you,' she said.

Occlesius smiled, and grasped her arm. 'Promise me you'll continue my life's work,' he said. 'In my name, see the wonders of the realms. There are so many sights to see, Miss Arclis. So many beautiful things, even amidst the darkness and chaos of war. I have yet to see more than a fraction of what there is out there. Now I know that I never will. But you can. You're going to achieve great things, I'm sure of it. I should have liked to accompany you, but it is enough for an old man to know there are others walking in his footsteps.'

'In your name,' Shev said. 'I swear it. I'll see it all.'

'Should I meet your father in the afterlife, I'll tell him all about our travels together. I'm sure he would be very proud of who you have become.'

'No more time,' said the creature, staring up at the heavens.

Shev held the Realms-Walker's hand while the storm broke over them.

Thunder rolled overhead, and where there once had been dark skies, cracks of searing light were breaking through. The golden ziggurats of Xoantica began to crumble and fall, collapsing in on each other level by level. Then the ground gave way beneath their feet, and once more they were falling into darkness. Shev saw the saurian's small, clever eyes one last time before they were swallowed up by enveloping night.

Chapter Thirty-Six

Toll's eyes opened and he was once again in the collapsing grand hall of Xoantica, the deafening sounds of disintegrating masonry filling his ears. He rolled to his feet, ignoring the sheet of white fire that enveloped his chest as he rose. At least three ribs broken. They ground and clicked against each other when he moved. The agony was exquisite, and stole his breath.

Hate came to his rescue, lighting its own fire inside him and burning away the weakness of pain. Vermyre was still alive, and the bastard thought he was going to escape justice once again. Toll had decided that he was very much willing to die to see his former ally served his due.

'Ortam!' he bellowed, throwing his useless pistol aside and drawing his rapier.

Vermyre turned, a mad light shining in his eyes, somehow even more unsettling than the ruin his face had been. He laughed, taking in the witch hunter's battered appearance.

'I should have known you wouldn't lie down so easily,' he

said. 'You know, you're a very stubborn man, Hanniver. It can be most irritating.'

'I see you've given up using a blade,' said Toll. 'You used to consider yourself quite the swordsman, if I recall. Of course, I cut your face the last time we duelled.'

Vermyre's eyes narrowed. 'Toll, are you trying to anger me? That's really quite unnecessary.'

'You know, you did have me fooled, Ortam. I admit it. Your betrayal shocked me to the core of my soul. You had every advantage over me. And still you failed.'

The traitor was advancing upon him now, his frenzy of destruction forgotten. He swung the Silver Shard low, and as it moved, its form flowed into that of a duelling sabre, still rippling with molten energy.

'You had the city at your mercy. You had your moment – the moment you'd spent your life in preparation for – and you let it slip from your fingers. I would say your wretched god is very angry with you, Ortam. And as powerful as your new toy is, I don't think it'll stay his wrath.'

'I care nothing for the gods,' spat Vermyre. 'I only ever cared for what they could grant me. And now I no longer require the Changemaker's aid. Here, let me show you what I mean.'

He lunged forward. Toll had forgotten how fast the man was; he was a born duellist. Last time they had fought, during the last fight for Excelsis, only good fortune had seen Toll escape with a narrow victory.

This time luck was not with him.

He managed to pull back from the blow, but not far enough. Vermyre's blade sank deep into the meat of his upper arm, burning as it tore through flesh and bone. Toll gasped and fell to his knees, his own rapier tumbling from his hand. Vermyre's face leered at him, and through the mask of illusion he briefly saw again the monstrous form beneath.

'You took my moment of glory from me,' said Vermyre, his teeth bared like a rabid hound. 'Let me take something from you, old friend.'

He stepped back and brought his blade around in a tight arc. White-hot agony engulfed Toll's arm, and he heard something thud to the floor. Knowing what he would see but somehow also not believing it, Toll glanced down to see his severed arm, lying in a pool of spreading blood.

Callis was too slow. He saw the blade fall, and Toll's arm fly free, trailing an arc of spurting blood. The witch hunter sagged to one knee, gasping in pain. One hand went to the torn stump below his shoulder. Vermyre circled, twirling his blade in a duellist's flourish, delight writ large upon his features.

'It's a terrible thing, is it not, to find one's body altered forever?' he said.

Callis charged across the floor and leapt at Vermyre. He crashed into him, bearing him to the floor and raining heavy punches into his face. It was like striking stone. He felt his knuckles crack, but knew that the moment he let up, he was dead, or worse. Callis had to buy time. He rolled, slipping through Vermyre's guard and wrapping his forearm around the man's throat in a chokehold. He hauled back with all his might, but it was futile.

Vermyre twisted his shoulder and hurled Callis free. The throw sent him tumbling painfully across the floor, but he turned the painful impact into an awkward roll and came up firing from the hip, discharging both barrels of his duardin piece. The bullets struck a wall of invisible force, and erupted into bursts of blinding colour.

'It's very touching, this,' said Vermyre. 'The protégé, defending his master. What do you suppose your chances are, in this instance?'

'Better than yours,' Callis replied, seeing a flicker of movement behind the sorcerer.

Shev pressed her weapon against Vermyre's back and fired. Blood splattered across the floor, and Vermyre staggered, growling in pain.

Miss Arclis, came Occlesius' voice.

The Realms-Walker's voice was strained and weak inside her head.

His will is so strong. I can feel it pressing down upon me, even now. There is something unutterably powerful growing inside his flesh. The creature was right. We must finish him, for the good of all.

'Oh, Shevanya,' Vermyre hissed, standing upright with a grimace. 'I had no intention of killing you along with these fools. But I see now that you cannot be trusted.'

He moved like flowing water, so fast she barely had time to flinch before his punch struck her in the stomach, sending her skidding across the floor, groaning in agony.

'And so,' Vermyre continued. 'I am disinclined to offer you that luxury. You should have chosen my side, Shevanya.'

'Don't call me that,' she growled, wiping blood from her mouth and clambering to her feet.

If she was to die here, she would do so spitting in this monster's face.

He was closing on her. She could smell the foul, perfumed reek of him, and she wondered how she had ever been able to stand it. His eyes were bloodshot, crazed. They stared straight through her.

This is it, Shevanya, said Occlesius the Realms-Walker, and though his voice was weak there was a calm acceptance to it. *I would like to thank you for this last journey. It has been most delightful to spend time in your company, and I wish you nothing but the best of fortune in the years to come.*

'I'm sorry,' she whispered, feeling numb and helpless, and hating herself for it. 'I'm sorry I couldn't help you.'

Nonsense, my dear. Nothing to be done about it. If nothing else, this is surely a fitting end for a life as rich and – dare I say it? – glorious as mine. Goodbye, Miss Arclis.

Something lifted Shev and sent her sliding away across the floor. The shadeglass crystal flew from her grip.

Toll felt the blood pouring from his arm in gushing torrents, and knew that it was over. Even if they somehow made it out of this room alive, there would be no making it back across the city before he bled out. Callis' face swam into focus. He was shouting something, but Toll couldn't quite make out the words. Blackness seeped into the corners of his vision.

Then there was a ragged, terrified scream. Blearily, Toll looked up from where he lay, and saw the ruined form of the Lord Pa'tha'quen'tos, once more seated upon the remnant of its stone palanquin, which was held together by arcing streams of lightning. It hovered in place before Ortam Vermyre, who was enveloped in a field of that same fulminating energy. The stench of burning flesh was overwhelming. Even as the man struggled and writhed, Pa'tha'quen'tos raised its stubby arms high, weaving an incredibly complex series of gestures in the air. Occlesius' shadeglass gem floated in the air in front of the creature, crackling with energy.

At first, nothing happened. Then there was a whistling shriek of tortured air. Slowly, but with gathering inevitability, a tear began to open in the world. Where the aura surrounding the Silver Shard had been that of misplaced, overlapping realities, this breach spilled only thick, all-encompassing darkness into the world. Vermyre struggled free of the web of energy, and swung his silver blade into the chest of Pa'tha'quen'tos, but the creature did not even seem to register the surely fatal blow even as blood bubbled in its wide maw and poured down its chest. Instead, they could hear a low, throaty murmuring, and it continued to craft a final spell.

Something silver-white rushed out from the crystal, and ricocheted across the room like a bouncing ball of lightning. Vermyre was dragged forwards. His hideous face began to twist and deform, flesh drawn from his bones towards the crystal.

Vermyre shrieked, and tried desperately to drag himself away, but his feet slipped on the smooth floor and he could make no progress. Toll could see the panic in his old friend's eyes as he realised his doom. He felt no pride or delight in witnessing this. Only relief that he had, at last, earned justice for the dead of Excelsis, before the end.

The black hole was still growing now, and it seemed to drain all the light and sound from the chamber. Shev was crawling towards them, looking over her shoulder in fear at the spreading vortex. At this pace, it would soon devour them all.

In one final, desperate attempt to escape his fate, Vermyre began to hack wildly at Pa'tha'quen'tos, carving through flesh and stone. The wizened creature, somehow still alive, simply rested its hands upon the man's chest, and with its dying breath mouthed one last arcane phrase. With one final agonised scream, Vermyre's spirit was torn from his body, disappearing into the shadeglass gem, which flared and crackled with energy. His lifeless body crumpled and was sucked into the vortex, before Pa'tha'quen'tos reached out a stubby hand to grasp the scintillating blade of the Silver Shard. Its flesh began to bubble and boil away, but the creature seemed to ignore the pain. The spreading orb of oblivion now enveloped the raised dais entirely. Pa'tha'quen'tos released his hold upon the floating crystal containing whatever remained of Vermyre's essence, which followed after the man's corpse.

Then, his great eyes closed and the Silver Shard clutched to his chest, the master of Xoantica was drained into the vortex of devouring nothingness, his body tumbling and whirling away into the distance.

'To the void with you, Vermyre,' Toll whispered, and then began his own journey into darkness.

Chapter Thirty-Seven

The rift continued to widen, tendrils of antimatter reaching out to steal the life and colour from the world. Enormous masonry chunks dropped from the ceiling to smash upon the chamber floor, sending up great explosions of dust and shards of splintered stone.

'Toll! Toll!' Callis was shouting, slapping the oblivious witch hunter about the face in an attempt to bring him out of his stupor. Shev put a hand to the prone man's chest. She felt him breathing, but it was shallow and faint. She did not think he had more than a few minutes to live.

'Armand,' she shouted, gripping the soldier by his shoulders and shaking him. He stared at her, blood and dust smeared all across his face. 'We have to get out of here. Or we'll all follow Vermyre into oblivion.'

He nodded, and stooped to gather Toll in his arms, straining as he hefted the comatose man onto his back. They struggled to move, for each of them now felt the pull of the widening vortex, reaching out to tug at their bodies.

Shev thought to say that they should leave Toll here, but Callis had a look of formidable determination about him, and she knew he would countenance no such thing. Together they half-ran, half-staggered to the stairway, and began to descend. The ground shook beneath their feet. Shev had lived through an earthquake before, and she knew that they had almost no chance of outrunning the blast radius. The sole comfort she found was that she felt awake and focused in a way that she had not in all the time they had spent in Xoantica. Something had changed, as if she had just awoken for the very first time. That sense of crushing doom she had felt ever since she had followed Vermyre into the depths of the forgotten city had mercifully ceased. Where before the journey up this staircase had felt like some kind of purgatorial nightmare, now she could see all the way down to the entrance hall far below. It was littered with corpses, and there was no movement down there.

They were perhaps a third of the way down the spiralling stairway when there was another, fiercer tremor that sent them skidding to their knees. Shev looked up and saw the black orb of nothingness stretching out to consume the apex of the tower. The arched roof tore away into the void, and Shev saw the inky blackness of the rift meet a slate-grey sky, its all-consuming darkness seeping into the world like oil into water.

Callis helped her upright, somehow still managing to drag Toll's body alongside him.

They bounded down the steps as fast as their aching legs allowed, bursting out into the charnel pit that was the entrance-way. Shev noticed that there were none of the saurian creatures amongst the dead. Apparently, they had left Xoantica alongside their master. Neither could she see the bulky armour of Admiral Bengtsson, or the night-black leathers of Arika

Zenthe – both of whom, according to Callis, had been left to guard the stairway – though there was no time to search the scene.

At last they burst out into open air, racing down the steps while the building came apart behind him. The shadow of the vortex swept across the plaza, bathing the square in darkness, but beyond she could see the city stretching away into the distance – and beyond that, the mist-wreathed mountains of the Fatescars.

'Get a godsdamned move on!' came a voice from far ahead, barely loud enough to be heard over the roar of the collapsing city. It was Zenthe, on the far side of the plaza, leaning heavily on Bengtsson, clutching her side in a manner that indicated she had taken a nasty wound.

They raced across the open ground and reached the battered pair of shipmasters, who were covered in blood and grime. Bengtsson's helm had been marked by a vicious diagonal cut that had almost breached his armour, and he was favouring one leg and breathing heavily. Zenthe was grimacing in pain, and it looked as though she had been run through or pierced by an arrow, for her coat was soaked in blood and her breathing was wet and ragged.

'I think that our fine fellowship now comes to an end,' she growled. 'There's no way we're outrunning death this time.'

Bengtsson grunted, a sound that might have been affirmation. Zenthe was right, Shev knew. She turned, and gazed up at the orb of nothingness, which had grown to envelop the domed hall. As they watched, the structure disintegrated, clouds of bricks and shattered glass draining away into the hungry void, the great marble face of the building cracking and crumbling. With a thunderous explosion, the front of the building came apart, and the entire structure was swallowed up into darkness.

Still not sated, the crackling tendrils of the void stretched out, seeking fresh sustenance.

'There's no escaping that,' panted Callis. His hands were trembling with exhaustion. Shev had no idea how the man had managed to haul his companion so far without pausing for breath.

'No,' she whispered, and sat down on the flagstones, sighing as she massaged her aching muscles. Even now the rift was eating up the distance between them, ripping tiles and stones from the plaza.

'You know, since I joined your one-armed master's mad crusade of vengeance I've lost my ship, been hurled in the dungeons, been stabbed by a bird-faced mutant and now I'm about to be swallowed up by the abyss,' said Zenthe, spitting up a mouthful of blood. 'Oblivion will come as something of a relief.'

'Well, if you're all so intent on dying along with this city mayhap I should leave upon the *Indefatigable* by myself,' said Bengtsson.

They turned as one to stare at him, and he jerked an armoured hand towards the mountains. There, sailing out of the mist amidst a cloud of thick, grey smoke, was the admiral's flagship, making straight for their position.

'If there's one thing you can rely upon, it's that my crew will want to ensure my survival,' said Bengtsson.

'Wonder if my own sea-wolves would be so loyal,' muttered Zenthe.

'Loyalty?' asked the admiral, as if he had never heard the word before. 'No, no, no, my dear Captain Zenthe. Pragmatism is a far more reliable motivator. I earned command by *mehret*, and every soul aboard that vessel knows that their profits would sink like a harpooned tuvahsk without me leading them.'

He reached into his belt and withdrew a small, brass-handled pistol with a wide, stubby barrel. He raised it into the air and fired, and a flare of bright red raced into the air and detonated in a shower of sparks.

Closer and closer the airship came. They ran to meet it while the rift widened and stretched behind them, gaining with every passing moment.

The great, bulbous shape of the duardin ironclad dropped out of the clouds, turning broadside in the middle of the central thoroughfare. Shev saw armoured figures with those familiar sphere-shaped backpacks dashing across the deck, launching themselves over the side and soaring out towards their band. They gathered Bengtsson and Zenthe first, grasping the pair under the arms and lifting them into the air. Then, like a flock of oversized insects, the rest of the engineers descended. Shev felt rough hands grasp her by the shoulders, and then her feet left the ground, and she was kicking empty air as she rose up towards the deck of the *Indefatigable*.

As she soared over the deck, the grip released, and the studded iron surface rushed up with fearsome speed. She hit hard, but turned the fall into an awkward roll.

'Pull away,' Bengtsson ordered, slapping away the attention of his crew, who were checking him for signs of injury.

The engine-spheres flared, and the ship's iron hull began to creak and groan as the great vessel swung back, away from the growing disaster enveloping Xoantica. Callis and Toll were dropped to the deck, the latter only slightly more carefully than Shev had been. She rushed over and checked Toll's pulse. Astonishingly, there was a faint beat there, though the man's flesh was cold and dry as a corpse.

'He needs a healer,' said Callis, who was slumped against the gunwale, breathing heavily, too exhausted to move.

Shev dragged herself to the rail of the ship and slumped against it as the crew of the *Indefatigable* rushed to their stations, and the huge sky-ship slowly began to haul itself away from the dying city. The vortex was now a howling globe that dominated the skyline all around them, and its tendrils crackled and grasped empty air mere yards from the gleaming hull of the Ironclad. She could feel their monstrous pull tugging at her flesh, sending her hair whipping over her head. She gripped the edge of the gunwale so hard it hurt. The engine-spheres above protested loudly, and as one of the tendrils of darkness brushed against the dull brass surface it loosed panels and rune-etched vents, which tumbled away into nothingness. The city itself was crumbling apart all around, buildings collapsing in on themselves, streets dissolving brick by brick. Snaking rivers of shattered marble and gold trailed to the mouth of the great maw. The *Indefatigable* pitched terribly, sending duardin crew stumbling and sliding across its deck, and for an awful moment she thought that it was going to tip over and spill them all out into empty space.

But then the spherical engine roared with fresh power, and the great vessel began to pull away towards the mountains, rising into the sky and away from the dead city of Xoantica.

The growing vortex began to split the entire floating mountain apart. Enormous splinters ran through the bedrock of the island. Great valleys were torn open in the ragged earth, and towering shelves of rock bent and gave way under the unthinkable pressure. The majestic stone face upon which the lost city had sheltered began to morph and leer as it was rent asunder. Now the sky-vortex was bigger than Xoantica itself, a nucleus of pure darkness at the heart of the mountain, still feeding upon the raw matter of existence. There was a crack louder than a myriad of thunderstorms discharging at once, and the floating island split apart, the lower half of the titanic face sundered as if it had been struck by an enormous axe. The stern brow and forehead of the mountain, which made up the crown of the floating island, were swallowed into the void.

It was as if this final act of consumption finally sated the black hole's voracious hunger. The orb of destruction began to flicker and collapse, falling in upon itself. A shockwave rushed out to buffet the *Indefatigable*, spinning the ship about. Steel plates groaned as the helmsman struggled to compensate for the buffeting winds. The lower half of the mountain collapsed, whatever magic held its brethren up entirely obliterated by the unthinkable eruption that had occurred. It fell from the skies in terrible slow motion and struck the sweeping lowland jungle below. An enormous cloud of dust spread as a secondary shockwave was unleashed, flattening trees and sending rippling tidal waves arcing out to sea. Shev watched in horror as the waters of the Taloncoast churned into a boiling tsunami and swept across the land, to the horizon and beyond.

Callis leaned alongside Shev, his bloodied face pressed against the cold metal. He whistled softly as the devastation unfurled beneath them.

'That's something you don't see every day,' he muttered.

Chapter Thirty-Eight

Four months later...

Callis awoke with a start, sitting bolt upright, his heart hammering in his chest. The sheets were damp with sweat even though a brisk breeze was drifting through the open window. Judging by the lilac glow that filled the room, it was some time in the early morning. He could already hear the clatter of carts passing along the cobbled road outside, and the shouts of tradesmen on their way to the Circle Market. He blinked sleep out of his eyes, and tried to banish the image that had dragged him into wakefulness.

A single, yellow eye, wreathed in fire and madness, staring into his very soul. He wondered if the terror of that moment would ever leave him. Worse still, he wondered if he would ever stop imagining what horror had been obscured at the heart of that mist-shrouded chamber. The daemon's true form...

'Nightmares again?' said Shev.

Callis gave a start, torn from his uneasy thoughts. The aelf was dressing, pulling on her tunic and securing her belt, her body silhouetted by the early morning light. On the sill of the tavern window rested a travel bag of cured leather.

'You're leaving,' he said, and it wasn't a question. He had expected this, though that fact didn't stop it from hurting. They'd only had a few blessed weeks to share one another's company, and he found that he would miss the experience intensely.

She sighed, and turned.

'I would never have left before you awoke,' she said.

'You could stay,' he offered, but the words sounded weak and futile even to him. They both knew the truth; their lives were simply heading down different paths. He sighed and sat upright, bunching the sheets around him.

'I made a promise to a friend,' she said. 'To chart the realms, and to carry on the great legacy that Occlesius started all those years ago. I intend to keep my word. And anyway, this life you lead, it's not one I can share. I know it's something you believe in, so I won't ask you to leave it behind and come with me. We had our moment, and I'm so glad to have met you.'

She moved to him, leaned down and kissed him, long and fiercely. Then she moved back to the window and gathered her satchel.

'Where will you go?' he asked.

'Wherever the wind takes me. There's an expedition heading into the Tiungra Valley in search of the Seeing-Stones of Prensis that's caught my interest. Or perhaps I'll read through my father's notes. He always talked about tracking down the Seven Tombs of the Ulkirian Faroahs.'

'Just try and keep out of trouble, will you?' he said. 'No more accepting dubious offers of assistance from masked figures. That never ends well.'

Shev smiled at that.

'I believe that we will see each other again, Armand,' she said. 'The realms are infinite, but we'll bend them to our will, you'll see. I wonder who we'll be when fate brings us together a second time? It's exciting to think that, isn't it?'

Callis thought the chance of them seeing each other again extremely unlikely, but thought better of saying it. This parting was painful enough already.

'Take care of yourself, Shevanya,' he said.

'You too, Armand.'

And with that, she was gone.

Toll was indeed at his usual spot at the Hammerhead, a duardin-run tavern that overlooked the dock district on the eastern rise of Trader's Row. It was mid-morning now, and already the piers and jetties were thick with bodies, muscular shiphands hauling produce and nimble-tongued merchants trying to score themselves a good deal. The sky was clear, a rarity in Excelsis, and in the far distance one could see the sails of Zenthe's privateer fleet flitting between the rows of moored vessels, keeping a close watch on their flock.

The witch hunter had taken a table in the shade at the far side of a small balcony, covered by a canopy of coloured shark-hide. He leaned back in his chair, sipping from a glass of crystal-clear water. As Callis arrived, Toll pushed out the nearest stool with his foot, not taking his gaze from the bustling harbour. They sat awhile in silence, listening to the sounds of civilisation. It had taken many harsh months for the city to recover from the horror of war and the shock of Vermyre's betrayal. Life continued of course – you could hardly afford the luxuries of grief and self-pity in the wilds of the Beastlands – but before Callis had left there had been a foreboding sense of gloom, a lack of trust between even those who had formerly been trusted neighbours. It seemed, at last, that the wounds were healing.

'She's gone, then?' said Toll.

Callis raised an eyebrow.

'Shev told you she was leaving?'

'No, but you're up and out of bed before the sun's reached its apex, and you've got a general hangdog look about you that I happen to recognise quite well.'

Callis sighed, and gestured to the barkeep for a mug of ale.

'I'm at peace with it,' he said. 'It was her decision. I knew she wasn't the type to stick around for long. I think Excelsis still holds bad memories for her. She says we may see each other again, one day.'

Toll nodded, and had the good grace to not point out how incredibly unlikely that was.

'I'm sorry, Armand,' he said, scratching at the stump of his arm, where his coat had been folded over and stitched up.

'How is it?' Callis asked, suddenly quite keen to change the subject.

'The arm? Having two was far more convenient, if I'm being honest, but I'll manage. The tales were right, though. You still feel it after it's gone. Sometimes I wake up in the middle of the night, reach for a cup of water and realise...'

He looked like he was about to speak further, but simply shook his head.

'Will you... get a replacement?' asked Callis. He had seen several Ironweld engineers and Freeguild officers who had been grafted with intricate mechanical arms to replace those lost through war or unfortunate accident. They were awkward and cumbersome for the most part, but still mostly effective.

Toll shook his head. 'For now, it's a fair reminder of what happens when I drop my guard. Before I rush to fix this wound,

I want to get used to what it means, the difficulties it poses me. I mistrust simple, swift solutions.'

They sat another while in silence. It was a pleasure simply to be amongst civilisation again, after so many months at sea. Callis peered off into the distance, seeing a violent crimson sail on the horizon.

'That's the *Blood Drake*,' he said, gesturing towards the departing vessel. 'Zenthe's new flagship, formerly the property of our old friend, High Captain Kaskin. The good captain's off again on her travels.'

Toll nodded. 'I paid my debt to her in full. She's not one to stay still too long, if she can help it.'

'What was it? The city treasury? A blood sacrifice? Your first-born child?'

The witch hunter gave a slight twitch of amusement. 'No. I gave her the location of her father.'

'Zenthe has a father? I assumed she was descended from a ghyreshark. Not much of a price for ferrying us halfway across the realm.'

'It is for Arika. She's off to claim his head and nail it to her prow.'

Callis glanced at Toll, who waved a hand wearily.

'It's a long story. I'll tell it to you another time.'

A duardin steam-cog was pulling into port ahead of them, kicking gouts of greyish smoke into the air from a row of short black funnels. Its wide-open bay was filled with piles of black coal that shimmered with a faint silver light. The dockmaster, a wizened little man who insisted upon being carried everywhere in a sedan chair, arrived as if summoned from the aether. Leaning out of the window of his chair, he began to shout and holler at the stoically unimpressed duardin captain, who was covered head to toe in grime so thick it seemed as if he was wearing pitch-black overalls. Callis couldn't stifle a grin.

'I never thanked you, Armand,' said Toll, meeting Callis' gaze for the first time. 'It would have been the sensible thing to leave me behind in that place, but you didn't. You risked your life to save mine, and I won't forget it.'

Callis didn't really know what to say to that, so he simply gave his companion a brief, awkward nod, and accepted the proffered ale brought over by the broad-shouldered innkeep, passing the man a handful of glimmerings.

They watched as the dockmaster and his hirelings continued to wage their war of words with the duardin steamheads, which grew steadily more foul-mouthed and inarticulate, until it suddenly and unexpectedly culminated in a shake of hands and a transition of coin and goods. Triumphant, the elderly dockmaster was carried forth on his mighty steed, onwards to the next glorious victory.

Diplomacy writ small, Callis thought with a smile.

'We have orders,' said Toll, fetching a clutch of papers from his coat. 'We're leaving Excelsis again. The *Indefatigable*'s refuelling and finalising repairs as we speak. I managed to talk Admiral Bengtsson into giving us passage. The least he could do, considering the king's ransom he earned from our last voyage. I'd make all the goodbyes to this city you think necessary, because we won't be coming back here for quite some time.'

'That's all right,' said Callis. 'I'm ready to move on.'

'Good. Because we'll travel further than we ever have before. Our path takes us across realms, Armand. Beyond the edge of this map and onto a whole new one. To the Jade Kingdoms and beyond.'

ABOUT THE AUTHOR

Nick Horth is the author of the Age of Sigmar novella *City of Secrets* and the novel *Callis & Toll: The Silver Shard*. Nick works as a background writer for Games Workshop, crafting the worlds of Warhammer Age of Sigmar and Warhammer 40,000. He lives in Nottingham, UK.

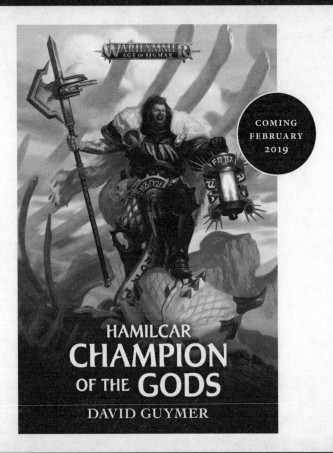

COMING FEBRUARY 2019

HAMILCAR CHAMPION OF THE GODS
by David Guymer

There are few heroes so mighty as Hamilcar Bear-Eater –
but when an ancient skaven warlock with a thirst for godhood
seeks Hamilcar's immortal soul, will his martial prowess
and uncanny skill be enough to ensure survival?

An extract from
Hamilcar: Champion of the Gods
by David Guymer

I arced over the gurgling water like a zephyrgryph with his claws unfurled. The air was ice, the sky a weird shade of green, amber leaking into the night with the dawn. My face was the painful side of numb as my arms and legs paddled the thin air. All I could hear from beneath me was the creak of ice, the rush of the river and the wind slipping through my fingers. I started to laugh, my mouth thus conveniently wide for a roar of triumph as my boots slammed into the frozen slush of the Nevermarsh. Cracks spread through the frost-veined mud, but it was already hard as rock and did not break.

Just as well – sinking to my greaves in mud or getting into a tug-of-war for my boot was hardly the look I had been going for.

'Yes!'

The cry exploded from my chest and I spun around with my fists in the air.

'Let it be known that Hamilcar Bear-Eater is first across every river, first into every charge, first unto every blade!' I bellowed.

Broudiccan's slow handclap wasn't quite the enthusiastic reaction that I felt the feat deserved. My second-in-command cut an imposing figure on the other side of the water, a fortress of a man in the thrice-blessed maroon and gold of the Astral Templars. His Mask Impassive, the grim facial covering of the Stormcast Eternals, was anything but; a gouge from a beast's claw had cloven the stoic purple mask in two, leaving a disdainful aspect which suited his taciturnity to the ground.

If he thought he could leap twenty feet across ice-cold rapids then I would have very much liked to see him try.

'Bravo, Lord Hamilcar,' Frankos shouted through cupped hands, separated from the burly Decimator by the haggard width of a tree. 'Congratulations on being the first of Sigmar's Stormhosts to set foot in the Nevermarsh.'

Distinctions of age and experience counted for little within a company of immortals, but the Knight-Heraldor had always been possessed of a youthful effervescence that made me feel old. I nodded my thanks, pausing to glare at my second.

'May the Heraldor Temples always proclaim it so,' I bellowed back.

'They shall, my lord,' he cried with gusto. 'They shall.'

Frankos was also quite unique amongst my warrior chamber in taking everything I said in deadly earnest. He continues to do so, in fact, even after the later reversal in our fortunes.

The sigmarite mountain called Broudiccan rumbled as the giant sighed.

His masked gaze slipped towards the frothing water.

Feral-looking birds with wicked red eyes twittered back and forth between the two banks. Their beaks were perfectly made for the stripping of flesh, the cracking of bone, and I suspected they could even chew the cure right off a man's armour. Generally, the birds were happy enough scavenging for fish and insects amongst the densely tangled buttress roots that clawed out of the riverbank and into the water, but the Freeguild army I was leading through the Gorwood might as well have been one giant victuallers' caravan for all they were concerned. More than one poor soldier had already lost a finger or an eye. Broudiccan swatted at one, which knew better than to test its toothed beak on sigmarite and flapped out of reach to shrill from the leafless canopy.

'I'll wait for the bridge,' he grumbled, after a while.

I barely heard him over the white roar of the water, but I am a Stormcast Eternal, and my ears are sharp enough.

'I wonder about you sometimes,' I laughed. 'Are you a plodding Knight-Excelsior, summoned to my warrior chamber in error?'

Broudiccan shrugged. 'Even Sigmar can make mistakes. The pain of reforging is proof enough of this.'

'Ha! Indeed. I remember my last day as a mortal, when I feasted with Him and ten thousand warriors in the Heldenhall.' The memories of my mortal life were dimmer back then than they are now, jumbled like a stained glass that had been broken and thrown back together, most of the pieces still missing, but this I remembered. 'He has a delicate stomach. For a god.'

Frankos frowned at nothing. 'I do not remember my final night.'

'Parts of mine are a little blurry also. It was that aelf nectar wine. I swear there was nothing like it where–'

A racket worthy of Gorkamorka drowned me out as the rest of the army made their way through the trees.

I looked past the two Astral Templars, my sentence unfinished.

About nineteen hundred soldiers, two of the five Freeguild regiments of the Seven Words, had followed me into the

Gorwood. Their baggage train and camp followers amounted to about the same again although I generally deferred the small details to Frankos and the mortal generals themselves. The fifty warriors of my Chamber, the Bear-Eaters, were strung out over several leagues of woodland. The trees that grew here at the boundary of the Low Gorwood were twisted runts compared to the predatory bowers that canopied the high slopes of the Gorkomon, but no less deadly. For all my efforts, the Gorwood was – and would always be – a wild place, home to as many hungry creatures as it had been when the Beastlord Uxor Untamed had ruled these heights. And I wouldn't have had it any other way. The men and women that emerged wore a collage of colours – torn, faded, chewed on – over armour of tough leather and the occasional skin. There were a few wooden or leather shields, but most carried two-handed spears, javelins or hunting bows. Despite the cold and the predations of the forest they were still laughing – Ghurites all of them, none tougher – whistling catcalls at those behind and pointing at me on the other side of the river.

Coming in behind the vanguard was a trio of ogors in tattered surcoats, hauling a bridge of coppery lumber behind them. Their faces were snarled with effort, muscles standing like boulders from a mountainside. A few of the soldiers dropped their gear to run in and help push, the ogors hissing something that probably wasn't all that complimentary through their teeth.

I put my hands on my hips and watched them, my heart ready to burst with pride.

I loved them all.

Only slightly less than they loved me.

'Who is first upon the Nevermarsh?' I called out to them, thumping my breastplate. 'He who waits upon no man, beast nor creature of Ruin.' I thrust my gauntleted fists in the air, wringing the musty stink of bear from my cloak.

'Hamilcar!'

Cheers rippled through the treeline. The ogors took the opportunity to draw up and wipe the sweat from their sledgehammer-like brows, before readjusting the draw-chains wrapped round their fists.

I made a grand show of pulling off my gauntlets, rubbing my hands together and blowing into them, despite the fact I have little feeling for the cold. I am a champion of Heaven, and to be of Heaven is to be cold as starlight. And yet it means something to the common soldier to see his hardships shared. Most Storm-cast Eternals, broken from humanity in order to be elevated to that space beyond, would never even have considered such a gesture. There are better warriors than I in Sigmar's Storm-hosts. I'll not name them, and I'll only deny saying it should it get back to them. Let's just say I have all the fingers I need to count them. But if you think that any of them can get as much as I can from a mortal man, then I would say you have passed too many times over the Anvil of Apotheosis, my friend.

'The winter is cold,' I yelled. 'The Ghurlands are dangerous. But you know cold, you know danger. Every man and woman here is a veteran of the Gorwood. You have fought beside me against beastman and skaven and orruk, yet here you all are with me still. Why?' My breath shrouded my tattooed fist in fog. 'Because Hamilcar Bear-Eater is your brother and your champion, ahead of you every step of the way!'

'Hamilcar!'

The cry came back louder now, men still spilling out of the forest to hear my words.

I unhooked the halberd from its bracket across my back. The black wood of the haft scraped over my armour as I drew it.

The head sang as it came free. The blade was sigmarite, forged by the first of the Six Smiths under the Auroral Tempest, imbuing the metal with the storm's vicious power. Bands of amber and violet rippled through the blade as I turned it and held it aloft. A pair of predator birds that I had managed to trap and kill myself dangled from the head on chains. Runes of my own inscription decorated the haft. They imparted no power I know of, and I had no idea from which ice hole of my memory they emerged, only that in those days you could not leave me with a flat surface and a knife and not return to find the former filled with the strange pictograms.

I had always assumed them to be a facet of my lost life as a mortal, which would of course prove to be correct, though I never gave it much thought at the time.

'The Nevermarsh is another challenge again. No army of Sigmar has ever crossed its border, and yet...' I spread my arms to indicate the river running across me. The soldiers chuckled, a few of them still shouting my name. A cloaked and helmeted veteran in a glittery cuirass of leather and glass and a rash of insect bites on his browned face choked on laughter. Even I didn't think my remark was that amusing, but I acknowledged the old-timer with the point of my halberd. I recognised him from some battle or other, and I always liked to give the impression of familiarity with every woman or man who bore the Twin-Tailed Comet in my name.

'This is where our enemies seek to hide from us, so this is where we hound them. We will run them to the ground, my friends. We will kill them, we will butcher them, and we will feed their bloody carcasses to the carniferns of the Gorwood!'

The bank erupted with a mighty cheer.

'For Sigmar!'

'Sigmar!'

'For the God-King!'

My voice was the coming of thunder. I held the final syllable until my throat was hoarse and my body shook with passion.

I rehoused my halberd, leaving my fist raised in salute.

The men would all be warm now. If my Vanguards were right about the position of the hole that our enemy had found to hide in, and they generally were, then I expected the fire I had put in the soldiers' bellies to last them until it was needed.

'A good speech, lord,' Frankos shouted to me.

I could almost sense Broudiccan's eyes rolling.

'Go and aid with the bridge,' I told the Heraldor. 'You're as strong as any ogor, brother.' One hand on the pommel of his broadsword, Frankos bowed low, his white crest bobbing in the frozen muck. I called after him as he departed. 'Be sure that it's good and flat. I would hate for Broudiccan to fall off.'

I chuckled to myself, Broudiccan still wearing that disdainful look of his.

Now ordinarily, these sullen spells were precisely the reason I chose the Paladin for my second. The long silences gave me more room to talk, but a man can only bear so much.

'Spit it out, brother,' I barked.

'It is nothing.'

'With you, it's never nothing.'

The big Paladin grumbled. 'You are like a boy on his first hunt, lord.'

I smiled wistfully. 'You remember your first hunt?'

'No.'

'Nor I mine.' I cocked a grin as though he had just made my point for me. 'Every time is the first now. The realms are so vast, the enemy so numerous. It is always new.'

'You are a Lord-Castellant, not an Azyros or a Venator to go seeking out new dangers.'

I blew out through my lips. 'The best defence...' Broudic-can's eyes narrowed reproachfully, and I motioned towards the Freeguild further uphill, dragging the bridge towards us with renewed vigour. 'They will work faster knowing I'm here on the far side. I don't forget my calling, brother.'

Frankos had joined the labourers as I spoke, jostling in between the ogors and taking up some of the chain to help pull.

'He is a bad influence upon you,' said Broudiccan.

I laughed at that. 'I suspect most would say it was the other way around.'

'I have known Frankos longer than you. He is perfectly incorruptible. You, on the other hand, will do anything for an audience.'

I frowned across the water, but Broudiccan had nothing more to add. Frankly, I should have been astonished to have got as many words out of him as I had, but I was justifiably distracted by what happened next.